Spells of Wonder

WITHDRAWN

By Bestselling,
Award-Winning Masters of Fantasy,
Including:

- **"What Good Is a Glass Dagger?"** by Larry Niven: An idealistic werewolf sets out to destroy Magic—and becomes its last protector . . .
- **"Armaja Das"** by Joe Haldeman: The world's leading computer tycoon finds the spell to counter a gypsy's lethal curse—but there's a glitch . . .
- **"Wizard's World"** by Andre Norton: A transdimensional fugitive must conquer a realm of incredible power and deadly illusions . . .
- **"RATED"** by F. Paul Wilson: Amazing Secret of the Rich and Famous!!! UNLIMITED WEALTH CAN BE YOURS—WITH NO MONEY DOWN!!! Don't delay!!! Operators are standing by!!! ACT NOW!!!
- **"The Alchemist and the Witch"** by Christopher Stasheff: Sometimes a magician can get into more trouble if he *doesn't* sell his soul . . .

And many more, including such unforgettable,
must-read classics as Ray Bradbury's "The Vacation,"
Fritz Leiber's "Bazaar of the Bizarre," Jack Vance's "Mazirian
the Magician," Zenna Henderson's "The Anything Box,"
Ursula K. Le Guin's "The Word of Unbinding," and
Roger Zelazny's "The Last Defender of Camelot."

A Magic Lover's Treasury Of The Fantastic

EDITED BY
MARGARET WEIS

ASPECT®

WARNER BOOKS

A Time Warner Company

Copyright © 1998 by Margaret Weis and Tekno Books
All rights reserved.

"What Good Is a Glass Dagger?" by Larry Niven. Copyright © 1971 by Larry Niven. Reprinted by permission of the author and his agent, Eleanor Wood, Spectrum Literary Agency.

"The Princess and the Bear" by Orson Scott Card. Copyright © 1980 by Orson Scott Card. Reprinted by permission of the author.

"The Summoning" by Katherine Kurtz. Copyright © 1991 by Katherine Kurtz. Reprinted by permission of the author and her agent, Russ Galen, Scovil-Chichak-Galen Literary Agency, Inc.

Copyright information continued on page 422.

Aspect® name and logo are registered trademarks of Warner Books, Inc.

Warner Books, Inc., 1271 Avenue of the Americas, New York, NY 10020

Visit our Web site at
http://warnerbooks.com

 A Time Warner Company

Printed in the United States of America

First Printing: January 1998

10 9 8 7 6 5 4 3 2 1

Library of Congress Cataloging-in-Publication Data
A magic-lover's treasury of the fantastic / edited by Margaret Weis.
   p.   cm.
  ISBN 0-446-67284-X
  1. Fantastic fiction, American. 2. Magicians—Fiction. 3. Magic—Fiction I. Weis, Margaret.
PS648.M25M35 1998
813'.087660837—dc21   97-12855
                                          CIP

Cover design by Don Puckey
Cover illustration by Keith Birdsong
Book design and text composition by H. Roberts

CONTENTS

Introduction	Margaret Weis	vii
What Good Is a Glass Dagger?	Larry Niven	1
The Princess and the Bear	Orson Scott Card	41
The Summoning	Katherine Kurtz	72
As Is	Robert Silverberg	85
The Alchemist and the Witch	Christopher Stasheff	102
Fiddler Fair	Mercedes Lackey	133
Wizard's World	Andre Norton	151
Geroldo's Incredible Trick	Raymond E. Feist	202
Willow	C.J. Cherryh	211
The Vacation	Ray Bradbury	232
Mazirian the Magician	Jack Vance	240
The Bazaar of the Bizarre	Fritz Leiber	257
The Lady's Gifts	Melanie Rawn	282
The Walker Behind	Marion Zimmer Bradley	295
The Anything Box	Zenna Henderson	312
The White Horse Child	Greg Bear	327
Armaja Das	Joe Haldeman	347
REATERO	F. Paul Wilson	366
The Word of Unbinding	Ursula K. Le Guin	391
The Last Defender of Camelot	Roger Zelazny	398

INTRODUCTION

Margaret Weis

Magic. It was once a part of everyday life.

In the Middle Ages, evil magic or "black magic" was condemned by the church. At the same time, natural magic—magic that did not harm anyone and was instead used to benefit people—was generally condoned. Such magic might include the making of an image, under the right astrological sign, to benefit a person or putting medicine on a weapon in the belief that this would aid the person injured by that weapon. People turned readily to magic to aid them when the real world failed.

And then came science, to prove to us that the real world operates under strict laws—laws that cannot be broken. Under such laws, an arrow is an arrow, an impersonal object, and anointing it with salve will not have the slightest effect on the victim with an arrow wound in the gut. There are no mysteries or miracles left in the world. Science has an explanation for them all.

We bow to science. We rise up and call science blessed. But, oh, how we long for magic!

Perhaps it is the strong presence of science in *our* everyday lives that has renewed our interest in magic. We know for a fact that a person cannot shoot bolts of electricity from his fingertips or produce wondrous fireworks without benefit of a gunpowder factory somewhere in China. Yet we enjoy stories that portray people, ordinary people like ourselves, casting spells and enchantments and, in our hearts, we believe. It is the rebel in us all. We are ruled by the laws of physics. We love to see those laws broken!

Yet magic presents the odd dichotomy that in breaking the laws of physics, we must create laws for magic. We must try to govern that which is, by definition, ungovernable. Such laws are necessary in order to give magic credibility, define its limits. Among these laws is one that states, as does a modern novelist, "even wizards must suffer."

Just as money may not buy happiness, so magic may not conjure up happiness. Perhaps it is racial memory, but we fear magic almost as much as we long to use it. We don't like the thought of any person having that much power over us or over the laws of nature. We do not give away such power lightly, not even to those who live only in our imaginations. They must work for their power; they must be willing to make sacrifices for that power.

For me, the creation of these laws and the people who are bound by them is one of the greatest pleasures in reading fantasy and in writing it.

A MAGIC-LOVER'S TREASURY
OF THE FANTASTIC

WHAT GOOD IS A GLASS DAGGER?

Larry Niven

I

Twelve thousand years before the birth of Christ, in an age when miracles were somewhat more common, a warlock used an ancient secret to save his life.

In later years he regretted that. He had kept the secret of the Warlock's Wheel for several normal lifetimes. The demon-sword Glirendree and its stupid barbarian captive would have killed him, no question of that. But no mere demon could have been as dangerous as that secret.

Now it was out, spreading like ripples on a pond. The battle between Glirendree and the Warlock was too good a tale not to tell. Soon no man would call himself a magician who did not know that magic could be used up. So simple, so dangerous a secret. The wonder was that nobody had noticed it before.

A year after the battle with Glirendree, near the end of a summer day, Aran the Peacemonger came to Shayl Village to steal the Warlock's Wheel.

* * *

Aran was a skinny eighteen-year-old, lightly built. His face was lean and long, with a pointed chin. His dark eyes peered out from under a prominent shelf of bone. His short, straight dark hair dropped almost to his brows in a pronounced widow's peak. What he was was no secret; and anyone who touched hands with him would have known at once, for there was short fine hair on his palms. But had anyone known his mission, he would have been thought mad.

For the Warlock was a leader in the Sorcerer's Guild. It was known that he had a name; but no human throat could pronounce it. The shadow demon who had been his name-father had later been imprisoned in tattooed runes on the Warlock's own back: an uncommonly dangerous bodyguard.

Yet Aran came well protected. The leather wallet that hung from his shoulder was old and scarred, and the seams were loose. By its look it held nuts and hard cheese and bread and almost no money. What it actually held was charms. Magic would serve him better than nuts and cheese, and Aran could feed himself as he traveled, at night.

He reached the Warlock's cave shortly after sunset. He had been told how to use his magic to circumvent the Warlock's safeguards. His need for magic implied a need for voice and hands, so that Aran was forced to keep the human shape; and this made him doubly nervous. At moonrise he chanted the words he had been taught, and drew a live bat from his pouch and tossed it gently through the barred entrance to the cave.

The bat exploded into a mist of blood that drifted slant-wise across the stone floor. Aran's stomach lurched. He almost ran then; but he quelled his fear and followed it in, squeezing between the bars.

Those who had sent him had repeatedly diagrammed the cave for him. He could have robbed it blindfolded. He would have preferred darkness to the flickering blue light from what seemed to be a captured lightning bolt tethered in the middle of the cavern. He moved quickly, scrupulously tracing what he had been told was a path of safety.

Though Aran had seen sorcerous tools in the training laboratory in the School for Mercantile Grammaree in Atlantis, most of the Warlock's tools were unfamiliar. It was not an age of mass production. He paused by a workbench, wondering. Why would the Warlock be grinding a glass dagger?

But Aran found a tarnish-blackened metal disc hanging above the workbench, and the runes inscribed around its rim convinced him that it was what he had come for. He took it down and quickly strapped it against his thigh, leaving his hands free to fight if need be. He was turning to go, when a laughing voice spoke out of the air.

"Put that down, you mangy son of a bitch—"

Aran converted to wolf.

Agony seared his thigh!

In human form Aran was a lightly built boy. As a wolf he was formidably large and dangerous. It did him little good this time. The pain was blinding, stupefying. Aran the wolf screamed and tried to run from the pain.

He woke gradually, with an ache in his head and a greater agony in his thigh and a tightness at his wrists and ankles. It came to him that he must have knocked himself out against a wall.

He lay on his side with his eyes closed, giving no sign that he was awake. Gently he tried to pull his hands apart. He was bound, wrists and ankles. Well, he had been taught a word for unbinding ropes.

Best not to use it until he knew more.

He opened his eyes a slit.

The Warlock was beside him, seated in lotus position, studying Aran with a slight smile. In one hand he held a slender willow rod.

The Warlock was a tall man in robust good health. He was deeply tanned. Legend said that the Warlock never wore anything above the waist. The years seemed to blur on him; he might have been twenty or fifty. In fact he was one hundred and ninety years old, and bragged of it. His condition indicated the power of his magic.

Behind him, Aran saw that the Warlock's Wheel had been returned to its place on the wall.

Waiting for its next victim? The real Warlock's Wheel was of copper; those who had sent Aran had known that much. But this decoy must be tarnished silver, to have seared him so.

The Warlock wore a dreamy, absent look. There might still be a chance, if he could be taken by surprise. Aran said, "Kplir—"

The Warlock lashed him across the throat.

The willow wand had plenty of spring in it. Aran choked and gagged; he tossed his head, fighting for air.

"That word has four syllables," the Warlock informed him in a voice he recognized. "You'll never get it out."

"Gluck," said Aran.

"I want to know who sent you."

Aran did not answer, though he had his wind back.

"You're no ordinary thief. But you're no magician either," the Warlock said almost musingly. "I heard you. You were chanting by rote. You used basic spells, spells that are easy to get right, but they were the right spells each time.

"Somebody's been using prescience and farsight to spy on me. Someone knows too many of my defenses," the ancient magician said gently. "I don't like that. I want to know who, and why."

When Aran did not reply, the Warlock said, "He had all the knowledge, and he knew what he was after, but he had better sense than to come himself. He sent a fool." The Warlock was watching Aran's eyes. "Or perhaps he thought a werewolf would have a better chance at me. By the way, there's silver braid in those cords, so you'd best stay human for the nonce."

"You knew I was coming."

"Oh, I had ample warning. Didn't it occur to you that I've got prescience and farsight too? It occurred to your master," said the Warlock. "He set up protections around you, a moving region where prescience doesn't work."

"Then what went wrong?"

"I foresaw the dead region, you ninny. I couldn't get a glimpse of what was stealing into my cave. But I could look around it. I could follow its path through the cavern. That path was most direct. I knew what you were after.

"Then, there were bare footprints left behind. I could study them before they were made. You waited for moonrise instead of trying to get in after dusk. On a night of the full moon, too.

"Other than that, it wasn't a bad try. Sending a werewolf was bright. It would take a kid your size to squeeze between the bars, and then a kid your size couldn't win a fight if something went wrong. A wolf your size could."

"A lot of good it did me."

"What I want to know is, how did they talk an Atlantean into this? They must have known what they were after. Didn't they tell you what the Wheel does?"

"Sucks up magic," said Aran. He was chagrined, but not surprised, that the Warlock had placed his accent.

"Sucks up *mana*," the Warlock corrected him. "Do you know what *mana* is?"

"The power behind magic."

"So they taught you that much. Did they also tell you that when the *mana* is gone from a region, it doesn't come back? Ever?"

Aran rolled on his side. Being convinced that he was about to die, he felt he had nothing to lose by speaking boldly. "I don't understand why you'd want to keep it a secret. A thing like the Warlock's Wheel, it could make war obsolete! It's the greatest purely defensive weapon ever invented!"

The Warlock didn't seem to understand. Aran said, "You *must* have thought of that. Why, no enemy's curses could touch Atlantis, if the Warlock's Wheel were there to absorb it!"

"Obviously you weren't sent by the Atlantean Minister of Offense. He'd know better." The Warlock watched him shrewdly. "Or were you sent by the Greek Isles?"

"I don't understand."

"Don't you know that Atlantis is tectonically unstable? For the last half a thousand years, the only thing that's kept Atlantis above the waves has been the spells of the sorcerer-kings."

"You're lying."

"You obviously aren't." The Warlock made a gesture of dismissal. "But the Wheel would be bad for any nation, not just Atlantis. Spin the Wheel, and a wide area is dead to magic for—as far as I've been able to tell—the rest of eternity. Who would want to bring about such a thing?"

"I would."

"You would. Why?"

"We're sick of war," Aran said roughly. Unaware that he had said *we*. "The Warlock's Wheel would end war. Can you imagine an army trying to fight with nothing but swords and daggers? No hurling of death spells. No prescients spying out the enemy's battle plans. No killer demons beating at unseen protective walls." Aran's eyes glowed. "Man to man, sword against sword, blood and bronze, and no healing spells. Why, no king would ever fight on such terms! We'd give up war forever!"

"Some basic pessimism deep within me forces me to doubt it."

"You're laughing at me. You don't *want* to believe it," Aran said scornfully. "No more *mana* means the end of your youth spells. You'd be an old man, too old to live!"

"That must be it. Well, let's see who you are." The Warlock touched Aran's wallet with the willow wand, let it rest there a few moments. Aran wondered frantically what the Warlock could learn from his wallet. If the lockspells didn't hold, then—

They didn't, of course. The Warlock reached in, pulled out another live bat, then several sheets of parchment marked with what might have been geometry lessons and with script printed in a large, precise hand.

"Schoolboy script," he commented. "Lines drawn with painful accuracy, mistakes scraped out and redrawn . . . The idiot! He forgot the hooked tail on the Whirlpool design. A wonder it didn't eat him." The Warlock looked up. "Am I being attacked by children? These spells were prepared by half a dozen apprentices!"

Aran didn't answer; but he lost hope of concealing anything further.

"They have talent, though. So. You're a member of the Peacemongers, aren't you? All the army-age youngsters. I'll wager you're backed by half the graduating class of the School of Mercantile Grammaree. They must have been watching me for months now, to have my defenses down so pat.

"And you want to end the war against the Greek Isles. Did you think you'd help matters by taking the Warlock's Wheel to Atlantis? Why, I'm half minded to let you walk out with the thing. It would serve you right for trying to rob me."

He looked hard into Aran's eyes. "Why, you'd do it, wouldn't you? Why? I said *why?*"

"We could still use it."

"You'd sink Atlantis. Are the Peacemongers traitors now?"

"I'm no traitor." Aran spoke low and furious. "We want to change Atlantis, not destroy it. But if we owned the Warlock's Wheel, the Palace would listen to us!"

He wriggled in his tight bonds, and thought once again of the word that would free him. Then, convert to werewolf and run! Between the bars, down the hill, into the woods and freedom.

"I think I'll make a conservative of you," the Warlock said suddenly.

He stood up. He brushed the willow wand lightly across Aran's lips. Aran found that he could not open his mouth. He remembered now that he was entirely in the Warlock's power—and that he was a captured thief.

The Warlock turned, and Aran saw the design on his back. It was an elaborately curlicued five-sided tattoo in red and green and gold inks. Aran remembered what he had been told of the Warlock's bodyguard.

"Recently I dreamed," said the Warlock. "I dreamed that I would find a use for a glass dagger. I thought that the dream might be prophetic, and so I carved—"

"That's silly," Aran broke in. "What good is a glass dagger?"

He had noticed the dagger on the way in. It had a honed square point and honed edges and a fused-looking hilt with a guard. Two clamps padded with fox leather held it in place on the work table. The uppermost cutting edge was not yet finished.

Now the Warlock removed the dagger from its clamps. While Aran watched, the Warlock scratched designs on the blade with a pointed chunk of diamond that must have cost him dearly. He spoke low and softly to it, words that Aran couldn't hear. Then he picked it up like— a dagger.

Frightened as he was, Aran could not quite believe what the Warlock was doing. He felt like a sacrificial goat. There was *mana* in sacrifice . . . and more *mana* in human sacrifice . . . but he wouldn't. He wouldn't!

The Warlock raised the knife high, and brought it down hard in Aran's chest.

Aran screamed. He had felt it! A whisper of sensation, a slight ghostly tug—the knife was an insubstantial shadow. But there was a knife in Aran the Peacemonger's heart! The hilt stood up out of his chest!

The Warlock muttered low and fast. The glass hilt faded and was gone, apparently.

"It's easy to make glass invisible. Glass is half invisible already. It's still in your heart," said the Warlock. "But don't worry about it. Don't give it a thought. Nobody will notice. Only, be sure to spend the rest of your life in *mana*-rich territory. Because if you ever walk into a place where magic doesn't work—well, it'll reappear, that's all."

Aran struggled to open his mouth.

"Now, you came for the secret of the Warlock's Wheel, so you might as well have it. It's just a simple kinetic sorcery, but open-ended." He gave it. "The Wheel spins faster and faster until it's used up all the *mana* in the area. It tends to tear itself apart, so you need another spell to hold it together—" and he gave that, speaking slowly and distinctly. Then he seemed to notice that Aran was flopping about like a fish. He said, "Kplirapranthry."

The ropes fell away. Aran stood up shakily. He found he could speak again, and what he said was, "Take it out. Please."

"Now, there's one thing about taking that secret back to Atlantis. I assume you still want to? But you'd have to describe it before you could use it as a threat. You can see how easy it is to make. A big nation like Atlantis tends to have enemies, doesn't it? And you'd be telling them how to sink Atlantis in a single night."

Aran pawed at his chest, but he could feel nothing. "Take it out."

"I don't think so. Now we face the same death, wolf boy. Goodby, and give my best to the School for Mercantile Grammaree. And, oh yes, don't go back by way of Hvirin Gap."

"Grandson of an ape!" Aran screamed. He would not beg again. He was wolf by the time he reached the bars, and he did not touch them going through. With his mind he felt the knife in his chest, and he heard the Warlock's laughter following him down the hill and into the trees.

When next he saw the Warlock, it was thirty years later and a thousand miles away.

II

Aran traveled as a wolf, when he could. It was an age of greater magic; a werewolf could change shape whenever the moon was in the sky. In the wolf shape Aran could forage, reserving his remaining coins to buy his way home.

His thoughts were a running curse against the Warlock.

Once he turned about on a small hill, and stood facing north toward Shayl Village. He bristled, remembering the Warlock's laugh; but he remembered the glass dagger. He visualized the Warlock's throat, and imagined the taste of arterial blood; but the glowing, twisting design on the Warlock's back flashed at the back of Aran's eyes, and Aran tasted defeat. He could not fight a shadow demon. Aran howled, once, and turned south.

Nildiss Range, the backbone of a continent, rose before him as he traveled. Beyond the Range was the sea, and a choice of boats to take him home with what he had learned of the Warlock. Perhaps the next thief would have better luck . . .

And so he came to Hvirin Gap.

Once the range had been a formidable barrier to trade. Then, almost a thousand years ago, a sorcerer of Rynildissen had worked an impressive magic. The Range had been split as if by a cleaver. Where the mountains to either side sloped precipitously upward, Hvirin Gap sloped smoothly down to the coast, between rock walls flat enough to have a polished look.

Periodically the bandits had to be cleaned out of Hvirin Gap. This was more difficult every year; for the spells against banditry didn't work well there, and swords had to be used instead. The only compensation was that the dangerous mountain dragons had disappeared too.

Aran stopped at the opening. He sat on his haunches, considering.

For the Warlock might have been lying. He might have thought it funny to send Aran the long way over Nildiss Range.

But the dragon bones. Where magic didn't work, dragons died. The bones were there, huge and reptilian. They had fused with the rock of the pass somehow, so that they looked tens of millions of years old.

Aran had traveled the Gap in wolf form. If Hvirin Gap was dead of magic, he should have been forced into the man form. Or would he find it impossible to change at all?

"But I can go through as a wolf," Aran thought. "That way I can't be killed by anything but silver and platinum. The glass dagger should hurt, but—

"Damn! I'm invulnerable, but is it *magic*? If it doesn't work in Hvirin Gap—" and he shuddered.

The dagger had never been more than a whisper of sensation, that had faded in half an hour and never returned. But Aran knew it was there. Invisible, a knife in his heart, waiting.

It might reappear in his chest, and he could still survive—as a wolf. But it would hurt! And he could never be human again.

Aran turned and padded away from Hvirin Gap. He had passed a village yesterday. Perhaps the resident magician could help him.

"A glass dagger!" the magician chortled. He was a portly, jolly, balding man, clearly used to good living. "Now I've heard everything. Well, what were you worried about? It's got a handle, doesn't it? Was it a complex spell?"

"I don't think so. He wrote runes on the blade, then stabbed me with it."

"Fine. You pay in advance. And you'd better convert to wolf, just to play safe." He named a sum that would have left Aran without money for passage home. Aran managed to argue him down to something not far above reason, and they went to work.

The magician gave up some six hours later. His voice was hoarse, his eyes were red from oddly colored, oddly scented smokes, and his hands were discolored with dyes. "I can't touch the hilt, I can't make it visible, I can't get any sign that it's there at all. If I use any stronger spell, it's likely to kill you. I quit, wolf boy. Whoever put this spell on you, he knows more than a simple village magician."

Aran rubbed his chest where the skin was stained by mildly corrosive dyes. "They call him the Warlock."

The portly magician stiffened. "The Warlock? *The* Warlock? And you didn't think to tell me. Get out."

"What about my money?"

"I wouldn't have tried it for ten times the fee! Me, a mere hedge-magician, and you turned me loose against the Warlock! We might both have been killed. If you think you're entitled to your money, let's go to the headman and state our case. Otherwise, get out."

Aran left, shouting insults.

"Try other magicians if you like," the other shouted after him. "Try Rynildissen City! But tell them what they're doing first!"

III

It had been a difficult decision for the Warlock. But his secret was out and spreading. The best he could do was see to it that world sorcery understood the implications.

The Warlock addressed the Sorcerers' Guild on the subject of *mana* depletion and the Warlock's Wheel.

"Think of it every time you work magic," he thundered in what amounted to baby talk after his severely technical description of the Wheel. "Only finite *mana* in the world, and less of it every year, as a thousand magicians drain it away. There were beings who ruled the world as gods, long ago, until the raging power of their own being used up the *mana* that kept them alive.

"One day it'll all be gone. Then all the demons and dragons and unicorns, trolls and rocs and centaurs will vanish quite away, because their metabolism is partly based on magic. Then all the dream-castles will evaporate, and nobody will ever know they were there. Then all the magicians will become tinkers and smiths, and the world will be a dull place to live. You have the power to bring that day nearer!"

That night he dreamed.

A duel between magicians makes a fascinating tale. Such tales are common—and rarely true. The winner of such a duel is not likely to give up trade secrets. The loser is dead, at the very least.

Novices in sorcery are constantly amazed at how much preparation goes into a duel, and how little action. The duel with the Hill Magician started with a dream, the night after the Warlock's speech made that duel inevitable. It ended thirty years later.

In that dream the enemy did not appear. But the Warlock saw a cheerful, harmless-looking fairy castle perched on an impossible hill. From a fertile, hummocky landscape, the hill rose like a breaking wave, leaning so far that the castle at its crest had empty space below it.

In his sleep the Warlock frowned. Such a hill would topple without magic. The fool who built it was wasting *mana*.

And in his sleep he concentrated, memorizing details. A narrow path curled up the hillside. Facts twisted, dreamlike. There was a companion with him; or there wasn't. The Warlock lived until he passed through the gate; or he died at the gate, in agony, with great ivory teeth grinding together through his rib cage.

He woke himself up trying to sort it out.

The shadowy companion was necessary, at least as far as the gate. Beyond the enemy's gate he could see nothing. A Warlock's Wheel must have been used there, to block his magic so thoroughly.

Poetic justice?

He spent three full days working spells to block the Hill Magician's prescient sense. During that time his own sleep was dreamless. The other's magic was as effective as his own.

IV

Great ships floated at anchor in the harbor.

There were cargo ships whose strange demonic figureheads had limited power of movement, just enough to reach the rats that tried to swarm up the mooring lines. A large Atlantean passenger liner was equipped with twin outriggers made from whole tree trunks. By the nearest dock a magician's slender yacht floated eerily above the water. Aran watched them all rather wistfully.

He had spent too much money traveling over the mountains. A week after his arrival in Rynildissen City he had taken a post as body-guard/watchdog to a rug merchant. He had been down to his last coin, and hungry.

Now Lloraginezee the rug merchant and Ra-Harroo his secretary talked trade secrets with the captain of a Nile cargo ship. Aran waited on the dock, watching ships with indifferent patience.

His ears came to point. The bearded man walking past him wore a captain's kilt. Aran hailed him: "Ho, Captain! Are you sailing to Atlantis?"

The bearded man frowned. "And what's that to you?"

"I would send a message there."

"Deal with a magician."

"I'd rather not," said Aran. He could hardly tell a magician that he wanted to send instructions on how to rob a magician. Otherwise the message would have gone months ago.

"I'll charge you more, and it will take longer," the bearded man said with some satisfaction. "Who in Atlantis, and where?"

Aran gave him an address in the city. He passed over the sealed message pouch he had been carrying for three months now.

Aran too had made some difficult decisions. In final draft his mes-sage warned of the tectonic instability of the continent, and suggested steps the Peacemongers could take to learn if the Warlock had lied. Aran had not included instructions for making a Warlock's Wheel.

Far out in the harbor, dolphins and mermen played rough and com-plicated games. The Atlantean craft hoisted sail. A wind rose from nowhere to fill the sails. It died slowly, following the passenger craft out to sea.

Soon enough, Aran would have the fare. He would almost have it now, except that he had twice paid out sorcerer's fees, with the result that the money was gone and the glass dagger was not. Meanwhile, Lloraginezee did not give trade secrets to his bodyguard. He knew that Aran would be on his way as soon as he had the money.

Here they came down the gangplank: Lloraginezee with less waddle than might be expected of a man of his girth; the girl walking with quiet grace, balancing the rug samples on her head. Ra-Harroo was saying something as Aran joined them, something Aran may have been intended to hear.

"Beginning tomorrow, I'll be off work for five days. *You* know," she told Lloraginezee—and blushed.

"Fine, fine," said Lloraginezee, nodding absently.

Aran knew too. He smiled but did not look at her. He might embarrass her . . . and he knew well enough what Ra-Harroo looked like. Her hair was black and short and coarse. Her nose was large but flat, almost merging into her face. Her eyes were brown and soft, her brows dark and thick. Her ears were delicately formed and convoluted, and came to a point. She was a lovely girl, especially to another of the wolf people.

They held hands as they walked. Her nails were narrow and strong, and the fine hair on her palm tickled.

In Atlantis he would have considered marrying her, had he the money to support her. Here, it was out of the question. For most of the month they were friends and co-workers. The night life of Rynildissen City was more convenient for a couple, and there were times when Lloraginezee could spare them both.

Perhaps Lloraginezee made such occasions. He was not of the wolf people. He probably enjoyed thinking that sex had reared its lovely, disturbing head. But sex could not be involved—except at a certain time of the month. Aran didn't see her then. She was locked up in her father's house. He didn't even know where she lived.

*   *   *

He found out five nights later.

He had guarded Lloraginezee's way to Adrienne's House of Pleasures. Lloraginezee would spend the night . . . on an air mattress floating on mercury, a bed Aran had only heard described. A pleasant sleep was not the least of pleasures.

The night was warm and balmy. Aran took a long way home, walking wide of the vacant lot behind Adrienne's. That broad, flat plot of ground had housed the palace of Shilbree the Dreamer, three hundred years ago. The palace had been all magic, and quite an achievement even in its day. Eventually it had . . . worn out, Shilbree would have said.

One day it was gone. And not even the simplest of spells would work in that vacant lot.

Someone had told Aran that households of wolf people occupied several blocks of the residential district. It seemed to be true, for he caught identifying smells as he crossed certain paths. He followed one, curious to see what kind of house a wealthy werewolf would build in Rynildissen.

The elusive scent led him past a high, angular house with a brass door . . . and then it was too late, for another scent was in his nostrils and in his blood and brain. He spent that whole night howling at the door. Nobody tried to stop him. The neighbors must have been used to it; or they may have known that he would kill rather than be driven away.

More than once he heard a yearning voice answering from high up in the house. It was Ra-Harroo's voice. With what remained of his mind, Aran knew that he would be finding apologies in a few days. She would think he had come deliberately.

Aran howled a song of sadness and deprivation and shame.

V

The first was a small village called Gath, and a Guild 'prentice who came seeking black opals. He found them, and free for the taking too, for Gath was dead empty. The 'prentice sorcerer wondered about that, and he looked about him, and presently he found a dead spot with a crumbled castle in it. It might have been centuries fallen. Or it might have been raised by magic, and collapsed when the *mana* went out of it, yesterday or last week.

It was a queer tale, and it got around. The 'prentice grew rich on the opals, for black opals are very useful for cursing. But the empty village bothered him.

"I thought it was slavers at first," he said once, in the Warlock's hearing as it turned out. "There were no corpses, none anywhere. Slave traders don't kill if they can help it.

"But why would a troop of slavers leave valuables lying where they were? The opals were all over the street, mixed with hay. I think a jeweler must have been moving them in secret when—*something* smashed his wagon. But why didn't they pick up the jewels?"

It was the crumbled castle the Warlock remembered three years later, when he heard about Shiskabil. He heard of that one directly, from a magpie that fluttered out of the sky onto his shoulder and whispered, "Warlock?"

And when he had heard, he went.

Shiskabil was a village of stone houses within a stone wall. It must have been abandoned suddenly. Dinners had dried or rotted on their plates; meat had been burnt to ash in ovens. There were no living inhabitants, and no dead. The wall had not been breached. But there were signs of violence everywhere: broken furniture, doors with broken locks or splintered hinges, crusted spears and swords and makeshift clubs, and blood. Dried black blood everywhere, as if it had rained blood.

Clubfoot was a younger Guild member, thin and earnest. Though talented, he was still a little afraid of the power he commanded through magic. He was not happy in Shiskabil. He walked with shoulders hunched, trying to avoid the places where blood had pooled.

"Weird, isn't it? But I had a special reason to send for you," he said. "There's a dead region outside the wall. I had the idea someone might have used a Warlock's Wheel there."

A rectangular plot of fertile ground, utterly dead, a foretaste of a world dead to magic. In the center were crumbled stones with green plants growing between.

The Warlock circled the place, unwilling to step where magic did not work. He had used the Wheel once before, against Glirendree, after the demon-sword had killed his shadow demon. The Wheel had sucked the youth from him, left the Warlock two hundred years old in a few seconds.

"There was magic worked in the village," said Clubfoot. "I tried a few simple spells. The *mana* level's very low. I don't remember any famous sorcerers from Shiskabil; do you?"

"No."

"Then whatever happened here was done by magic." Clubfoot almost whispered the word. Magic could be very evil—as he knew.

They found a zigzag path through the dead borderline, and a faintly live region inside. At a gesture from the Warlock, the crumbled stones stirred feebly, trying to rise.

"So it was somebody's castle," said Clubfoot. "I wonder how he got this effect?"

"I thought of something like it once. Say you put a heavy kinetic spell on a smaller Wheel. The Wheel would spin very fast, would use up *mana* in a very tight area—"

Clubfoot was nodding. "I see it. He could have run it on a track, a close path. It would give him a kind of hedge against magic around a live region."

"And he left the border open so he could get his tools in and out. He zigzagged the entrance so no spells could get through. Nobody could use farsight on him. I wonder . . . "

"I wonder what he had to hide?"

"I wonder what happened in Shiskabil," said the Warlock. And he remembered the dead barrier that hid the Hill Magician's castle. His leisurely duel with a faceless enemy was twelve years old.

It was twenty-three years old before they found the third village.

Hathzoril was bigger than Shiskabil, and better known. When a shipment of carvings in ivory and gem woods did not arrive, the Warlock heard of it.

The village could not have been abandoned more than a few days when the Warlock arrived. He and Clubfoot found meals half cooked, meals half eaten, broken furniture, weapons that had been taken from their racks, broken doors—

"But no blood. I wonder why?"

Clubfoot was jittery. "Otherwise it's just the same. The whole population gone in an instant, probably against their will. Ten whole years; no, more. I'd half forgotten . . . You got here before I did. Did you find a dead area and a crumbled castle?"

"No. I looked."

The younger magician rubbed his birth-maimed foot—which he could have cured in half an hour, but it would have robbed him of half his powers. "We could be wrong. If it's him, he's changed his techniques."

That night the Warlock dreamed a scrambled dream in pyrotechnic colors. He woke thinking of the Hill Magician.

"Let's climb some hills," he told Clubfoot in the morning. "I've got to know if the Hill Magician has something to do with these empty villages. We're looking for a dead spot on top of a hill."

That mistake almost killed him.

The last hill Clubfoot tried to climb was tumbled, crumbled soil and rock that slid and rolled under his feet. He tried it near sunset, in sheer desperation, for they had run out of hills and patience.

He was still near the base when the Warlock came clambering to join him. "Come down from there!" he laughed. "Nobody would build on this sand heap."

Clubfoot looked around, and shouted, "Get out of here! You're older!"

The Warlock rubbed his face and felt the wrinkles. He picked his way back in haste and in care, wanting to hurry, but fearful of breaking fragile bones. He left a trail of fallen silver hair.

Once beyond the *mana*-poor region, he cackled in falsetto. "My mistake. I know what he did now. Clubfoot, we'll find the dead spot inside the hill."

"First we'll work you a rejuvenation spell." Clubfoot laid his tools out on a rock. A charcoal block, a silver knife, packets of leaves . . .

"That border's bad. It sucks up *mana* from inside. He must have to move pretty often. So he raised up a hill like a breaking wave. When the magic ran out the hill just rolled over the castle and covered up everything. He'll do it again, too."

"Clever. What do you think happened in Hathzoril Village?"

"We may never know." The Warlock rubbed new wrinkles at the corners of his eyes. "Something bad, I think. Something very bad."

VI

He was strolling through the merchants' quarter that afternoon, looking at rugs.

Normally this was a cheerful task. Hanging rugs formed a brightly colored maze through this part of the quarter. As Aran the rug merchant moved through the maze, well-known voices would call his name. Then there would be gossip and canny trading.

He had traded in Rynildissen City for nearly thirty years, first as Lloraginezee's apprentice, later as his own man. The finest rugs and the cheapest, from all over this continent and nearby islands, came by ship and camel's back to Rynildissen City. Wholesalers, retailers, and the odd nobleman who wished to furnish a palace would travel to Rynildissen City to buy. Today they glowed in the hot sunlight . . . but today they only depressed him. Aran was thinking of moving away.

A bald man stepped into view from behind a block of cured sphinx pelts.

Bald as a roc's egg he was, yet young, and in the prime of muscular good health. He was shirtless like a stevedore, but his pantaloons were of high quality and his walk was pure arrogance. Aran felt he was staring rather rudely. Yet there was something familiar about the man.

He passed Aran without a glance.

Aran glanced back once, and was jolted. The design seemed to leap out at him: a five-sided multicolored tattoo on the man's back.

Aran called, "Warlock!"

He regretted it the next moment. The Warlock turned on him the look one gives a presumptuous stranger.

The Warlock had not changed at all, except for the loss of his hair. But Aran remembered that thirty years had passed; that he himself was a man of fifty, with the hollows of his face filled out by rich living. He remembered that his greying hair had receded, leaving his widow's peak as a shock of hair all alone on his forehead. And he remembered, in great detail, the circumstances under which he had met the Warlock.

He had spent a thousand nights plotting vengeance against the Warlock; yet now his only thought was to get away. He said, "Your pardon, sir—"

But something else occurred to him, so that he said firmly, "But we *have* met."

"Under what circumstance? I do not recall it," the Warlock said coldly.

Aran's answer was a measure of the self-confidence that comes with wealth and respect. He said, "I was robbing your cave."

"Were you!" The Warlock came closer. "Ah, the boy from Atlantis. Have you robbed any magicians lately?"

"I have adopted a somewhat safer way of life," Aran said equably. "And I do have reason for presuming on our brief acquaintance."

"Our brief—" The Warlock laughed so that heads turned all over the marketplace. Still laughing, he took Aran's arm and led him away.

They strolled slowly through the merchants' quarter, the Warlock leading. "I have to follow a certain path," he explained. "A project of my own. Well, my boy, what have you been doing for thirty years?"

"Trying to get rid of your glass dagger."

"Glass dagger? . . . Oh, yes, I remember. Surely you found time for other hobbies?"

Aran almost struck the Warlock then. But there was something he wanted from the Warlock; and so he held his temper.

"My whole life has been warped by your damned glass dagger," he said. "I had to circle Hvirin Gap on my way home. When I finally got here I was out of money. No money for passage to Atlantis, and no money to pay for a magician, which meant that I couldn't get the glass knife removed.

"So I hired out to Lloraginezee the rug merchant as a bodyguard/watchdog. Now I'm the leading rug merchant in Rynildissen City, I've got two wives and eight children and a few grandchildren, and I don't suppose I'll ever get back to Atlantis."

They bought wine from a peddler carrying two fat wineskins on his shoulders. They took turns drinking from the great copper goblet the man carried.

The Warlock asked, "Did you ever get rid of the knife?"

"No, and you ought to know it! What kind of a spell did you *put* on that thing? The best magicians in this continent haven't been able to so much as *touch* that knife, let alone pull it out. I wouldn't be a rug merchant if they had."

"Why not?"

"Well, I'd have earned my passage to Atlantis soon enough, except that every time I heard about a new magician in the vicinity I'd go to him to see if he could take that knife out. Selling rugs was a way to get the money to pay the magicians. Eventually I gave up on the magicians and kept the money. All I'd accomplished was to spread your reputation in all directions."

"Thank you," the Warlock said politely.

Aran did not like the Warlock's amusement. He decided to end the conversation quickly. "I'm glad we ran into each other," he said, "because I have a problem that is really in your province. Can you tell me something about a magician named Wavyhill?"

It may be that the Warlock stiffened. "What is it that you want to know?"

"Whether his spells use excessive power."

The Warlock lifted an interrogatory eyebrow.

"You see, we try to restrict the use of magic in Rynildissen City. The whole nation could suffer if a key region like Rynildissen City went dead to magic. There'd be no way to stop a flood, or a hurricane, or an invasion of barbarians. Do you find something amusing?"

"No, no. But could a glass dagger possibly have anything to do with your conservative attitude?"

"That's entirely my own business, Warlock. Unless you'd care to read my mind?"

"No, thank you. My apologies."

"I'd like to point out that more than just the welfare of Rynildissen City is involved. If this region went dead to magic, the harbor mermen would have to move away. They have quite an extensive city of their own, down there beyond the docks. Furthermore, they run most of the docking facilities and the *entire* fishing industry—"

"Relax. I agree with you completely. You know that," the magician laughed. "You ought to!"

"Sorry. I preach at the drop of a hat. It's been ten years since anyone saw a dragon near Rynildissen City. Even further out, they're warped, changed. When I first came here the dragons had a mercenary's booth in the city itself! What are you doing?"

The Warlock had handed the empty goblet back to the vendor and was pulling at Aran's arm. "Come this way, please. Quickly, before I lose the path."

"Path?"

"I'm following a fogged prescient vision. I could get killed if I lose the path—or if I don't, for that matter. Now, just what was your problem?"

"That," said Aran, pointing among the fruit stalls.

The troll was an ape's head on a human body, covered from head to toe in coarse brown hair. From its size it was probably female, but it had no more breasts than a female ape. It held a wicker basket in one quite human hand. Its bright brown eyes glanced up at Aran's pointing finger—startlingly human eyes—then dropped to the melon it was considering.

Perhaps the sight should have roused reverence. A troll was ancestral to humanity: *Homo habilis*, long extinct. But they were too common. Millions of the species had been fossilized in the drylands of Africa. Magicians of a few centuries ago had learned that they could be reconstituted by magic.

"I think you've just solved one of my own problems," the Warlock said quietly. He no longer showed any trace of amusement.

"Wonderful," Aran said without sincerity. "My own problem is, how much *mana* are Wavyhill's trolls using up? The *mana* level in Rynildissen City was never high to start with. Wavyhill must be using terrifically powerful spells just to keep them walking." Aran's fingertips brushed his chest in an unconscious gesture. "I'd hate to leave Rynildissen City, but if magic stops working here I won't have any choice."

"I'd have to know the spells involved. Tell me something about Wavyhill, will you? Everything you can remember."

To most of Rynildissen City the advent of Wavyhill the magician was very welcome.

Once upon a time troll servants had been common. They were terrifically strong. Suffering no pain, they could use hysterical strength for the most mundane tasks. Being inhuman, they could work on official holidays. They needed no sleep. They did not steal.

But Rynildissen City was old, and the *mana* was running low. For many years no troll had walked in Rynildissen City. At the gate they turned to blowing dust.

Then came Wavyhill with a seemingly endless supply of trolls, which did *not* disintegrate at the gate. The people paid him high prices in gold and in honors.

"For half a century thieves have worked freely on holidays," Aran told the Warlock. "Now we've got a trollish police force again. Can you blame people for being grateful? They made him a Councilman—over my objections. Which means that there's very little short of murder that Wavyhill can't do in Rynildissen City."

"I'm sorry to hear that. Why did you say *over your objections?* Are you on the Council?"

"Yes. I'm the one who rammed through the laws restricting magic in Rynildissen City. And failed to ram through some others, I might add. The trouble is that Wavyhill doesn't make the trolls in the city. Nobody knows where they come from. If he's depleting the *mana* level, he's doing it somewhere else."

"Then what's your problem?"

"Suppose the trolls use up *mana* just by existing? . . . I should be asking, *do they?*"

"I think so," said the Warlock.

"I *knew* it. Warlock, will you testify before the Council? Because—"

"No, I won't."

"But you've got to! I'll never convince anyone by myself. Wavyhill is the most respected magician around, and he'll be testifying against me! Besides which, the Council all own trolls themselves. They won't want to believe they've been suckered, and they have been if we're right. The trolls will collapse as soon as they've lowered the *mana* level enough."

At that point Aran ran down, for he had seen with what stony patience the Warlock was waiting for him to finish.

The Warlock waited three seconds longer, using silence as an exclamation point. Then he said, "It's gone beyond that. Talking to the Council would be like shouting obscenities at a forest fire. I could get results that way. You couldn't."

"Is he *that* dangerous?"

"I think so."

Aran wondered if he was being had. But the Warlock's face was so grave . . . and Aran had seen that face in too many nightmares. *What am I doing here?* he wondered. *I had a technical question about trolls. So I asked a magician . . . and now . . .*

"Keep talking. I need to know more about Wavyhill. And walk faster," said the Warlock. "How long has he been here?"

"Wavyhill came to Rynildissen City seven years ago. Nobody knows where he came from; he doesn't have any particular accent. His palace sits on a hill that looks like it's about to fall over. What are you nodding at?"

"I know that hill. Keep talking."

"We don't see him often. He comes with a troupe of trolls, to sell them; or he comes to vote with the Council on important matters. He's short and dark—."

"That could be a seeming. Never mind, describe him anyway. I've never seen him."

"Short and dark, with a pointed nose and a pointed chin and very curly dark hair. He wears a dark robe of some soft material, a tall pointed hat, and sandals, and he carries a sword."

"Does he!" The Warlock laughed out loud.

"What's the joke? I carry a sword myself sometimes.—Oh, that's right, magicians have a *thing* about swordsmen."

"That's not why I laughed. It's a trade joke. A sword can be a symbol of masculine virility."

"Oh?"

"You see the point, don't you? A sorcerer doesn't need a sword. He knows more powerful protections. When a sorcerer takes to carrying a sword, it's pretty plain he's using it as a cure for impotence."

"And it works?"

"Of course it works. It's straight one-for-one similarity magic, isn't it? But you've got to take the sword to bed with you!" laughed the Warlock. But his eyes found a troll servant, and his laughter slipped oddly.

He watched as the troll hurried through a gate in a high white wall. They had passed out of the merchants' quarter.

"I think Wavyhill's a necromancer," he said abruptly.

"Necromancer. What is it? It sounds ugly."

"A technical term for a new branch of magic. And it is ugly. Turn sharp left here."

They ducked into a narrow alley. Two- and three-story houses leaned over them from both sides. The floor of the alley was filthy, until the Warlock snarled and gestured. Then the dirt and garbage flowed to both sides.

The Warlock hurried them deep into the alley. "We can stop here, I think. Sit down if you like. We'll be here for some time—or I will."

"Warlock, are you playing games with me? What does this new dance have to do with a duel of sorcery?"

"A fair question. Do you know what lies that way?"

Aran's sense of direction was good, and he knew the city. "The Judging Place?"

"Right. And that way, the vacant lot just this side of Adrienne's

House of Pleasures—you know it? The deadest spot in Rynildissen City. The palace of Shilbree the Dreamer once stood there."

"*Might* I ask—"

"The courthouse is void of *mana* too, naturally. Ten thousand defendants and thirty thousand lawyers all praying for conviction or acquittal doesn't leave much magic in *any* courthouse. If I can keep either of those spots between me and Wavyhill, I can keep him from using farsight on me."

Aran thought about it. "But you have to know where he is."

"No, I only have to know where I ought to be. Most of the time, I don't. Wavyhill and I have managed to fog each other's prescient senses pretty well. But I'm supposed to be meeting an unknown ally along about now, and I've taken great care that Wavyhill can't spy on me.

"You see, I invented the Wheel. Wavyhill has taken the Wheel concept and improved it in at least two ways that I know of. Naturally he uses up *mana* at a ferocious rate.

"He may also be a mass murderer. And he's my fault. That's why I've got to kill him."

Aran remembered then that his wives were waiting dinner. He remembered that he had decided to end this conversation hours ago. And he remembered a story he had been told, of a layman caught in a sorcerer's duel, and what had befallen him.

"Well, I've got to be going," he said, standing up. "I wish you the best of luck in your duel, Warlock. And if there's anything I can do to help . . . "

"Fight with me," the Warlock said instantly.

Aran gaped. Then he burst out laughing.

The Warlock waited with his own abnormal patience. When he had some chance of being heard, he said, "I dreamed that an ally would meet me during this time. That ally would accompany me to the gate of Wavyhill's castle. I don't have many of those dreams to help me, Aran. Wavyhill's good. If I go alone, my forecast is that I'll be killed."

"Another ally," Aran suggested.

"No. Too late. The time has passed."

"Look." Aran slapped his belly with the flat of his hand. The flesh rippled. "It's not that much extra weight," he said, "for a man. I'm not *unsightly*. But as a wolf I'd look ten years pregnant! I haven't turned wolf in years."

"What am I doing? I don't have to convince you of anything," Aran said abruptly. And he walked away fast.

The Warlock caught him up at the mouth of the alley. "I swear you won't regret staying. There's something you don't know yet."

"Don't follow me too far, Warlock. You'll lose your path." Aran laughed in the magician's face. "Why should I fight by your side? If you really need me to win, I couldn't be more delighted! I've seen your face in a thousand nightmares, you and your glass dagger! So die, Warlock. It's my dinner time."

"Shh," said the Warlock. And Aran saw that the Warlock was not looking at him, but over his shoulder.

Aran felt the urge to murder. But his eyes flicked to follow the Warlock's gaze, and the imprecations died in his throat.

It was a troll. Only a troll, a male, with a tremendous pack on its back. Coming toward them.

And the Warlock was gesturing to it. Or were those magical passes?

"Good," he said, "Now, I could tell you that it's futile to fight fate, and you might even believe me, because I'm an expert. But I'd be lying. Or I could offer you a chance to get rid of the dagger—"

"Go to Hell. I learned to live with that dagger—"

"Wolf man, if you never learn anything else from me, learn never to blaspheme in the presence of a magician! Excuse me." The troll had walked straight to the mouth of the alley. Now the Warlock took it by the arm and led it inside. "Will you help me? I want to get the pack off its back."

They lifted it down, while Aran wondered at himself. Had he been bewitched into obedience? The pack was very heavy. It took all of Aran's strength, even though the Warlock bore the brunt of the load. The troll watched them with blank brown eyes.

"Good. If I tried this anywhere else in the city, Wavyhill would know it. But this time I know where he is. He's in Adrienne's House of

Pleasures, searching for me, the fool! He's already searched the court-house."

"Never mind that. Do you know of a village named Gath?"

"No."

"Or Shiskabil?"

"No Wait." A Shiska had bought six matching green rugs from him once. "Yes. A small village north of here. Something . . . happened to it . . . "

"The population walked out one night, leaving all their valuables and a good deal of unexplained blood."

"That's right." Aran felt sudden horrible doubt. "It was never explained."

"Gath was first. Then Shiskabil, then Hathzoril. Bigger cities each time. At Hathzoril he was clever. He found a way to hide where his palace had been, and he didn't leave any blood."

"But what does he *do?* Where do the people go?"

"What do you know about *mana*, Aran? You know that it's the power behind magic, and you know it can be used up. What else?"

"I'm not a magician. I sell rugs."

"*Mana* can be used for good or evil; it can be drained, or transferred from one object to another, or from one man to another. Some men seem to carry *mana* with them. You can find concentrations in oddly shaped stones, or in objects of reverence, or in meteoroids.

"There is much *mana* associated with murder," said the Warlock. "Too much for safety, in my day. My teacher used to warn us against working near the site of a murder, or the corpse of a murdered man, or murder weapons—as opposed to weapons of war, I might add. War and murder are different in intent.

"Necromancy uses murder as a source of magic. It's the most powerful form of magic—so powerful that it could never have developed until now, when the *mana* level everywhere in the world is so low.

"I think Wavyhill is a necromancer," said the Warlock. And he turned to the troll. "We'll know in a moment."

The troll stood passive, its long arms relaxed at its sides, watching the Warlock with strangely human brown eyes and with a human dignity that contrasted oddly with its low animal brow and hairy body. It did not flinch as the Warlock dropped a kind of necklace over its head.

The change came instantly. Aran backed away, sucking air. The Warlock's necklace hung around a man's neck—a man in his middle thirties, blond-haired and bearded, wearing a porter's kilt—and that man's belly had been cut wide open by one clean swing of a sword or scimitar. Aran caught the smell of him: he had been dead for three or four days, plus whatever time the preserving effects of magic had been at work on him. Yet he stood, passively waiting, and his expression had not changed.

"Wavyhill has invented a kind of perpetual motion," the Warlock said dryly; but he backed away hastily from the smell of the dead man. "There's enough power in a murdered man to make him an obedient slave, and plenty left over to cast on him the seeming of a troll. He takes more *mana* from the environment, but what of that? When the *mana* runs out in Gath, Wavyhill's trolls kill their masters. Then twice as many trolls move on to Shiskabil. In Hathzoril they probably used strangling cords; they wouldn't spill any blood that way, and they wouldn't bleed themselves. I wonder where he'll go after Rynildissen?"

"Nowhere! We'll tell the Council!"

"And Wavyhill a Councilman? No. And you can't spread the word to individual members, because eventually one of them would tip Wavyhill that you're slandering him."

"They'd believe *you*."

"All it takes is one who doesn't. Then he tells Wavyhill, and Wavyhill turns loose the trolls. No. You'll do three things," said the Warlock in tones not of command but of prophecy. "You'll go home. You'll spend the next week getting your wives and children out of Rynildissen City."

"My gods, yes!"

"I swore you wouldn't regret hearing me out. The third thing, if you so decide, is to join me at dawn, at the north gate, a week from today. Come by way of Adrienne's House of Pleasures," the Warlock ordered, "and stay awhile. The dead area will break your trail.

"Do that today, too. I don't want Wavyhill to follow you by prescience. Go *now*," said the Warlock.

"I can't decide!"

"Take a week."

"I may not be here. How can I contact you?"

"You can't. It doesn't matter. I'll go with you or without you." Abruptly the Warlock stripped the necklace from the neck of the standing corpse, turned and strode off down the alley. Following the path.

The dead man was a troll again. It followed Aran with large, disturbingly human brown eyes.

VII

That predawn morning, Adrienne's House of Pleasures was wrapped in thick black fog. Aran the rug merchant hesitated at the door; then, shivering, squared his shoulders and walked out into it.

He walked with his sword ready for tapping or killing. The fog grew lighter as he went, but no less dense. Several times he thought he saw monstrous vague shapes pacing him. But there was no attack. At dawn he was at the north gate.

The Warlock's mounts were either lizards enlarged by magic or dragons mutated by no magic. They were freaks, big as twin bungalows. One carried baggage; the other, two saddles in tandem.

"Mount up," the Warlock urged. "We want to get there before nightfall." Despite the chill of morning he was bare to the waist. He turned in his saddle as Aran settled behind him. "Have you lost weight?"

"I fasted for six days, and exercised too. And my wives and children are four days on their way to Atlantis by sea. You can guess what pleasures I chose at Adrienne's." •

"I wouldn't have believed it. Your belly's as flat as a board."

"A wolf can fast for a long time. I ate an unbelievable meal last night. Today I won't eat at all."

The fog cleared as they left Rynildissen, and the morning turned clear and bright and hot. When Aran mentioned it, the Warlock said, "That fog was mine. I wanted to blur things for Wavyhill."

"I thought I saw shapes in the fog. Were those yours too?"

"No."

"Thanks."

"Wavyhill meant to frighten you, Aran. He wouldn't attack you. He *knows* you won't be killed before we reach the gate."

"That explains the pack lizards. I wondered how you could possibly expect to sneak up on him."

"I don't. He knows we're coming. He's waiting."

The land was rich in magic near Wavyhill's castle. You could tell by the vegetation: giant mushrooms, vying for variety of shape and color; lichens growing in the shapes of men or beasts; trees with contorted trunks and branches, trees that moved menacingly as the pack-lizards came near.

"I could make them talk," said the Warlock. "But I couldn't trust them. They'll be Wavyhill's allies."

In the red light of sunset, Wavyhill's castle seemed all rose marble, perched at the top of a fairy mountain. The slender tower seemed made for kidnapped damsels. The mountain itself, as Aran saw it now for the first time, was less a breaking wave than a fist raised to the sky in defiance.

"We couldn't use the Wheel here," said the Warlock. "The whole mountain would fall on us."

"I wouldn't have let you use the Wheel."

"I didn't bring one."

"Which way?"

"Up the path. He knows we're coming."

"Is your shadow demon ready?"

"Shadow demon?" The Warlock seemed to think. "Oh. For a moment I didn't know what you were talking about. That shadow demon was killed in the battle with Glirendree, thirty years ago."

Words caught in Aran's throat, then broke loose in a snarl. *"Then why don't you put on a shirt?"*

"Habit. I've got lots of strange habits. Why so vehement?"

"I don't know. I've been staring at your back since morning. I guess I was counting on the shadow demon." Aran swallowed. "It's just us, then?"

"Just us."

"Aren't you even going to take a sword? Or a dagger?"

"No. Shall we go?"

The other side of the hill was a sixty degree slope. The narrow, meandering path could not support the lizard beasts. Aran and the Warlock dismounted and began to climb.

The Warlock said, "There's no point in subtlety. We know we'll get as far as the gate. So does Wavyhill . . . excuse me." He threw a handful of silver dust ahead of them. "The road was about to throw us off. Apparently Wavyhill doesn't take anything for granted."

But Aran had only the Warlock's word for it; and that was the only danger that threatened their climb.

There was a rectangular pond blocking the solid copper gates. An arched bridge led across the pond. They were approaching the bridge when their first challenger pushed between the gates.

"What is it?" Aran whispered. "I've never *heard* of anything like it."

"There isn't. It's a changed one. Call it a snail dragon . . ."

. . . A snail dragon. Its spiral shell was just wide enough to block the gate completely. Its slender, supple body was fully exposed, reared high to study the intruders. Shiny leaflike scales covered the head and neck; but the rest of the body was naked, a soft greyish-brown. Its eyes were like black marbles. Its teeth were white and pointed, and the longest pair had been polished to a liquid glow.

From the other side of the small arched bridge, the Warlock called, "Ho, guardian! Were you told of our coming?"

"No," said the dragon. "Were you welcome, I would have been told."

"Welcome!" The Warlock guffawed. "We came to kill your master. Now, the interesting thing is that he knows of our coming. Why did he not warn you?"

The snail dragon tilted its mailed head.

The Warlock answered himself. "He knows that we will pass this gate. He suspects that we must pass over your dead body. He chose not to tell you so."

"That was kind of him." The dragon's voice was low and very gravelly, a sound like rocks being crushed.

"Kind, yes. But since we are foredoomed to pass, why not step aside? Or make for the hills, and we will keep your secret."

"It cannot be."

"You're a changed one, snail dragon. Beasts whose energy of life is partly magical breed oddly where the *mana* is low. Most changed ones are not viable. So it is with you," said the Warlock. "The shell could not protect you from a determined and patient enemy. Or were you counting on speed to save you?"

"You raise a salient point," said the guardian. "If I were to leave now, what then? My master will very probably kill you when you reach his sanctum. Then, by and by, this week or the next, he will wonder how you came to pass his guardian. Then, next week or the week following, he will come to see, or to remove the discarded shell. By then, with luck and a good tail wind, I could be halfway to the woods. Perchance he will miss me in the tall grass," said the bungalow-sized beast. "No. Better to take my chances here in the gate. At least I know the direction of attack."

"Damn, you're right," said the Warlock. "My sympathies, snail dragon."

And he set about fixing the bridge into solidity. Half of it, the half on the side away from the gate, really was solid. The other half was a reflected illusion, until the Warlock—did things.

"The dead border runs under the water," he told Aran. "Don't fall into it."

The snail dragon withdrew most of itself into its shell. Only his scaly head showed now, as Aran and the Warlock crossed.

Aran came running.

He was still a man. It was not certain that Wavyhill knew that Aran was a werewolf. It *was* certain that they would pass the gate. So he reserved his last defense, and came at the dragon with a naked sword.

The dragon blew fire.

Aran went through it. He carried a charm against dragon fire.

But he couldn't *see* through it. It shocked hell out of him when teeth closed on his shoulder. The dragon had stretched incredibly. Aran screamed and bounced his blade off the metallic scales and—the teeth loosed him, snapped ineffectually at the Warlock, who danced back laughing, waving—

But the Warlock had been unarmed!

The dragon collapsed. His thick neck was cut half in two, behind the scales. The Warlock wiped his weapon on his pantaloons and held it up.

Aran felt suddenly queasy.

The Warlock laughed again. "'What good is a glass dagger?' The fun thing about being a magician is that everyone always expects you to use magic."

"But, but—"

"It's just a glass dagger. No spells on it, nothing Wavyhill could detect. I had a friend drop it in the pond two days ago. Glass in water is near enough to invisible to fool the likes of Wavyhill."

"Excuse my open mouth. I just don't like glass daggers. Now what?"

The corpse and shell of the snail dragon still blocked the gate.

"If we try to squeeze around, we could be trapped. I suppose we'll have to go over."

"Fast," said Aran.

"Right, fast. Keep in mind that he could be *anywhere*." The Warlock took a running start and ran/climbed up the curve of the shell.

Aran followed almost as quickly.

In his sanctum, the snail dragon had said. The picture he had evoked was still with Aran as he went up the shell. Wavyhill would be hidden in his basement or his tower room, in some place of safety. Aran and the Warlock would have to fight their way through whatever the enemy could raise against them, while Wavyhill watched to gauge their defenses. There were similar tales of magicians' battles . . .

Aran was ravenously hungry. It gave him a driving energy he hadn't had in years, decades. His pumping legs drove a body that seemed feather-light. He reached the top of the shell just as the Warlock was turning full about in apparent panic.

Then he saw them: a horde of armed and armored skeletons

coming at them up a wooden plank. There must have been several score of them. Aran shouted and drew his sword. *How do you kill a skeleton?*

The Warlock shouted too. Strange words, in the Guild language.

The skeletons howled. A whirlwind seemed to grip them and lift them and fling them forward. Already they were losing form, like smoke rings. Aran turned to see the last of them vanishing into the Warlock's back.

My name is legion. They must have been animated by a single demon. And the Warlock had pulled that demon into a demon trap, empty and waiting for thirty years.

The problem was that both Aran and the Warlock had been concentrating on the plural demon.

The Warlock's back was turned, and Aran could do nothing. He spotted Wavyhill gesticulating from across the courtyard, in the instant before Wavyhill completed his spell.

Aran turned to shout a warning; and so he saw what the spell did to the Warlock. The Warlock was old in an instant. The flesh seemed to fade into his bones. He looked bewildered, spat a mouthful of blackened pebbles—no, teeth—closed his eyes and started to fall.

Aran caught him.

It was like catching an armload of bones. He eased the Warlock onto his back on the great snail shell. The Warlock's breathing was stertorous; he could not have long to live.

"Aran the Merchant!"

Aran looked down. "What did you do to him?"

The magician Wavyhill was dressed as usual, in dark robe and sandals and pointed hat. A belt with a shoulder loop held his big-hilted sword just clear of the ground. He called, "That is precisely what I wish to discuss. I have found an incantation that behaves as the Warlock's Wheel behaves, but directionally. Is this over your head?"

"I understand you."

"In layman's terms, I've sucked the magic from him. That leaves him two hundred and twenty-six years old. I believe that gives me the win.

"My problem is whether to let you live. Aran, do you understand what my spell will do to you?"

Aran did, but—"Tell me anyway. Then tell me how you found out."

"From some of my colleagues, of course, after I determined that you were my enemy. You must have consulted an incredible number of magicians regarding the ghostly knife in your heart."

"More than a dozen. Well?"

"Leave in peace. Don't come back."

"I have to take the Warlock."

"He is my enemy."

"He's my ally. I won't leave him," said Aran.

"Take him then."

Aran stooped. He was forty-eight years old, and the bitterness of defeat had replaced the manic energy of battle. But the Warlock was little more than a snoring mummy, dry and light. The problem would be to get the fragile old man down from the snail shell.

Wavyhill was chanting!

Aran stood—in time to see the final gesture: Then the spell hit him.

For an instant he thought that the knife had truly reappeared in his heart. But the pain was all through him! like a million taut strings snapping inside him! The shape of his neck changed grindingly; all of his legs snapped forward; his skull flattened, his eyes lost color vision, his nose stretched, his lips pulled back from bared teeth.

The change had never come so fast, had never been more complete. A blackness fell on Aran's mind. It was a wolf that rolled helplessly off the giant snail shell and into the courtyard. A wolf bounced heavily and rolled to its feet, snarled deep in its throat and began walking stiff-legged toward Wavyhill.

Wavyhill was amazed! He started the incantation over, speaking very fast, as Aran approached. He finished as Aran came within leaping distance.

This time there was no change at all. Except that Aran leapt, and Wavyhill jumped back just short of far enough, and Aran tore his throat out.

* * *

For Aran the nightmare began then. What had gone before was as sweet dreams.

Wavyhill should have been dead. His severed carotid arteries pumped frantically, his windpipe made horrid bubbling sounds, and— Wavyhill drew his sword and attacked.

Aran the wolf circled and moved in and slashed—and backed away howling, for Wavyhill's sword had run him through the heart. The wound healed instantly. Aran the wolf was not surprised. He leapt away, and circled, and slashed and was stabbed again, and circled . . .

It went on and on.

Wavyhill's blood had stopped flowing. He'd run out. Yet he was still alive. So was his sword, or so it seemed. Aran never attacked unless it seemed safe, but the sword bit him every time. And every time he attacked, he came away with a mouthful of Wavyhill.

He was going to win. He could not help but win. His wounds healed as fast as they were made. Wavyhill's did not. Aran was stripping the flesh from the magician's bones.

There was a darkness on his brain. He moved by animal cunning. Again and again he herded Wavyhill back onto the slippery flagstones where Wavyhill had spilled five quarts of his blood. Four feet were surer than two. It was that cunning that led him to bar Wavyhill from leaving the courtyard. He tried. He must have stored healing magic somewhere in the castle. But Aran would not let him reach it.

He had done something to himself that would not let him die. He must be regretting it terribly. Aran the wolf had crippled him now, slashing at his ankles until there was not a shred of muscle left to work the bones. Wavyhill was fighting on his knees. Now Aran came closer, suffering the bite of the sword to reach the magician . . .

Nightmare.

Aran the Peacemonger had been wrong. If Aran the rug merchant could work on and on, stripping the living flesh from a man in agony, taking a stab wound for every bite—if Aran could suffer such agonies to do this to *anyone*, for *any* cause—

Then neither the end of magic, nor anything else, would ever persuade men to give up war. They would fight on, with swords and stones and whatever they could find, for as long as there were men.

The blackness had lifted from Aran's brain. It must have been the sword: the *mana* in an enchanted sword had replaced the *mana* sucked from him by Wavyhill's variant of the Warlock's Wheel.

And, finally, he realized that the sword was fighting alone.

Wavyhill was little more than bloody bones. He might not be dead, but he certainly couldn't move. The sword waved itself at the end of the stripped bones of his arm, still trying to keep Aran away.

Aran slid past the blade. He gripped the hilt in his teeth and pulled it from the magician's still-fleshy hand. The hand fought back with a senseless determined grip, but it wasn't enough.

He had to convert to human to climb the dragon shell.

The Warlock was still alive, but his breathing was a thing of desperation. Aran laid the blade across the Warlock's body and waited.

The Warlock grew young. Not as young as he had been. But he no longer looked—dead. He was in the neighborhood of seventy years old when he opened his eyes, blinked, and asked, "What happened?"

"You missed all the excitement," said Aran.

"I take it you beat him. My apologies. It's been thirty years since I fought Glirendree. With every magician in the civilized world trying to duplicate the Warlock's Wheel, one or another was bound to improve on the design."

"He used it on me, too."

"Oh?" The Warlock chuckled. "I suppose you're wondering about the knife."

"It did come to mind. Where is it?"

"In my belt. Did you think I'd leave it in your chest? I'd had a dream that I would need it. So I kept it. And sure enough—"

"But it was in my heart!"

"I made an image of it. I put the image in your heart, then faded it out."

Aran's fingernails raked his chest. "You miserable son of an ape! You let me think that knife was in me for thirty years!"

"You came to my house as a thief," the Warlock reminded him. "Not an invited guest."

Aran the merchant had acquired somewhat the same attitude toward thieves. With diminished bitterness he said, "Just a little magician's joke, was it? No wonder nobody could get it out. All right. Now tell me why Wavyhill's spell turned me into a wolf."

The Warlock sat up carefully. He said, "What?"

"He waved his arms at me and sucked all the *mana* out of me, and I turned into a wolf. I even lost my human intelligence. Probably my invulnerability too. If he hadn't been using an enchanted sword he'd have cut me to ribbons."

"I don't understand that. You should have been frozen into human form. Unless . . . "

Then, visibly, the answer hit him. His pale cheeks paled further. Presently he said, "You're not going to like this, Aran."

Aran could see it in the Warlock's face, seventy years old and very tired and full of pity. "Go on," he said.

"The Wheel is a new thing. Even the dead spots aren't *that* old. The situation has never come up before, that's all. People automatically assume that werewolves are people who can turn themselves into wolves.

"It seems obvious enough. You can't even make the change without moonlight. You keep your human intelligence. But there's never been proof, one way or another, until now."

"You're saying I'm a wolf."

"Without magic, you're a wolf," the Warlock agreed.

"Does it matter? I've spent most of my life as a man," Aran whispered. "What difference does it make—oh. Oh, yes."

"It wouldn't matter if you didn't have children."

"Eight. And they'll have children. And one day the *mana* will be gone everywhere on Earth. Then what, Warlock?"

"You know already."

"They'll be wild dogs for the rest of eternity!"

"And nothing anyone can do about it."

"Oh, yes, there is! I'm going to see to it that no magician ever enters Rynildissen again!" Aran stood up on the dragon's shell. "Do you hear me, Warlock? Your kind will be barred. Magic will be barred. We'll save the *mana* for the sea people and the dragons!"

It may be that he succeeded. Fourteen thousand years later, there are still tales of werewolves where Rynildissen City once stood. Certainly there are no magicians.

The Princess and the Bear

Orson Scott Card

I know you've seen the lions. All over the place: beside the doors, flanking the throne, roaring out of the plates in the pantry, spouting water from under the caves.

Haven't you ever wondered why the statue atop the city gates is a bear? Many years ago in this very city, in the very palace that you can see rising granite and gray behind the old crumbly walls of the king's garden, there lived a princess. It was so long ago that who can ever remember her name? She was just the princess. These days it isn't in fashion to think that princesses are beautiful, and in fact they tend to be a bit horse-faced and gangling. But in those days it was an absolute requirement that a princess look fetching, at least when wearing the most expensive clothes available.

This princess, however, would have been beautiful dressed like a slum child or a shepherd girl. She was beautiful the moment she was born. She only got more beautiful as she grew up.

And there was also a prince. He was not her brother, though. He was the son of a king in a far-off land, and his father was the thirteenth cousin twice removed of the princess' father. The boy had been sent here to our land to get an education—because the princess' father, King Ethelred, was known far and wide as a wise man and a good king.

And if the princess was marvelously beautiful, so was the prince. He was the kind of boy that every mother wants to hug, the kind of boy who gets his hair tousled by every man that meets him.

He and the princess grew up together. They took lessons together from the teachers in the palace, and when the princess was slow, the prince would help her, and when the prince was slow, the princess would help him. They had no secrets from each other, but they had a million secrets that they two kept from the rest of the world. Secrets like where the bluebirds' nest was this year, and what color underwear the cook wore, and that if you duck under the stairway to the armory there's a little underground path that comes up in the wine cellar. They speculated endlessly about which of the princess' ancestors had used that path for surreptitious imbibing.

After not too many years the princess stopped being just a little girl and the prince stopped being just a little boy, and then they fell in love. All at once all their million secrets became just one secret, and they told that secret every time they looked at each other, and everyone who saw them said, "Ah, if I were only young again." That is because so many people think that love belongs to the young: sometime during their lives they stopped loving people, and they think it was just because they got old.

The prince and the princess decided one day to get married.

But the very next morning, the prince got a letter from the far-off country where his father lived. The letter told him that his father no longer lived at all, and that the boy was now a man; and not just a man, but a king.

So the prince got up the next morning, and the servants put his favorite books in a parcel, and his favorite clothes were packed in a trunk, and the trunk, and the parcel, and the prince were all put on a coach with bright red wheels and gold tassels at the corner and the prince was taken away.

The princess did not cry until after he was out of sight. Then she went into her room and cried for a long time, and only her nurse could come in with food and chatter and cheerfulness. At last the chatter brought smiles to the princess, and she went into her father's study where he sat by the fire at night and said, "He promised he would write, every day, and I must write every day as well."

She did, and the prince did, and once a month a parcel of thirty letters would arrive for her, and the postrider would take away a parcel of thirty letters (heavily perfumed) from her.

And one day the Bear came to the palace. Now he wasn't a bear, of course, he was *the* Bear, with a capital B. He was probably only thirty-five or so, because his hair was still golden brown and his face was only lined around the eyes. But he was massive and grizzly, with great thick arms that looked like he could lift a horse, and great thick legs that looked like he could carry that horse a hundred miles. His eyes were deep, and they looked brightly out from under his bushy eyebrows, and the first time the nurse saw him she squealed and said, "Oh, my, he looks like a *bear*."

He came to the door of the palace and the doorman refused to let him in, because he didn't have an appointment. But he scribbled a note on a piece of paper that looked like it had held a sandwich for a few days, and the doorman—with grave misgivings—carried the paper to the king.

The paper said, "If Boris and 5,000 stood on the highway from Rimperdell, would you like to know which way they were going?"

King Ethelred wanted to know.

The doorman let the stranger into the palace, and the king brought him into his study and they talked for many hours.

In the morning the king arose early and went to his captains of cavalry and captains of infantry, and he sent a lord to the knights and their squires, and by dawn all of Ethelred's little army was gathered on the highway, the one that leads to Rimperdell. They marched for three hours that morning, and then they came to a place and the stranger with golden brown hair spoke to the king and King Ethelred commanded the army to stop. They stopped, and the infantry was sent into the forest on one side of the road, and the cavalry was sent into the tall cornfields on the other side of the road, where they dismounted. Then the king, and the stranger, and the knights waited in the road.

Soon they saw a dust cloud in the distance, and then the dust cloud grew near, and they saw that it was an army coming down the road. And at the head of the army was King Boris of Rimperdell. And behind him the army seemed to be five thousand men.

"Hail," King Ethelred said, looking more than a little irritated, since King Boris' army was well inside our country's boundaries.

"Hail," King Boris said, looking more than a little irritated, since no one was supposed to know that he was coming.

"What do you think you're doing?" asked King Ethelred.

"You're blocking the road," said King Boris.

"It's my road," said King Ethelred.

"Not anymore," said King Boris.

"I and my knights say that this road belongs to me," said King Ethelred.

King Boris looked at Ethelred's fifty knights, and then he looked back at his own five thousand men, and he said, "I say you and your knights are dead men unless you move aside."

"Then you want to be at war with me?" asked King Ethelred.

"War?" said King Boris. "Can we really call it a war? It will be like stepping on a nasty cockroach."

"I wouldn't know," said King Ethelred, "because we haven't ever had cockroaches in our kingdom."

Then he added, "Until now, of course."

Then King Ethelred lifted his arm, and the infantry shot arrows and threw lances from the wood, and many of Boris' men were slain. And the moment all of his troops were ready to fight the army in the forest, the cavalry came from the field and attacked from the rear, and soon Boris' army, what was left of it, surrendered, and Boris himself lay mortally wounded in the road.

"If you had won this battle," King Ethelred said, "what would you have done to me?"

King Boris gasped for breath and said, "I would have had you beheaded."

"Ah," said King Ethelred. "We are very different men. For I will let you live."

But the stranger stood beside King Ethelred, and he said, "No, King

Ethelred, that is not in your power, for Boris is about to die. And if he were not, I would have killed him myself, for as long as a man like him is alive, no one is safe in all the world."

Then Boris died, and he was buried in the road with no marker, and his men were sent home without their swords.

And King Ethelred came back home to crowds of people cheering the great victory, and shouting, "Long live King Ethelred the conqueror."

King Ethelred only smiled at them. Then he took the stranger into the palace, and gave him a room where he could sleep, and made him the chief counselor to the king, because the stranger had proved that he was wise, and that he was loyal, and that he loved the king better than the king loved himself, for the king would have let Boris live.

No one knew what to call the man, because when a few brave souls asked him his name, he only frowned and said, "I will wear the name you pick for me."

Many names were tried, like George, and Fred, and even Rocky and Todd. But none of the names seemed right. For a long time, everyone called him Sir, because when somebody is that big and that strong and that wise and that quiet, you feel like calling him sir and offering him your chair when he comes in the room.

And then after a while everyone called him the name the nurse had chosen for him just by accident: they called him the Bear. At first they only called him that behind his back, but eventually someone slipped and called him that at the dinner table, and he smiled, and answered to the name, and so everyone called him that.

Except the princess. She didn't call him anything, because she didn't speak to him if she could help it, and when she talked about him, she stuck out her lower lip and called him That Man.

This is because the princess hated the Bear.

She didn't hate him because he had done anything bad to her. In fact, she was pretty sure that he didn't even notice she was living in the palace. He never turned and started when she walked into the room, like all the other men did. But that isn't why she hated him, either.

She hated him because she thought he was making her father weak.

King Ethelred was a great king, and his people loved him. He always stood very tall at ceremonies, and he sat for hours making judgments with great wisdom. He always spoke softly when softness was needed, and shouted at the times when only shouting would be heard.

In all he was a stately man, and so the princess was shocked with the way he was around the Bear.

King Ethelred and the Bear would sit for hours in the king's study, every night when there wasn't a great banquet or an ambassador. They would both drink from huge mugs of ale—but instead of having a servant refill the mugs, the princess was shocked that her own father stood up and poured from the pitcher! A king, doing the work of a servant, and then giving the mug to a commoner, a man whose name no one knew!

The princess saw this because she sat in the king's study with them, listening and watching without saying a word as they talked. Sometimes she would spend the whole time combing her father's long white hair. Sometimes she would knit long woolen stockings for her father for the winter. Sometimes she would read—for her father believed that even women should learn to read. But all the time she listened, and became angry, and hated the Bear more and more.

King Ethelred and the Bear didn't talk much about affairs of state. They talked about hunting rabbits in the forest. They told jokes about lords and ladies in the kingdom—and some of the jokes weren't even nice, the princess told herself bitterly. They talked about what they should do about the ugly carpet in the courtroom—as if the Bear had a perfect right to have an opinion about what the new carpet should be.

And when they did talk about affairs of state, the Bear treated King Ethelred like an *equal*. When he disagreed with the king, he would leap to his feet saying, "No, no, no, no, you just don't see at all." When he thought the king had said something right, he clapped him on the shoulder and said, "You'll make a great king yet, Ethelred."

And sometimes King Ethelred would sigh and stare into the fire, and whisper a few words, and a dark and tired look would steal across his face. Then the Bear would put his arm around the king's shoulder, and stare into the fire with him, until finally the king would sigh again, and then lift himself, groaning, out of his chair, and say, "It's time that this old man put his corpse between the sheets."

The next day the princess would talk furiously to her nurse, who never told a soul what the princess said. The princess would say, "That Man is out to make my father a weakling! He's out to make my father look stupid. That Man is making my father forget that he is a king." Then she would wrinkle her forehead and say, "That Man is a traitor."

She never said a word about this to her father, however. If she had, he would have patted her head and said, "Oh, yes, he does indeed make me forget that I am a king." But he would also have said, "He makes me remember what a king should be." And Ethelred would not have called him a traitor. He would have called the Bear his friend.

As if it wasn't bad enough that her father was forgetting himself around a commoner, that was the very time that things started going bad with the prince. She suddenly noticed that the last several packets of mail had not held thirty letters each—they only held twenty, and then fifteen, and then ten. And the letters weren't five pages long anymore. They were only three, and then two, and then one.

He's just busy, she thought

Then she noticed that he no longer began her letters with, "My dearest darling sweetheart pickle-eating princess." (The pickle-eating part was an old joke from something that happened when they were both nine.) Now he started them, "My dear lady," or "Dear princess." Once she said to her nurse, "He might as well address them to Occupant."

He's just tired, she thought.

And then she realized that he never told her he loved her anymore, and she went out on the balcony and cried where only the garden could hear, and where only the birds in the trees could see.

She began to keep to her rooms, because the world didn't seem like a very nice place anymore. Why should she have anything to do with the world, when it was a nasty place where fathers turned into mere men, and lovers forgot they were in love?

And she cried herself to sleep every night that she slept. And some nights she didn't sleep at all, just stared at the ceiling trying to forget the prince. And you know that if you want to remember something, the best way is to try very, very hard to forget it.

Then one day, as she went to the door of her room, she found a basket of autumn leaves just inside her door. There was no note on them, but they were very brightly colored, and they rustled loudly when she touched the basket, and she said to herself, "It must be autumn."

She went to the window and looked, and it was autumn, and it was beautiful. She had already seen the leaves a hundred times a day, but she hadn't remembered to notice.

And then a few weeks later she woke up and it was cold in her room. Shivering, she went to her door to call for a servant to build her fire up higher—and just inside the door was a large pan, and on the pan there stood a little snowman, which was grinning a grin made of little chunks of coal, and his eyes were big pieces of coal, and all in all it was so comical the princess had to laugh. That day she forgot her misery for a while and went outside and threw snowballs at the knights, who of course let her hit them and who never managed to hit her, but of course that's all part of being a princess—no one would ever put snow down your back or dump you in the canal or anything.

She asked her nurse who brought these things, but the nurse just shook her head and smiled. "It wasn't me," she said. "Of course it was," the princess answered, and gave her a hug, and thanked her. The nurse smiled and said, "Thanks for your thanks, but it wasn't me." But the princess knew better, and loved her nurse all the more.

Then the letters stopped coming altogether. And the princess stopped writing letters. And she began taking walks in the woods.

At first she only took walks in the garden, which is where princesses are supposed to take walks. But in a few days of walking and walking and walking she knew every brick of the garden path by heart, and she kept coming to the garden wall and wishing she were outside it.

So one day she walked to the gate and went out of the garden and wandered into the forest. The forest was not at all like the garden. Where the garden was neatly tended and didn't have a weed in it, the forest was all weeds, all untrimmed and loose, with animals that ran from her, and birds that scurried to lead her away from their young, and best of all, only grass or soft brown earth under her feet. Out in the forest she could forget the garden where every tree reminded her of talks she had had with the prince while sitting in the branches. Out in the forest she could forget the palace where every room had held its own joke or its own secret or its own promise that had been broken.

That was why she was in the forest the day the wolf came out of the hills.

She was already heading back to the palace, because it was getting on toward dark, when she caught a glimpse of something moving. She looked, and realized that it was a huge gray wolf, walking along beside her not fifteen yards off. When she stopped, the wolf stopped. When she moved, the wolf moved. And the farther she walked, the closer the wolf came.

She turned and walked away from the wolf.

After a few moments she looked behind her, and saw the wolf only a dozen feet away, its mouth open, its tongue hanging out, its teeth shining white in the gloom of the late afternoon forest.

She began to run. But not even a princess can hope to outrun a wolf. She ran and ran until she could hardly breathe, and the wolf was still right behind her, panting a little but hardly tired. She ran and ran some more until her legs refused to obey her and she fell to the ground. She looked back, and realized that this was what the wolf had been waiting for—for her to be tired enough to fall, for her to be easy prey, for her to be a dinner he didn't have to work for.

And so the wolf got a gleam in its eye, and sprang forward.

Just as the wolf leaped, a huge brown shape lumbered out of the forest and stepped over the princess. She screamed. It was a huge brown bear, with heavy fur and vicious teeth. The bear swung its great hairy arm at the wolf, and struck it in the head. The wolf flew back a dozen yards, and from the way its head bobbed about as it flew, the princess realized its neck had been broken.

And then the huge bear turned toward her, and she saw with despair that she had only traded one monstrous animal for another.

And she fainted. Which is about all that a person can do when a bear that is standing five feet away looks at you. And looks hungry.

She woke up in bed at the palace and figured it had all been a dream. But then she felt a terrible pain in her legs, and felt her face stinging with scratches from the branches. It had not been a dream— she really had run through the forest.

"What happened?" she asked feebly. "Am I dead?" Which wasn't all that silly a question, because she really had expected to be.

"No," said her father, who was sitting by the bed.

"No," said the nurse. "And why in the world, why should you be dead?"

"I was in the forest," said the princess, "and there was a wolf, and I ran and ran but he was still there. And then a bear came and killed the wolf, and it came toward me like it was going to eat me, and I guess I fainted."

"Ah," said the nurse, as if that explained everything.

"Ah," said her father, King Ethelred. "Now I understand. We were taking turns watching you after we found you unconscious and scratched up by the garden gate. You kept crying out in your sleep, 'Make the bear go away! Make the bear leave me alone!' Of course, we thought you meant *the* Bear, our Bear, and we had to ask the poor man not to take his turn anymore, as we thought it might make you upset. We all thought you hated him, for a while there." And King Ethelred chuckled. "I'll have to tell him it was all a mistake."

Then the king left. Great, thought the princess, he's going to tell the Bear it was all a mistake, and I really do hate him to pieces.

The nurse walked over to the bed and knelt beside it. "There's another part of the story. They made me promise not to tell you," the nurse said, "but you know and I know that I'll always tell you everything. It seems that it was two guards that found you, and they both said that they saw something running away. Or not running, exactly, galloping. Or something. They said it looked like a bear, running on all fours."

"Oh, no," said the princess. "How horrible!"

"No," said the nurse. "It was their opinion, and Robbo Knockle swears it's true, that the bear they saw had brought you to the gate and set you down gentle as you please. Whoever brought you there smoothed your skirt, you know, and put a pile of leaves under your head like a pillow, and you were surely in no state to do all that yourself."

"Don't be silly," said the princess. "How could a bear do all that?"

"I know," said the nurse, "so it must not have been an ordinary bear. It must have been a magic bear." She said this last in a whisper, because the nurse believed that magic should be talked about quietly, lest something awful should hear and come calling.

"Nonsense," said the princess. "I've had an education, and I don't believe in magic bears or magic brews or any kind of magic at all. It's just old-lady foolishness."

The nurse stood up and her mouth wrinkled all up. "Well, then, this foolish old lady will take her foolish stories to somebody foolish, who wants to listen."

"Oh, there, there," the princess said, for she didn't like to hurt any-one's feelings, especially not Nurse's. And they were friends again. But the princess still didn't believe about the bear. However, she hadn't been eaten, after all, so the bear must not have been hungry.

It was only two days later, when the princess was up and around again—though there were nasty scabs all over her face from the scratches–that the prince came back to the palace.

He came riding up on a lathered horse that dropped to the ground and died right in front of the palace door. He looked exhausted, and there were great purple circles under his eyes. He had no baggage. He had no cloak. Just the clothes on his back and a dead horse.

"I've come home," he said to the doorman, and fainted into his arms. (By the way, it's perfectly all right for a man to faint, as long as he has ridden on horseback for five days, without a bite to eat, and with hundreds of soldiers chasing him.)

"It's treason," he said when he woke up and ate and bathed and dressed. "My allies turned against me, even my own subjects. They drove me out of my kingdom. I'm lucky to be alive."

"Why?" asked King Ethelred.

"Because they would have killed me. If they had caught me."

"No, no, no, no, don't be stupid," said the Bear, who was listening from a chair a few feet away. "Why did they turn against you?"

The prince turned toward the Bear and sneered. It was an ugly sneer, and it twisted up the prince's face in a way it had never twisted when he lived with King Ethelred and was in love with the princess.

"I wasn't aware that I was being stupid," he said archly. "And I cer-tainly wasn't aware that *you* had been invited into the conversation."

The Bear didn't say anything after that, just nodded an unspoken apology and watched.

And the prince never did explain why the people had turned against him. Just something vague about power-hungry demagogues and mob rule.

The princess came to see the prince that very morning.

"You look exhausted," she said.

"You look beautiful," he said.

"I have scrabs all over my face and I haven't done my hair in days," she said.

"I love you," he said.

"You stopped writing," she said.

"I guess I lost my pen," he said. "No, I remember now. I lost my mind. I forgot how beautiful you are. A man would have to be mad to forget."

The he kissed her, and she kissed him back, and she forgave him for all the sorrow he had caused her and it was like he had never been away.

For about three days.

Because in three days she began to realize that he was different somehow.

She would open her eyes after kissing him (princesses always close their eyes when they kiss someone) and she would notice that he was looking off somewhere with a distant expression on his face. As if he barely noticed that he was kissing her. That does not make any woman, even a princess, feel very good.

She noticed that sometimes he seemed to forget she was even there. She passed him in a corridor and he wouldn't speak, and unless she touched his arm and said good morning he might have walked on by without a word.

And then sometimes, for no reason, he would feel slighted or offended, or a servant would make a noise or spill something and he would fly into a rage and throw things against the wall. He had never even raised his voice in anger when he was a boy.

He often said cruel things to the princess, and she wondered why she loved him, and what was wrong, but then he would come to her and apologize, and she would forgive him because after all he had lost a kingdom because of traitors, and he couldn't be expected to always feel sweet and nice. She decided, though, that if it was up to her, and it was, he would never feel unsweet and unnice again.

Then one night the Bear and her father went into the study and locked the door behind them. The princess had never been locked out of her father's study before, and she became angry at the Bear because he was taking her father away from her, and so she listened at the door. She figured that if the Bear wanted to keep her out, she would see to it that she heard everything anyway.

This is what she heard.

"I have the information," the Bear said.

"It must be bad, or you wouldn't have asked to speak to me alone," said King Ethelred. Aha, thought the princess, the Bear *did* plot to keep me out.

The Bear stood by the fire, leaning on the mantel, while King Ethelred sat down.

"Well?" asked King Ethelred.

"I know how much the boy means to you. And to the princess. I'm sorry to bring such a tale."

The boy! thought the princess. They couldn't possibly be calling her prince a boy, could they? Why, he had been a king, except for treason, and here a commoner was calling him a boy.

"He means much to us," said King Ethelred, "which is all the more reason for me to know the truth, be it good or bad."

"Well, then," said the Bear, "I must tell you that he was a very bad king."

The princess went white with rage.

"I think he was just too young. Or something," said the Bear. "Perhaps there was a side to him that you never saw, because the moment he had power it went to his head. He thought his kingdom was too small, because he began to make war with little neighboring counties and duchies and took their lands and made them part of his kingdom. He plotted against other kings who had been good and true friends of his father. And he kept raising taxes on his people to support huge armies. He kept starting wars and mothers kept weeping because their sons had fallen in battle.

"And finally," said the Bear, "the people had had enough, and so had the other kings, and there was a revolution and a war all at the same time. The only part of the boy's tale that is true is that he was lucky to escape with his life, because every person that I talked to spoke of him with hatred, as if he were the most evil person they had ever seen."

King Ethelred shook his head. "Could you be wrong? I can't believe this of a boy I practically raised myself."

"I wish it were not true," said the Bear, "for I know that the princess loves him dearly. But it seems obvious to me that the boy doesn't love her—he is here because he knew he would be safe here, and because he knows that if he married her, he would be able to rule when you are dead."

"Well," said King Ethelred, "that will never happen. My daughter will never marry a man who would destroy the kingdom."

"Not even if she loves him very much?" asked the Bear.

"It is the price of being a princess," said the king. "She must think first of the kingdom, or she will never be fit to be queen."

At that moment, however, being queen was the last thing the princess cared about. All she knew was that she hated the Bear for taking away her father, and now the same man had persuaded her father to keep her from marrying the man she loved.

She beat on the door, crying out, "Liar! Liar!" King Ethelred and the Bear both leaped for the door. King Ethelred opened it, and the princess burst into the room and started hitting the Bear as hard as she could. Of course the blows fell very lightly, because she was not all that strong, and he was very large and sturdy and the blows could have caused him no pain. But as she struck at him his face looked as if he were being stabbed through the heart at every blow.

"Daughter, daughter," said King Ethelred. "What is this? Why did you listen at the door?"

But she didn't answer; she only beat at the Bear until she was crying too hard to hit him anymore. And then, between sobs, she began to yell at him. And because she didn't usually yell her voice became harsh and hoarse and she whispered. But yelling or whispering, her words were clear, and every word said hatred.

She accused the Bear of making her father little, nothing, worse than nothing, a weakling king who had to turn to a filthy commoner to make any decision at all. She accused the Bear of hating her and trying to ruin her life by keeping her from marrying the only man she could ever love. She accused the Bear of being a traitor, who was plotting to be king himself and rule the kingdom. She accused the Bear of making up vile lies about the prince because she knew that he would be a better king than her weakling father, and that if she married the prince all the Bear's plans for ruling the kingdom would come to nothing.

And finally she accused the Bear of having such a filthy mind that he imagined that he could eventually marry her himself, and so become king.

But that would never happen, she whispered bitterly, at the end. "That will never happen," she said, "never, never, never, because I hate you and I loathe you and if you don't get out of this kingdom and never come back I'll kill myself, I swear it."

And then she grabbed a sword from the mantel and tried to slash her wrists, and the Bear reached out and stopped her by holding her arms in his huge hands that gripped like iron. Then she spit at him and tried to bite his fingers and beat her head against his chest until King Ethelred took her hands and the Bear let go and backed away.

"I'm sorry," King Ethelred kept saying, though he himself wasn't certain who he was apologizing to or what he was apologizing for. "I'm sorry." And then he realized that he was apologizing for himself, because somehow he knew that his kingdom was ruined right then.

If he listened to the Bear and sent the prince away, the princess would never forgive him, would hate him, in fact, and he couldn't bear that. But if he didn't listen to the Bear, then the princess would surely marry the prince, and the prince would surely ruin his kingdom. And he couldn't endure that.

But worst of all, he couldn't stand the terrible look on the Bear's face.

The princess stood sobbing in her father's arms.

The king stood wishing there were something he could do or undo.

And the Bear simply stood.

And then the Bear nodded, and said, "I understand. Good-bye."

And then the Bear walked out of the room, and out of the palace, and out of the garden walls, and out of the city, and out of any land that the king had heard of.

He took nothing with him—no food, no horse, no extra clothing. He just wore his clothing and carried his sword. He left as he came.

And the princess cried with relief. The Bear was gone. Life could go on, just like it was before ever the prince left and before ever the Bear came.

So she thought.

She didn't really realize how her father felt until he died only four months later, suddenly very old and very tired and very lonely and despairing for his kingdom.

She didn't realize that the prince was not the same man she loved before until she married him three months after her father died.

On the day of their wedding she proudly crowned him king herself, and led him to the throne, where he sat.

"I love you," she said proudly, "and you look like a king."

"I am a king," he said. "I am King Edward the first."

"Edward?" she said. "Why Edward? That's not your name."

"That's a king's name," he said, "and I am a king. Do I not have power to change my name?"

"Of course," she said. "But I liked your own name better."

"But you will call me Edward," he said, and she did.

When she saw him. For he didn't come to her very often. As soon as he wore the crown he began to keep her out of the court, and conducted the business of the kingdom where she couldn't hear. She didn't understand this, because her father had always let her attend everything and hear everything in the government, so she could be a good queen.

"A good queen," said King Edward, her husband, "is a quiet woman who has babies, one of whom will be king."

And so the princess, who was now the queen, had babies, and one of them was a boy, and she tried to help him grow up to be a king.

But as the years passed by she realized that King Edward was not the lovely boy she had loved in the garden. He was a cruel and greedy man. And she didn't like him very much.

He raised the taxes, and the people became poor.

He built up the army, so it became very strong.

He used the army to take over the land of Count Edred, who had been her godfather.

He also took over the land of Duke Adlow, who had once let her pet one of his tame swans.

He also took over the land of Earl Thlaffway, who had wept openly at her father's funeral, and said that her father was the only man he had ever worshipped, because he was such a good king.

And Edred and Adlow and Thlaffway all disappeared, and were never heard of again.

"He's even against the common people," the nurse grumbled one day as she did up the queen's hair. "Some shepherds came to court yesterday to tell him a marvel, which is their duty, isn't it, to tell the king of anything strange that happens in the land?"

"Yes," said the queen, remembering how as a child she and the prince had run to their father often to tell him a marvel—how grass springs up all at once in the spring, how water just disappeared on a hot day, how a butterfly comes all awkward from the cocoon.

"Well," said the nurse, "they told him that there was a bear along the edge of the forest, a bear that doesn't eat meat, but only berries and roots. And this bear, they said, killed wolves. Every year they lose dozens of sheep to the wolves, but this year they had lost not one lamb, because the bear killed the wolves. Now that's a marvel, I'd say," said the nurse.

"Oh yes," said the princess who was now a queen.

"But what did the king do," said the nurse, "but order his knights to hunt down that bear and kill it. Kill it!"

"Why?" asked the queen.

"Why, why, why?" asked the nurse. "The best question in the world. The shepherds asked it, and the king said, 'Can't have a bear loose around here. He might kill children.'

"'Oh no,' says the shepherds, 'the bear don't eat meat.'

"'Then, it'll wind up stealing grain,' the king says in reply, and there it is, my lady—the hunters are out after a perfectly harmless bear! You can bet the shepherds don't like it. A perfectly harmless bear!"

The queen nodded. "A magic bear."

"Why, yes," said the nurse. "Now you mention it, it does seem like the bear that saved you that day—"

"Nurse," said the queen, "there was no bear that day. I was dreaming I was mad with despair. There wasn't a wolf chasing me. And there was definitely no magic bear."

The nurse bit her lip. Of course there had been a bear, she thought. And a wolf. But the queen, her princess, was determined not to believe in any kind thing.

"Sure there was a bear," said the nurse.

"No, there was no bear," said the queen, "and now I know who put the idea of a magic bear into the children's head."

"They've heard of him?"

"They came to me with a silly tale of a bear that climbs over the wall into the garden when no one else is around, and who plays with them and lets him ride on his back. Obviously you told them your silly tale about the magic bear who supposedly saved me. So I told them that magic bears were a full tall-tale and that even grownups liked to tell them, but that they must be careful to remember the difference between truth and falsehood, and they should wink if they're fibbing."

"What did they say?" the nurse said.

"I made them all wink about the bear," said the queen, "of course. But I would appreciate it if you wouldn't fill their heads with silly stories. You did tell them your stupid story, didn't you?"

"Yes," said the nurse sadly.

"What a trouble your wagging tongue can cause," said the queen, and the nurse burst into tears and left the room.

They made it up later but there was no talk of bears. The nurse understood well enough, though. The thought of bears reminded the queen of *the* Bear, and everyone knew that she was the one who drove that wise counselor away. If only the Bear were still here, thought the nurse—and hundreds of other people in the kingdom—if he were still here we wouldn't have these troubles in the kingdom.

And there were troubles. The soldiers patrolled the streets of the cities and locked people up for saying things about King Edward. And when a servant in the palace did anything wrong he would bellow and storm, and even throw things and beat them with a rod.

One day when King Edward didn't like the soup he threw the whole tureen at the cook. The cook promptly took his leave, saying for anyone to hear, "I've served kings and queens, lords and ladies, soldiers, and servants, and in all that time this is the first time I've ever been called upon to serve a pig."

The day after he left he was back, at swordpoint—not cooking in the kitchen, of course, since cooks are too close to the king's food. No, the cook was sweeping the stables. And the servants were told in no uncertain terms that none of them was free to leave. If they didn't like their jobs, they could be given another one to do. And they all looked at the work the cook was doing, and kept their tongues.

Except the nurse, who talked to the queen about everything.

"We might as well be slaves," said the nurse. "Right down to the wages. He's cut us all in half, some even more, and we've got barely enough to feed ourselves. I'm all right, mind you, my lady, for I have no one but me to feed, but there's some who's hard put to get a stick of wood for the fire and a morsel of bread for a hungry mouth or six."

The queen thought of pleading with her husband, but then she realized that King Edward would only punish the servants for complaining. So she began giving her nurse jewels to sell. Then the nurse quietly gave the money to the servants who had the least or who had the largest families, and whispered to them, even though the queen had told her not to give a hint, "This money's from the queen, you know. *She* remembers us servants, even if her husband's a lout and a pimple." And the servants remembered that the queen was kind.

The people didn't hate King Edward quite as much as the servants did, of course, because even though taxes were high, there are always silly people who are proud fit to bust when their army has a victory. And of course King Edward had quite a few victories at first. He would pick a fight with a neighboring king or lord and then march in and take over. People had thought old King Boris' army of five thousand was bad, back in the old days. But because of his high taxes, King Edward was able to hire an army of fifty thousand men, and war was a different thing then. They lived off the land in enemy country, and killed and plundered where they liked. Most of the soldiers weren't local men, anyway—they were the riffraff of the highways, men who begged or stole, and now were being paid for stealing.

But King Edward tripled the size of the kingdom, and there were a good many citizens who followed the war news and cheered whenever King Edward rode through the streets.

They cheered the queen, too, of course, but they didn't see her very much, about once a year or so. She was still beautiful, of course, more beautiful than ever before. No one particularly noticed that her eyes were sad these days, or else those who noticed said nothing and soon forgot it.

But King Edward's victories had been won against weak, and peaceful, and unprepared men. And at last the neighboring kings got together, and the rebels from conquered lands got together, and they planned King Edward's doom.

When next King Edward went a-conquering, they were ready, and on the very battlefield where King Ethelred had defeated Boris they ambushed King Edward's army. Edward's fifty thousand hired men faced a hundred thousand where before they had never faced more than half their number. Their bought courage melted away, and those who lived through the first of the battle ran for their lives.

King Edward was captured and brought back to the city in a cage, which was hung above the city gate, right where the statue of the bear is today.

The queen came out to the leaders of the army that had defeated King Edward and knelt before them in the dust and wept, pleading for her husband. And because she was beautiful, and good, and because they themselves were only good men trying to protect their own lives and property, they granted him his life. For her sake they even let him remain king, but they imposed a huge tribute on him. To save his own life, he agreed.

So taxes were raised even higher, in order to pay the tribute, and King Edward could only keep enough soldiers to police his kingdom, and the tribute went to paying for soldiers of the victorious kings to stay on the borders to keep watch on our land. For they figured, and rightly so, that if they let up their vigilance for a minute, King Edward would raise an army and stab them in the back.

But they didn't let up their vigilance, you see. And King Edward was trapped.

A dark evil fell upon him then, for a greedy man craves all the more the thing he can't have. And King Edward craved power. Because he couldn't have power over other kings, he began to use more power over his own kingdom, and his own household, and his own family.

He began to have prisoners tortured until they confessed to conspiracies that didn't exist, and until they denounced people who were innocent. And people in this kingdom began to lock their doors at night, and hide when someone knocked. There was fear in the kingdom, and people began to move away, until King Edward took to hunting down and beheading anyone who tried to leave the kingdom.

And it was bad in the palace, too. For the servants were beaten savagely for the slightest things, and King Edward even yelled at his own son and daughters whenever he saw them, so that the queen kept them hidden away with her most of the time.

Everyone was afraid of King Edward. And people almost always hate anyone they fear.

Except the queen. For though she feared him she remembered his youth, and she said to herself, or sometimes to the nurse, "Somewhere in that sad and ugly man there is the beautiful boy I love. Somehow I must help him find that beautiful boy and bring him out again."

But neither the nurse nor the queen could think how such a thing could possibly happen.

Until the queen discovered that she was going to have a baby. Of course, she thought. With a new baby he will remember his family and remember to love us.

So she told him. And he railed at her about how stupid she was to bring another child to see their humiliation, a royal family with enemy troops perched on the border, with no real power in the world.

And then he took her roughly by the arm into the court, where the lords and ladies were gathered, and there he told them that his wife was going to have a baby to mock him, for she still had the power of a woman, even if he didn't have the power of a man. She cried out that it wasn't true. He hit her, and she fell to the ground.

And the problem was solved, for she lost the baby before it was born and lay on her bed for days, delirious and fevered and at the point of death. No one knew that King Edward hated himself for what he had done, that he tore at his face and his hair at the thought that the queen might die because of his fury. They only saw that he was drunk all through the queen's illness, and that he never came to her bedside.

While the queen was delirious, she dreamed many times and many things. But one dream that kept coming back to her was of a wolf following her in the forest, and she ran and ran until she fell, but just as the wolf was about to eat her, a huge brown bear came and killed the wolf and flung him away, and then picked her up gently and laid her down at her father's door, carefully arranging her dress and putting leaves under her head as a pillow.

When she finally woke up, though, she only remembered that there was no magic bear that would come out of the forest to save her. Magic was for the common people—brews to cure gout and plague and to make a lady love you, spells said in the night to keep dark things from the door. Foolishness, the queen told herself. For she had an education, and knew better. There is nothing to keep the dark things from the door, there is no cure for gout and plague, and there is no brew that will make your husband love you. She told this to herself and despaired.

King Edward soon forgot his grief at the thought his wife might die. As soon as she was up and about he was as surly as ever, and he didn't stop drinking, either, even when the reason for it was gone. He just remembered that he had hurt her badly and he felt guilty, and so whenever he saw her he felt bad, and because he felt bad he treated her badly, as if it were her fault.

Things were about as bad as they could get. There were rebellions here and there all over the kingdom, and rebels were being beheaded every week. Some soldiers had even mutinied and got away over the border with the people they were supposed to stop. And so one morning King Edward was in the foulest, blackest mood he had ever been in.

The queen walked into the dining room for breakfast looking as beautiful as ever, for grief had only deepened her beauty, and made you want to cry for the pain of her exquisite face and for the suffering in her proud, straight bearing. King Edward saw that pain and suffering but even more he saw that beauty, and for a moment he remembered the girl who had grown up without a care or a sorrow or an evil thought. And he knew that he had caused every bit of the pain she bore.

So he began to find fault with her, and before he knew it he was ordering her into the kitchen to cook.

"I can't," she said.

"If a servant can, you can," he snarled in reply.

She began to cry. "I've never cooked. I've never started a fire. I'm a queen."

"You're not a queen," the king said savagely, hating himself as he said it. "You're not a queen and I'm not a king, because we're a bunch of powerless lackeys taking orders from those scum across the border! Well, if I've got to live like a servant in my own palace, so have you!"

And so he took her roughly into the kitchen and ordered her to come back in with a breakfast she had cooked herself.

The queen was shattered, but not so shattered that she could forget her pride. She spoke to the cooks cowering in the corner. "You heard the king. I must cook him breakfast with my own hands. But I don't know how. You must tell me what to do."

So they told her, and she tried her best to do what they said, but her untrained hands made a botch of everything. She burned herself at the fire and scalded herself with the porridge. She put too much salt on the bacon and there were shells left in the eggs. She also burned the muffins. And then she carried it all in to her husband and he began to eat.

And of course it was awful.

And at that moment he realized finally that the queen was a queen and could be nothing else, just as a cook had no hope of being a queen. Just so he looked at himself and realized that he could never be anything but a king. The queen, however, was a good queen—while he was a terrible king. He would always be a king but he would never be good at it. And as he chewed up the eggshells he reached the lowest despair.

Another man, hating himself as King Edward did, might have taken his own life. But that was not King Edward's way. Instead he picked up his rod and began to beat the queen. He struck her again and again, and her back bled, and she fell to the ground, screaming.

The servants came in and so did the guards, and the servants, seeing the queen treated so, tried to stop the king. But the king ordered the guards to kill anyone who tried to interfere. Even so, the chief steward, a cook, and the butler were dead before the others stopped trying.

And the king kept beating and beating the queen until everyone was sure he would beat her to death.

And in her heart as she lay on the stone floor, numb to the pain of her body because of the pain of her heart, she wished that the bear would come again, stepping over her to kill the wolf that was running forward to devour her.

At that moment the door broke in pieces and a terrible roar filled the dining hall. The king stopped beating the queen, and the guards and the servants looked at the door, for there stood a huge brown bear on its hind legs, towering over them all, and roaring in fury.

The servants ran from the room.

"Kill him," the king bellowed at the guards.

The guards drew their swords and advanced on the bear.

The bear disarmed them all, though there were so many that some drew blood before their swords were slapped out of their hands. Some of them might even have tried to fight the bear without weapons, because they were brave men, but the bear struck them on the head, and the rest fled away.

Yet the queen, dazed though she was, thought that for some reason the bear had not struck yet with all his force, that the huge animal was saving his strength for another battle.

And that battle was with King Edward, who stood with his sharp sword in his hand, eager for battle, hoping to die, with the desperation and self-hatred in him that would make him a terrible opponent, even for a bear.

A bear, thought the queen. I wished for a bear and he is here.

Then she lay, weak and helpless and bleeding on the stone floor as her husband, her prince, fought the bear. She did not know who she hoped would win. For even now, she did not hate her husband. And yet she knew that her life and the lives of her subjects would be unendurable as long as he lived.

They circled around the room, the bear moving clumsily yet quickly, King Edward moving faster still, his blade whipping steel circles through the air. Three times the blade landed hard and deep on the bear, before the animal seized the blade between his paws. King Edward tried to draw back the sword, and as he did it bit deeply into the animal's paws. But it was a battle of strength, and the bear was sure to win it in the end. He pulled the sword out of Edward's hand, and then grasped the king in a mighty embrace and carried him screaming from the room.

And at that last moment, as Edward tugged hopelessly at his sword and blood poured from the bear's paws, the queen found herself hoping that the bear would hold on, would take away the sword, that the bear would win out and free the kingdom—her kingdom—and her family and even herself, from the man who had been devouring them all.

Yet when King Edward screamed in the bear's grip, she heard only the voice of the boy in the garden in the eternal and too-quick summer of her childhood. She fainted with a dim memory of his smile dancing crazily before her eyes.

She awoke as she had awakened once before, thinking that it had been a dream, and then remembering the truth of it when the pain where her husband had beaten her nearly made her fall unconscious again. But she fought the faintness and stayed awake, and asked for water.

The nurse brought water, and then several lords of high rank and the captain of the army and the chief servants came in and asked her what they should do.

"Why do you ask me?" she said.

"Because," the nurse answered her, "the king is dead."

The queen waited.

"The bear left him at the gate," the captain of the army said.

"His neck was broken," the chief said.

"And now," one of the lords said, "now we must know what to do. We haven't even told the people, and no one has been allowed inside or outside the palace."

The queen thought, and closed her eyes as she did so. But what she saw when she closed her eyes was the body of her beautiful prince with his head loose as the wolf's had been that day in the forest. She did not want to see that, so she opened her eyes.

"You must proclaim that the king is dead throughout the land," she said.

To the captain of the army she said, "There will be no more

beheading for treason. Anyone who is in prison for treason is to be set free, now. And any other prisoners whose terms are soon to expire should be set free at once."

The captain of the army bowed and left. He did not smile until he was out the door, but then he smiled until tears ran down his cheeks.

To the chief cook she said, "All the servants in the palace are free to leave now, if they want. But please ask them, in my name, to stay. I will restore them as they were, if they'll stay."

The cook started a heartfelt speech of thanks, but then thought better of it and left the room to tell the others.

To the lords she said, "Go to the kings whose armies guard our borders, and tell them that King Edward is dead and they can go home now. Tell them that if I need their help I will call on them, but that until I do I will govern my kingdom alone."

And the lords came and kissed her hands tenderly, and left the room.

And she was alone with the nurse.

"I'm so sorry," said the nurse, when enough silence had passed.

"For what?" asked the queen.

"For the death of your husband."

"Ah, that," said the queen. "Ah, yes, my husband."

And then the queen wept with all her heart. Not for the cruel and greedy man who had warred and killed and savaged everywhere he could. But for the boy who had somehow turned into that man, the boy whose gentle hand had comforted her childhood hurts, the boy whose frightened voice had cried out to her at the end of his life, as if he wondered why he had gotten lost inside himself, as if he realized that it was too, too late to get out again.

When she had done weeping that day, she never cried for him again.

In three days she was up again, though she had to wear loose clothing because of the pain. She held court anyway, and it was then that the shepherds brought her the Bear. Not the bear, the animal, that had killed the king, but *the* Bear, the counselor, who had left the kingdom so many years before.

"We found him on the hillside, with our sheep nosing him and lapping his face," the oldest of the shepherds told her. "Looks like he's been set on by robbers, he's cut and battered so. Miracle he's alive," he said.

"What is that he's wearing?" asked the queen, standing by the bed where she had had the servants lay him.

"Oh," said one of the other shepherds. "That's me cloak. They left him nekkid, but we didn't think it right to bring him before you in such a state."

She thanked the shepherds and offered to pay them a reward, but they said no thanks, explaining, "We remember him, we do, and it wouldn't be right to take money for helping him, don't you see, because he was a good man back in your father's day."

The queen had the servants—who had all stayed on, by the way—clean his wounds and bind them and tend to his wants. And because he was a strong man, he lived, though the wounds might have killed a smaller, weaker man. Even so, he never got back the use of his right hand, and had to learn to write with his left; and he limped ever after. But he often said he was lucky to be alive and wasn't ashamed of his infirmities, though he sometimes said that something ought to be done about the robbers who run loose in the hills.

As soon as he was able, the queen had him attend court, where he listened to the ambassadors from other lands and to the cases she heard and judged.

Then at night she had him come to King Ethelred's study, and there she asked him about the questions of that day and what he would have done differently, and he told her what he thought she did well, too. And so she learned from him as her father had learned.

One day she even said to him, "I have never asked forgiveness of many in my life. But I ask for yours."

"For what?" he said, surprised.

"For hating you, and thinking you served me and my father badly, and driving you from this kingdom. If we had listened to you," she said, "none of this would have happened."

"Oh," he said, "all that's past. You were young, and in love, and that's as inevitable as fate itself."

"I know," she said, "and for love I'd probably do it again, but now that I'm wiser I can still ask for forgiveness for my youth."

The Bear smiled at her. "You were forgiven before you asked. But since you ask I gladly forgive you again."

"Is there any reward I can give you for your service so many years ago, when you left unthanked?" she asked.

"Yes," he answered. "If you could let me stay and serve you as I served your father, that would be reward enough."

"How can that be a reward?" she asked. "I was going to ask you to do that for *me*. And now you ask it for yourself."

"Let us say," said the Bear, "that I loved your father like my brother, and you like my niece, and I long to stay with the only family that I have."

Then the queen took the pitcher and poured him a mug of ale, and they sat by the fire and talked far into the night.

Because the queen was a widow, because despite the problems of the past the kingdom was large and rich, many suitors came asking for her hand. Some were dukes, some were earls, and some were kings or sons of kings. And she was as beautiful as ever, only in her thirties, a prize herself even if there had been no kingdom to covet.

But though she considered long and hard over some of them, and even liked several men who came, she turned them all down and sent them all away.

And she reigned alone, as queen, with the Bear to advise her.

And she also did what her husband had told her a queen should do—she raised her son to be king and her daughters to be worthy to be queens. And the Bear helped her with that, too, teaching her son to hunt, and teaching him how to see beyond men's words into their hearts, and teaching him to love peace and serve the people.

And the boy grew up as beautiful as his father and as wise as the Bear, and the people knew he would be a great king, perhaps even greater than King Ethelred had been.

The queen grew old, and turned much of the matter of the kingdom over to her son, who was now a man. The prince married the daughter of a neighboring king. She was a good woman, and the queen saw her grandchildren growing up.

She knew perfectly well that she was old, because she was sagging and no longer beautiful as she had been in her youth—though there were many who said that she was far more lovely as an old lady than any mere girl could hope to be.

But somehow it never occurred to her that the Bear, too, was growing old. Didn't he still stride through the garden with one of her grandchildren on each shoulder? Didn't he still come into the study with her and her son and teach them statecraft and tell them, yes, that's good, yes, that's right, yes, you'll make a great queen yet, yes, you'll be a fine king, worthy of your grandfather's kingdom—didn't he?

Yet one day he didn't get up from his bed, and a servant came to her with a whispered message, "Please come."

She went to him and found him gray-faced and shaking in his bed.

"Thirty years ago," he said, "I would have said it's nothing but a fever and I would have ignored it and gone riding. But now, my lady, I know I'm going to die."

"Nonsense," she said, "you'll never die," knowing as well as he did that he was dying, and knowing that he knew that she knew it.

"I have a confession to make," he said to her.

"I know it already," she said.

"Do you?"

"Yes," she said softly, "and much to my surprise, I find that I love you too. Even an old lady like me," she said, laughing.

"Oh," he said, "that was not my confession. I already knew that you knew I loved you. Why else would I have come back when you called?"

And then she felt a chill in the room and remembered the only time she had ever called for help.

"Yes," he said, "you remember. How I laughed when they named me. If they only knew, I thought at the time."

She shook her head. "How could it be?"

"I wondered myself," he said. "But it is. I met a wise old man in the woods when I was but a lad. An orphan, too, so that there was no one to ask about me when I stayed with him. I stayed until he died five years later, and I learned all his magic."

"There's no magic," she said as if by rote, and he laughed.

"If you mean brews and spells and curses, then you're right," he said. "But there is magic of another sort. The magic of becoming what most you are. My old man in the woods, his magic was to be an owl, and to fly by night seeing the world and coming to understand it. The owlness was in him, and the magic was letting that part of himself that was most himself come forward. And he taught me."

The Bear had stopped shaking because his body had given up trying to overcome the illness.

"So I looked inside me and wondered who I was. And then I found it out. Your nurse found it, too. One glance and she knew I was a bear."

"You killed my husband," she said to him.

"No," he said. "I fought your husband and carried him from the palace, but as he stared death in the face he discovered, too, what he was and who he was, and his real self came out."

The Bear shook his head.

"I killed a wolf at the palace gate, and left a wolf with a broken neck behind when I went away into the hills."

"A wolf both times," she said. "But he was such a beautiful boy."

"A puppy is cute enough whatever he plans to grow up to be," said the Bear.

"And what am I?" asked the queen.

"You?" asked the Bear. "Don't you know?"

"No," she answered. "Am I a swan? A porcupine? These days I walk like a crippled, old biddy hen. Who am I, after all these years? What animal should I turn into by night?"

"You're laughing," said the Bear, "and I would laugh too, but I have to be stingy with my breath. I don't know what animal you are, if you don't know yourself, but I think—"

And he stopped talking and his body shook in a great heave.

"No!" cried the queen.

"All right," said the Bear. "I'm not dead yet. I think that deep down inside you, you are a woman, and so you have been wearing your real self out in the open all your life. And you are beautiful."

"What an old fool you are after all," said the queen. "Why didn't I ever marry you?"

"Your judgment was too good," said the Bear.

But the queen called the priest and her children and married the Bear on his deathbed, and her son who had learned kingship from him called him father, and then they remembered the bear who had come to play with them in their childhood and the queen's daughters called him father; and the queen called him husband, and the Bear laughed and allowed as how he wasn't an orphan anymore. Then he died.

And that's why there's a statue of a bear over the gate of the city.

THE SUMMONING

Katherine Kurtz

 he old man sat on a stump beside the frozen river, watching black water race past a hole in the ice. It was twilight, the last day of the year 1773, and the bone-chilling cold of the coming night was descending; but the old man only wrapped his cloak more closely around himself and waited— watching, willing—as the last weak rays of sunlight finally retreated from the ice-rimmed hole and left the surface a black mirror.

"Now show thyself to me," he whispered, sketching the sign of the Dragon in the air before him, centered over his blackened mirror. "Show thyself, who shall come at the appointed hour to accept thy destiny. Show thyself. . . ."

Sitting back then, he waited, eyes fixed on his mirror, summoning the image of the one who would come. Absently his hand sought the silver chain around his neck, his thumb caressing the coin-sized medallion with its image of a knight confronting a dragon. Slowly the image came—of a tall, commanding figure in a full-cut black cloak with shoulder capelets, striding along a snow-covered street.

A smart tricorn hat crowned reddish-brown hair pulled back in a queue. Well-polished boots with spurs showed below fawn-colored breeches as he set one toe in a polished stirrup and swung up on a tall, raw-boned grey. The gloved hands that gathered up the reins were big, almost a little awkward, the thighs gripping the grey's sides thick and powerful.

The old man nodded as the image wavered and then faded, touching the silver medallion to his lips and bowing his head in thanks for the Vision. Very shortly, he was roused from his meditation by the crunching footfall of someone approaching from behind him in the snow.

"Yes, daughter, I know what time it is," he said, even as he turned to greet her. "I was just ready to come in. Is all in readiness?"

The girl was just eighteen, small like her mother had been, with hair of a rich bronzy-gold pulled up in a loose knot at the crown. Her cloak was a deep forest-green, the gown beneath it the saffron hue of marigolds or sunflower petals. The eyes that gazed at him adoringly were a clear, startling blue. He had named her Amanda, for the mother she had never known. Today's Amanda bore a wreath of fresh laurel leaves in her slender hands, looking very much as her mother had looked at a similar age, so many years before. The radiance of her smile made it seem that the sun had turned backward in its path, bringing the dawn once more.

"Well, this is done, at any rate. I hope it's what you wanted," she said, displaying the wreath hopefully. "I only took slips from young laurel trees, as you suggested. That helped to keep everything supple, and made the weaving easier."

"Did you remember to take from thirteen different trees?" he asked, arching an eyebrow.

"Of course!" she replied, drawing the wreath away momentarily in mock indignation. "And also asked permission before I cut them. Whose daughter do you think I am, to forget something that important? Seriously, though"—she flashed him a smile and offered the wreath again—"will it be all right?"

He took the wreath from her and held it up for inspection, breathing deeply of the pungent, familiar scent. He was white haired and bearded, with a nobility about his bearing that recalled gentle origins in the Old World—and indeed, he had been born noble, though castles and lands and titles had been left behind with his wife's grave, across a broad ocean that he knew he would never cross again.

Nor had he any desire to re-cross it. That phase of his life had closed with Amanda's death. Here, he was simply Jakob, sometimes referred to as the Hermit of the Ridge. There were others of his kind farther along the Wissahikon, some of whom had banded together in a semi-monastic community—and others, still, who had abandoned the pretense of Christian facade and pursued their ancient skills more openly—and more precariously. But though a younger Jakob had considered both options, he had deemed neither course suitable for the father of a young son and infant daughter.

Accordingly, in the nearly two decades since his arrival in these Pennsylvania woods, he had carved out a sheltered and solitary life for himself and his children, diligently setting himself a routine of study, work, and prayer, teaching his children to reverence the same, bequeathing them a richness of spiritual freedom that was not possible in the Old World, with its hypocrisies and religious intolerance. One still must be careful, even here—distant cousins had burned in Salem, less than a century before—but the old man's pious demeanor and willingness to help anyone in need, and the reassuring little chapel, with its simple cross of iron, had long ago disarmed any local suspicion or resentment.

"The wreath is marvelous, my dear," the old man murmured, bending to kiss the top of her burnished head. "Exactly as I envisioned. Now, what about your brother? Has he finished at the chapel?"

Her face clouded briefly at that, but she made a brave attempt at a new smile and nodded. "Of course he has, Father. You know that you have only to ask, and either Ephraim or I would do anything for you, but—"

"But?" he repeated, smiling gently and caressing her cheek with one veined hand.

She hooked her arm in his as they started back toward the snug, sod-walled blockhouse that was their home, sighing as she scuffed her little boots along the snow-encrusted path.

"I wish I had your confidence," she said, searching for the words. "I know what the prophecies say, and I respect our ancient ways. But how can you be so certain he will heed the Call? He is not one of us. The Dragon's breath does not stir his lungs. The blood of the Dragon does not run in his veins."

"No, he is not kin to the Dragon," the old man agreed, "but nonetheless, he will play a vital role in the New Order. Besides, this is not the Dragon's land—though it is meet that the Dragon should find refuge here. The one who is to come is kin to the Eagle, I suspect— though perhaps the Dragon may help teach the Eagle to soar. But doubt it not, he will come, my darling. I have seen his visage, and he will come."

They reached the blockhouse then and went in, and the old man sat beside the well-scrubbed table and contemplated the laurel wreath while the girl built up the fire. She was drawing the curtains at the front windows to shut out the gloomy forest and the falling night when her brother returned with an armload of wood, cheeks red from the cold outside, eyes blazing with his news. He was a tall, handsome youth, as dark as Amanda was fair, with the same guileless blue gaze that all three of them shared. The graceful hands were callused from honest work, but every line of his slender form confirmed his gentle breeding.

"I ran into Caleb Matheson, when I went down to chop the wood," he announced, depositing his wood in a sturdy basket beside the fire and throwing off his heavy cloak. "Do you know what's happening up in Boston?"

As he sat himself eagerly on a stool opposite his father, the old man nodded slowly.

"A little over a fortnight ago, in outraged and righteous protest against scandalous new British taxes, a great deal of tea was flung into Boston Harbor," he said blandly. "So that it would appear that Red Indians were to blame, the perpetrators blacked and painted their faces, and communicated by means of grunts and 'ugh-ugh,' and exchanged the phrase 'me know you,' as a countersign.

"In truth, however, the plan was hatched in a tavern called the Green Dragon, by Bostonians of several different radical groups and

Masonic Lodges, united by the resolve that the tea should not be off-loaded and the tax should not be tolerated. It is believed that some of the participants foregathered at a meeting of the Saint Andrew's Lodge—which was adjourned early, there being few members present—ending their night's escapade at a chowder supper hosted by the brothers Bradlee. What came between Lodge and chowder, few will own openly, but the names of such notables as Dr. Joseph Warren and Mr. Paul Revere have been mentioned in connection with the affair, and it is certain that some three hundred forty-two chests of tea ended up in Boston Harbor, to the value of some eighteen thousand pounds sterling. Rumor also has it that old Mother Bradlee kept a kettle of water hot, so that 'the boys' could wash off their face-black and war paint, afterwards."

Young Ephraim's jaw had dropped as his father's recital became more and more specific, and he shook his head as his sire finally wound down. At twenty-two, he was sometimes inclined to believe that his youthful agility gave him an edge on gathering news; but somehow his father usually managed to know about important events long before the local grapevine carried it to Ephraim's ears.

"You knew!" he blurted, half-indignant. "How in the world did you know? I only found out the details this afternoon."

The old man only smiled, touching a fingertip lightly along the leaves of the laurel wreath and watching his son. The smile was infectious, and Ephraim soon broke into his own perplexed grin.

"It's clear that I still have a great deal to learn," the youth said amiably. "I suppose you've also heard that it's feared the British will close the Port of Boston in retaliation, and make them pay back the eighteen thousand pounds?"

The old man raised one eyebrow in question.

"You hadn't heard?" The young man's delight was palpable. "Well, Caleb had it from his father, who heard it in Philadelphia. Apparently the State House is all a-buzz with talk of a blockade, once Parliament finds out what's happened. The Virginia Burgesses are calling the threat an attack made on all British America, and wondering who'll be next. In fact, all the Colonies are supporting what Boston did. There's even talk of a Continental Congress in the new year."

The old man drew a deep breath as the youth finished, lowering his eyes in contemplation, and a silence fell around the little table. When he raised his eyes to them once more, the fire of his calling smoldered in their blue depths, and he carefully folded his hands on the table before him.

"It all is coming to pass, even sooner than I dreamed," he murmured, shifting his gaze into the circlet of the laurel wreath, focusing beyond the scrubbed pine of the tabletop. "The events in Boston have already triggered the change. No more shall the Old World extend its wickedness to the New. Those who revere the cause of freedom shall enshrine it upon these shores, and hereon the footsteps of kings shall never tread. God has spoken and it is so. Say Amen!"

"Amen," his children repeated softly, not daring to gainsay him.

There would be no supper tonight, for fasting would hone and focus their energies for the night's work. Bread and water only would he allow, though he made of this sparse fare a sacrament, as he blessed and broke the bread for them, then blessed and passed the cup filled from the sacred spring outside their door.

Afterward, when they had spent an hour in meditation, threesome hands joined around the table, Amanda silently helped father and brother pull on the ritual garments set aside for their most important work—white hooded robes sewn from nubbly virgin wool, carded, spun, and loomed by her virgin hands. The scarlet cinctures they knotted about their waists had been plaited of more of the wool, each one the prayerful work of the individual who should wear it, dyed with the last of the precious cochineal Jakob had brought with him twenty years before. Amanda donned her robe as well, but she did not go with them to the chapel; her place was to keep watch here in the house, adding her prayers to theirs, and to join them when he had come. She set a candle in the window as they went out, sinking to her knees to focus on the flame.

The two men did not speak as they made their way across the snow, Ephraim carrying a lantern and his father bearing the laurel wreath, both wrapped in cloaks over their robes. The chapel was a small, round building made of sod, but with a good thatched roof and a chimney thrusting skyward on the right. A little wooden vestibule guarded the doorway, and as Ephraim opened the door, light from the candles left burning on the altar streamed out across the snow. The night wind swept a flurry of snow inside and stirred the white cloth adorning the altar, and Ephraim shut the door before setting the lantern squarely in the center of the little chamber.

The walls and floor were planked with pine, with a modest brick fireplace built into the wall on the right as they entered. A large cross of iron hung above the altar, clean-lined and simple, centered on a hanging of nubbly white wool. As Ephraim went to feed the fire back to life, his father carried the laurel wreath to the altar and laid it beside a slender silver flagon and a large, richly bound Bible. The latter had been a family heirloom for nearly two hundred years, bound in crimson leather and stamped in gold, the corners and clasps fashioned of silver-gilt, but the old man paid it only passing interest as he shifted its bulk a little nearer the altar's front edge. For beyond the book and the wreath and the flagon, almost invisible in the angle between surface and wall, lay a naked sword of an earlier age. And in the nearer angle of quillons and blade lay three smooth-polished quartz pebbles that had not been there earlier in the afternoon.

Blessing the messenger, the old man smiled and bowed his respect to the altar, touched his fingertips to his lips and to the crossing of the sword hilt, then scooped up the pebbles and closed them in his hand before turning to face his son.

"The one we have awaited will come at the third hour after midnight," he said quietly. At his son's look askance, he repeated, "Doubt it not, he will come. At the third hour of the new year, as the clock concludes its strike, he will come through yonder door to take upon himself his sacred mission. All is prepared for his coming. We have only to keep our faith, to continue the Call, and he cannot but come."

He and his son knelt in prayer then, while behind them, close beside the door, the ancient grandfather clock that usually graced a corner of their sitting room ticked off the minutes and the hours. At eleven, the old man extinguished the lantern and moved it aside, throwing open the door to the winter night and beginning to pace back and forth across the width of the chapel. His son fed the fire again, remaining nearer its warmth to continue his prayers. The altar candles filled the little chapel with a softer glow than had the lantern, spilling a golden path onto the snow outside—a beacon to anyone approaching.

The old man paced on, head bowed and hands clasped in prayer. When the clock finally struck twelve, ushering in the new year, Ephraim lifted his head and glanced toward his father, compassion welling up—for though the appointed time was yet three hours away, youthful impatience worried that the old man might be wrong.

"Father, what if he doesn't come?" he whispered, tottering unsteadily to his feet to flex his knees, stiff after kneeling so long.

The old man glanced back at the open doorway, at the path of candlelight streaming out onto the snow, then turned back to the altar and the sacred objects it held.

"He will come," the old man declared. "At the third hour after midnight, the Deliverer will come."

Silently he resumed his measured pacing; and as Ephraim watched and listened, he realized that the steps and his father's breathing had fallen into an engaging rhythm. The pattern was at once compelling and reassuring, weaving its own call in counterpoint to the ticking of the clock.

Renewed in spirit, the youth knelt once more near the fire, out of the direct draught of the open door, and resumed his meditations, letting himself fall into the rhythm of the spell, lifting his spirit to soar with his sire's call, searching out the one who was to come. Detached from physical perception, he quested outward, casting in an ever-widening net.

By one o'clock, the altar candles had nearly burned down. Carefully, reverently, the old man changed them, inserting fresh tapers in the pewter candlesticks, making certain they stood straight, that everything was as it should be. The honey scent of beeswax continued to fill the little chamber with its sweet incense as he again resumed his pacing.

The clock struck two. Now the old man stood before the fireplace, bowed head resting on the hands clasped to the edge of the pine mantel, shifting to a different sort of concentration, never ceasing to send forth his call. The wind had risen with the turn of the year, and the candles danced in the breeze, the altar cloth billowing along the front edge and ends. The stillness in the tiny chamber became more profound, each tick of the clock carrying father and son deeper into concentration, strengthening the spell.

When the clock at last began to strike the hour, the old man slowly raised his head and turned to face the open door, his white head cocked in a listening attitude. And as the third stroke hung and died away on air suddenly gone very, very still, there came hesitant footsteps in the little vestibule, stamping snow from boots; and then a tall stranger of majestic presence ducked his head to enter the room, grey-blue eyes sweeping the little chamber in respect and wonder.

"Pray, pardon my intrusion, friends, but I seem to have lost my way in the forest," he said uncertainly, removing his tricorne and making the old man a courteous bow. "Can you direct me to the right way?"

"I can, if thou wouldst find the way to thy destiny," the old man said, catching and holding the grey-blue eyes in his compelling gaze. "Come in and close the door. The winter night is cold, and we have waited long for thy coming."

The stranger's eyes widened, but he turned without demur and closed the door, coming in then to the center of the chamber, to stand unresisting before the old man's inspection. The red-brown hair was powdered now, the linen at his throat more formal, the line of his dark blue coat more stylish than the image the old man had seen in his black water mirror.

But the gloved hands were the same, and the black cloak with its several shoulder capelets, and the spurred black boots—though the latter now were caked with snow. A smallsword hung at his side, its silver hilt just visible through the parting of the cloak.

"It is late to be out on such a night," the old man said.

The stranger nodded, fingering his hat a little nervously, his expression suggesting that even he was not certain why or how he had come here.

"Yes, it is."

"And some desperate burden lies upon thy heart, to bring thee to this place at this time," the old man continued softly. "Is it not thy country's welfare?"

Looking a little startled, the stranger gave a cautious nod.

"And it troubles thee, does it not, that a subject might feel bound to raise his hand against his king?"

"How do you know that?" the man demanded, staring at the old man in amazement. "Who are you, to know what troubles me?"

"I am but an instrument, sent to prepare thee," the old man said. "Thy calling comes from One far higher than I. Put aside thy sword and kneel before this altar. With thy right hand upon the Volume of Sacred Law, pledge thy faith; and having pledged, receive that threefold confirmation which shall sustain thee in the times to come, as future deliverer of a nation's freedom!"

A little dazed-looking, the stranger complied, laying his hat aside and letting the youth divest him of his sword, which then was laid reverently upon the altar. Of his own volition he stripped off his gloves as he sank to one knee, stuffing them distractedly into the front of his coat as he set his bare right hand upon the Bible. Throughout, the grey-blue eyes remained locked on the old man's blue ones, the craggy face still and expectant.

"Know that before half a year has passed, thou shalt be called to lead thy fellow countrymen to war!" the old man said, both admiring and pitying him. "Soon shalt thou ride forth to battle at the head of mighty armies. Soon shall thy sword be raised as a shining beacon to those who shall help thee win a nation's freedom!"

As the stranger's face went a little paler, the old man laid his own hand atop the one resting on the Book, though no compulsion accompanied the questions he now put to the chosen one.

"Dost thou promise that, when the appointed time doth come, thou shalt be found ready, sword in hand, to fight for thy country and thy God?"

Without hesitation the answer came, the voice steady, the grey-blue eyes clear.

"I do."

"Dost thou promise to persevere through defeats as well as victories, knowing that both shall have caused thee to send good men to their deaths?"

The stranger's "I do" was softer this time, but no less determined.

"And dost thou promise that, even in the hour of victory, when a nation shall bow before thee, thou shalt remember that thou art but the instrument of God in achieving this Great Work of a nation's freedom?"

"I do promise," came the answer, clearly and firmly.

"Then in His Name Who hath given the New World as the last altar of human rights," the old man said, taking up the flagon from the altar, "I do consecrate thee its Champion and Deliverer."

Moistening his thumb with oil from the flagon, he slowly and deliberately traced a cross and then a circle on the stranger's brow, sealing the vows and imparting his blessing with the sacred symbol. A shiver went through the stranger at the other's touch, and the eyes half-closed. His breathing deepened as the old man replaced the flagon on the altar and took up the laurel wreath, and he bowed his head and clasped trembling hands in an attitude of prayerful reverence as the old man lifted the wreath above him.

"In times ahead shall come a victor's crown," the old man said, his gaze flicking expectantly to the door. "But let it be no conqueror's blood-stained wreath—though blood thou shalt shed. Rather, this brighter crown of fadeless laurel."

But before he could place it on the stranger's head, wind gusted through the suddenly open door, billowing the altar cloth and setting the candles to guttering, and Amanda was standing in the doorway. She had wrapped her green cloak over her robe to make her way from the house, and her loosened hair floated on the wind like a tawny halo.

The old man paused as he saw her, her brother's eyes also turning in her direction. Then the old man lowered the wreath and made her a profound bow.

"Come to us, as *la Déesse de la Liberté*," he said. "For it is fitting that a nation's Champion and Deliverer should receive his crown of laurel from the hands of a stainless woman."

Lifting her head, she drew the door closed behind her and let fall her cloak, at the same time assuming the psychic mantle he had bade her take upon herself for the office to which she was called. As she came softly to her father's side and took the laurel wreath from him, the stranger's eyes lifted to hers, not comprehending; but as she willed him to see past the merely visible, the grey-blue eyes widened—not in fear, but in profound recognition.

He was trembling as she lifted the laurel wreath above his head, and a shudder went through his body as she placed the leafy crown on his powdered hair—a shudder stilled by the touch of her hands upon his shoulders, and by the kiss she pressed gently to his forehead, atop the imprint of the sacred oil.

Then, as the straightened and backed away a step to stand beside her father, her brother moved before the altar, unsheathing the stranger's sword and laying it nearer the front edge, moving the antique sword close beside it. The scabbard and belt he gave into his sister's keeping, sparing only a brief glance at his father before extending his hands flat over the antique blade as he had been taught, closing his eyes.

His lips moved silently in prayer; the stranger watched numbly, the big hands still clasped loosely at his heart in an attitude of reverence.

Then the young man's eyes opened and the hands slowly were lifted, drawing an ethereal ghost-image of the antique sword out of the physical steel to float a hand-span above. A gesture of his left hand held the image steady while his right hand traced the Dragon sign over the ghost-hilt, severing the connection with the original weapon.

Slowly he drew the ghost image to overlap the stranger's sword, superimposing the energy of the first over that of the second, pressing the image into the second sword's steel, making of the stranger's blade a magical implement akin to the first. Blue sparks arced as his hands touched the steel of the stranger's sword, startling even him.

But then he took up the weapon by its hilt, touched his lips to the crossing, and sheathed the blade in the scabbard his sister offered, letting the ends of the sword belt dangle free as he shifted it to his left hand, grasping it below the hilt, and turned to give the stranger his right hand. His eyes locked with the other man's, compelling his attention, ensuring that his words should be engraved on the other's memory for all time as he raised him up.

"Rise now, Champion and Deliverer of a people. To thee I give the hand of loyalty and service, which shall be a sign for the hands and loyalties to come, to sustain thee in thy mission. I know not thy name," he went on, releasing the other's hand, "yet on this Book I swear to be faithful to the cause you have made your own, even unto death."

He touched the fingertips of his right hand briefly to his lips, to the sacred Book, then bent to buckle the sword to the stranger's side. When he had finished, he stood back and made him a little bow. It was the signal for the girl also to bow, after which the three of them, in unison, made the stranger a sign of respect.

The stranger looked at all of them a little dazedly—and at the altar, at the Book, at the iron cross witnessing all—then raised his chin in growing confidence, the laurel wreath resting like a royal diadem on his noble head.

"I know not whether I wake or dream," he whispered, "but this I vow, by all that is sacred—I shall be true to the charge you have set before me."

So saying, and taking his example from the young man, he touched the fingers of his right hand to his lips and laid that hand flat on the Bible for a moment, his eyes closing briefly.

Then he was turning to stride out of the little chapel without a backward glance, blindly taking the hat that the young man pressed into his hands. The sound of his retreating footsteps mingled with the moaning wind as he opened the door and passed into the night of the new year, taking their magic with him.

When he had gone, the girl and the young man turned to their father.

"Will he remember what has happened here tonight, Father?" Amanda asked.

"He will," the old man replied. "It may be but the whisper of a fleeting dream, when the time is right—sparked, perhaps, by the scent of mountain laurel—but he will remember."

"And he will, indeed, take up the sword?" Ephraim persisted.

The old man nodded, his aged eyes staring far beyond the path of candlelight still streaming onto the snow outside.

"He will take it up," he whispered. "By the Dragon, he will become the Deliverer. It is his destiny."

As Is

Robert Silverberg

s is," the auto dealer said, jamming his thumbs under his belt. "Two hundred fifty bucks and drive it away. I'm not pretending it's perfect, but I got to tell you, you're getting a damned good hunk of car for the price."

"As is," Sam Norton said.

"As is. Strictly as is."

Norton looked a little doubtful. "Maybe she drives well, but with a trunk that doesn't open—"

"So what?" the dealer snorted. "You told me yourself you're renting a U-Haul to get your stuff to California. What do you need a trunk for? Look, when you get out to the Coast and have a little time, take the car to a garage, tell 'em the story, and maybe five minutes with a blow-torch—"

"Why didn't you do that while you had the car in stock?"

The dealer looked evasive. "We don't have time to fool with details like that."

Norton let the point pass. He walked around the car again, giving it a close look from all angles. It was a smallish dark-green four-door sedan, with the finish and trim in good condition, a decent set of tires, and a general glow that comes only when a car has been well cared for. The upholstery was respectable, the radio was in working order, the engine was—as far as he could judge—okay, and a test drive had been smooth and easy. The car seemed to be a reasonably late model, too; it had shoulder-harness safety belts and emergency blinkers.

There was only one small thing wrong with it. The trunk didn't open. It wasn't just a case of a jammed lock, either; somebody had fixed this car so the trunk *couldn't* open. With great care the previous owner had apparently welded the trunk shut; nothing was visible back there except a dim line to mark the place where the lid might once have lifted.

What the hell, though. The car was otherwise in fine shape, and he wasn't in a position to be too picky. Overnight, practically, they had transferred him to the Los Angeles office, which was fine in terms of getting out of New York in the middle of a lousy winter, but not so good as far as his immediate finances went. The company didn't pay moving costs, only transportation; he had been handed four one-way tourist-class tickets, and that was that. So he had put Ellen and the kids aboard the first jet to L.A., cashing in his own ticket so he could use the money for the moving job. He figured to do it the slow but cheap way: rent a U-Haul trailer, stuff the family belongings into it, and set out via turnpike for California, hoping that Ellen had found an apartment by the time he got there. Only he couldn't trust his present clunker of a car to get him very far west of Parsippany, New Jersey, let alone through the Mojave Desert. So here he was, trying to pick up an honest used job for about five hundred bucks, which was all he could afford to lay out on the spot.

And here was the man at the used-car place offering him this very attractive vehicle—with its single peculiar defect—for only two and a half bills, which would leave him with that much extra cash cushion for the expenses of his transcontinental journey. And he didn't *really* need a trunk, driving alone. He could keep his suitcase on the back seat and stash everything else in the U-Haul. And it shouldn't be all that hard to have some mechanic in L.A. cut the trunk open for him and get it working again. On the other hand, Ellen was likely to chew him out for having bought a car that was sealed up that way; she had let him have it before on other "bargains" of that sort. On the third hand, the mystery of the sealed trunk appealed to him. Who knew what he'd find in there once he opened it up? Maybe the car had belonged to a smuggler who had had to hide a hot cargo fast, and the trunk was full of lovely golden ingots, or diamonds, or ninety-year-old cognac, which the smuggler had planned to reclaim a few weeks later, except that something unexpected had come up. On the fourth hand—

The dealer said, "How'd you like to take her out for another test spin, then?"

Norton shook his head. "Don't think I need to. I've got a good idea of how she rides."

"Well, then, let's step into the office and close the deal."

Sidestepping the maneuver, Norton said, "What year did you say she was?"

"Oh, about a 'sixty-four, 'sixty-five."

"You aren't sure?"

"You can't really tell with these foreign jobs, sometimes. You know, they don't change the model for five, six, ten years in a row, except in little ways that only an expert would notice. Take Volkswagen, for instance—"

"And I just realized," Norton cut in, "that you never told me what make she is, either."

"Peugeot, maybe, or some kind of Fiat," said the dealer hazily. "One of those kind."

"You don't *know?*"

A shrug. "Well, we checked a lot of the style books going back a few years, but there are so damn many of these foreign cars around, and some of them they import only a few thousand, and—well, so we couldn't quite figure it out."

Norton wondered how he was going to get spare parts for a car of unknown make and uncertain date. Then he realized that he was thinking of the car as his, already, even though the more he considered the deal, the less he liked it. And then he thought of those ingots in the trunk. The rare cognac. The suitcase full of rubies and sapphires.

He said, "Shouldn't the registration say something about the year and make?"

The dealer shifted his weight from foot to foot. "Matter of fact, we don't have the registration. But it's perfectly legitimate. Hey, look, I'd like to get this car out of my lot, so maybe we call it two twenty-five, huh?"

"It all sounds pretty mysterious. Where'd you get the car, anyway?"

"There was this little guy who brought it in, about a year ago, a year last November, I think it was. Give it a valve job, he said. I'll be back in a month—got to take a sudden business trip. Paid in advance for tune-up and a month's storage and everything. Wouldn't you know that was the last we ever saw of him? Well, we stored his damn car here free for ten, eleven months, but that's it, now we got to get it out of the place. The lawyer says we can take possession for the storage charge."

"If I buy it, you give me a paper saying you had the right to sell it?"

"Sure. Sure."

"And what about getting the registration? Shifting the insurance over from my old heap? All the red tape?"

"I'll handle everything," the dealer said. "Just you take the car outa here."

"Two hundred," Norton said. "As is."

The dealer sighed. "It's a deal. As is."

A light snow was falling when Norton began his cross-country hegira three days later. It was an omen, but he was not sure what kind; he decided that the snow was intended as his last view of a dreary winter phenomenon he wouldn't be seeing again, for a while. According to the *Times*, yesterday's temperature range in L.A. had been sixty-six low, seventy-nine high. Not bad for January.

He slouched down behind the wheel, let his foot rest lightly on the accelerator, and sped westward at a sane, sensible forty-five miles per hour. That was about as fast as he dared go with the bulky U-Haul trailing behind. He hadn't had much experience driving with a trailer—he was a computer salesman, and computer salesmen don't carry sample computers—but he got the hang of it pretty fast. You just had to remember that your vehicle was now a segmented organism, and make your turns accordingly. God bless turnpikes, anyhow. Just drive on, straight and straight and straight, heading toward the land of the sunset with only a few gentle curves and half a dozen traffic lights along the way.

The snow thickened some. But the car responded beautifully, hugging the road, and the windshield wipers kept his view clear. He hadn't expected to buy a foreign car for the trip at all; when he had set out, it was to get a good solid Plymouth or Chevvie, something heavy and sturdy to take him through the wide open spaces. But he had no regrets about this smaller car. It had all the power and pickup he needed, and with that trailer bouncing along behind him he wouldn't have much use for all that extra horsepower, anyway.

He was in a cheerful, relaxed mood. The car seemed comforting and protective, a warm enclosing environment that would contain and shelter him through the thousands of miles ahead. He was still close enough to New York to be able to get Mozart on the radio, which was nice. The car's heater worked well. There wasn't much traffic. The snow itself, new and white and fluffy, was all the more beautiful for the knowledge that he was leaving it behind. He even enjoyed the solitude. It would be restful, in a way, driving on and on through Ohio and Kansas and Colorado or Arizona or whatever states lay between him and Los Angeles. Five or six days of peace and quiet, no need to make small talk, no kids to amuse—

His frame of mind began to darken not long after he got on the Pennsylvania Turnpike. If you have enough time to think, you will eventually think of the things you should have thought of before; and now, as he rolled through the thickening snow on this gray and silent afternoon, certain aspects of a trunkless car occurred to him that in his rush to get on the road he had succeeded in overlooking earlier. What about a tool kit, for instance? If he had a flat, what would he use for a jack and a wrench? That led him to a much more chilling thought: what would he use for a spare tire? A trunk was something more than a cavity back of the rear seat; in most cars it contained highly useful objects.

None of which he had with him.

None of which he had even thought about, until just this minute.

He contemplated the prospects of driving from coast to coast without a spare tire and without tools, and his mood of warm security evaporated abruptly. At the next exit, he decided, he'd hunt for a service station and pick up a tire, fast. There would be room for it on the back seat next to his luggage. And while he was at it, he might as well buy—

The U-Haul, he suddenly observed, was jackknifing around awkwardly in back, as though its wheels had just lost traction. A moment later the car was doing the same, and he found himself moving laterally in a beautiful skid across an unsanded slick patch on the highway. Steer in the direction of the skid, that's what you're supposed to do, he told himself, strangely calm. Somehow he managed to keep his foot off the brake despite all natural inclinations, and watched in quiet horror as car and trailer slid placidly across the empty lane to his right and came to rest, upright and facing forward, in the piled-up snowbank along the shoulder of the road.

He let out his breath slowly, scratched his chin, and gently fed some gas. The spinning wheels made a high-pitched whining sound against the snow. He went nowhere. He was stuck.

The little man had a ruddy-checked face, white hair so long it curled at the ends, and metal-rimmed spectacles. He glanced at the snow covered autos in the used-car lot, scowled, and trudged toward the showroom.

"Came to pick up my car," he announced. "Valve job. Delayed by business in another part of the world."

The dealer looked uncomfortable. "The car's not here."

"So I see. Get it, then."

"We more or less sold it about a week ago."

"*Sold it?* Sold my car? My *car?*"

"Which you abandoned. Which we stored here for a whole year. This ain't no parking lot here. Look, I talked to my lawyer first, and he said—"

"All right. All right. Who was the purchaser?"

"A guy, he was transferred to California and had to get a car fast to drive out. He—"

"His name?"

"Look, I can't tell you that. He bought the car in good faith. You got no call bothering him now."

The little man said, "If I chose, I could draw the information from you in a number of ways. But never mind. I'll locate the car easily enough. And you'll certainly regret this scandalous breach of custodial duties. You certainly shall."

He went stamping out of the showroom, muttering indignantly.

Several minutes later a flash of lightning blazed across the sky. "Lightning?" the auto dealer wondered. "In January? During a snowstorm?"

When the thunder came rumbling in, every pane of plate glass in every window of the showroom shattered and fell out in the same instant.

Sam Norton sat spinning his wheels for a while in mounting fury. He knew it did no good, but he wasn't sure what else he could do, at this point, except hit the gas and hope for the car to pull itself out of the snow. His only other hope was for the highway patrol to come along, see his plight, and summon a tow truck. But the highway was all but empty, and those few cars that drove by shot past him without stopping.

When ten minutes had passed, he decided to have a closer look at the situation. He wondered vaguely if he could somehow scuff away enough snow with his foot to allow the wheels to get a little purchase. It didn't sound plausible, but there wasn't much else he could do. He got out and headed to the back of the car.

And noticed for the first time that the trunk was open.

The lid had popped up about a foot, along that neat welded line of demarcation. In astonishment Norton pushed it higher and peered inside.

The interior had a dank, musty smell. He couldn't see much of what might be in there, for the light was dim and the lid would lift no higher. It seemed to him that there were odd lumpy objects scattered about, objects of no particular size or shape, but he felt nothing when he groped around. He had the impression that the things in the trunk were moving away from his hand, vanishing into the darkest corners as he reached for them. But then his fingers encountered something cold and smooth, and he heard a welcome clink of metal on metal. He pulled.

A set of tire chains came forth.

He grinned at his good luck. Just what he needed! Quickly he unwound the chains and crouched by the back wheels of the car to fasten them in place. The lid of the trunk slammed shut as he worked—hinge must be loose, he thought—but that was of no importance. In five minutes he had the chains attached. Getting behind the wheel, he started the car again, fed some gas, delicately let in the clutch, and bit down hard on his lower lip by way of helping the car out of the snowbank. The car eased forward until it was in the clear. He left the chains on until he reached a service area eight miles up the turnpike. There he undid them; and when he stood up, he found that the trunk had popped open again. Norton tossed the chains inside and knelt in another attempt to see what else might be in the trunk; but not even by squinting did he discover anything. When he touched the lid, it snapped shut, and once more the rear of the car presented that puzzling welded-tight look.

Mine not to reason why, he told himself. He headed into the station and asked the attendant to sell him a spare tire and a set of tools. The attendant, frowning a bit, studied the car through the station window and said, "Don't know as we got one to fit. We got standards and we got smalls, but you got an in-between. Never saw a size tire like that, really."

"Maybe you ought to take a closer look," Norton suggested. "Just in case it's really a standard foreign-car size, and—"

"Nope. I can see from here. What you driving, anyway? One of them Japanese jobs?"

"Something like that."

"Look, maybe you can get a tire in Harrisburg. They got a place there, it caters to foreign cars, get yourself a muffler, shocks, anything you need."

"Thanks," Norton said, and went out.

He didn't fell like stopping when the turnoff for Harrisburg came by. It made him a little queasy to be driving without a spare, but somehow he wasn't as worried about it as he'd been before. The trunk had had tire chains when he needed them. There was no telling what else might turn up back there at the right time. He drove on.

Since the little man's own vehicle wasn't available to him, he had to arrange a rental. That was no problem, though. There were agencies in every city that specialized in such things. Very shortly he was in touch with one, not exactly by telephone, and was explaining his dilemma. "The difficulty," the little man said, "is that he's got a head start of several days. I've traced him to a point west of Chicago, and he's moving forward at a pretty steady four hundred fifty miles a day."

"You'd better fly, then."

"That's what I've been thinking, too," said the little man. "What's available fast?"

"Could have given you a nice Persian job, but it's out having its tassels restrung. But you don't care much for carpets anyway, do you? I forgot."

"Don't trust 'em in thermals," said the little man. "I caught an updraft once in Sikkim and I was halfway up the Himalayas before I got things under control. Looked for a while like I'd end up in orbit. What's at the stable?"

"Well, some pretty decent jobs. There's this classy stallion that's been resting up all winter, though actually he's a little cranky—maybe you'd prefer the bay gelding. Why don't you stop around and decide for yourself?"

"Will do," the little man said. "You still take Diner's Club, don't you?"

"All major credit cards, as always. You bet."

Norton was in southern Illinois, an hour out of St. Louis on a foggy, humid morning, when the front right-hand tire blew. He had been expecting it to go for a day and a half, now, ever since he'd stopped in Altoona for gas. The kid at the service station had tapped the tire's treads and showed him the weak spot, and Norton had nodded and asked about his chances of buying a spare, and the kid had shrugged and said, "It's a funny size. Try in Pittsburgh, maybe." He tried in Pittsburgh, killing an hour and a half there, and hearing from several men who probably ought to know that tires just weren't made to that size, nohow. Norton was beginning to wonder how the previous owner of the car had managed to find replacements. Maybe this was still the original set, he figured. But he was morbidly sure of one thing: that weak spot was going to give out, beyond any doubt, before he saw L.A.

When it blew, he was doing about thirty-five, and he realized at once what had happened. He slowed the car to a halt without losing control. The shoulder was wide here, but even so Norton was grateful that the flat was on the right-hand side of the car; he didn't much feature having to change a tire with his rump to the traffic. He was still congratulating himself on that small bit of good luck when he remembered that he had no spare tire.

Somehow he couldn't get very disturbed about it. Spending a dozen hours a day behind the wheel was evidently having a tranquilizing effect on him; at this point nothing worried him much, not even the prospect of being stranded an hour east of St. Louis. He would merely walk to the nearest telephone, wherever that might happen to be, and he would phone the local automobile club and explain his predicament, and they would come out and get him and tow him to civilization. Then he would settle in a motel for a day or two, phoning Ellen at her sister's place in L.A. to say that he was all right but was going to be a little late. Either he would have the tire patched or the automobile club would find a place in St. Louis that sold odd sizes, and everything would turn out for the best. Why get into a dither?

He stepped out of the car and inspected the flat, which looked very flat indeed. Then, observing that the trunk had popped open again, he went around back. Reaching in experimentally, he expected to find the tire chains at the outer edge of the trunk, where he had left them. They weren't there. Instead his fingers closed on a massive metal bar. Norton tugged it partway out of the trunk and discovered that he had found a jack. Exactly so, he thought. And the spare tire ought to be right in back of it, over here, yes? He looked, but the lid was up only eighteen inches or so, and he couldn't see much. His fingers encountered good rubber, though. Yes, here it is. Nice and plump, brand new, deep treads—very pretty. And next to it, if my luck holds, I ought to find a chest of golden doubloons—

The doubloons weren't there. Maybe next time, he told himself. He hauled out the tire and spent a sweaty half hour putting it on. When he was done, he dumped the jack, the wrench, and the blown tire into the trunk, which immediately shut to the usual hermetic degree of sealing. An hour later, without further incident, he crossed the Mississippi into St. Louis, found a room in a shiny new motel overlooking the Gateway Arch, treated himself to a hot shower and a couple of cold Gibsons, and put in a collect call to Ellen's sister. Ellen had just come back from some unsuccessful apartment hunting, and she sounded tired and discouraged. Children were howling in the background as she said, "You're driving carefully, aren't you?"

"Of course I am."

"And the new car is behaving okay?"

"Its behavior," Norton said, "is beyond reproach."

"My sister wants to know what kind it is. She says a Volvo is a good kind of car, if you want a foreign car. That's a Norwegian car."

"Swedish," he corrected.

He heard Ellen say to her sister, "He bought a Swedish car." The reply was unintelligible, but a moment later Ellen said, "She says you did a smart thing. Those Swedes, they make good cars too."

The flight ceiling was low, with visibility less than half a mile in thick fog. Airports were socked in all over Pennsylvania and eastern Ohio. The little man flew westward, though, keeping just above the fleecy whiteness spreading to the horizon. He was making good time, and it was a relief not to have to worry about those damned private planes.

The bay gelding had plenty of stamina, too. He was a fuel-guzzler, that was his only trouble. You didn't get a whole lot of miles to the bale with the horses available nowadays, the little man thought sadly. Everything was in a state of decline, and you had to accept the situation.

His original flight plan had called for him to overtake his car somewhere in the Texas Panhandle. But he had stopped off in Chicago on a sudden whim to visit friends, and now he calculated he wouldn't catch up with the car until Arizona. He couldn't wait to get behind the wheel again, after all these months.

The more he thought about the trunk and the tricks it had played, the more bothered by it all Sam Norton was. The chains, the spare tire, the jack—what next? In Amarillo he had offered a mechanic twenty bucks to get the trunk open. The mechanic had run his fingers along that smooth seam in disbelief. "What are you, one of those television fellers?" he asked. "Having some fun with me?"

"Not at all," Norton said. "I just want that trunk opened up."

"Well, I reckon maybe with an acetylene torch—"

But Norton felt an obscure terror at the idea of cutting into the car that way. He didn't know why the thought frightened him so much, but it did, and he drove out of Amarillo with the car whole and the mechanic muttering and spraying his boots with tobacco juice. A hundred miles on, when he was over the New Mexico border and moving through bleak, forlorn, winter-browned country, he decided to put the trunk to a test.

LAST GAS BEFORE ROSWELL, a peeling sign warned. FILL UP NOW!

The gas gauge told him that the tank was nearly empty. Roswell was somewhere far ahead. There wasn't another human being in sight, no town, not even a shack. This, Norton decided, is the right place to run out of gas.

He shot past the gas station at fifty miles an hour.

In a few minutes he was two and a half mountains away from the filling station and beginning to have doubts not merely of the wisdom of his course but even of his sanity. Deliberately letting himself run out of gas was against all reason; it was harder even to do than deliberately letting the telephone go unanswered. A dozen times he ordered himself to swing around and go back to fill his tank, and a dozen times he refused.

The needle crept lower, until it was reading E for Empty, and still he drove ahead. The needle slipped through the red warning zone below the E. He had used up even the extra couple of gallons of gas that the tank didn't register—the safety margin for careless drivers. And any moment now the car would—

—stop.

For the first time in his life Sam Norton had run out of gas. Okay, trunk, let's see what you can do, he thought. He pushed the door open and felt the chilly zip of the mountain breeze. It was quiet here, ominously so; except for the gray ribbon of the road itself, this neighborhood had a darkly prehistoric look, all sagebrush and pinyon pine and not a trace of man's impact. Norton walked around to the rear of his car.

The trunk was open again.

It figures. Now I reach inside and find that a ten-gallon can of gas has mysteriously materialized, and—

He couldn't feel any can of gas in the trunk. He groped a good long while and came up with nothing more useful than a coil of thick rope.

Rope?

What good is rope to a man who's out of gas in the desert?

Norton hefted the rope, seeking answers from it and not getting any. It occurred to him that perhaps this time the trunk hadn't *wanted* to help him. The skid, the blowout—those hadn't been his fault. But he had with malice aforethought let the car run out of gas, just to see what would happen, and maybe that didn't fall within the scope of the trunk's services.

Why the rope, though?

Some kind of grisly joke? Was the trunk telling him to go string himself up? He couldn't even do that properly here; there wasn't a tree in sight tall enough for a man to hang himself from, not even a telephone pole. Norton felt like kicking himself. Here he was, and here he'd remain for hours, maybe even for days, until another car came along. Of all the dumb stunts!

Angrily he hurled the rope into the air. It uncoiled as he let go of it, and one end rose straight up. The rope hovered about a yard off the ground, rigid, pointing skyward. A faint turquoise cloud formed at the upper end, and a thin, muscular olive-skinned boy in a turban and a loincloth climbed down to confront the gaping Norton.

"Well, what's the trouble?" the boy asked brusquely.

"I'm . . . out . . . of . . . gas."

"There's a filling station twenty miles back. Why didn't you tank up there?"

"I . . . that is . . . "

"What a damned fool," the boy said in disgust. "Why do I get stuck with jobs like this? All right, don't go anywhere and I'll see what I can do."

He went up the rope again and vanished.

When he returned, some three minutes later, he was carrying a tin of gasoline. Glowering at Norton, he slid the gas-tank cover aside and poured in the gas.

"This'll get you to Roswell," he said. "From now on look at your dashboard once in a while. Idiot!"

He scrambled up the rope. When he disappeared, the rope went limp and fell. Norton shakily picked it up and slipped it into the trunk, whose lid shut with an aggressive slam.

Half an hour went by before Norton felt it was safe to get behind the wheel again. He paced around the car something more than a thousand times, not getting a whole lot steadier in the nerves, and ultimately, with night coming on, got in and switched on the ignition. The engine coughed and turned over. He began to drive toward Roswell at a sober and steadfast fifteen miles an hour.

He was willing to believe anything, now.

And so it did not upset him at all when a handsome reddish-brown horse with the wingspread of a DC-3 came soaring through the air, circled above the car a couple of times, and made a neat landing on the highway alongside him. The horse trotted along, keeping pace with him, while the small white-haired man in the saddle yelled, "Open your window wider, young fellow! I've got to talk to you!"

Norton opened the window.

The little man said, "Your name Sam Norton?"

"That's right."

"Well, listen, Sam Norton, you're driving my car!"

Norton saw a dirt turnoff up ahead and pulled into it. As he got out, the pegasus came trotting up and halted to let its rider dismount. It cropped moodily at sagebrush, fluttering its huge wings a couple of times before folding them neatly along its back.

The little man said, "My car, all right. Had her specially made a few years back, when I was on the road a lot. Dropped her off at the garage last winter account of I had a business trip to make abroad, but I never figured they'd sell her out from under me before I got back. It's a decadent age, that's the truth."

"Your . . . car . . ." Norton said.

"My car, yep. Afraid I'll have to take it from you, son. Car like this, you don't want to own it, anyway. Too complicated. Get yourself a decent little standard-make flivver, eh? Well, now, let's unhitch this trailer thing of yours, and then—"

"Wait a second," Norton said. "I bought this car legally. I've got a bill of sale to prove it, and a letter from the dealer's lawyer, explaining that—"

"Don't matter one bit," said the little man. "One crook hires another crook to testify to his character, that's not too impressive. I know you're an innocent party, son, but the fact remains that the car is my property, and I hope I don't have to use special persuasion to get you to relinquish it."

"You just want me to get out and walk, is that it? In the middle of the New Mexico desert at sundown? Dragging the damned U-Haul with my bare hands?"

"Hadn't really considered that problem much," the little man said. "Wouldn't altogether be fair to you, would it?"

"It sure wouldn't." He thought a moment. "And what about the two hundred bucks I paid for the car?"

The little man laughed. "Shucks, it cost me more than that to rent the pegasus to come chasing you! And the overhead! You know how much hay that critter—"

"That's your problem," Norton said. "Mine is that you want to strand me in the desert and that you want to take away a car that I bought in good faith for two hundred dollars, and even if it's a goddam magic car I—"

"Hush, now," said the little man. "You're gettin' all upset, Sam! We can work this thing out. You're going to L.A., that it?"

"Ye-es."

"So am I. Okay, we travel together. I'll deliver you and your trailer, here, and then the car's mine again, and you forget anything you might have seen these last few days."

"And my two hundred dol—"

"Oh, all right." The little man walked to the back of the car. The trunk opened; he slipped in a hand and pulled forth a sheaf of crisp new bills, a dozen twenties, which he handed to Norton "Here. With a little something extra, thrown in. And don't look at them so suspiciously, hear? That's good legal tender U.S. money. They even got different serial numbers, every one." He winked and strolled over to the grazing pegasus, which he slapped briskly on the rump. "Git along, now. Head for home. You cost me enough already!"

The horse began to canter along the highway. As it broke into a gallop it spread its superb wings; they beat furiously a moment, and the horse took off, rising in a superb arc until it was no bigger than a hawk against the darkening sky, and then was gone.

The little man slipped into the driver's seat of the car and fondled the wheel in obvious affection. At a nod, Norton took the seat beside him, and off they went.

"I understand you peddle computers," the little man said when he had driven a couple of miles. "Mighty interesting things, computers. I've been considering computerizing our operation too, you know? It's a pretty big outfit, a lot of consulting stuff all over the world, mostly dowsing now, some thaumaturgy, now and then a little transmutation, things like that, and though we use traditional methods we don't object to the scientific approach. Now, let me tell you a bit about our inventory flow, and maybe you can make a few intelligent suggestions, young fellow, and you might just be landing a nice contract for yourself—"

Norton had the roughs for the system worked out before they hit Arizona. From Phoenix he phoned Ellen and found out that she had rented an apartment just outside Beverly Hills, in what *looked* like a terribly expensive neighborhood but really wasn't, at least, not by comparison with some of the other things she'd seen, and—

"It's okay," he said. "I'm in the process of closing a pretty big sale. I . . . ah . . . picked up a hitchhiker, and turns out he's thinking of going computer soon, a fairly large company—"

"Sam, you haven't been drinking, have you?"

"Not a drop."

"A hitchhiker and you sold him a computer. Next you'll tell me about the flying saucer you saw."

"Don't be silly," Norton said. "Flying saucers aren't real."

They drove into L.A. in midmorning, two days later. By then he had written the whole order, and everything was set; the commission, he figured, would be enough to see him through a new car, maybe one of those Swedish jobs Ellen's sister had heard about. The little man seemed to have no difficulty finding the address of the apartment Ellen had taken; he negotiated the maze of the freeways with complete ease and assurance, and pulled up outside the house.

"Been a most pleasant trip, young fellow," the little man said. "I'll be talking to my bankers later today about that wonderful machine of yours. Meanwhile here we part. You'll have to unhitch the trailer, now."

"What am I supposed to tell my wife about the car I drove here in?"

"Oh, just say that you sold it to that hitchhiker at a good profit. I think she'll appreciate that."

They got out. While Norton undid the U-Haul's couplings, the little man took something from the trunk, which had opened a moment before. It was a large rubbery tarpaulin. The little man began to spread it over the car. "Give us a hand here, will you?" he said. "Spread it nice and neat, so it covers the fenders and everything." He got inside, while Norton, baffled, carefully tucked the tarpaulin into place.

"You want me to cover the windshield too?" he asked.

"Everything," said the little man, and Norton covered the windshield. Now the car was wholly hidden.

There was a hissing sound, as of air being let out of tires. The tarpaulin began to flatten. As it sank toward the ground, there came a cheery voice from underneath, calling, "Good luck, young fellow!"

In moments the tarpaulin was less than three feet high. In a minute more it lay flat against the pavement. There was no sign of the car. It might have evaporated, or vanished into the earth. Slowly, uncomprehendingly, Norton picked up the tarpaulin, folded it until he could fit it under his arm, and walked into the house to tell his wife that he had arrived in Los Angeles.

Sam Norton never met the little man again, but he made the sale, and the commission saw him through a new car with something left over. He still has the tarpaulin, too. He keeps it folded up and carefully locked away in his basement. He's afraid to get rid of it, but he doesn't like to think of what might happen if someone came across it and spread it out.

THE ALCHEMIST
AND THE WITCH

Christopher Stasheff

he wind howled around the log cottage, straining at the eaves and rattling the shutters and the door. It made the pine trees that were gathered around the cottage moan and sway. It pushed at the chinking between the logs, then swirled up to test the shingles of the roof. Finally, it swept panting down the chimney.

Inside the cottage, Amer heard it and turned to close the flue. The wind struck against the metal plates and stopped in surprise, then began to rattle and beat at them. Finally it gave up and turned back up the chimney, shrieking with anger.

Amer looked up as he heard it. He sighed, shook his head, and clucked his tongue, thinking that the wind would never learn. He finished the seam of the brass tube he was working on and laid down his torch.

"Master," said Willow, "wha'cha makin'?"

She was a globe of light in a large glass jar. If you looked closely, you could see, within the globe, a diminutive, very dainty, humanoid form, but only in rough outline.

"A blowpipe, Willow." Amer looked the tube over carefully. He was a good-looking man, but overly solemn for one in his early thirties.

"Wha'cha gonna blow through it?"

"Air." Amer puffed through the pipe, checking to see that there were no leaks. Outside, the wind heard him and swept against the cracks and crevices of the cottage with a blast of redoubled fury at a being who dared mimic it. But Amer paid it no heed.

"Well, of course you're gonna blow air through it," Willow said, disgusted. "What else is there to blow? What I want to know is, 'Why?'"

"To make glassware." Amer went over to the hearth for a look at the kettle of liquid glass that was bubbling thickly over the flames. He found the fireplace filled with smoke from the glowing coals and opened the flue to let it out.

With a joyful shriek, the wind bounded down the chimney again. A second later, it came tumbling back out, coughing and spluttering with the smoke.

"Oh, I like glass!" the ball of light sang.

"It *is* attractive, isn't it?" Amer closed the flue and dipped the pipe into the glass. He lifted out a lump of the amorphous mass and began to blow gently into the pipe, swinging it in slow, cautious circles. Gradually the glass took the form of a globe.

"It's magic!" Willow breathed.

"No, just practice." Amer shook the pipe, and the globe slipped to the side. Then, with a wooden forceps, he drew it away, so that the narrowing tube of glass connected globe and pipe. He broke the tube and placed the finished object on a pile of sand on the floor, to cool.

"It's pretty," Willow said doubtfully, "but what *is* it?"

"An alembic," Amer said. "It's for boiling solutions and channeling their fumes where I want them to go." He dipped the pipe into the glass again, and soon, test tubes, flasks, beakers, and all the rest of the paraphernalia so vital to the alchemist had joined the retort on the sand pile.

"Oh, they're lovely!" the ball of light enthused. "But why are you making so many?"

"Because I have to replace all my apparatus," Amer explained. "The goodfolk of Salem town made that necessary."

The citizens of Salem had, with great civic zeal, destroyed all Amer's glassware in the process of razing his house. Due to the unselfish dedication of the goodfolk of the town, Amer had lost everything—laboratory, wardrobe, notebooks, and dwelling—which ten years of work and wonder had won from the New England wilderness. Barely escaping with his life, he had found his way at once to this hidden spot deep within the mountain forest, and in defiance of the rain and wind which had until then been undisputed masters of the forest, built a small house of logs and reproduced as well as possible his lost notebooks.

There was more to do, of course. There was always more to do.

Taking up a knife and a stick of wood, Amer went to the armchair by the fireplace, sat down, and began to whittle.

"*Now* wha'cha makin'?"

"A model of a human skeleton, Willow." Amer made a careful scrape along the tiny wooden bone with his carving knife, held back the piece to evaluate it, compared it with the drawings in Galen's text on anatomy beside him, and nodded, satisfied. He put it down and took up the next roughly cut blocky bone and began to whittle its details.

"Wha'cha makin' *that* for?"

"To better understand human anatomy, my dear."

"Why in firedamp do you want to understand *that?*"

Amer smiled. "So I can write a book about it."

A miniature skull began to grow out of the wood under his knife. On the table at his elbow lay a diminutive rib cage, a pelvis, and an assortment of other bones. There was also a large stack of drawings and pages, all written in the alchemist's hand. Amer was preparing his own text on anatomy.

"Oh," said the ball of light, "I'm writin' a book, too. I'm gonna call it *Bizarre Behavior of the Bipedal Beast.*"

"Indeed!" Amer looked up from his work. "And where are you finding your information?"

"From watching *you.* You're about as bizarre as they come. Let's see . . . 'makes little skeletons . . .'"

Amer smiled, wondering what his little captive was using for pen and ink—or paper, for that matter. He, of course, had never heard of electricity, let alone the concept of rearranging electrical charges that store her words. "You're not exactly a conformist yourself. Will-o'-the-wisps aren't supposed to write books, you know."

"Must be the company I keep."

"*Touché*." Amer smiled. "I am a trifle eccentric, I suppose."

"No 'suppose' about it. You do a *lot* of things people aren't supposed to do."

"Do I really!"

"Uh-huh." The ball of light bobbed. "Like, for one thing, they're not supposed to go messing around with smelly ol' potions and things. They're *also* not supposed to catch will-o'-the-wisps and keep 'em in bottles!"

"Beakers," Amer corrected automatically. "You wouldn't want me to be lonely, would you?"

"Yeah," the will-o'-the-wisp said pensively. "That's another thing people aren't supposed to do."

"What? Be lonely?"

"Uh-huh," said Willow. "They're supposed to live in towns, or maybe farmhouses, with other people—but not high up on mountainsides, all alone."

"Well, yes," Amer conceded. "I must admit that's true. But the people of Salem didn't want me there, Willow."

"Aw, I'll bet they did. You just *think* they didn't."

"No," Amer said, frowning. "I'm afraid they made their opinion quite clear. They burned my house and notebooks, and broke my instruments. I barely escaped with my life."

"No!" Willow said, shocked.

"Why, yes," said Amer mildly.

"But why, Master?"

"Because," said Amer, "Samona told them I was a warlock." He frowned. "Actually, I don't think they'd have taken action on her unsupported word—she's never been terribly well-liked, except by the young men, and then in the worst possible way. She must have had some help, some others telling the goodfolk that I had made a pact with Satan."

"Master!" Willow gasped. "You didn't, did you?"

"Of course not, Willow. I'm an alchemist, not a warlock."

The will-o'-the-wisp sounded puzzled. "What's the difference?"

"A warlock gains magical powers by selling his soul to the Devil," Amer explained. "An alchemist gains magical results by studying the phenomena of nature and mind."

"By how?" The will-o'-the-wisp was totally at a loss.

"By constructing logical generalizations encompassing ever more natural and supernatural phenomena."

"If you say so." But the will-o'-the-wisp sounded doubtful. "You sure you're safe here, though?"

"Oh, yes," Amer murmured. "Quite safe."

For Amer had done more than merely rebuild. He had set an elaborate network of traps and warning devices around his cottage in a wide circle, for it was highly possible that the good colonists would not rest until they had hunted him down and burned him at the stake.

"It is possible," he told Willow, "that the Salem folk may still be pursuing me. I'm quite certain that Samona, at least, will not rest until she has settled with me."

"But who *is* this Samona? And why'd she say you're a whosiwhatsis if you're not?"

"Samona," said Amer, "is a very beautiful young witch who lives in Salem—only they don't know she's a witch. And she told them I was a warlock because she hates me."

"Hates *you?*" Willow demanded, incredulous.

"Hates me," Amer confirmed. Not that he had ever done anything to Samona that should cause her to hate him; indeed, he was supremely indifferent to any being that walked on two feet, and especially so to those who wore skirts. Samona despised him for this; but then, she held the whole colony in contempt for similar reasons.

And this Amer could never understand, for though Samona loathed the Puritans for their reserve, she was herself extremely reticent, so much so that more than a few of the stern young men still bore the scars of her fingernails for their boyhood audacity in paying her a courtly compliment.

"Why does she hate you, Master?"

Amer made a guess. "Because she hates all men."

"Well—yeah, I can understand that. But why you especially?"

"Because my magic is just as powerful as hers."

"But that's no reason to hate you!"

"That's just the way women are, Willow." Amer sighed.

"Aw, it is not!" Willow said stoutly. "I'm not, and I'm a woman!"

"That's different," Amer explained. "You're a will-o'-the-wisp."

"What woman isn't?" Willow returned. "There's gotta be another reason why she hates you, Master."

"Well, there is, really. You see, she sold her soul to the Devil, and I didn't."

Notwithstanding his refusal to sell his soul, Amer had garnered more knowledge of magic through his experiments than Samona had gained through her pact with Satan. "I think we were both born with the ability to work magic, actually—it was just a matter of learning how. She thought she paid a much lower tuition than I, but she's begun to realize that the bill will come due eventually, and will be rather exorbitant. Mine took longer, but is paid in full as it goes."

"Oh." That gave the will-o'-the-wisp pause.

"No wonder she hates you."

Amer looked up, surprised. "I don't see any logic in it. . . ."

"That's all right, Master," Willow assured him. "There isn't any."

"Then it is absolutely necessary that I keep an eye on her." Amer put down the tiny bone and went back to the hearth. He placed the new glassware on a tray and took it over to a keg-spigot he had hammered into one of the logs that formed the wall. He twisted the handle, and clear, sparkling water gushed out, though the spigot met only solid wood within the log. It was fed by a clear mountain stream, a mile away; the alchemist had learned well from his research.

He washed the new glassware with water and sand, then set it up on metal stands on a bench that ran the full length of the wall. He lost no time in setting an alembic bubbling merrily into a cooling tube with a beaker at its end, to collect the distillate.

While he waited for the beaker to fill, he turned to another workbench, one that bore racks of vials, another alembic, several glass tubes, and a small crucible. It was backed by shelves of jars and boxes, each carefully labelled. Amer took another, larger beaker, filled it with water, and set it over an elaborately carved alcohol lamp. Then the alchemist began to ladle powders into a beaker. "Let's see . . . green pepper . . . sugar . . . cinnamon . . ."

"Sounds good, Master."

". . . powdered batwings . . ."

"Gaaaaaack!"

"Oil of ambergris . . ."

"Uh, Master . . ."

"Eye of eagle . . ."

"Master . . ."

"Monosodium glutamate . . ."

"M-A-A-A-A-STER!"

"Oh." Amer looked up, blinking. "Yes, Willow?"

"Wha'cha makin'!?!"

"Making?" Amer looked down at the frothy liquid in his beaker. "A far-sight potion, Willow."

"A what?"

"A far-sight potion. So I can watch Samona, wherever she is."

Willow gasped. "You're a peepin' Tom?"

"Willow!" Amer remonstrated, scandalized. "I am merely performing a vital mission of strategic reconnaissance."

"That's what I said. Wha'cha wanna look at her for, anyway?"

"I'm afraid it's necessary," Amer said, thin-lipped. He peered into the beaker. "You see, she's always trying to find some way to enslave me."

"Enslave *you*? What's she want to do *that* for?"

"Because she's a woman."

"*That's* no reason," Willow maintained.

"Samona thinks it is," Amer explained. "As I've said, she hates all men."

"And you most of all, 'cause you're not a warlock?"

"For that," Amer said judiciously, "and because I'm the only man she can't enslave with her magic."

"Why's that?"

"Because *I've* got magic, too."

Willow sounded puzzled. "I thought you said you weren't a witch."

"Warlock," Amer corrected absently. "That's the male equivalent. And no, I'm not. I'm an alchemist."

"Same thing."

"Not at all." Amer sighed, striving for patience and trying to find a slightly different way to explain something he'd already explicated. "A witch gets her power from the Devil. But an alchemist gets his magic by working experiments."

"Gotta get this down," Willow muttered. "Chapter Four: Magic, Male and Female . . . Now—you're an alchemist?"

"That's right."

"And she's a witch?"

"Mmm-hmm."

"And that's why she hates you?"

Amer looked up, startled. "You know, Willow, you may have something there. If I got my magic from the Devil, she probably wouldn't even notice me."

"Why not?" The will-o'-the-wisp was totally perplexed.

"That, my dear," said Amer, "is one of the peculiarities of the female mind."

"You mean," said Willow, "you don't know."

"Precisely."

A gentle bubbling announced that the beaker was ready. Amer recited an incantation and peered into the fluid. "Now let me see . . ." He found it filled with a swirling of unearthly colors. He sighed patiently and muttered a refinement of the earlier spell—with no results. He tried a second and a third spell, and then, losing patience, slapped the side of the beaker. Instantly the colors swirled together, stretched and wriggled, and snapped into focus in the form of Samona.

She was dressed in a low-cut, red velvet gown with a high Elizabethan collar that framed her head in a scarlet halo. The bodice was molded to her as though it had been born on her and had grown as she had grown, narrowing as her waist had narrowed and flaring out into the skirt as her hips had become wider and fuller, curving softly, and then sweeping up in a futile attempt to hide her high, swelling breasts. But where cloth had failed, long shimmering hair had succeeded, flowing down to hide her in soft, luxuriant black waves. Her face was smooth, gently tinted, with slanting black eyes and wide, full, blood-red lips.

All this Amer noted, and had noted every day of his childhood and youth almost without knowing it. She'd changed her eyebrows again, and the mahogany highlights were back in her hair.

"Still so easily bored," he murmured, staring into the beaker.

"Not you, Master!"

"No, no! Samona."

"Master! You really shouldn't!"

"Fo," Amer said, frowning at what he saw. "I think I should."

For the miniature Samona's hands were moving lightly and quickly among the bottles on the shelves alongside her fireplace, measuring their contents into a small cauldron that boiled and chortled softly over an unearthly green flame. She stirred the brew, dropped in a pinch of a white, glittering powder, and stood counting her pulse-beats as she watched the thickening liquid.

"What's she doing, Master?"

"I thought you said spying was wrong, Willow."

"Well, yes, but gossip is another matter. Tell me!"

Amer smiled. "She's making a potion, too. But what kind? Let's see . . . she's using essence of sweet zephyrs . . . powdered tears . . . rhadlakum. . . . What can it be?"

"That's what I was wonderin'," Willow muttered.

"My heavens!" Amer looked up, eyes wide. "Another aphrodisiac!"

In the beaker, the miniature Samona, judging the time to be right, swung the cauldron off the flame, let it stand for a few minutes, and then skimmed the surface with a ladle and poured the skimmings into a small vial. She held it up to the light; it glittered with ruby liquid, steaming. Her eyes glowed; she eyed the vial with a smug smile, then began to laugh.

Suddenly, there was a flash of green light, and she was gone.

Amer stood looking into the beaker for a few seconds more.

"What is it, Master?" Willow cried. "Master? Master!"

For Amer had taken a clean beaker and started pulling powders off the shelves.

"What kind of potion is an aphro-whatever?" Willow demanded.

"An aphrodisiac, Willow."

"What's *it* for?"

"Me, I'm afraid."

"No, no! I mean, what does it *do?*"

"Stra-a-a-ange things," Amer said.

"Like what?"

"Well," said Amer, and "well," again. Then, "It will, uh . . . make me, uh . . . like her."

"Wonderful! Then you'll be friends again?"

"Well, something like that, yes."

"Master," the will-o'-the-wisp accused, "you're not bein' honest with me."

"Very well, Willow." Amer sighed, looking up from his work for a moment. "An aphrodisiac makes a man desire a woman carnally. And the particular kinds that Samona brews are also love philtres."

"A love filter? What's it do, take the love out of the carnal-whatever?"

"Desire. And no, a 'philtre' adds love in to where it wasn't before."

"That doesn't make much sense to me."

"Nor to me, either," Amer confessed. "But here's the manner of it: if she can trick me into drinking that potion, I'll become her slave."

"I thought you said her magic didn't work on you."

"It hasn't—so far. And only because I counter her spells and potions with my own. But there is always the possibility that she might be able to concoct a *new* potion that *would* work on me."

"So what're *you* doin'?"

"Making an anti-aphrodisiac, Willow."

"A *what?*"

"A protective drug," Amer explained. "It will ward me from the effects of her potion. Let's see . . . where did I put the saltpeter?"

"But," said Willow, "don't you *want* to fall in love with her?"

"Willow," said Amer, "don't ask embarrassing questions."

"But I don't understand."

"That makes two of us."

"Why does she want to make you like her?"

"Because she's a woman."

"No, no! I mean, besides that!"

"Willow," Amer said between his teeth, "it is not tactful to remind a scholar of just how much he doesn't know."

"Well, I'm sorry! Y' know, this whole thing seems really silly to me. She mixes a potion so you'll fall in love with her, and you mix one so you won't. You could save a lot of time and trouble if neither of you mixed the potions."

"Very true," Amer agreed. "Unfortunately, Samona doesn't see it that way."

"Why not?"

"Well . . . I suppose it's that if she can't enslave me one way, she'll try another."

"And an aphro-whatsis will do that?"

"It's a good start," Amer allowed.

"I don't understand," said the poor, confused will-o'-the-wisp.

"I only wish I did!" Amer said fervently. "Let's see . . . wormwood . . . a pinch of gall . . . wolfbane . . ."

"Love potions." Willow was engraving in her book of energy impulses. "Protective drugs . . . Wait till Harvard hears about this!" She spoke of the College that had been established for many years.

Amer gave the potion a final stir, lifted it to his lips, and drank it off in a single draft. His face twisted in a wry grimace; he coughed, and came up smiling. "There! I'm safe!"

A tone, so low that it was more felt than heard, filled the room. Willow vibrated with panic, but Amer breathed, "Just in time."

"Good afternoon, Amer," murmured a low, husky voice.

"Good afternoon, Samona." Amer noted that her tones were deeper and fuller than usual, sending a shiver through his system; he reminded himself that his potion needed a few more minutes to take its full effect.

She came over to the side of his chair, and the flowing skirts clung to her as she came.

"You aren't very polite," she said. "A host usually offers his guest some refreshment after a long journey."

"Of course," Amer said. "Forgive me." He rose and took a decanter and two glasses from the mantel. "Will amontillado do?"

"Quite well," Samona said, and a smiled flickered for an instant over her lips. It lasted no longer than the tick of a watch, but that was long enough for Amer to be certain it had been there.

He filled the glasses and gave her one. "To your power—may it increase."

"Hypocrite!" she said. "Toast something else, Amer, for you know as well as I that I'll never be stronger than I am now."

"Oh, come," Amer said. "You're young yet."

"Yes, but I've reached my peak. You're young, too, Amer, but somehow your power keeps growing. I should know, I've been trying to defeat you long enough."

"Oh, now, Samona!" Amer protested. "You mustn't give up so easily! You might win yet, you know."

"Indeed? It doesn't seem very likely."

"Don't believe her, Master!" Willow whispered, just behind his back. "Remember her potion!"

That jarred Amer out of his shock. "Yes! Well, uh, Samona—I'm glad to see you've finally given up chasing a will-o'-the-wisp."

Someone cleared a miniature throat behind his back.

"I beg your pardon, Willow," Amer hissed out of the corner of his mouth.

Samona didn't notice; she had turned away, pacing toward the hearth. "You're right, Amer. I've become wise in the hard school of frustration. I know when I'm beaten."

"Surely . . ."

"No," she said, bowing her head forlornly, "I've come to admit defeat, Amer."

For a moment he panicked, thinking she meant it. But then he remembered the fleeting, gloating smile as he poured the wine, and said, "Well, I'm glad to see that you've finally become wise, Samona. It's not good for you to keep wearing yourself out getting nowhere."

"So I've learned," she said with a touch of bitterness. "No, I've come for a truce. And to prove that I mean you well, I've brought news of danger."

"Danger? From whom?"

"From Death."

Amer smiled. "There's always danger of that, Samona."

"You don't understand." Samona turned away impatiently.

"I'm willing to learn."

"Yes, and eager, too, I know," she said, bitter again. But she smoothed her face with a smile. "Then learn, scholar, that in this eldritch world we inhabit, Death is not a force, but a being."

"Fantastic . . ."

"But real enough, for us." Samona turned to face him again. "Death doesn't come in the usual way when he comes for a witch. He comes in person, and you may never know he's there until you feel the cold, damp bones of his hand clutching your shoulder."

"Come now," Amer said. "Surely, with all your powers, you could invent some sort of protection for yourselves."

"True," she said, "but if we ever relax for so much as a second, he is upon us. If we forget ourselves in our delight with our own cleverness, if we lose our heads in glee as we watch a victim shudder, we will almost certainly feel the chill on our shoulders and feel it creep to our hearts, and will hear a cry of triumph as we sink to the depths of Hell." She stood gazing at the fire, pale and trembling, as though she could see the hollow eyes of Death staring at her.

"But if Death is always lying in wait, as you say," said Amer, softly, "how is it that you have never thought it necessary to speak of him until now?"

"Because he struck among us last night," Samona said in a hushed, almost strangled voice. "This morning Goody Coister was found sitting in the old rocking chair in front of her fireplace. She was stone dead." Samona's eyes reflected the fire burning quietly on the hearth. "I saw her myself," she whispered. "You could still see the marks of his fingers on her shoulder."

"Goody Coister?" Amer whispered in shock and disbelief.

Samona smiled with malicious satisfaction. "Yes, Goody Coister, that virtuous old bag. That venerable symbol of New England purity. Shall I tell you how many bastards she and old Moggard have spawned?"

"Moggard?"

"Yes, Moggard. Warlock-General of New England and Vice-

Chairman of the Universal Brotherhood of Sorcerers. He begat quite a few on the old biddy—not that any of them lived to know of it, of course." For a moment, Samona seemed sad and forlorn.

"But Goody Cloister taught me my catechism!"

"Of course. The worst ones always look to be the most respectable. Shall I tell you about Sexton Karrier?"

Amer shuddered. "Please don't."

Samona's eyes gleamed, and her smile deepened with satisfaction. She turned away, and when she turned back to face Amer again she looked quietly humble once more.

"Ah, well," she said, "I just wanted to warn you. Come, Amer, fill my glass again, and let's drink to friendship."

Amer shook off the mood of apprehension and forced a smile. He nodded and took the decanter from the mantelpiece and poured them each a glass. "As red as your lips, my dear, and as sparkling as your eyes."

"Gallant," she noted, and lifted her glass. "To our truce."

"*Pax nobiscum*," Amer said, and drank.

Samona nearly choked on her wine. "Please!" she said between splutters, "must you use Church language?"

"I'm sorry," Amer said. "Really I am." He patted her back gently.

"Don't touch me!" she screamed, and turned on him like a cornered vixen. For a moment, Amer could have sworn that he saw the Devil looking out at him from her midnight eyes.

But she regained her composure immediately. "I'm sorry, Amer. But you know I could never bear to be touched. And it's become worse since I . . . joined the coven."

"Yes, quite so." Amer had a brief, nightmarish vision of what her initiation must have been like, and how much of herself she had lost. He shuddered. "I'd forgotten. My apologies."

"Accepted," she said, looking up at him, and, "Oh, Hell!" in a slightly reverent tone. "I've split my wine all over you."

"That's all right," Amer said, recovering himself with equal rapidity. "I've plenty more. Would you care for another glass?"

"Yes, please," she said. She put her hand to her forehead. "Yes, I—I think I need it."

"Why, you're pale," he said.

"No, I'm all right," she said. "It's nothing."

"Sit down," Amer said, pushing an armchair toward her. She all but fell into it. He picked up a notebook and fanned her gently.

"Just a moment's rest . . ."

"There, there," Amer soothed. "Too much excitement, that's all . . ."

"Yes. I—I'm fine now. Thank you."

Amer put the notebook down, took Samona's glass to the mantel, and filled it from the decanter. He knelt and gave it to her.

But as she took it, he noticed a ring on her hand, a ring with an exceptionally large stone—a huge emerald with a deep, almost liquid lustre. In all the time he had known her Amer had never seen Samona wear such a ring. "What a beautiful gem!"

"I—I'm glad you like it, Amer." Her eyes were wide with surprise and—was it alarm?

"That—uh—friend I've heard you speak of . . . Lucretia . . . ?"

"Yes, it was a present from her."

He smiled sadly as he looked at it.

"Amer . . ."

"Yes, of course." He tore his gaze away and went over to a cabinet that stood next to the table on which Willow rested. "You'll need something stronger than wine."

As soon as he'd turned away, Samona sat up, pressed the stone out of its setting with feverish haste, and emptied the drop of potion it contained into his glass of wine.

"Master," Willow hissed, "she's pouring something into your wineglass."

"I thought she would," Amer muttered. "Fortunate that I didn't drink it all."

"Aren't you worried?"

"No, not especially, Willow. Let me see . . . I suppose I've given her enough time. . . ."

Only just; Samona had scarcely replaced the stone and fallen back into the chair before Amer returned.

He took a glass from the mantel and filled it from the bottle of whiskey he'd taken out of the cabinet. "Here." He pressed it into her hand, which trembled as she brought the glass to her lips. Amer took his wineglass from the table and raised it, wondering what kind of spell the potion was supposed to cast over him. "To your quick recovery," he said, and downed it.

Samona watched him out of the corner of her eye and muttered a short incantation as he drank. Then she leaned back in the armchair and sipped her whiskey slowly, waiting for the potion to take effect. Beneath the dark waves of hair that covered them, her breasts rose and fell softly with her breathing, and Amer was shocked when he realized that he'd been wondering just what the low-cut gown would reveal if she wore her hair back over her shoulders.

Finally Samona set down her glass, took a deep breath, bit her lip, and said, "Amer, I—I don't feel too well. Would you see how my pulse is?"

"Certainly," Amer said, and he took her wrist, frankly puzzled as to what she was up to. He probed for the large vein, probed again, and frowned. "I can't seem to find it."

"I never seem to be able to, either," she said, "not there. See if you can feel my heartbeat." She slid his hand under the heavy black tresses, and Amer found that the gown was cut very low indeed.

For a moment he was stunned, completely at a loss. Then, with a sort of numb amazement, he realized the purpose of the potion, and began to be very glad he'd taken the antidote. For one way or another, Samona meant to have his soul. He would play along to see if she had more tricks prepared.

Amer caressed her, slowly moving his hand to part the rich black waves and stroke them away to her shoulders; then he let his hand slide over the swelling softness of her. He felt her shiver under his touch. He knelt and watched her cream-white breasts as they rose and fell, straining against their velvet prison.

Then he looked at her face, and it was dead white. He realized with a shock that he was the first ever to touch her with tenderness, and that her trembling was not from passion alone. Finally, with a sense of awe, he realized her courage.

Then she looked at him with fear in her eyes, and her trembling lips parted softly. He slid his free hand to her back, between her shoulders, and pressed her to him. Their lips met in moist sweetness.

They broke apart, and he pulled her head down onto his shoulder. "So," he said, with wonder, "that's what it's like. . . ."

"What . . . ?" Samona half-gasped.

"Your scapula," Amer breathed. "It articulates with your clavicle by ligament! And I thought it was connected by cartilage. . . ."

For a moment, Samona sat very, very still.

Then she was out of the chair and over against the wall with a wild-cat's scream. "Take your hands off me and get away from me, you tin-bellied machine!" She clasped at the wall behind her with fingers hooked into claws, glaring at him and hissing, "I wish you were in Hell!" And, for a moment, Amer could have sworn he saw hellfire in her eyes.

Then a cloud of green smoke exploded. When it cleared, she had vanished.

"Thank Heaven!" Willow sighed. "Master, she's gone!"

But Amer only stared at the place where she had been, murmuring, "Strange . . . strange, very strange . . ."

"What, Master?"

"My emotions, Willow."

"Why, Master?" the will-o'-the-wisp cried in alarm. "What's wrong?"

"I must write this down," Amer hurried to his writing desk and snatched up a quill. "It's priceless information . . . I'll probably never have the same experience again."

"I'll say!" Willow said fervently. "But what's the matter?"

"Well, Willow . . ."

"Now, now, Master, you've had a nasty shock. Just lie down and relax. You've had a hard day. I'll write it down for you." Willow prepared to make alterations in the electrical potentials within her.

Amer took her at her word, going over to the narrow cot against the wall and lying back, head pillowed on a horsehair cushion. "It started when she told me that she'd come to declare a truce. . . ."

"Just let it flow, Master," the will-o'-the-wisp said, oozing sympathy.

"She looked up at me, and her eyes looked so innocent, and she seemed so submissive . . ."

"Mm-hmmm."

". . . and she said she'd come to surrender. . . ."

"Yes, Master . . ."

"And, well, Willow, for just a moment there, I felt *panic!*"

"Really!"

"And, Willow—that *worries* me . . ."

The wind swept around the cottage, infuriated at being balked. But it was gaining strength, because other winds were coming, ushered by the towering black clouds that drifted from the west, obscuring the moon. The wind welcomed its kin, and together they tore at the cabin, howling and tearing. Then a great black cloud arrived and broke open a drum of rain, with a huge crack of thunder. Torrents gushed down, lashing the little cabin, and the winds howled in glee.

Inside, Amer slept on in blissful but disturbing dreams, unheeding of the winds. Enraged, they redoubled their force. Still Amer slept— until Willow came to attention, startled. She listened, was sure she'd heard right, and called, "Master! Wake up!"

It came again, from the door—a knocking.

"Master! Wake up! There's someone here!"

"What? Here? Where?" Amer lifted his head, dull with sleep.

"At the door!"

"Here?" Amer stared at the portal.

It shook as the knocking sounded again, louder and quicker.

"Oh, my heavens! And at this hour of the night!" Amer shoved himself out of bed, shuddering as his feet touched the cold boards, shoved them into slippers, and stood. He shuffled over to the door as the pounding came again, insistent, impatient. "Patience, please! Patience! I'm coming!" Finally, he pulled out the bar.

The door slammed open, and the wind howled in triumph, whirling toward the doorway—and swooping away as something blocked it from entering. It howled in frustration, but a flash of lightning drowned it out with a huge clap of thunder—and showed Amer the robed and hooded silhouette standing in his doorway.

The alchemist froze. Then he turned to catch up his dressing gown and don it. Knotting the sash, he turned back to the doorway.

"Please excuse my appearance," he said, "but I must admit that I was not expecting you."

"That's perfectly all right," the figure said. "Very few ever do."

Amer frowned. "I hope I'm not being too presumptuous," he said, "but would it be too much trouble for you to tell me who you are, and what you've come here for?"

"Not at all," the figure said, and, in sepulchral tones, "My name is Death, and I've come for you."

Amer raised his eyebrows.

"Indeed?" he said, and then, a little taken aback, "Well, I—I'm quite honored."

But then, recovering himself, he saw that Death still stood outside the door.

"Oh, my heavens!" he cried, "you must think me terribly rude. Come in out of the rain, won't you?"

Somewhat puzzled, Death stepped into the cabin, and Amer pushed the door shut behind him. The wind screamed as the door shut on it, then howled and battered against the door in rage. But Amer dropped the oaken bar into its brackets, then turned and went over to the fireplace to throw on another log. "Come stand by the hearth and dry yourself. May I get you a drink?"

"Why, yes," Death said, pleasantly surprised. "Wormwood, if you have it."

"Of course," said Amer, taking another decanter from the mantel. He filled a glass and handed it to Death, then poured one for himself. Reaching up, he took a vial from the mantelpiece, shook a little of the fine, chickory-scented powder it contained over the stool, and muttered a short, unintelligible phrase. The outline of the stool blurred, then began to stretch and bulge as though it were alive. Within thirty seconds, it had assumed the shape of a high-backed wing chair. It sprouted cushions, which grew and blossomed into a luxuriant golden velvet. The outlines hardened again, and a soft, comfortably padded armchair stood by the hearth.

"Sit down, won't you?" Amer said.

Death didn't answer. He stood staring at the armchair. At last he cleared his throat and said, in a businesslike tone, "Yes. This brings me to the matter about which I came, Master Amer."

"Please sit down," Amer said. "It pains me to see a guest standing."

r another. Or the principle of similarity, which makes it possible for me o do something to someone—say, removing a wart—just by doing the ame thing to a model of that person, once I've learned how to focus my houghts properly. That's really just an application of a larger principle, ctually—a sort of rule of symbolism: 'The symbol *is* the thing it repre-ents,' in some metaphysical way I haven't discovered yet. I've reason to elieve there are other worlds, other universes, in which the rules of nagic don't apply—in which the symbol is *not* the thing, for example."

"Fantasy," Death snapped.

"For us, yes. But we are no doubt fantasies for them. In this world n which an alchemist can talk to Death, the laws of magic work well nough."

Death eyed him warily. "You haven't sold your soul, then?"

"Not in the least," Amer said. "*Invictus.*"

Death paced the hearth for a long time, wrapped in thought. Amer was twisting the last toe into place when the skull spoke again.

"It may be," he said. "But I've heard the story before, and it's almost always a lie. I'm afraid you'll have to come with me, after all."

Amer smiled sadly. "Perhaps I shouldn't have been so hospitable," he said. "Then you might have been willing to give me the benefit of the doubt." He twisted a loop of wire around the little skeleton's leg and laid it on the table.

"Perhaps," Death said, "though I'm not worried about bribery—I'm immune to it. But come, you've finished your plaything. The time's come."

"Not quite," Amer said, twisting the other end of the wire around the table leg. He took the vial of powder from his dressing-gown pocket and sprinkled it over the model.

"Milyochim sloh Yachim," he said.

"What?"

"Milyochim sloh Yachim," Amer said again (repeated obligingly).

"What does that mean?" Death said.

"Well, for all practical purposes," Amer said, "it means you can't move from that spot."

"I don't know how you expect to convince me that you're not a sorcerer," Death said, "if you keep on materializing liqueurs that way."

"No, thank you," Death said. "My cloak isn't quite dry yet. But about this—ah—strange gift of yours, Master Amer."

"How rude of me!" Amer said. "Please forgive me. Being freshly wakened, I'm afraid I'm not thinking very clearly." He turned to a closet in the wall near the workbench and drew out a leather labora-tory coat. "Please put this on and let your wet cloak hang by the fire."

"No, thank you," Death said, a little hastily. "However, it *is* getting rather warm, and I must admit that I'm beginning to feel like a steamed chestnut." He opened his hood and the front of his cloak, and Amer stared, fascinated. For Death's head was a skull, and his body was a complete, articulated skeleton.

"Excuse me," Amer said, "but would you mind holding your arm straight out to the side?"

Death frowned. "Like this?"

"Yes, exactly." Amer picked up a notebook and pen and began drawing. "Now, would you move your arm in a circle? Yes, that's fine. You see, I'm in the midst of an investigation of the relationship between the scapula and the bones of the upper arm, and . . ."

"Please!" Death drew his cloak tightly about himself and turned away, and the white skull became suffused with a touch of pink.

"Oh, curse me!" Amer cried, and his face turned bright magenta. "When I become absorbed in an investigation, sir, I'm apt to forget everything else, including my manners. I beg your forgiveness."

"That's quite all right," Death said, turning back to him. "We all have our faults. But if you're really sorry, Master Amer, you may prove it at the price of a little more wormwood."

"Certainly, certainly," Amer said, filling Death's glass again. "Are you sure you won't sit down?"

"No, thank you," Death said. "But perhaps you should. I'm afraid I have some rather unpleasant news for you."

"Oh!" Amer sank into the armchair Samona had occupied earlier in the day. "Unpleasant news? What would it be?"

"Well," Death cleared his throat and began to pace to and fro in front of the fireplace, skeletal hands clasped behind his back. "Well," he said, "I'm afraid this may seem rather ungrateful in view of your excellent hospitality, but—well, duty is duty, and . . . Certainly you're aware, Master Amer, that none of us can live forever."

"Yes," said Amer, smiling blithely but blankly.

"Well . . . that's how it is," Death said, with a note of exasperation in his voice. "We must all die sometime, and . . . well . . . Confound it, Amer, now's your time."

Amer sat in a stunned silence for a minute, and then, in a hollow voice, he said, "I see . . ."

"Master!" Willow wailed. "What're we gonna do?"

"Well, Willow," Amer said slowly, "it would seem as though you're finally going to have your freedom."

"Oh, I don't want it, I don't want it! Not at that price!"

"Well . . . I'm sorry, old man," Death said gruffly, "but what must be, must be."

"Oh, that's all right, that's all right," Amer said, staring at the fire with an unwavering gaze. "But . . . isn't that strange?"

"What?"

"Samona. For some reason, all I can think is that I should have kissed Samona—just once, without my protection drug. I never did, you know." He turned and looked, frowning, at Death. "Now, why should I be thinking of that?"

A tear formed at the edge of the skull's hollow eye and rolled down the hard white cheekbone. "Come, come, let's have done with it quickly! Give me your hand."

Amer ignored the outstretched, bony fingers, and his eyes began to wander aimlessly around the room. "But I've so much left to do. . . ."

"So said Caesar when I came for him, and so said Peter and so said Charlemagne. Come, cease torturing yourself!"

Amer's wandering gaze fell on the miniature bones he had carved earlier in the day. The look of intelligence returned slowly to his eyes as, very carefully, he lifted the model bone-pile into his lap. He took a roll of fine wire from the table and began to string the little skeleton together.

"Just let me finish this," he said. "Just one more work completed— then I'll go."

"All right, but be quick," Death said, drawing back his hand. There was a note of relief in his voice.

He began to pace the floor again. "If you'd just had sense eno[ugh] keep your fingers out of magic, none of this would be necessary."

"Why, what's wrong with magic?" Amer fixed the collarbone in [

"It's not the magic, it's the way you go about getting it that [the boys upstairs."

Amer looked up. Death spun toward him and pointed an ac[cusing] finger. "You could at least have had the good sense to guard you[r Your master would have given you as many spells as you wanted [express purpose of keeping me out!"

Amer smiled sadly and shook his head. "But I don't have a m[

"It's complete and utter carelessness! If you—What did you s[

"I don't have a master."

"Indeed! And I suppose you're not a sorcerer?"

"Quite right—I'm not." Amer threaded the pelvis onto the s[

"Oh?" said Death. "Then how did you come by your magic?"[

"I was born with it, I think. In fact, I'm growing increasin[gly cer]tain that every magic-user is conceived with the talent for [either have it, or you don't—but if you do, the raw ability isn't [you have to learn how to use it." He warmed to his subject. "T[the witches and warlocks in the neighborhood gain by their pa[ct with the Devil—instruction. Of course, there are many who have n[o talent whatsoever; Satan and the older witches merely delude the[m into believing they're able to work magic." He frowned, gazing [into space. "I've learned, in the last few years, that there are holy [men in the East who know how to work wonders, though that's not t[he purpose of their study—and they do teach those who truly wis[h to cul]tivate the life of the spirit. So their magic is gained by s[piritual advancement, without condemning their souls to eternal agon[y in the afterlife. But I knew nothing of them, when I wished to learn."

"Then where did you find your teacher?" Death demanded. [

"I taught myself." Amer said, stringing up a femur. "I le[arned by investigation and hard thought. I experimented until I found [by which the world operates. I win my own knowledge, sir. I do[

"Rules?" Death snapped. "What sort of rules?"

"Oh, there are many of them—the principle of equivale[nce, for example: for every effect you work, you will always have to pay in [

"Oh, I'm not really materializing them." The alchemist snapped his fingers, and a flask of absinthe appeared on the table. "I'm transporting them. There's a spirits merchant in Boston, you see, who keeps finding bottles missing from his stock."

"Thief!" Death accused.

"Not at all; he finds gold wherever there's a bottle missing. You've noticed that I always place a nugget on the table before I transport the bottle?"

"And it disappears." Death gave him a severe stare. "I was wondering about that."

"The mass of the bottle must be replaced with an equivalent mass," Amer explained. "I suppose I could use stone, but it's much more honest to use gold. I believe he makes quite a profit on the transaction."

"I should think so. But where do you find the gold?"

"I dig it up—after I've dowsed for it, of course."

"Where did you learn dowsing?" Death demanded.

"It came naturally," Amer explained. "I was very young when I began to notice that hazel twigs twitched when I held them—perhaps three years old."

"And you will *still* have me believe your powers have nothing of the supernatural about them?"

"For that matter," Amer countered, "how do you expect me to believe that you're supernatural when you continue to consume such vast quantities?"

"Bah," Death said. "We've only had a couple of drinks."

"Uh-uh!" the will-o'-the-wisp slurred. "I been keepin' track!"

"And partaking, too." Death turned to Amer. "So that was why you poured the brandy into that beaker."

"Even a will-o'-the-wisp needs fuel. . . ."

"Your fifth glass of cointreau was emptied three hours ago," Willow said brightly if blearily. "Since then you've downed six glasses of chartreuse, four of cognac, and four of absinthe—right now, you're starting your fifth."

"Willow," said Death, "you have missed your calling. You would have made an excellent conscience."

"And to top it all," the alchemist said, "you're not the slightest bit tipsy."

"Naturally not," Death said.

"Don't you mean 'supernaturally not'?"

"I meant what I said." Death set down his glass. "Would it be natural for Death to become intoxicated?"

"Is it natural for Death to be a connoisseur of fine liqueurs?"

"Certainly, as long as I'm not affected by them. In fact, I've quite an affinity for spirits. But come, Master Amer," Death said, "pour me another absinthe, for we stand in great danger of becoming philosophical just now."

"My heavens! We must prevent *that* at all costs!" Amer filled Death's glass again. The Pale Horseman sipped the liqueur and settled back in his chair with a satisfied sigh.

"You know, Master Amer," he said, "I'm beginning to like you quite well."

"That's not surprising," Amer said.

Death looked at him sharply. "Sorcerer," he said, in a tone of great severity, "have you been casting more spells in my direction?"

"Oh, no! Nothing of the sort," Amer said. "It's merely that absinthe makes the heart grow fonder."

"I'll overlook that remark," Death said, "if you'll fill my glass again. But wormwood this time."

"Try it with some juniper-flavored gin." Amer poured three measures into a glass.

"I notice that you are showing no more effects of your drinking than I do," Death noted.

"Mashter'zh on'y had two shnifterzh o'brandy," Willow slurred.

"I haven't much tolerance," Amer confessed. He followed the gin with a dash of wormwood, and handed it to his guest.

Death tasted a drop. "Not bad." He tasted another. "In fact, it's quite good. Is this your own invention, Master Amer?"

"It is," Amer said, very pleased.

"What do you call it?"

"Well, I named it for the saint on whose day I first tried the mixture."

"And that was . . . ?"

"Saint Martin's Day."

"No, thank you," Death said. "My cloak isn't quite dry yet. But about this—ah—strange gift of yours, Master Amer."

"How rude of me!" Amer said. "Please forgive me. Being freshly wakened, I'm afraid I'm not thinking very clearly." He turned to a closet in the wall near the workbench and drew out a leather laboratory coat. "Please put this on and let your wet cloak hang by the fire."

"No, thank you," Death said, a little hastily. "However, it *is* getting rather warm, and I must admit that I'm beginning to feel like a steamed chestnut." He opened his hood and the front of his cloak, and Amer stared, fascinated. For Death's head was a skull, and his body was a complete, articulated skeleton.

"Excuse me," Amer said, "but would you mind holding your arm straight out to the side?"

Death frowned. "Like this?"

"Yes, exactly." Amer picked up a notebook and pen and began drawing. "Now, would you move your arm in a circle? Yes, that's fine. You see, I'm in the midst of an investigation of the relationship between the scapula and the bones of the upper arm, and . . ."

"Please!" Death drew his cloak tightly about himself and turned away, and the white skull became suffused with a touch of pink.

"Oh, curse me!" Amer cried, and his face turned bright magenta. "When I become absorbed in an investigation, sir, I'm apt to forget everything else, including my manners. I beg your forgiveness."

"That's quite all right," Death said, turning back to him. "We all have our faults. But if you're really sorry, Master Amer, you may prove it at the price of a little more wormwood."

"Certainly, certainly," Amer said, filling Death's glass again. "Are you sure you won't sit down?"

"No, thank you," Death said. "But perhaps you should. I'm afraid I have some rather unpleasant news for you."

"Oh!" Amer sank into the armchair Samona had occupied earlier in the day. "Unpleasant news? What would it be?"

"Well," Death cleared his throat and began to pace to and fro in front of the fireplace, skeletal hands clasped behind his back. "Well," he said, "I'm afraid this may seem rather ungrateful in view of your excellent hospitality, but—well, duty is duty, and . . . Certainly you're aware, Master Amer, that none of us can live forever."

"Yes," said Amer, smiling blithely but blankly.

"Well . . . that's how it is," Death said, with a note of exasperation in his voice. "We must all die sometime, and . . . well . . . Confound it, Amer, now's your time."

Amer sat in a stunned silence for a minute, and then, in a hollow voice, he said, "I see . . ."

"Master!" Willow wailed. "What're we gonna *do?*"

"Well, Willow," Amer said slowly, "it would seem as though you're finally going to have your freedom."

"Oh, I don't want it, I don't want it! Not at *that* price!"

"Well . . . I'm sorry, old man," Death said gruffly, "but what must be, must be."

"Oh, that's all right, that's all right," Amer said, staring at the fire with an unwavering gaze. "But . . . isn't that strange?"

"What?"

"Samona. For some reason, all I can think is that I should have kissed Samona—just once, without my protection drug. I never did, you know." He turned and looked, frowning, at Death. "Now, why should I be thinking of that?"

A tear formed at the edge of the skull's hollow eye and rolled down the hard white cheekbone. "Come, come, let's have done with it quickly! Give me your hand."

Amer ignored the outstretched, bony fingers, and his eyes began to wander aimlessly around the room. "But I've so much left to do. . . ."

"So said Caesar when I came for him, and so said Peter and so said Charlemagne. Come, cease torturing yourself!"

Amer's wandering gaze fell on the miniature bones he had carved earlier in the day. The look of intelligence returned slowly to his eyes as, very carefully, he lifted the model bone-pile into his lap. He took a roll of fine wire from the table and began to string the little skeleton together.

"Just let me finish this," he said. "Just one more work completed—then I'll go."

"All right, but be quick," Death said, drawing back his hand. There was a note of relief in his voice.

He began to pace the floor again. "If you'd just had sense enough to keep your fingers out of magic, none of this would be necessary."

"Why, what's wrong with magic?" Amer fixed the collarbone in place.

"It's not the magic, it's the way you go about getting it that ruffles the boys upstairs."

Amer looked up. Death spun toward him and pointed an accusing finger. "You could at least have had the good sense to guard your door! Your master would have given you as many spells as you wanted for the express purpose of keeping me out!"

Amer smiled sadly and shook his head. "But I don't have a master."

"It's complete and utter carelessness! If you—*What* did you say?"

"I don't have a master."

"Indeed! And I suppose you're not a sorcerer?"

"Quite right—I'm not." Amer threaded the pelvis onto the spine.

"Oh?" said Death. "Then how did you come by your magic?"

"I was born with it, I think. In fact, I'm growing increasingly certain that every magic-user is conceived with the talent for it. You either have it, or you don't—but if you do, the raw ability isn't enough; you have to learn how to use it." He warmed to his subject. "That's all the witches and warlocks in the neighborhood gain by their pact with the Devil—instruction. Of course, there are many who have no power whatsoever; Satan and the older witches merely delude them into believing they're able to work magic." He frowned, gazing off into space. "I've learned, in the last few years, that there are holy men in the East who know how to work wonders, though that's not the main purpose of their study—and they do teach those who truly wish to cultivate the life of the spirit. So their magic is gained by spiritual advancement, without condemning their souls to eternal agony in the afterlife. But I knew nothing of them, when I wished to learn."

"Then where did you find your teacher?" Death demanded.

"I taught myself." Amer said, stringing up a femur. "I learned by investigation and hard thought. I experimented until I found the rules by which the world operates. I win my own knowledge, sir. I don't beg."

"Rules?" Death snapped. "What sort of rules?"

"Oh, there are many of them—the principle of equivalence, for example: for every effect you work, you will always have to pay in one way or another. Or the principle of similarity, which makes it possible for me to do something to someone—say, removing a wart—just by doing the same thing to a model of that person, once I've learned how to focus my thoughts properly. That's really just an application of a larger principle, actually—a sort of rule of symbolism: 'The symbol *is* the thing it represents,' in some metaphysical way I haven't discovered yet. I've reason to believe there are other worlds, other universes, in which the rules of magic don't apply—in which the symbol is *not* the thing, for example."

"Fantasy," Death snapped.

"For us, yes. But we are no doubt fantasies for them. In this world in which an alchemist can talk to Death, the laws of magic work well enough."

Death eyed him warily. "You haven't sold your soul, then?"

"Not in the least," Amer said. "*Invictus.*"

Death paced the hearth for a long time, wrapped in thought. Amer was twisting the last toe into place when the skull spoke again.

"It may be," he said. "But I've heard the story before, and it's almost always a lie. I'm afraid you'll have to come with me, after all."

Amer smiled sadly. "Perhaps I shouldn't have been so hospitable," he said. "Then you might have been willing to give me the benefit of the doubt." He twisted a loop of wire around the little skeleton's leg and laid it on the table.

"Perhaps," Death said, "though I'm not worried about bribery—I'm immune to it. But come, you've finished your plaything. The time's come."

"Not quite," Amer said, twisting the other end of the wire around the table leg. He took the vial of powder from his dressing-gown pocket and sprinkled it over the model.

"Milyochim sloh Yachim," he said.

"What?"

"Milyochim sloh Yachim," Amer said again (repeated obligingly).

"What does that mean?" Death said.

"Well, for all practical purposes," Amer said, "it means you can't move from that spot."

"I don't know how you expect to convince me that you're not a sorcerer," Death said, "if you keep on materializing liqueurs that way."

"Oh, I'm not really materializing them." The alchemist snapped his fingers, and a flask of absinthe appeared on the table. "I'm transporting them. There's a spirits merchant in Boston, you see, who keeps finding bottles missing from his stock."

"Thief!" Death accused.

"Not at all; he finds gold wherever there's a bottle missing. You've noticed that I always place a nugget on the table before I transport the bottle?"

"And it disappears." Death gave him a severe stare. "I was wondering about that."

"The mass of the bottle must be replaced with an equivalent mass," Amer explained. "I suppose I could use stone, but it's much more honest to use gold. I believe he makes quite a profit on the transaction."

"I should think so. But where do you find the gold?"

"I dig it up—after I've dowsed for it, of course."

"Where did you learn dowsing?" Death demanded.

"It came naturally," Amer explained. "I was very young when I began to notice that hazel twigs twitched when I held them—perhaps three years old."

"And you will *still* have me believe your powers have nothing of the supernatural about them?"

"For that matter," Amer countered, "how do you expect me to believe that you're supernatural when you continue to consume such vast quantities?"

"Bah," Death said. "We've only had a couple of drinks."

"Uh-uh!" the will-o'-the-wisp slurred. "I been keepin' track!"

"And partaking, too." Death turned to Amer. "So that was why you poured the brandy into that beaker."

"Even a will-o'-the-wisp needs fuel. . . ."

"Your fifth glass of cointreau was emptied three hours ago," Willow said brightly if blearily. "Since then you've downed six glasses of chartreuse, four of cognac, and four of absinthe—right now, you're starting your fifth."

"Willow," said Death, "you have missed your calling. You would have made an excellent conscience."

"And to top it all," the alchemist said, "you're not the slightest bit tipsy."

"Naturally not," Death said.

"Don't you mean 'supernaturally not'?"

"I meant what I said." Death set down his glass. "Would it be natural for Death to become intoxicated?"

"Is it natural for Death to be a connoisseur of fine liqueurs?"

"Certainly, as long as I'm not affected by them. In fact, I've quite an affinity for spirits. But come, Master Amer," Death said, "pour me another absinthe, for we stand in great danger of becoming philosophical just now."

"My heavens! We must prevent *that* at all costs!" Amer filled Death's glass again. The Pale Horseman sipped the liqueur and settled back in his chair with a satisfied sigh.

"You know, Master Amer," he said, "I'm beginning to like you quite well."

"That's not surprising," Amer said.

Death looked at him sharply. "Sorcerer," he said, in a tone of great severity, "have you been casting more spells in my direction?"

"Oh, no! Nothing of the sort," Amer said. "It's merely that absinthe makes the heart grow fonder."

"I'll overlook that remark," Death said, "if you'll fill my glass again. But wormwood this time."

"Try it with some juniper-flavored gin." Amer poured three measures into a glass.

"I notice that you are showing no more effects of your drinking than I do," Death noted.

"Mashter'zh on'y had two shnifterzh o'brandy," Willow slurred.

"I haven't much tolerance," Amer confessed. He followed the gin with a dash of wormwood, and handed it to his guest.

Death tasted a drop. "Not bad." He tasted another. "In fact, it's quite good. Is this your own invention, Master Amer?"

"It is," Amer said, very pleased.

"What do you call it?"

"Well, I named it for the saint on whose day I first tried the mixture."

"And that was . . . ?"

"Saint Martin's Day."

"It appears to be excellent," said a fat, rasping voice. "May I have some?"

"Why, certainly," said Amer. He had poured the wormwood into the glass before it occurred to him to wonder where the voice had come from.

He turned and saw an enormously fat man dressed in a huge black cape and conical, flat-topped, broad-brimmed hat with a tarnished brass buckle. His whole face seemed to sag, giving him the mournful appearance of a bloodhound. But the sadness of his face was belied by his mouth, which curved in a wide grin of insane glee.

"Amer," said another voice, a feminine one. "May I introduce you to Master Moggard, Warlock-General of New England and Vice-Chairman of the Universal Brotherhood of Sorcerers."

Amer turned and saw Samona standing nearby, the glow of victory in her eyes.

"Who is it?" said Death, for he sat facing the fireplace in a high-backed wing chair, and Samona and the sorcerer were behind him.

"Samona and a—um—friend," Amer said, looking at Death. "They seem to have . . ." But he stopped there, for he saw pits of fire at the back of the skull's hollow eyes.

"Master Moggard," Samona said, "this is Amer, the man of whom I told you."

Moggard waddled forward, holding out a stubby, hairy paw. "Charmed," he croaked.

"I'm glad you are," Amer murmured, rising to grasp the acid-stained appendage.

"No, no," Moggard said. "Not *I*. It's you who are charmed—or will be shortly."

"Indeed?" Amer said, freeing himself of the warlock's clammy grasp. He turned and poured the juniper gin into the glass with the wormwood. Turning again, he placed it in Moggard's hand.

"Would you care for something, Samona?"

"I believe I would," she said.

"Amontillado?"

"Of course."

Moggard waddled about the cabin, inspecting apparatus, thumbing through notebooks, examining powders. He turned back to them as Amer was handing Samona her glass.

"Excellent, excellent," he said, rolling up to them. "You have a superb laboratory, Master Amer."

"Thank you," Amer said, bowing in acknowledgment of the compliment. He remained wary.

Moggard turned to the bookshelf and leafed through another notebook. "Yes, indeed! You have amassed an amazing deal of knowledge, Master Amer." Then, thoughtfully, "Perhaps a bit too much."

"Oh?" said Amer. "May I ask exactly how I am to interpret that statement?"

Moggard sighed—or rather, wheezed—as he replaced the volume.

"You are not, if I am correct, a member of the Brotherhood, Master Amer?"

"The Brotherhood?"

"That is to say, you have gathered your knowledge with no other— ah—'being's' help?"

"Certainly. I have extracted all of it by myself." Amer's voice rang with a note of pride.

"Ah. So I feared," Moggard said. "I am sure, Master Amer, that you can appreciate our predicament. We cannot have a man practicing without—ah—having been initiated."

Amer's gaze sharpened. "I wasn't aware you had any jurisdiction over the situation."

"Not technically, perhaps." Moggard's smile turned toothy. "But we have ways of influencing affairs, for people who disagree with us. For example, I'm certain you have realized that your expulsion from Salem was not purely spontaneous."

Amer frowned. "That the goodfolk did not originate the notion of my being a warlock? I was aware Samona had put the idea into their heads. . . ."

"But you also must have realized that a female, so young and with so little influence, would not have sufficed to arouse so fierce a movement." Moggard crowded closer. "No, no, she had a great deal of support from some very influential citizens, very influential."

"Such as . . . Goody Coister? And Sexton Karrier?"

"Them, yes." Moggard nodded vigorously. "And others—there were several others, all substantial citizens."

"And all members of your coven."

"Not mine, no; my coven is elsewhere. But of the Salem coven, yes. We did wish it to be lethal . . ."

Samona looked up, shocked.

". . . so that the problem you represent would have had a final solution—but unfortunately, you were too adroit for the mob."

"The action was ill-considered." Amer frowned. "It will rebound on you—not immediately, perhaps, but it will rebound."

"Oh, I think you underestimate us—as we underestimated you. No, the knowledge and skill you have demonstrated make you a problem of great significance."

"Why, thank you!"

"I assure you, though it is a compliment, it is also a statement of menace—so you will understand that we must revoke your powers."

Amer smiled slowly. "May I ask how you propose to accomplish this?"

Moggard pursed his blubber lips thoughtfully. Then he said, "It's somewhat irregular, but a man of your ability merits the courtesy."

Meaning, Amer realized, that Moggard hoped to frighten Amer out of his dedication to God and goodness, and add both him and his powers to the coven.

Grinning again, Moggard said, "Master Amer, all your powers are based on knowledge of certain laws which your investigations have revealed, are they not?"

"They are."

"Then I am certain you realize what the consequences would be if these laws were suspended in a certain area, and if that area were to surround you, rather like a cloud, no matter where you were to go."

The smile faded from Amer's lips. "You have the power to do this?"

"Yes, my—ah—superior has arranged it for me."

"And of course you would not hesitate to use it."

"Of course." Moggard's grin widened. "Unless, of course, you were to apply for membership in the Brotherhood."

"I see." Amer's voice was calm, but his face was white. He turned away and looked at the fire in the grate. "And if I don't choose to apply, you will cancel my powers by suspending all natural and super-natural laws within my immediate area."

"That is correct."

"The forces that hold the tiniest bits of matter together would lose their hold—and everything about me would turn to dust."

"To a dust so fine that we could not see it," the warlock agreed.

"Including food."

"Ah, I see you have grasped the essence of the situation," Moggard chortled.

"In short, if I refuse to sell my soul, I die by slow starvation."

"Indeed you would! Admirable perception, sir! Really, you delight me."

"Starve!" Samona turned to the warlock sharply. She was white-faced, and her lips trembled as she spoke. "No, Moggard! You said you would do no more than make him powerless!"

"True, my dear, but at that time I had no idea that he had garnered so much—ah—wisdom."

"I'll not let you harm him!"

A new glint appeared in Moggard's eye, and he waddled up to her with a rapt, fascinated stare.

"Oh, do try to stop me, my dear!" he gurgled. "Such an act would make you liable to discipline"—and his voice dropped to a low, giggling tone—"of my choosing."

Samona backed away from him, revolted and trembling. Giggling, Moggard followed her.

"Let her be!" Amer shouted, brandishing the poker.

Moggard spun, and then he waddled up to Amer, and his giggling became almost hysterical.

"So you, too, wish a display of my powers?"

Amer fell back. A bony hand shot out and closed round his wrist. He stared down into the flaming eyes of Death.

"Loose me!" Death said in a low, angry voice. "Loose me and I'll rid you of him forever!"

Amer stared at Death, and then he looked up at Samona, pressed blanched and trembling against the wall. He shook his head slowly.

"Are you a fool?" Death hissed. Then, in a tone of mild disgust, "Don't worry, these two have convinced me you're no sorcerer."

Amer just shook his head again.

"Why?" Death's voice was hoarse with rage. But then he realized that Amer was looking at the witch, not the warlock. He sat back in his chair, glowering at the alchemist.

"I see," he said bitterly. "Thus are men made powerless. I'd thought better of you than that, Amer."

"Come, sir!" Moggard gurgled. "Will you sign your name in our—ah—'captain's' book? Or will you die?"

Cold determination crystallized within Amer. He stood straight and tall, giving the sorcerer a stony glance. "I have never had any dealings with the Devil, Master Moggard, and I will not have any now—even at the cost of my life."

"As you will, then," Moggard giggled, and his voice had the sound of twigs crackling in a fire. He stretched out his paw and spoke a polysyllable that was mostly consonants, and Amer saw the objects around him dissolve as all laws, natural and supernatural, ceased. In a few seconds everything near him was powder.

Including the miniature skeleton, the wire, and the table—and with them, the spell that held Death bound.

Death shot to his feet, and the skeleton hand closed on Moggard's neck. The sorcerer turned to stare into the flaming eye sockets, and his face had scarcely registered his horror before he fainted.

"You see what comes of cowardice, Amer," Death said. "Had you loosed me when I asked, I might have spared your witch for you. But now she too must come with me." And he stalked toward Samona.

"Wait!" Amer shouted. "Give her a chance. Can't you spare her if she gives up her witchcraft?"

Death halted. He fixed his blazing stare on Samona.

"Your absinthe was good," he said. "This one time I'll be clement."

Amer breathed a sigh of relief.

"Come then, she-devil," Death said. "Which will it be? Life or damnation?"

Samona looked from Death to Amer and back again, and then she stood away from the wall and straightened her back.

"I don't have much choice, do I?" she said, and the look she threw at Amer was pure hate. "Yes, I renounce the darkness."

"Well enough!" Death turned and stalked to the door, dragging Moggard along like a rag doll. He paused with his hand on the latch and turned to Amer.

"Farewell, alchemist. You've won your witch. But I wish you luck, for you've made a bad bargain." And Death threw open the door and in two long strides was lost in the stormy night. The cabin returned to normal, but only for seconds. Then the wind shrieked in joy and tore into the cabin.

It raced around the room, overturning furniture, smashing glassware, and triumphantly hurling notebooks into the fire. It fanned the flames and howled with glee.

Amer fought his way to the door and shoved it closed. The wind screamed in rage as the door pinched it off, and blasted the cabin with the finest imprecations in its vocabulary as the alchemist shot the bolt.

Amer leaned against the door, catching his breath. Then, with a smile which, considering the smiler, could be judged as sizzling, he turned to Samona. But the smiled faded and Amer fell back against the door as he looked at her, for the wind had blown her hair back over her shoulders, and Amer suddenly became acutely aware of her femininity.

Samona frowned, puzzled—Amer had never behaved in such fashion before.

"Wha'sa matter?" Willow asked.

"My protection drug," Amer gasped. "It wore off an hour ago!"

Then Samona realized her advantage. She advanced on him relentlessly, with a smile on her lips and victory in her eyes, and she pulled his mouth down to hers and kissed him very thoroughly.

And in her arms we must leave our friend Amer, for he has finally been completely and very capably bewitched.

FIDDLER FAIR

Mercedes Lackey

ll the world comes to Ithkar Fair.

That's what they said, anyway—and it certainly seemed that way to Rune as she traveled the Main Trade Road down from her home near Galzar Pass. She wasn't walking on the dusty, hard-packed road itself; she'd likely have been trampled by the press of beasts, then run over by the carts into the bargain. Instead, she walked with the rest of the foot travelers on the road's verge. It was no less dusty—what grass there had been had long since been trampled into powder by all the pilgrims and fair-goers—but at least a traveler was able to move along without risk of acquiring hoofprints on his anatomy.

Rune was close enough now to see the gates of the fair itself, and the fair-ward beside them. This seemed like a good moment to separate herself from the rest of the throng, rest her tired feet, and plan her next moves before entering the fairgrounds.

She elbowed her way out of the line of people, some of whom complained and elbowed back, and moved away from the road to a place where she had a good view of the fair and a rock to sit on. The sun beat down with enough heat to be felt through her soft leather hat as she plopped herself down on the rock and began massaging her tired feet while she looked the fair over.

It was a bit overwhelming. Certainly it was much bigger than she'd imagined it would be. It was equally certain that there would be nothing dispensed for free behind those log palings, and the few coppers Rune had left would have to serve to feed her through the three days of trials for admission to the Bardic Guild. After that . . .

Well, after that, she should be an apprentice, and food and shelter would be for her master to worry about. If not—

She refused to admit the possibility of failing the trials. She couldn't—the Three surely *wouldn't* let her fail. Not after getting this far.

But for now, she needed to get herself cleaned of the road dust and a place to sleep, both with no price tags attached. Right now, she was the same gray brown from head to toe, the darker brown of her hair completely camouflaged by the dust, or at least it felt that way. Even her eyes felt dusty.

She strolled down to the river, her lute thumping her shoulder softly on one side, her pack doing the same on the other. Close to the docks the water was muddy and roiled; there was too much traffic on the river to make an undisturbed bath a viable possibility, and too many wharf rats about to make leaving one's belongings a wise move. She backtracked upstream a bit, while the noise of the fair faded behind her, crossed over the canal, and went hunting the rapids that the canal bypassed. The bank of the river was wilder here and overgrown, not like the carefully tended area of the canal side. Finally she found a place where the river had cut a tiny cove into the bank. It was secluded; trees overhung the water, their branches making a good thick screen that touched the water, the ground beneath them bare of growth, and hollows between some of the roots just big enough to cradle her sleeping roll. Camp, bath, and water, all together, and within climbing distance on one of the trees was a hollow large enough to hide her bedroll and those belongings she didn't want to carry into the fair.

She waited until dusk fell before venturing into the river and kept her eyes and ears open while she scrubbed herself down. Once clean, she debated whether or not to change into the special clothing she'd brought; it might be better to save it. . . . Then the thought of donning the sweat-soaked, dusty traveling gear became too distasteful, and she rejected it out of hand.

She felt strange and altogether different once she'd put on the new costume. Part of that was due to the materials—except for when she'd tried the clothing on for fit, this was the first time she'd ever worn silk and velvet. Granted, the materials were all old; bought from a secondhand vendor and cut down from much larger garments. The velvet of the breeches wasn't *too* rubbed, the ribbons on the sleeves of the shirt and the embroidery should cover the faded places, and the vest should cover the stain on the back panel completely. Her hat, once the dust was beaten out of it and the plumes she'd snatched from the tails of several disgruntled roosters were tucked into the band, looked brave enough. Her boots, at least, were new and, when the dust was brushed from them, looked quite well. She tucked her remaining changes of clothing and her bedroll into her pack, hid the lot in the tree hollow, and felt ready to face the fair.

The fair-ward at the gate eyed her carefully. "Minstrel?" he asked suspiciously, looking at the lute and fiddle she carried in their cases, slung from her shoulders.

She shook her head. "Here for the trials, m'lord."

"Ah." He appeared satisfied. "You come in good time, boy. The trials begin tomorrow. The guild has its tent pitched hard by the main gate of the temple; you should have no trouble finding it."

The wizard-of-the-gate ignored her, looking bored. Rune did not correct the fair-ward's assumption that she was a boy; it was her intent to pass as male until she'd safely passed the trials. She'd never heard of the Bardic Guild admitting a girl, but as far as she'd been able to determine, there was nothing in the rules and charter of the guild against it. So once she'd been accepted, once the trials were safely passed, she'd reveal her sex, but until then she'd play the safe course.

She thanked him, but he had already turned his attention to the next traveler in line. She passed inside the log walls and entered the fair itself.

The first impressions she had were of noise and light; torches burned all along the aisle she traversed; the booths to either side were lit by lanterns, candles, or other, more arcane methods. The crowd was noisy; so were the merchants. Even by torchlight it was plain that these booths featured shoddier goods: secondhand finery, brass jewelry, flash and tinsel. The entertainers here were . . . surprising. She averted her eyes from a set of dancers. It wasn't so much that they wore little but imagination, but the *way* they were dancing embarrassed even her; and a tavern-bred child has seen a great deal in its life.

She kept a tight grip on her pouch and instruments, tried to ignore the crush, and let the flow of fairgoers carry her along.

Eventually the crowd thinned out a bit (though not before she'd felt a ghostly hand or two try for her pouch and give it up as a bad cause). She followed her nose then, looking for the row that held the cookshop tents and the ale-sellers. She hadn't eaten since morning, and her stomach was lying in uncomfortably close proximity to her spine.

She learned that the merchants of tavern row were shrewd judges of clothing; hers wasn't fine enough to be offered a free taste but wasn't poor enough to be shooed away. Sternly admonishing her stomach to be less impatient, she strolled the length of the row twice, carefully comparing prices and quantities before settling on a humble tent that offered meat pasties (best not ask what beast the meat came from, not at these prices) and fruit juice or milk as well as ale and wine. Best of all, it offered seating at rough trestle tables. Rune took her flaky pastry and her mug of juice (no wine or ale for her, not even had she the coppers to spare for it—she dared not be the least muddle-headed, not with a secret to keep and a competition on the morn) and found herself a spot at an empty table where she could eat and watch the crowd passing by. The pie was more crust than meat, but it was filling and well made and fresh; that counted for a great deal. She noted with amusement that there were two sorts of the clumsy, crude clay mugs. One sort, the kind in which they served the milk and juice, was ugly and shapeless (too ugly to be worth stealing) but was just as capacious as the exterior promised. The other, for wine and ale, was just the same ugly shape and size on the *outside* (though a different shade of toad-back green) but had a far thicker bottom, effectively reducing the interior capacity by at least a third.

"Come for the trials, lad?" asked a quiet voice in her ear.

Rune jumped, nearly knocking her mug over and snatching at it just in time to save the contents from drenching her shopworn finery. (And however would she have gotten it clean again in time for the

morrow's competition?) There hadn't been a sound or a hint of movement or even the shifting of the bench to warn her, but now there was
a man sitting beside her.

He was of middle years, red hair going to gray, smile wrinkles around
his mouth and gray-green eyes, with a candid, triangular face. Well, that
said nothing. Rune had known highwaymen with equally friendly and
open faces. His dress was similar to her own: leather breeches instead of
velvet, good linen instead of worn silk, a vest and a leather hat that
could have been twin to hers, knots of ribbon on the sleeves of his
shirt—and the neck of a lute peeking over his shoulder. A minstrel!

Of the guild? Rune rechecked the ribbons on his sleeves and was
disappointed. Blue and scarlet and green, not the purple and silver of a
guild minstrel, nor the purple and gold of a guild bard. This was only a
common songster, a mere street player. Still, he'd bespoken her kindly
enough, and the Three knew not everyone with the music passion had
the skill or the talent to pass the trials. . . .

"Aye, sir," she replied politely. "I've hopes to pass; I think I've the
talent, and others have said as much."

His eyes measured her keenly, and she had the disquieting feeling
that her boy ruse was fooling *him* not at all. "Ah, well," he said, "there's
a-many before you have thought the same, and failed."

"That may be"—she answered the challenge in his eyes—"but I'd
bet fair coin that none of *them* fiddled for a murdering ghost, and not
only came out by the grace of their skill but were rewarded by that
same spirit for amusing him!"

"Oh, so?" A lifted eyebrow was all the indication he gave of being
impressed, but somehow that lifted brow conveyed volumes. "You've
made a song of it, surely?"

"Have I not! It's to be my entry for the third day of testing."

"Well then . . ." He said no more than that, but his wordless attitude of waiting compelled Rune to unsling her fiddle case, extract her
instrument, and tune it without further prompting.

"It's the fiddle that's my first instrument," she said apologetically,
"and since 'twas the fiddle that made the tale—"

"Never apologize for a song, child," he admonished, interrupting
her. "Let it speak out for itself. Now let's hear this ghost tale."

It wasn't easy to sing while fiddling, but Rune had managed the trick of it some time ago. She closed her eyes a half moment, fixing in her mind the necessary changes she'd made to the lyrics—for unchanged, the song would have given her sex away—and began.

> "I sit here on a rock, and curse my stupid, bragging tongue,
> And curse the pride that would not let me back down from
>   a boast
> And wonder where my wits went, when took that challenge up
> And swore that I would go and fiddle for the Skull Hill
>   Ghost!"

Oh, aye, that had been a damn fool move—to let those idiots who patronized the tavern where her mother worked goad her into boasting that there wasn't anyone, living or dead, she couldn't cozen with her fiddling. Too much ale, Rune, and too little sense. And too tender a pride, as well, to let them rub salt in the wound of being the tavern wench's bastard.

> "It's midnight, and there's not a sound up here upon Skull
>   Hill
> Then comes a wind that chills my blood and makes the
>   leaves blow wild."

Not a good word choice, but a change that had to be made—that was one of the giveaway verses.

> "And rising up in front of me, a thing like shrouded Death.
> A voice says, 'Give me reason why I shouldn't kill you, child.'"

Holy Three, that thing had been ghastly: cold and old and totally heartless. It had smelled of death and the grave, and had shaken her right down to her toenails. She made the fiddle sing about what words alone could never convey and saw her audience of one actually shiver.

The next verse described Rune's answer to the spirit, and the fiddle wailed of fear and determination and things that didn't rightly belong on earth. Then came the description of that nightlong, lightless ordeal she'd passed through, and the fiddle shook with the weariness she'd felt, playing the whole night long; and the tune rose with dawning triumph when the thing not only didn't kill her outright, but began to warm to the music she'd made. Now she had an audience of more than one, though she was only half-aware of the fact.

> "At last the dawn light strikes my eyes; I stop, and see the sun.
> The light begins to chase away the dark and midnight cold—
> And then the light strikes something more—I stare in dumb surprise—
> For where the ghost had stood there is a heap of shining gold!"

The fiddle laughed at death cheated, thumbed its nose at spirits, and chortled over the revelation that even the dead could be impressed and forced to reward courage and talent.

Rune stopped and shook back brown locks dark with sweat, looking about her in astonishment at the applauding patrons of the cookshop. She was even more astonished when they began to toss coppers in her open fiddle case, and the cookshop's owner brought her over a full pitcher of juice and a second pie.

"I'd'a brought ye wine, laddie, but Master Talaysen there says ye go to trials and must'na be amuddled," she whispered, and hurried back to her counter.

"I hadn't meant—"

"Surely this isn't the first time you've played for your supper, child?" The minstrel's eyes were full of amused irony.

"Well, no, but—"

"So take your well-earned reward and don't go arguing with folk who have a bit of copper to fling at you, and who recognize the gift when they hear it. No mistake, youngling, you *have* the gift. And sit and eat; you've more bones than flesh. A good tale, that."

"Well"—Rune blushed—"I did exaggerate a bit at the end. 'Twasn't gold, it was silver. But silver won't rhyme. And it was that silver that got me here—bought me my second instrument, paid for lessoning, kept me fed while I was learning. I'd be just another tavern musician, otherwise. . . ."

"Like me, you are too polite to say?" The minstrel smiled, then the smile faded. "There are worse things, child, than to be a free musician. I don't think there's much doubt your gift will get you past the trials—but you might not find the guild to be all you think it to be."

Rune shook her head stubbornly, wondering briefly why she'd told this stranger so much and why she so badly wanted his good opinion. "Only a guild minstrel would be able to earn a place in a noble's train. Only a guild bard would have the chance to sing for royalty. I'm sorry to contradict you, sir, but I've had my taste of wandering, singing my songs out only to know they'll be forgotten in the next drink, wondering where my next meal is coming from. I'll never get a secure life except through the guild, and I'll never see my songs live beyond me without their patronage."

He sighed. "I hope you never regret your decision, child. But if you should—or if you need help, ever . . . well, just ask for Talaysen. I'll stand your friend."

With those surprising words, he rose soundlessly, as gracefully as a bird in flight, and slipped out of the tent. Just before he passed out of sight among the press of people, Rune saw him pull his lute around and begin to strum it. She managed to hear the first few notes of a love song, the words rising golden and glorious from his throat, before the crowd hid him from view and the babble of voices obscured the music.

Rune was waiting impatiently outside the guild tent the next morning, long before there was anyone there to take her name for the trials. It was, as the fair-ward had said, hard to miss: purple in the main, with pennons and edgings of silver and gilt. Almost . . . *too* much; almost gaudy. She was joined shortly by three more striplings, one well dressed and confident, two sweating and nervous. More trickled in as the sun rose higher, until there was a line of twenty or thirty waiting when the guild registrar, an old and sour-looking scribe, raised the tent-flap to let them file inside. He wasn't wearing guild colors, but rather a robe of dusty brown velvet: a hireling therefore.

He took his time, sharpening his quill until Rune was ready to scream with impatience, before looking her up and down and asking her name.

"Rune, child of Lista Jesaril, tavern-keeper." That sounded a trifle better than her mother's *real* position, serving wench.

"From whence?"

"Karthar, east and north—below Galzar Pass."

"Primary instrument?"

"Fiddle."

"Secondary?"

"Lute."

He raised an eyebrow. The usual order was lute, primary; fiddle, secondary. For that matter, fiddle wasn't all that common even as a secondary instrument.

"And you will perform . . . ?"

"First day, primary, 'Lament of the Maiden Esme.' Second day, secondary, 'The Unkind Lover.' Third day, original, 'The Skull Hill Ghost.'" An awful title, but she could hardly use "Fiddler Girl," its real name. "Accompanied on primary, fiddle."

"Take your place."

She sat on the backless wooden bench trying to keep herself calm. Before her was the raised wooden platform on which they would all perform; to either side of it were the backless benches like the one she warmed, for the aspirants to the guild. The back of the tent made the third side, and the fourth faced the row of well-padded chairs for the guild judges. Although she was first here, it was inevitable that others would have the preferred first few slots: those with fathers already in the guild or those who had coins for bribes. Still, she shouldn't have to wait too long—rising with the dawn had given her that much of an edge, at least.

She got to play by midmorning. "Lament" was perfect for fiddle, the words were simple and few, and the wailing melody gave her lots of scope for improvisation. The row of guild judges, solemn in tunics or robes of purple, white silk shirts trimmed with gold or silver ribbon depending on whether they were minstrels or bards, was a formidable audience. Their faces were much alike, well fed and very conscious of their own importance; you could see it in their eyes. As they sat below the platform and took unobtrusive notes, they seemed at least mildly impressed. Even more heartening, several of the boys yet to perform looked satisfyingly worried when she'd finished.

She packed up her fiddle and betook herself briskly out—to find herself a corner of temple wall to lean against as her knees sagged when the excitement that had sustained her wore off. It was several long moments before she could get her legs to bear her weight and her hands to stop shaking. It was then she realized that she hadn't eaten since the night before—and that she was suddenly ravenous. Before she'd played, the very thought of food had been revolting.

The same cookshop tent as before seemed like a reasonable proposition. She paid for her breakfast with some of the windfall coppers of the night before. This morning the tent was crowded and she was lucky to get a scant corner of a bench to herself. She ate hurriedly and joined the strollers through the fair.

Once or twice she thought she glimpsed the red hair of Talaysen, but if it was he, he was gone by the time she reached the spot where she had thought he'd been. There were plenty of other street singers, though. She thought wistfully of the harvest of coin she'd garnered the night before as she noted that none of them seemed to be lacking for patronage. But now that she was a duly registered entrant in the trials, it would be going against custom, if not the rules, to set herself up among them.

So instead she strolled, and listened, and made mental notes for further songs. There was many a tale she overheard that would have worked well in song form; many a glimpse of silk-bedecked lady, strangely sad or hectically gay, or velvet-clad lord, sly and foxlike or bold and pompous, that brought snatches of rhyme to mind. By early evening her head was crammed full—and it was time to see how the guild had ranked the aspirants of the morning.

The list was posted outside the closed tent-flaps, and Rune wasn't the only one interested in the outcome of the first day's trials. It took a bit of time to work her way in to look, but when she did—

By the Three! There she was, "Rune of Karthar"—listed *third.*

She all but floated back to her riverside tree roost.

The second day of the trials was worse than the first; the aspirants performed in order, lowest ranking to highest. That meant Rune had to spend most of the day sitting on the hard wooden bench, clutching the neck of her lute in nervous fingers, listening to contestant after contestant and sure that each one was *much* better on his secondary instrument than she was. She'd only had a year of training on it, after all. Still, the song she'd chosen was picked deliberately to play up her voice and deemphasize her lute strumming. It was going to be pretty difficult for any of these others to match her high contralto (a truly cunning imitation of a boy's soprano), since most of them had passed puberty.

At long last her turn came. She swallowed her nervousness as best she could, took the platform, and began.

Privately she thought it was a pretty silly song. Why on earth any man would put up with the things that lady did to him, and all for the sake of a "kiss on her cold, quiet hand," was beyond her. Still, she put all the acting ability she had into it and was rewarded by a murmur of approval when she'd finished.

"That voice—I've seldom heard one so pure at that late an age!" she overheard as she packed up her instrument. "If he passes the third day—you don't suppose he'd agree to become castrati, do you? I can think of half a dozen courts that would pay red gold to have him."

She smothered a smile—imagine their surprise to discover that it would *not* be necessary to eunuch her to preserve her voice!

She lingered to listen to the last of the entrants, then waited outside for the posting of the results.

She nearly fainted to discover that she'd moved up to second place.

"I told you," said a familiar quiet voice in her ear. "But are you still sure you want to go through with this?"

She whirled to find the minstrel Talaysen standing behind her, the sunset brightening his hair and the soft shadows on his face making him appear scarcely older than she.

"I'm sure," she replied firmly. "One of the judges said today that he could think of half a dozen courts that would pay red gold to have my voice."

"Bought and sold like so much mutton? Where's the living in that? Caged behind high stone walls and never let out of the sight of m'lord's guards, lest you take a notion to sell your services elsewhere? Is *that* the life you want to lead?"

"Trudging down roads in the pouring cold rain, frightened half to death that you'll take sickness and ruin your voice—maybe for good? Singing with your stomach growling so loud it drowns out the song? Watching some idiot with half your talent being clad in silk and velvet and eating at the high table, while you try and please some brutes of guardsmen in the kitchen in hopes of a few scraps and a corner by the fire?" she countered. "No, thank you. I'll take my chances with the guild. Besides, where else would I be able to *learn*? I've got no more silver to spend on instruments or teaching."

"There are those who would teach you for the love of it—welladay, you've made up your mind. As you will, child," he replied, but his eyes were sad as he turned away and vanished into the crowd again.

Once again she sat the hard bench for most of the day while those of lesser ranking performed. This time it was a little easier to bear; it was obvious from a great many of these performances that few, if any, of the boys had the gift to create. By the time it was Rune's turn to perform, she judged that, counting herself and the first-place holder, there could only be five real contestants for the three open bardic apprentice slots. The rest would be suitable only as minstrels, singing someone else's songs, unable to compose their own.

She took her place before the critical eyes of the judges and began.

She realized with a surge of panic as she finished the first verse that they did *not* approve. While she improvised, she mentally reviewed the verse, trying to determine what it was that had set those slight frowns on the judicial faces.

Then she realized: *boasting*. Guild bards simply did not admit to being boastful. Nor did they demean themselves by reacting to the taunts of lesser beings. Oh, holy Three—

Quickly she improvised a verse on the folly of youth; of how, had she been older and wiser, she'd never have gotten herself into such a predicament. She heaved an invisible sigh of relief as the frowns disappeared.

By the last chorus, they were actually nodding and smiling, and one of them was tapping a finger in time to the tune. She finished with a flourish worthy of a master and waited breathlessly.

And they *applauded*. Dropped their dignity and *applauded*.

The performance of the final contestant was an anticlimax.

None of them had left the tent since this last trial began. Instead of a list, the final results would be announced, and they waited in breathless anticipation to hear what they would be. Several of the boys had already approached Rune, offering smiling congratulations on her presumed first-place slot. A hush fell over them all as the chief of the judges took the platform, a list in his hand.

"First place, and first apprenticeship as bard—Rune, son of Lista Jesaril of Karthar—"

"Pardon, my lord," Rune called out clearly, bubbling over with happiness and unable to hold back the secret any longer, "but it's not son—it's *daughter*."

She had only a split second to take in the rage on their faces before the first staff descended on her head.

They flung her into the dust outside the tent, half-senseless, and her smashed instruments beside her. The passersby avoided even looking at her as she tried to get to her feet and fell three times. Her right arm dangled uselessly; it hurt so badly that she was certain it must be broken, but it hadn't hurt half as badly when they'd cracked it as it had when they'd smashed her fiddle; that had broken her heart. All she wanted to do now was to get to the river and throw herself in. With any luck at all, she'd drown.

But she couldn't even manage to stand.

"Gently, lass." Firm hands took her and supported her on both sides. "Lady be my witness, if ever I thought they'd have gone this far, I'd never have let you go through with this farce."

She turned her head, trying to see through tears of pain, both of heart and body, with eyes that had sparks dancing before them. The man supporting her on her left she didn't recognize, but the one on the right—

"T-Talaysen?" she faltered.

"I told you I'd help if you needed it, did I not? I think you have more than a little need at the moment—"

"Th-they broke my fiddle, Talaysen. And my lute. They broke them, and they broke my arm—"

"Oh, Rune, lass . . ." There were tears in *his* eyes, and yet he almost seemed to be laughing as well. "If *ever* I doubted you'd the makings of a bard, you just dispelled those doubts. *First* the fiddle, *then* the lute—and only *then* do you think of your own hurts. Ah, come away, lass, come where people can care for such a treasure as you—"

Stumbling through darkness, wrenched with pain, carefully supported and guided on either side, Rune was in no position to judge where or how far they went. After some unknown interval, however, she found herself in a many colored tent, lit with dozens of lanterns, partitioned off with curtains hung on wires that crisscrossed the entire dwelling. Just now most of these were pushed back, and a mixed crowd of men and women greeted their entrance with cries of welcome that turned to dismay at the sight of her condition.

She was pushed down into an improvised bed of soft wool blankets and huge, fat pillows, while a thin, dark girl dressed like a gypsy bathed her cuts and bruises with something that stung, then numbed them, and a gray-bearded man tsked over her arm, prodded it once or twice, then, without warning, pulled it into alignment. When he did that, the pain was so incredible that Rune nearly fainted.

By the time the multicolored fire flashing cleared from her eyes, he was binding her arm up tightly with thin strips of wood, while the girl was urging her to drink something that smelled of herbs and wine.

Before she had a chance to panic, Talaysen reappeared as if conjured at her side.

"Where—"

"You're with the free bards—the *real* bards, not those pompous pufftoads with the guild," he said. "Dear child, I thought all that would happen to you was that those inflated bladders of self-importance would give you a tongue-lashing and throw you out on your backside. If I'd had the slightest notion they'd do *this* to you, I'd have kidnapped you and had you drunk insensible till the trials were over. I may never forgive myself. Now, drink your medicine."

"But how—why—who *are* you?" Rune managed between gulps.

"'What are you?' might be the better place to start, I think. Tell her, will you, Erdric?"

"We're the free bards," said the gray-bearded man, "as Master

Talaysen told you—he's the one who banded us together, when he found that there were those who, like himself, had the gift and the talent but were disinclined to put up with the self-aggrandizement and politics and foolish slavishness to form of guild nonsense. We go where we wish and serve—or not serve—who we will, and sing as we damn well please, and no foolishness about who'll be offended. We also keep a sharp eye out for youngsters like you, with the gift, and with the spirit to fight the guild. We've had our eye on you these three years now."

"You—but how?"

"Myself, for one," said a new voice, and a bony fellow with hair that kept falling into his eyes joined the group around her. "You likely don't remember me, but I remember you—I heard you fiddle in your tavern when I was passing through Karthar, and I passed the word."

"And I'm another." This one Rune recognized; he was the man who'd sold her her lute, who had seemed to have been a gypsy peddler selling new and used instruments. Unaccountably, he had also stayed long enough to teach her the rudiments of playing it.

"You see, we keep an eye out for all the likely lads and lasses we've marked, knowing that soon or late, they'd come to the trials. Usually, though, they're not so stubborn as you." Talaysen smiled.

"I should hope to live!" agreed the lanky fellow. "They made the same remark my first day about wanting to have me stay a liltin' soprano the rest of me days. That was enough for me!"

"And they wouldn't even give *me* the same notice they'd have given a flea." The dark girl laughed. "Though I hadn't the wit to think of passing myself off as a boy for the trials."

"But—why are you—together?" Rune asked, bewildered.

"We band together to give each other help; a spot of silver to tide you over an empty month, a place to go when you're hurt or ill, someone to care for you when you're not as young as you used to be," said the gray-haired Erdric. "And to teach, and to learn. And we have more and better patronage than you, or even the guild, suspect; not everyone finds the precious style of the guild songsters to their taste, especially the farther you get from the large cities. Out in the countryside, away from the decadence of courts, they like their songs, like their food, substantial and heartening."

"But why does the guild let you get away with this, if you're taking patronage from them?" Rune's apprehension, given her recent treatment, was real and understandable.

"Bless you, child, they couldn't do without us!" Talaysen laughed. "No matter what you think, there isn't an original, creative master among 'em! Gwena, my heart, sing her 'The Unkind Lover'—your version, I mean, the real and original."

Gwena, the dark girl, flashed dazzling white teeth in a vulpine grin, plucked a gittern from somewhere behind her, and began.

Well, it was the same melody Rune had sung, and some of the words—the best phrases—were the same as well. But this was no ice-cold princess taunting her poor knightly admirer with what he'd never touch; no, this was a teasing shepherdess seeing how far she could harass her cowherd lover, and the teasing was kindly meant. And what the cowherd claimed at the end was a good deal more than a "kiss on her cold, quiet hand." In fact, you might say with justice that the proceedings got downright heated!

"That 'Lament' you did the first day is another song they've twisted and tormented; most of the popular ballads the guild touts as their own are ours," Talaysen told her with a grin.

"As you should know, seeing as you've written at least half of them!" Gwena snorted.

"But what would you have done if they had accepted me anyway?" Rune wanted to know.

"Oh, you wouldn't have lasted long; can a caged thrush sing? Soon or late, you'd have done what I did—escaped your gilded cage—and we'd have been waiting."

"Then *you* were a guild bard?" Somehow she felt she'd known that all along. "But I never heard of one called Talaysen, and if the 'Lament' is yours—"

"Well, I changed my name when I took my freedom. Likely, though, you wouldn't recognize it—"

"Oh, she wouldn't, you think? Or are you playing mock modest with us again?" Gwena shook back her abundant black hair. "I'll make it known to you that you're having your bruises tended by Master Bard Merridon himself."

"Merridon?" Rune's eyes went wide as she stared at the man, who coughed deprecatingly. "But—but—I thought Master Merridon was supposed to have gone into seclusion—"

"The guild would hardly want it known that their pride had rejected 'em for a pack of gypsy jongleurs, now would they?" the lanky fellow pointed out.

"So, can I tempt you to join with us, Rune lass?" the man she'd known as Talaysen asked gently.

"I'd like—but I can't," she replied despairingly. "How could I keep myself? It'll take months for my arm to heal. And—my instruments are splinters, anyway." She shook her head, tears in her eyes. "They weren't much, but they were all I had. I'll have to go home; they'll take me in the tavern. I can still turn a spit and fill a glass one-handed."

"Ah, lass, didn't you hear Erdric? We take care of each other—we'll care for you till you're whole again." The old man patted her shoulder, then hastily found her a rag when scanning their faces brought her belief—and tears.

"As for the instruments"—Talaysen vanished and returned again as her sobs quieted—"I'll admit to relief at your words. I was half-afraid you'd a real attachment to your poor, departed friends. 'They're splinters, and I loved them' can't be mended, but 'They're splinters, and they were all I had' is a different tune altogether. What think you of these twain?"

The fiddle and lute he laid in her lap weren't new, nor were they the kind of gilded, carved, and ornamented dainties guild musicians boasted, but they held their own kind of quiet beauty, a beauty of mellow wood and clean lines. Rune plucked a string on each, experimentally, and burst into tears again. The tone was lovely, smooth and golden, and these were the kind of instruments she'd never dreamed of touching, much less owning.

When the tears had been soothed away, the various medicines been applied both internally and externally, and introductions made all around, Rune found herself once again alone with Talaysen—or Merridon, though on reflection, she liked the name she'd first known him by better. The rest had drawn curtains on their wires close in about her little corner, making an alcove of privacy.

"If you'll let me join you . . ." she said shyly.

"Let!" He laughed. "Haven't we made it plain enough we've been trying to lure you like coney catchers? Oh, you're one of us, Rune lass. You'll not escape us now!"

"Then—what am I supposed to do?"

"You heal, that's the first thing. The second . . . well, we don't have formal apprenticeships amongst us. By the Three, there's no few things you could serve as master in, and no question about it! You could teach most of us a bit about fiddling, for one—"

"But"—she looked and felt dismayed—"one of the reasons I wanted to join the guild was to *learn!* I can't read or write music; there's so many instruments I can't play. . . ." Her voice rose to a soft wail. "How am I going to learn if a master won't take me as an apprentice?"

"Enough! Enough! No more weeping and wailing, my heart's over-soft as it is!" he said hastily. "If you're going to insist on being an apprentice, I suppose there's nothing for it. Will I do as a master to you?"

Rune was driven to speechlessness and could only nod.

"Holy Three, lass, you make a liar out of me, who swore never to take an apprentice! Wait a moment." He vanished around the curtain, then returned. "Here—" He set down a tiny harp. "This can be played one-handed, and learning the ways of her will keep you too busy to bedew me with any more tears while your arm mends. Treat her gently—she's my own very first instrument, and she deserves respect."

Rune cradled the harp in her good arm, too awe-stricken to reply.

"We'll send someone in the morning for your things, wherever it is you've cached 'em. Lean back there—oh, it's a proper nursemaid I am." He made her comfortable on her pillows, covering her with blankets and moving her two—no, three—new instruments to a place of safety, but still within sight. He seemed to understand how seeing them made her feel. "We'll find you clothing and the like as well. That sleepy-juice they gave you should have you nodding shortly. Just remember one thing before you doze off. I'm not going to be an easy master to serve. You won't be spending your days lazing about, you know! Come morning, I'll set you your very first task. You'll teach *me*"—his eyes lighted with unfeigned eagerness—"that ghost song!"

WIZARD'S WORLD

Andre Norton

I

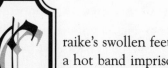raike's swollen feet were agony, every breath he drew fought a hot band imprisoning his laboring lungs. He clung weakly to a rough spur of rock in the canyon wall, swayed against it, raking his flesh raw on the stone. That weathered red and yellow rock was no more unyielding than the murderous wills behind him. And the stab of pain in his calves no less than the pain of their purpose in his dazed mind.

He had been on the run so long, ever since he had left the E-Camp. But until last night—no, two nights ago—when he had given himself away at the gas station, he had not known what it was to be actually hunted. The will-to-kill which fanned from those on his trail was so intense it shocked his Esper senses, panicking him completely.

Now he was trapped in wild country, and he was city-born. Water—Craike flinched at the thought of water. Espers should control their bodies, that was what he had been taught. But there come times when cravings of the flesh triumph over will.

He winced, and the spur grated against his half-naked breast. They had a "hound" on him right enough. And that brain-twisted Esper slave who fawned and served the mob masters would have no difficulty in trailing him straight to any pocket into which he might crawl. A last remnant of rebellion sent Craike reeling on over the gravel of the long-dried stream bed.

Espers had once been respected for their "wild talents," then tolerated warily. Now they were used under guard for slave labor. And the day was coming soon when the fears of the normals would demand their extermination. They had been trying to prepare against that.

First they had worked openly, petitioning to be included in space-ship crews, to be chosen for colonists on the Moon and Mars; then secretly when they realized the norms had no intention of allowing that. Their last hope was flight to the waste spots of the world, those refuse places resulting from the same atomic wars which had brought about the birth of their kind.

Craike had been smuggled out of an eastern E-Camp, provided with a cover, sent to explore the ravaged area about the onetime city of Reno. Only he had broken his cover for the protection of a girl, only to learn, too late, she was bait for an Esper trap. He had driven a stolen speeder until the last drop of fuel was gone, and after that he had kept blindly on, running, until now.

The contact with the Esper "hound" was clear; they must almost be in sight behind. Craike paused. They were not going to take him alive, wring from him knowledge of his people, recondition him into another "hound." There was only one way, he should have known that from the first.

His decision had shaken the "hound." Craike bared teeth in a death's-head grin. Now the mob would speed up. But their quarry had already chosen a part of the canyon wall where he might pull his tired and aching body up from one hold to another. He moved deliberately now, knowing that when he had lost hope; he could throw aside the need for haste. He would be able to accomplish his purpose before they brought a gas rifle to bear on him.

At last he stood on a ledge, the sand and gravel some fifty feet below. For a long moment he rested, steadying himself with both hands braced on the stone. The weird beauty of the desert country was a pattern of violent color under the afternoon sun. Craike breathed slowly; he had regained a measure of control. There came shouts as they sighted him.

He leaned forward and, as if he were diving into the river which had once run there, he hurled himself outward to the clean death he sought.

Water, water in his mouth! Dazed, he flailed water until his head broke surface. Instinct took over, and he swam, fought for air. The current of the stream pulled him against a boulder collared with froth, and he arched an arm over it, lifting himself, to stare about in stupefied bewilderment.

He was close to one bank of a river. Where the colorful cliff of the canyon had been there now rolled downs thickly covered with green growth. The baking heat of the desert had vanished; there was even a slight chill in the air.

Dumbly Craike left his rock anchorage and paddled ashore, to lie shivering on sand while the sun warmed his battered body. What *had* happened? When he tried to make sense of it, the effort hurt his mind almost as much as had the "hound's" probe.

The Esper "hound"! Craike jerked up, old panic stirring. First delicately and then urgently, he cast a thought-seek about him. There was life in plenty. He touched, classified and disregarded the flickers of awareness which mingled in confusion—animals, birds, river dwellers. But nowhere did he meet intelligence approaching his own. A wilderness world without man as far as Esper ability could reach.

Craike relaxed. Something had happened. He was too tired, too drained to speculate as to what. It was enough that he was saved from the death he had sought, that he was *here* instead of *there*.

He got stiffly to his feet. Time was the same, he thought—late afternoon. Shelter, food—he set off along the stream. He found and ate berries spilling from bushes where birds raided before him. Then, squatting above a side eddy of the stream, he scooped out a fish, eating the flesh raw.

The land along the river was rising, he could see the beginning of a gorge ahead. Later, when he had climbed those heights, he caught sight through the twilight of the fires. Four of them burning some miles to the southwest, set out in the form of a square!

Craike sent out a thought probe. Yes—men! But an alien touch. This was no hunting mob. And he was drawn to the security of the fires, the camp of men in the dangers of the night. Only, as Esper, he was not one with them but an outlaw. And he dare not risk joining them.

He retraced his path to the river and holed up in a hollow not large enough to be termed a cave. Automatically he probed again for danger. Found nothing, but animal life. He slept at last, drugged by exhaustion of mind and body.

The sky was gray when he roused, swung cramped arms, stretched. Craike had awakened with the need to know more of that camp. He climbed once again to the vantage point, shut his eyes to the early morning and sent out a seeking.

A camp of men far from home. But they were not hunters. Merchants—traders! Craike located one mind among the rest, read in it the details of a bargain to come. Merchants from another country, a caravan. But a sense of separation grew stronger as the fugitive Esper sorted out thought streams, absorbed scraps of knowledge thirstily. A herd of burden-bearing animals, nowhere any indication of machines. He sucked in a deep breath—he was—he was in another world!

Merchants traversing a wilderness—a wilderness? Though he had been driven into desert the day before, the land through which he had earlier fled could not be termed a wilderness. It was overpopulated because there were too many war-poisoned areas where mankind could not live.

But from these strangers he gained a concept of vast, barren territory broken only by small, sparse strips of cultivation. Craike hurried. They were breaking camp. And the impression of an unpeopled land they had given him made him want to trail the caravan.

There was trouble! An attack—the caravan animals stampeded. Craike received a startlingly vivid mind picture of a hissing, lizard thing he could not identify. But it was danger on four scaled feet. He winced at the fear in those minds ahead. There was a vigor of mental broadcast in these men which amazed him. Now, the lizard thing had been killed. But the pack animals were scattered. It would take hours to find them. The exasperation of the master trader was as strong to Craike as if he stood before the man and heard his outburst of complaint.

The Esper smiled slowly. Here—handed to him by Fate—was his chance to gain the good will of the travelers. Breaking contact with the men, Craike cast around probe webs, as a fisher might cast a net. One panic-crazed animal and then another—he touched minds, soothed, brought to bear his training. Within moments he heard the dull thud of hooves on the mossy ground, no longer pounding in a wild gallop. A shaggy mount, neither pony nor horse of his knowledge, but like in ways of each, its dull hide marked with a black stripe running from the root of shaggy mane to the base of its tail, came toward him, nickered questioningly. And then fell behind Craike, to be joined by another and another, as the Esper walked on—until he led the full train of runaways.

He met the first of the caravan men within a quarter of a mile and savored the fellow's astonishment at the sight. Yet, after the first surprise the man did not appear too amazed. He was short, dark of skin, a black beard of wiry, tightly curled hair clipped to a point thrusting out from his chin. Leggings covered his limbs, and he wore a sleeveless jerkin laced with thongs. This was belted by a broad strap gaudy with painted designs, from which hung a cross-hilted sword and a knife almost as long. A peaked cap of silky white fur was drawn far down so that a front flap shaded his eyes, and another, longer strip brushed his shoulders.

"Many thanks, Man of Power—" The words he spoke were in a clicking tongue, but Craike read their meaning mind to mind.

Then, as if puzzled on his closer examination of the Esper, the stranger frowned, his indecision slowly turning hostile.

"Outlaw! Begone, horned one!" The trader made a queer gesture with two fingers. "We pass free from your spells—"

"Be not so quick to pass judgment, Alfric—"

The newcomer was the Master Trader. As his man, he wore leather, but there was a gemmed clasp on his belt. His sword and knife hilt were of precious metal, as was a badge fastened to the fore of his yellow and black fur head gear.

"This one is no local outlaw." The Master stood, feet apart, studying the fugitive Esper as if he were a burden pony offered as a bargain. "Would such use his power for our aid? If he is a horned one—he is unlike any I have seen."

"I am not what you think—" Craike said slowly, fitting his tongue to the others' alien speech.

The Master Trader nodded. "That is true. And you intend us no harm, does not the sun-stone so testify?" His hand went to the badge on his cap. "In this one is no evil, Alfric, rather does he come to us in aid. Have I not spoken the truth to you, stranger from the wastes?"

Craike broadcast good will as strongly as he could. And they must have been somewhat influenced by that.

"I feel—he *does* have the power!" Alfric burst forth.

"He has power," the Master corrected him. "But has he striven to possess our minds as he could do? We are still our own men. No—this is no renegade Black Hood. Come!"

He beckoned to Craike, and the Esper, the animals still behind him, followed on into the camp, where the rest of the men seized upon the ponies to adjust their packs.

The Master filled a bowl from the contents of a three-legged pot set in the coals of a dying fire. Craike gulped an excellent and filling stew. When he had done, the Master indicated himself.

"I am Kaluf of the Children of Noe, a far trader and trail master. Is it your will, Man of Power, to travel this road with us?"

Craike nodded. This might all be a wild dream. But he was willing to see it to its end. A day with the caravan, the chance to gather more information from the men here, should give him some inkling as to what had happened to him and where he now was.

II

Craike's day with the traders became two and then three. Esper talents were accepted by this company matter-of-factly, even asked in aid. And from the travelers he gained a picture of this world which he could not reconcile with his own.

His first impression of a large continent broken by widely separated holdings of a frontier type remained. In addition there was knowledge of a feudal government, petty lordlings holding title to lands over men of lesser birth.

Kaluf and his men had a mild contempt for their customers. Their own homeland lay to the southeast, where, in some coastal cities, they had built up an overseas trade, retaining its cream for their own consumption, peddling the rest in the barbarous hinterland. Craike, his facility in their click speech growing, asked questions which the Master answered freely enough.

"These inland men know no difference between Saludian silk and the weaving of the looms in our own Kormonian quarter." He shrugged in scorn at such ignorance. "Why should we offer Salud when we can get Salud prices for Kormon lengths and the buyer is satisfied? Maybe— if these lords ever finish their private quarrels and live at peace so that there is more travel and they themselves come to visit in Larud or the other cities of the Children of Noe, then shall we not make a profit on lesser goods."

"Do these Lords never try to raid your caravans?"

Kaluf laughed. "They tried that once or twice. Certainly they saw there was the profit in seizing a train and paying nothing. But we purchased trail rights from the Black Hoods, and there was no more trouble. How is it with you, Ka-rak? Have you lords in your land who dare to stand against the power of the Hooded Ones?"

Craike, taking a chance, nodded. And knew he had been right when some reserve in Kaluf vanished.

"That explains much, perhaps even why such a man of power as you should be adrift in the wilderness. But you need not fear in this country, your brothers hold complete rule—"

A colony of Espers! Craike tensed. Had he, through some weird chance, found here the long-hoped-for refuge of his kind? But where *was* here? His old bewilderment was lost in a shout from the fore of the train.

"The outpost has sighted us and raised the trade banner." Kaluf quickened pace. "Within the hour we'll be at the walls of Sampur Illif!"

Craike made for the head of the line. Sampur, by the reckoning of the train, was a city of respectable size, the domain of a Lord Ludicar with whom Kaluf had had mutually satisfactory dealings for some time. And the Master anticipated a profitable stay. But the man who had ridden out to greet them was full of news.

Racially he was unlike the traders, taller, longer of arm. His bare chest was a thatch of blond-red hair as thick as a bear's pelt, long braids swung across his shoulders. A leather cap, reinforced with sewn rings of metal, was crammed down over his wealth of hair, and he carried a shield slung from his saddle pad. In addition to sword and knife, he nursed a spear in the crook of his arm, from the point of which trailed a banner strip of blue stuff.

"You come in good time, Master. The Hooded Ones have proclaimed a horning, and all the outbounders have gathered as witnesses. This is a good day for your trading, the Cloudy Ones have indeed favored you. But hurry, the Lord Ludicar is now riding in and soon there will be no good place from which to watch—"

Craike fell back. Punishment? An execution? No, not quite that. He wished he dared ask questions. Certainly the picture which had leaped into Kaluf's mind at the mention of "horning" could not be true!

Caution kept the Esper aloof. Sooner or later his alien origin must be noted, though Kaluf had supplied him with a fur cap, leather jerkin, and boots from the caravan surplus.

The ceremony was to take place just outside the main gate of the stockade, which formed the outer rampart of the town. A group of braided, ring-helmed warriors hemmed in a more imposing figure with a feather plume and a blue cloak, doubtless Lord Ludicar. Thronging at a respectful distance were the townfolk. But they were merely audience; the actors stood apart.

Craike's hands went to his head. The emotion which beat at him from that party brought the metallic taste of fear to his mouth, aroused his own memories. Then he steadied, probed. There was terror there, broadcast from two figures under guard. Just as an impact of Esper power came from the three black-hooded men who walked behind the captives.

He used his own talent carefully, dreading to attract the attention of the men in black. The townsfolk opened an aisle in their ranks, giving free passage to the open moorland and the green stretch of forest not too far away.

Fear—in one of those bound, stumbling prisoners it was abject, the same panic which had hounded Craike into the desert. But, though the other captive had no hope, there was a thick core of defiance, a desperate desire to strike back. And something in Craike arose to answer that.

Other men, wearing black jerkins and no hoods, crowded about the prisoners. When they stepped back Craike saw that the drab clothing of the two had been torn away. Shame, blotting out fear, came from the smaller captive. And there was no mistaking the sex of the curves that white body displayed. A girl, and very young. A violent shake of her head loosened her hair to flow, black and long, clothing her nakedness. Craike drew a deep breath as he had before that plunge into the canyon. Moving quickly he crouched behind a bush.

The Black Hoods went about their business with dispatch, each drawing in turn certain designs and lines in the dust of the road until they had created an intricate pattern about the feet of the prisoners.

A chant began in which the townspeople joined. The fear of the male captive was an almost visible cloud. But the outrage and anger of his feminine companion grew in relation to the chant, and Craike could sense her will battling against that of the assembly.

The watching Esper gasped. He could not be seeing what his eyes reported to his brain! The man was down on all fours, his legs and arms stretched, a mist clung to them, changed to red-brown hide. His head lengthened oddly, horns sprouted. No man, but an antlered stag stood there.

And the girl—?

Her transformation came more slowly. It began and then faded. The power of the Black Hoods held her, fastening on her the form they visualized. She fought. But in the end a white doe sprang down the path to the forest, the stag leaping before her. They whipped past the bush where Craike had gone to earth, and he was able to see through the illusion. Not a red stag and a white doe, but a man and woman running for their lives, yet already knowing in their hearts there was no hope in their flight.

Craike, hardly knowing why he did it or who he could aid, followed, sure that mind touch would provide him with a guide.

He had reached the murky shadow of the trees when a sound rang from the town. At its summoning he missed a step before he realized it was directed against those he trailed and not himself. A hunting horn! So this world also had its hunted and its hunters. More than ever he determined to aid those who fled.

But it was not enough to just run blindly on the track of stag and doe. He lacked weapons. And his wits had not sufficed to save him in his own world. But there he had been conditioned against turning on his hunters, hampered, cruelly designed from birth to accept the quarry role. That was not true here.

Esper power—Craike licked dry lips. Illusions so well done they had almost enthralled him. Could illusion undo what illusion had done? Again the call of the horn, ominous in its clear tone, rang in his ears, set his pulses to pounding. The fear of those who fled was a cord, drawing him on.

But as he trotted among the trees Craike concentrated on his own illusion. It was not a white doe he pursued but the slim, young figure he had seen when they stripped away the clumsy stuff which had cloaked her, before she had shaken loose her hair veil. No doe, but a woman. She was not racing on four hooved feet, but running free on two, her hair blowing behind her. No doe, but a maid!

And in that moment, as he constructed that picture clearly, he contacted her in thought. It was like being dashed by sea-spray, cool, remote, very clean. And, as spray, the contact vanished in an instant, only to return.

"Who are you?"

"One who follows," he answered, holding to his picture of the running girl.

"Follow no more, you have done what was needful!" There was a burst of joy, so overwhelming a release from terror that it halted him. Then the cord between them broke.

Frantically Craike cast about seeking contact. There was only a dead wall. Lost, he put out a hand to the rough bark of the nearest tree. Wood things lurked here, them only did his mind touch. What did he do now?

His decision was made for him. He picked up a wave of panic again—spreading terror. But this was the fear of feathered and furred things. It came to him as ripples might run on a pool.

Fire! He caught the thought distorted by bird and beast mind. Fire which leaped from tree crown to tree crown, cutting a gash across the forest. Craike started on, taking the way west, away from the menace.

Once he called out as a deer flashed by him, only to know in the same moment that this was no illusion but an animal. Small creatures tunneled through the grass. A dog fox trotted, spared him a measuring gaze from slit eyes. Birds whirred, and behind them was the scent of smoke.

A mountain of flesh, muscle and fur snarled, reared to face him. But Craike had nothing to fear from any animal. He confronted the great red bear until it whined, shuffled its feet and plodded on. More and more creatures crossed his path or ran beside him for a space.

It was their instinct which brought them, and Craike, to a river. Wolves, red deer, bears, great cats, foxes and all the rest came down to the saving water. A cat spat at the flood, but leaped in to swim. Craike lingered on the bank. The smoke was thicker, more animals broke from the wood to take to the water. But the doe—where was she?

He probed, only to meet that blank. Then a spurt of flame ran up a dead sapling, advance scout of the furnace. He yelped as a floating cinder stung his skin and took to the water. But he did not cross, rather did he swim upstream, hoping to pass the flank of the fire and pick up the missing trail again.

III

Smoke cleared as Craike trod water. He was beyond the path of the fire, but not out of danger. For the current against which he had fought his way beat here through an archway of masonry. Flanking that arch were two squat towers. As an erection it was far more ambitious than anything he had seen during his brief glimpse of Sampur. Yet, as he eyed it more closely, he could see it was a ruin. There were gaps in the narrow span across the river, a green bush sprouted from the summit of the far tower.

Craike came ashore, winning his way up the steep bank by hand-holds of vine and bush no alert castellan would have allowed to grow. As he reached a terrace of cobbles stippled with bunches of coarse grass, a sweetish scent of decay drew him around the base of the tower to look down at a broad ledge extending into the river. Piled on it were small baskets and bowls, some so rotted that only outlines were visible. Others new and all filled with moldering food stuffs. But those who left such offerings must have known that the tower was deserted.

Puzzled, Craike went back to the building. The stone was undressed, yet the huge blocks which formed its base were fitted together with such precision that he suspected he could not force the thin blade of a pocket knife into any crack. There had been no effort at ornamentation, at any lightening of the impression of sullen, brute force.

Wood, split and insect-bored, formed a door. As he put his hand to it Craike discovered the guardian the long-ago owners of the fortress had left in possession. His hands went to his head, the blow he felt might have been physical. Out of the stronghold before him came such a wave of utter terror and dark promise as to force him back. But no farther than the edge of the paved square about the building's foundation.

Grimly he faced that challenge, knowing it for stored emotion and not the weapon of an active will. He had his own defense against such a formless enemy. Breaking a dead branch from a bush, he twisted about it wisps of the sun-bleached grass until he had a torch of sorts. A piece of smoldering tinder blown from the fire gave him a light.

Craike put his shoulder to the powdery remnants of the door, bursting it wide. Light against dark. What lurked there was nourished by dark, fed upon the night fears of his species.

A round room, bare except for some crumbling sticks of wood, a series of steps jutting out from the wall to curl about and vanish above. Craike made no move toward further exploration, holding up the torch, seeking to see the real, not the threat of this place.

Those who had built it possessed Esper talents. And they had used that power for twisted purposes. He read terror and despair trapped here by the castellans' art, horror, an abiding fog of what his race considered evil.

Tentatively Craike began to fight. With the torch he brought light and heat into the dark and cold. Now he struggled to offer peace. Just as he had pictured a girl in flight in place of the doe, so did he now force upon those invisible clouds of stored suffering calm and hope. The gray window slits in the stone were uncurtained to the streaming sunlight.

Those who had set that guardian had not intended it to hold against an Esper. Once he began the task, Craike found the opposition melting. The terror seeped as if it sank into the floor wave by wave. He stood in a room which smelt of damp and, more faintly, of the rotting food piled below its window slits; but now it was only an empty shell.

Craike was tired, drained by his effort. And he was puzzled. Why had he fought for this? Of what importance to him was the cleansing of a ruined tower?

Though to stay here had certain advantages. It had been erected to control river traffic. Though that did not matter for the present, just now he needed food more—

He went back to the rock of offerings, treading a wary path through the disintegrating stuff. Close to the edge he came upon a clay bowl containing coarsely ground grain and, beside it, a basket of wilted leaves filled with overripe berries. He ate in gulps.

Grass made him a matted bed in the tower, and he kindled a fire. As he squatted before its flames, he sent out a questing thought. A big cat drank from the river. Craike shuddered away from that contact with blood lust. A night-hunting bird provided a trace of awareness. There were small rovers and hunters. But nothing human.

Tired as he was Craike could not sleep. There was the restless sensation of some demand about to be made, some task waiting. From time to time he fed the fire. Towards morning he dozed, to snap awake. A night creature drinking, a screech overhead. He heard the flutter of wings echo hollowly through the tower.

Beyond—darkness—blank, that curious blank which had fallen between him and the girl. Craike got to his feet eagerly. That blank could be traced.

Outside it was raining, and fog hung in murky bands among the river hollows. The blank spot veered. Craike started after it. The tower pavement became a trace of old road he followed, weaving through the fog.

There was the sour smell of old smoke. Charred wood, black muck clung to his feet. But his guide point was now stationary as the ground rose, studded with outcrops of rock. So Craike came to a mesa jutting up into a steel gray sky.

He hitched his way up by way of a long-ago slide. The rain had stopped, but there was no hint of sun. And he was unprepared for the greeting he met as he topped the lip of a small plateau.

A violent blow on the shoulder whirled him halfway around, and only by a finger's width did he escape a fall. A cry echoed his, and the blank broke. She was there.

Moving slowly, using the same technique he knew to soothe fright-ened animals, Craike raised himself again. The pain in his shoulder was sharp when he tried to put much weight upon his left arm. But now he saw her clearly.

She sat cross-legged, a boulder at her back, her hair a rippling cloud of black through which her hands and arms shone starkly white. She had the thin, three-cornered face of a child who has known much harshness; there was no beauty there—the flesh had been too much worn by spirit. Only her eyes, watchful-wary as those of a feline, considered him bleakly. In spite of his beam of good will, she gave him no welcome. And she tossed another stone from hand to hand with the ease of one who had already scored with such a weapon.

"Who are you?" She spoke aloud.

"He who followed you." Craike fingered the bruise wound on his shoulder, not taking his eyes from hers.

"You are no Black Hood." It was a statement not a question. "But you, also, have been horned." Another statement.

Craike nodded. In his own time and place he had indeed been "horned."

Just as her thrown stone had struck without warning, so came her second attack. There was a hiss. Within striking distance a snake flick-ered a forked tongue.

Craike did not give ground. The snake head expanded, fur ran over it; there were legs, a plume of tail fluffed. A dog fox yapped once at the girl and vanished. Craike read her recoil, the first faint uncertainty.

"You have the power!"

"I have power," he corrected her.

But her attention was no longer his. She was listening to something he could hear with neither ear nor mind. Then she ran to the edge of the mesa. He followed.

On this side the country was more rolling, and across it now came mounted men moving in and out of mist pools. They rode in silence, and over them was the same blanketing of thought as the girl had used.

Craike glance about. There were loose stones, and the girl had already proven her marksmanship with such. But they would be no answer to the weapons the others had. Only flight was no solution either.

The girl sobbed once, a broken cry so unlike the iron will she had shown that Craike started. She leaned perilously over the drop, staring down at the horsemen.

Then her hands moved with desperate speed. She tore hairs from her head, twisted and snarled them between her fingers, breathed on them, looped them with a stone for weight, casting the tangled mass out to land before the riders.

The mist curled, took on substance. Where there had been only rock there was now a thicket of thorn, so knotted that no fleshed creature could push through it. The hunters paused, then they rode on again, but now they drove a reeling, naked man, a man kept going by a lashing whip whenever he faltered.

Again the girl sobbed, burying her face in her hands. The wretched captive reached the thorn barrier. Under his touch it melted. He stood there, weaving drunkenly.

A whip sang. He went to his knees under its cut, a trapped animal's wail on the wind. Slowly, with a blind seeking, his hands went out to small stones about him. He gathered them, spread them anew in patterns. The girl had raised her head, watched dry-eyed, but seething with hate and the need to strike back. But she did not move.

Craike dared lay a hand on her narrow shoulder, feeling through her hair the chill of her skin, while the hair itself clung to his fingers as if it had the will to smother and imprison. He tried to pull her away, but he could not move her.

The naked man crouched in the midst of his pattern, and now he chanted, a compelling call the girl could not understand. She wrenched free of Craike's hold. But as she went she spared a thought for the man who had tried to save her. She struck out, her fist landing on the stone bruise. Pain sent him reeling back as she went over the rim of the mesa, her face a mask which no friend nor enemy might read. But there was no resignation in her eyes as she was forced to the meeting below.

IV

By the time Craike reached a vantage point the girl stood in the center of the stone ring. Outside crouched the man, his head on his knees. She looked down at him, no emotion showing on her wan face. Then she dropped her hand on his thatch of wild hair. He jerked under that touch as he had under the whip which had printed the scarlet weals across his back and loins. But he raised his head, and from his throat came a beast's mournful howl. At her gesture he was quiet, edging closer to her as if seeking some easement of his suffering.

The Black Hoods drew in. Craike's probe could make nothing of them. But they could not hide their emotions as well as they concealed their thoughts. And the Esper recoiled from the avid blood lust which lapped at the two by the cliff.

A semicircle of the black-jerkined retainers moved too. And the man who had led them lay on the earth now, moaning softly. But the girl faced them, head unbowed. Craike wanted to aid her. Had he time to climb down the cliff? Clenching his teeth against the pain movement brought to his shoulder, the Esper went back, holding a mind shield as a frail protection.

Directly before him now was one of the guards. His mount caught

Craike's scent, stirred uneasily, until the quieting thought of the Esper held it steady. Craike had never been forced into such action as he had these past few days; he had no real plan now, it must depend upon chance and fortune.

As if the force of her enemies' wills had slammed her back against the rock, the girl was braced by the cliff wall, a black-and-white figure.

Mist swirled, took on half substance of a monstrous form, was swept away in an instant. A clump of dried grass broke into flame, sending the ponies stamping and snorting. It was gone, leaving a black smudge on the earth. Illusions, realities—Craike watched. This was so far beyond his own experience that he could hardly comprehend the lightning moves of mind against mind. But he sensed these others could beat down the girl's resistance at any moment they desired, that her last futile struggles were being relished by those who decreed this as part of her punishment.

And Craike, who had believed that he could never hate more than he had when he had been touched by the fawning "hound" of the mob, was filled with a rage tempered into a chill of steel determination.

The girl went to her knees, still clutching her hair about her, facing her tormenters with her still-held defiance. Now the man who had wrought the magic which had drawn her there crawled, all humanity gone out of him, wriggling on his belly back to his captors.

Two of the guards jerked him up. He hung limp in their hands, his mouth open in an idiot's grin. Callously, as he might tread upon a worm, the nearest Black Hood waved a hand. A metal axe flashed, and there came the dull sound of cracking bone. The guards pitched the body from them so that the bloodied head almost touched the girl.

She writhed, a last frenzied attempt to break the force which pinned her. Without haste the guards advanced. One caught at her hair, pulling it tautly from her head.

Craike shivered. The thrill of her agony reached him. This was what she feared most, fought so long to prevent. If ever he must move now. And that part of his brain which had been feverishly seeking a plan went into action.

Ponies pawed, reared, went wild with panic. One of the Black Hoods swung around to face the terrorized animals. But his own mount struck out with teeth and hooves. Guardsmen shouted, and above their cries arose the shrill squeals of the animals.

Craike stood his ground, keeping the ponies in terror-stricken revolt. The guard who held the handful of hair slashed at the tress with his knife, severing it at a palm's distance away from her head. But in that same movement she moved. The knife leaped free from the man's grasp, while the severed hair twined itself about his hands, binding them until the blade buried itself in his throat; and he went down.

One of the Black Hoods was also finished, tramped into a feebly squirming thing by the ponies. Then from the ground burst a sheet of flame which split into balls, drifting through the air or rolling along the earth.

The Esper wet his lips—that was not his doing! He did not have to feed the panic of the animals now; they were truly mad. The girl was on her feet. Before his thought could reach her she was gone, swallowed up in a mist which arose to blanket the fireballs. Once more she cut their contact; there was a blank void where she had been.

Now the fog thickened. Through it came one of the ponies, foam dripping from its blunt muzzle. It bore down on Craike, eyes gleaming red through a tangled forelock. With a scream it reared.

Craike's hand grabbed a handful of mane as he leaped, avoiding teeth and hooves. Then, somehow, he gained the pad saddle, locking his fingers in the coarse hair, striving to hold his seat against the bucking enraged beast. It broke into a run, and the Esper plastered himself to the heaving body. For the moment he made no attempt at mind control.

Behind, the Black Hoods came out of their stunned bewilderment. They were questing feverishly, and he had to concentrate on holding his shield against them. A pony fleeing in terror would not excite them; a pony under control would provide them with a target.

Later he could circle about and try to pick up the trail of the witch girl. Flushed with success, Craike was sure he could provide her with a rear guard no Black Hood could pass.

The fog was thick, and the pace of the pony began to slacken.

Once or twice it bucked halfheartedly, giving up when it could not dislodge its rider. Craike drew his fingers in slow, soothing sweeps down the sweating curve of its neck.

There were no more trees about, and the unshod hooves pounded on sand. They were in a dried watercourse, and Craike did not try to turn from that path. Then his luck ran out.

What he had ignorantly supposed to be a rock ahead heaved up seven feet or more. A red mouth opened in a great roar. He had believed the bear he had seen fleeing the fire to be a giant, but this one was a nightmare monster.

The pony screamed with an almost human note of despair and whirled. Craike gripped the mane again and tried to mind-control the bear. But his surprise had lasted seconds too long. A vast clawed paw struck, ripping across pony hide and human thigh. Then Craike could only cling to the running mount.

How long he was able to keep his seat he never knew. Then he slipped; there was a throb of pain as he struck the ground, to be followed by blackness.

It was dusk when he opened his eyes, fighting agony in his head, his leg. But later there was moonlight. And that silver-white spotlighted a waiting shape. Green slits of eyes regarded him remotely. Dizzily he made contact.

A wolf—hungry—yet with a wariness which recognized in the prone man an enemy. Craike fought for control. The wolf whined, then it arose, its prick ears sharp-cut in the moonlight, its nose questing for the scent of other, less disturbing prey, and it was gone.

Craike edged up against a boulder and sorted out sounds. The rush of water. He moved a paper-dry tongue over cracked lips. Water to drink—to wash his wounds—water!

With a groan Craike worked his way to his feet, holding fast to the top of the rock when his torn leg threatened to buckle under him. The same inner drive which had kept him going through the desert brought him down to the river.

By sunrise he was seeking a shelter, wanting to lie up, as might the wolf, in some secret cave until his wounds healed. All chance of finding the witch girl was lost. But as he crawled along the shingle, leaning on a staff he had found in drift wood, he kept alert for any trace of the Black Hoods.

It was midmorning on the second day that his snail's progress brought him to the river towers. And it took another hour for him to reach the terrace. Gaunt and worn, his empty stomach complaining, he wanted nothing more than to sink down in the nest of grass he had gathered and cease to struggle.

Perhaps he might have done so had not a click-clack of sound from the river put him on the defensive, his staff now a club. But these were not Black Hoods. Farmers, local men bound for the market of Sampur with products of their fields. They had paused, were making a choice among the least appetizing of their wares for a tribute to be offered to the tower demon.

Craike hitched stiffly to a point where he could witness that sacrifice. But when he assessed the contents of their dugout, the heaping basket piled between the paddlers, his hunger took command.

Fob off a demon with a handful of meal and a too-ripe melon, would they? With three haunches of cured meat and all that other stuff on board!

Craike voiced a roar which could have done credit to the red bear, a roar which altered into a demand for meat. The paddlers nearly lost control of their crude craft. But one reached for a haunch and threw it blindly on the refuse-covered rock, while his companion added a basket of small cakes into the bargain.

"Enough, little men—" Craike's voice boomed hollowly. "You may pass free."

They needed no urging, they did not look at those threatening towers as their paddles bit into the water, adding impetus to the pull of the current.

Craike watched them well out of sight before he made a slow descent to the rock. The effort he was forced to expend warned him that a second such trip might be impossible, and he inched back to the terrace dragging both meat and cakes.

The cured haunch he worried into strips, using his pocket knife. It was tough, not too pleasant to the taste and unsalted. But he found it more appetizing than the cakes of baked meal. With this supply he could afford to lie up and favor his leg.

About the claw rents the flesh was red and puffed. Craike had no dressing but river water and the leaves he had tied over the tears. Sampur was beyond his power to reach, and to contact men traveling on the river would only bring the Black Hoods.

He lay in his grass nest and tried to sort out the events of the past few days. This was a land in which Esper powers were allowed free range. He had no idea of how he had come here, but it seemed to his feverish mind that he had been granted another chance—one in which the scales of justice were more balanced in his favor. If he could only find the girl, learn from her—

Tentatively, without real hope, he sent out a questing thought. Nothing. He moved impatiently, wrenching his leg, so that his head swam with pain. Throat and mouth were dry. The lap of water sounded in his ears. Water—he was thirsty again. But he could not crawl down-slope and up once more. Craike closed his eyes wearily.

V

Craike's memory of the hours which followed thereafter was dim. *Had* he seen a demon in the doorway? A slavering wolf? A red bear?

Then the girl sat there, cross-legged as he had seen her on the mesa, her cloak of hair about her. A hand emerged from the cloak to lay wood on the fire. Illusions?

But would an illusion turn to him, put firm, cool fingers upon his wound, somehow driving out by touch the pain and fire which burned there? Would an illusion raise his head, cradling it against her so that the soft silk of her hair lay against his cheek and throat, urging on him liquid out of a crude bowl? Would an illusion sing softly to herself while she drew a fish-bone comb back and forth through her hair, until the song and the sweep of the comb lulled him into a sleep so deep that no dream walked there?

He awoke, clear-headed. Yet that last illusion lingered. For she came from the sun-drenched world without, a bowl of fruit in her hand. For a long moment she stood gazing at him searchingly. But when he tried mind contact, he met that wall. Not unheeding—but a refusal to answer.

Her hair was now braided. But about her face the lock which the guardsman had shorn made an untidy fringe. While around her thin body was a strip of hide, purposefully arranged to mask all femininity.

"So," Craike spoke rustily, "you are real—"

She did not smile. "I am real. You no longer dream with fever."

"Who are you?" He asked the first of his long hoarded questions.

"I am Takya." She added nothing to that.

"You are Takya, and you are a witch—"

"I am Takya, and I have the power." It was an assertion of fact rather than agreement.

She settled in her favorite cross-legged position, selected a fruit from her bowl and examined it with the interest of a housewife who has shopped for supplies on a limited budget. Then she placed it in his hand before she chose another for herself. He bit into the plumlike globe. If she would only drop her barrier, let him communicate in the way which was fuller and deeper than speech.

"You also have the power—"

Craike decided to be no more communicative than she. He replied to that with a curt nod.

"Yet you have not been horned—"

"Not as you have been. But in my own world, yes."

"Your world?" Her eyes held some of the feral glow of a hunting cat's. "What world, and why were you horned there, man of sand and ash power?"

Without knowing why Craike related the events of the days past. Takya listened, he was certain, with more than ears alone. She picked up a stick from the pile of firewood and drew patterns in the sand and ash, patterns which had something to do with her listening.

"Your power was great enough to break a world wall." She snapped the stick between two fingers, threw it into the flames.

"A world wall?"

"We of the power have long known that different worlds lie together in such a fashion." She held up her hand with the fingers tight lying one to another. "Sometimes there comes a moment when two touch so closely that the power can carry one through if at that moment there is a desperate need for escape. But those places of meeting cannot be readily found, and the moment of their touch can lie only for an instant. Have you in your world no reports of men and women who have vanished almost in sight of their fellows?"

Remembering old tales, he nodded.

"I have seen a summoning from another world," she continued with a shiver, running both hands down the length of her braids as if so she evoked a shield for both mind and body. "To summon so is a great evil, for no man can hold in check the power of something alien. You broke the will of the Black Hoods when I was a beast running from their hunt. When I made the serpent to warn you off, you changed it into a fox. And when the Black Hoods would have shorn my power"— she looped the braids about her wrists, caressing, treasuring them against her small breasts—"again you broke their hold and set me free for a second time. But this you could not have done had you been born into this world, for our power must follow set laws. Yours lies outside our patterns and can cut across those laws—even as the knife cut this—" She touched the rough patch of hair at her temple.

"Follow patterns? Then it was those patterns in stone which drew you down from the mesa?"

"Yes. Takyi, my womb-brother, whom they slew there, was blood of my blood, bone of my bone. When they crushed him, then they could use him to draw me, and I could not resist. But in the slaying of his husk they freed me—to their great torment, as Tousuth shall discover in time."

"Tell me of this country. Who are the Black Hoods and why did they horn you? Are you not of their breed since you have the power?"

But Takya did not answer at once in words. Nor did she, as he had hoped, lower her mind barrier.

Her fingers now held one long hair she had pulled from her head, and this she began to weave in and out, swiftly, intricately, in a complicated series of loops and crossed strands. After a moment Craike did not see the white fingers, nor the black hair they passed in loops from one to another. Rather did he see the pictures she wrought in her weaving.

A wide land, largely wilderness. The impressions he had gathered from Kaluf and the traders crystalized into vivid life. Small holdings here and there, ruled by petty lords, new settlements carved out by a scattered people moving up from the south in great wheeled wains, bringing flocks and herds, their carefully treasured seed. Stopping here and there for a season to sow and reap, until they decided upon a site for their final rooting. Tiny city-states, protected by the Black Hoods—the Esper born who purposefully interbred their own gifted stock, keeping their children apart.

Takya and her brother coming, as was sometimes—if rarely—true, from the common people. Carefully watched by the Black Hoods. Then discovered to be a new mutation, condemned as such to be used for experimentation. But for a while protected by the local lord who wanted Takya.

But he might not take her unwilling. For the power that was hers as a virgin was wholly rift from her should she be forced. And he had wanted that power, obedient to him, as a check upon the monopoly of the Black Hoods. So with some patience he had set himself to a peaceful wooing. But the Black Hoods had moved first.

Had they accomplished her taking, the end they had intended for her was not as easy as death. And she wove a picture of it, with all its degradation and shame stark and open, for Craike's seeing.

"Then the Hooded Ones are evil?"

"Not wholly." She untwisted the hair and put it with care into the fire. "They do much good, and without them people would suffer. But I, Takya, am different. And after me, when I mate, there will be others also different. How different we are not yet sure. The Hooded Ones want no change, by their thinking that means disaster. So they would use me to their own purposes. Only I, Takya, shall not be so used!"

"No, you shall not." The vehemence of his own outburst startled him. Craike wanted nothing so much at that moment as to come to grips with the Black Hoods, who had planned this systematic hunt.

"What will you do now?" he asked more calmly, wishing she would share her thoughts with him.

"This is a strong place. Did you cleanse it?"

He nodded impatiently.

"So I thought. That was also a task one born to this world might not have performed. But those who pass are not yet aware of the cleansing. They will not trouble us, but pay tribute."

Craike found her complacency irritating. To lie up here and live on the offerings of river travelers did not appeal to him.

"This stone piling is older work than Sampur and much better," she continued. "It must have been a fortress for some of those forgotten ones who held lands and then vanished long before we came from the south. If it is repaired no lord of this district would have so good a roof."

"Two of us to rebuild it?" he laughed.

"Two of us—working thus."

A block of stone, the size of a brick, which had fallen from the sill of one of the needle-narrow windows, arose slowly in the air, settled into the space from which it had tumbled. Illusion or reality? Craike got to his feet and lurched to the window. His hand fell upon the stone, which moved easily in his grasp. He took it out, weighed it, and then gently returned it to its place. Not illusion.

"But illusion too—if need be." There was, for the first time, a warmth not of amusement in her tone. "Look on your tower, river lord!"

He limped to the door. Outside it was warm, sunny, but it was a site of ruins. Then the picture changed. Brown drifts of grass vanished from the terrace, the fallen stone was all in place. A hard-faced sentry stood wary-eyed on a repaired river arch. Another guardsman led out ponies saddle-padded and ready, other men were about garrison tasks.

Craike grinned. The sentry on the arch lost his helm, his jerkin. He now wore the tight tunic of the Security Police, his spear was a gas rifle. The ponies misted, and in their place a speedster sat on the stone. He heard her laugh.

"Your guard, your traveling machine. But how grim, ugly. This is better!"

Guards, machine; all were swept away. Craike caught his breath at the sight of delicate winged creatures dancing in the air, displaying a joy of life he had never known. Fawns, little people of the wild, came to mingle with such shapes of beauty and desire that at last he turned his head away.

"Illusion." Her voice was hard, mocking.

But Craike could not believe that what he had seen had been born from hardness and mockery.

"All illusions. We shall be better now with warriors. As for plans, can you suggest any better than to remain here and take what fortune sends—for a space?"

"Those winged dancers—where?"

"Illusions!" she returned harshly. "But such games tire one. I do not think we shall conjure up any garrison before they are needed. Come, do not tear open those wounds of yours anew, for healing is no illusion and drains one even more of the power."

The clawed furrows were healing cleanly, though he would bear their scars for life. He hobbled back to the grass bed and dropped upon it, but regretted the erasure of the sprites she had shown him.

Once he was safely in place, Takya left with the curt explanation she had things to do. But Craike was restless, too much so to remain long inside the tower. He waited until she had gone and then, with the aid of his staff, climbed to the end of the span above the river. From here the twin tower on the other bank looked the same as the one from which he had come. Whether it was also haunted Craike did not know. But, as he looked about, he could see the sense of Tayka's suggestion. A few illusion sentries would discourage any ordinary intrusion.

Takya's housekeeping had changed the rock of offerings. All the rotting debris was gone and none of the odor of decay now offended the nostrils at a change of wind. But at best it was a most uncertain source of supply. There could not be too many farms up river, nor too many travelers taking the water away.

As if to refute that, his Esper sense brought him sudden warning of strangers beyond the upper bend. But, Craike sensed, these were no peasants bound for the market at Sampur. Fear, pain, anger, such emotions heralded their coming. There were three, and one was hurt. But they were not Esper, nor did they serve the Black Hoods. Though they were, or had been, fighting men.

A brutal journey over the mountains where they had lost comrades, the finding of this river, the theft of the dugout they now used so expertly—it was all there for him to read. And beneath that something else, which, when he found it, gave Craike a quick decision in their favor—a deep hatred of the Black Hoods! Outlaws, very close to despair, keeping on a hopeless trail because it was not in them to surrender.

Craike contacted them subtly. They must not think they were heading into an Esper trap! Plant a little hope, a faint suggestion that there was a safe camping place ahead, that was all he could do at present. But so he drew them on.

"No!" A ruthless order cut across his line of contact, striking at the delicate thread with which he was playing the strangers in. But Craike stood firm. "Yes, yes, and yes!"

He was on guard instantly. Takya, mistress of illusion as she had proved herself to be, might act. But surprisingly she did not. The dugout came into view, carried more by the current than the efforts of its crew. One lay full-length in the bottom, while the bow paddler had slumped forward. But the man in the stern was bringing them in. And Craike strengthened his invisible, unheard invitation to urge him on.

VI

But Takya had not yet begun to fight. As the dugout swung in toward the offering ledge one of the Black Hoods' guardsmen appeared there, his drawn sword taking fire from the sun. The fugitive steersman faltered until the current drew his craft on. Craike caught the full force of the stranger's despair, all the keener for the hope of moments before. The Esper irritation against Takya flared into anger.

He made the illusion reel back, hands clutching at his breast from which protruded the shaft of an arrow. Craike had seen no bows here, but it was a weapon to suit this world. And this should prove to Takya he meant what he had said.

The steersman was hidden as the dugout passed under the arch. There was a scrap of beach, the same to which Craike had swum on his first coming. He urged the man to that, beaming good will.

But the paddler was almost done, and neither of his companions could aid him. He drove the crude craft to the bank, and its bow grated on the rough gravel. Then he crawled over the bodies of the other two and fell rather than jumped ashore, turning to pull up the canoe as best he could.

Craike started down. But he might have known that Takya was not so easily defeated. Though they maintained an alliance of sorts she accepted no order from him.

A brand was teleported from the tower fire, striking spear-wise in the dry brush along the slope. Craike's mouth set. He tried no more arguments. They had already tested power against power, and he was willing to so battle again. But this was not the time. However, the fire was no illusion, and he could not fight it, crippled as he was. Or could he?

It was not spreading too fast—though Takya might spur it by the forces at her command. Now—there was just the spot! Craike steadied himself against a mound of fallen masonry and swept out his staff, dislodging a boulder and a shower of gravel. He had guessed right. The stone rolled to crush out the brand, and the gravel he continued to push after it smothered the creeping flames.

Red tongues dashed spitefully high in a sheet of flame, and Craike laughed. *That* was illusion. She was angry. He produced a giant pail in the air, tilted it forward, splashed its contents into the heart of that conflagration. He felt the lash of her rage, standing under it unmoved. So might she bring her own breed to heel, but she would learn he was not of that ilk.

"Holla!" That call was no illusion, it begged help.

Craike picked a careful path downslope until he saw the dugout and the man who had landed it. The Esper waved an invitation, and at his summons the fugitive covered the distance between them.

He was a big man of the same brawny race as those of Sampur, his braids of reddish hair hanging well below his wide shoulders. There was the raw line of a half-healed wound down the angle of his jaw, and his sunken eyes were very tired. For a moment he stood downslope from Craike, his hands on his hips, his head back, measuring the Esper with the shrewdness of a canny officer who had long known how to judge and handle raw levies.

"I am Jorik of the Eagles' Tower." The statement was made with the same confidence as the announcement of rank might have come from one of the petty lords. "Though," he shrugged, "the Eagles' Tower stands no more with one stone upon the other. You have a stout lair here—" He hesitated before he concluded, "—friend."

"I am Craike," the Esper answered as simply, "and I am also one who has run from enemies. This lair is an old one, though still useful."

"Might the enemies from whom you run wear black hoods?" countered Jorik. "It seems to me that things I have just seen here have the stink of that about them."

"You are right. I am no friend to the Black Hoods."

"But you have the power—"

"I have power." Craike tried to make the distinction clear. "You are welcome, Jorik. So all are welcome here who are no friends to Black Hoods."

The big warrior shrugged. "We can no longer run. If the time has come to make a last stand, this is as good a place as any. My men are done." He glanced back at the two in the dugout. "They are good men, but we were pressed when they caught us in the upper pass. Once there were twenty hands of us." He held up his fist and spread the fingers wide for counting. "They drew us out of the tower with their sorcerers' tricks, and then put us to the hunt."

"Why did they wish to make an end to you?"

Jorik laughed shortly. "They dislike those who will not fit into their neat patterns. We are free mountain men, and no Black Hood helped us win the Eagles' Tower; none aided us to hunt. When we took our furs down to the valley they wanted to levy tribute. But what spell of theirs trapped the beasts in our deadfalls, or brought them to our spears? We pay not for what we have not bought. Neither would we have made war on them. Only, when we spoke out and said it so, there were others who were encouraged to do likewise, and the Black Hoods must put an end to us before their rule was broken. So they did."

"But they did not get all of you," Craike pointed out. "Can you bring your men up to the tower? I have been hurt and cannot walk without support or I would lend you a hand."

"We will come." Jorik returned to the dugout. Water was splashed vigorously into the face of the man in the bow, arousing him to crawl ashore. Then the leader of the fugitives swung the third man out of the craft and over his shoulder in a practiced carry.

When Craike had seen the unconscious man established on his own grass bed, he stirred up the fire and set out food while Jorik returned to the dugout to bring in their gear.

Neither of the other men was of the same size as their leader. The one who lay limp, his breath fluttering between his slack lips, was young, hardly out of boyhood, his thin frame showing bones rather than muscled flesh under the rags of clothing. The other was short, dark-skinned, akin by race to Kaluf's men, his jaw sprouting a curly beard. He measured Craike with suspicious glances from beneath lowered red lids, turning that study to the walls about him and the unknown reaches at the head of the stair.

Craike did not try mind touch. These men were rightly suspicious of Esper arts. But he did attempt to reach Takya, only to meet that nothingness with which she cloaked her actions. Craike was disturbed. Surely now that she was convinced he was determined to give the harborage to the fugitives, she would not oppose him. They had nothing to fear from Jorik and his men, but rather would gain by joining forces.

Until his wounds were entirely healed he could not go far. And without weapons they would have to rely solely upon Esper powers for defense. Having witnessed the efficiency of the Hooded Ones' attack, Craike doubted a victory in any engagement to which those masters came fully prepared. He had managed to upset their spells merely because they had not known of his existence. But the next time he would have no such advantage.

On the other hand the tower could be defended by force of arms. With bows—Craike savored the idea of archers giving a Hooded force a devastating surprise. The traders had had no such arm, as sophisticated as they were. And he had seen none among the warriors of Sampur. He'd have to ask Jorik if such were known.

In the meantime he sat among his guests, watching Jorik feed the semiconscious boy with soft fruit pulp and the other man wolf down dried meat. When the latter had done, he hitched himself closer to the fire and jerked a thumb at his chest.

"Zackuth," he identified himself.

"From Larud?" Craike named the only city of Kaluf's people he could remember.

The dark man's momentary surprise had no element of suspicion. "What do you know of the Children of Noe, stranger?"

"I journeyed the plains with one called Kaluf, a Master Trader of Larud."

"A fat man who laughs much and wears a falcon plume in his cap?"

"Not so." Craike allowed a measure of chill to ice his reply. "The Kaluf who led this caravan was a lean man who knew the edge of a good blade from its hilt. As for cap ornaments—he had a red stone to the fore of his. Also he swore by the Eyes of the Lady Lor."

Zackuth gave a great bray of laughter. "You are no stream fish to be easily hooked, are you, tower dweller? I am not of Larud, but I know Kaluf, and those who travel in his company do not wear one badge one day and another the next. But, by the looks of you, you have fared little better than we lately. Has Kaluf also fallen upon evil luck?"

"I traveled safely with his caravan to the gates of Sampur. How it fared with him thereafter I cannot tell you."

Jorik grinned and settled his patient back on the bed. "I believe you must have parted company in haste, Lord Ka-rak?"

Craike answered that with the truth. "There were two who were horned. I followed them to give what aid I could."

Jorik scowled, and Zackuth spat into the fire.

"We were not horned; we have no power," the latter remarked. "But they have other tricks to play. So you came here?"

"I was clawed by a bear," Craike supplied a meager portion of his adventures, "and came here to lie up until I can heal me of that hurt."

"This is a snug hole." Jorik was appreciative. "But how got you such eating?" He popped half a fruit into his mouth and licked his juicy fingers. "This is no wilderness feeding."

"The tower is thought to be demon-haunted. Those taking passage downstream leave tribute."

Zackuth slapped his knee. "The Gods of the Waves are good to you, Lord Ka-rak, that you should stumble into such fortune. There is more than one kind of demon for the haunting towers. How say you, Lord Jorik?"

"That we have also come into luck at last, since Lord Ka-rak has made us free of this hold. But perhaps you have some other thought in your head?" He spoke to the Esper.

Craike shrugged. "What the clouds decree shall fall as rain or snow," he quoted a saying of the caravan men.

It was close to sunset, and he was worried about Takya. He could not believe that she had gone permanently. And yet, if she returned, what would happen? He had been careful not to use Esper powers. Takya would have no such compunctions.

He could not analyze his feelings about her. She disturbed him, awoke emotions he refused to face. There was a certain way she had of looking sidewise— But her calm assumption of superiority pricked beneath his surface armor. And the antagonism fretted against the feeling which had drawn him after her from the gates of Sampur. Once again he sent out a quest-thought and, to his surprise, was answered.

"They must go!"

"They are outlaws, even as we. One is ill, the others worn with long running. But they stood against the Black Hoods. As such they have a claim on roof, fire and food from us."

"They are not as we!" Again arrogance. "Send them or I shall drive them. I have the power—"

"Perhaps you have the power, but so do I!" He put all the assurance he could muster into that. "I tell you, no better thing could happen than for us to give these men aid. They are proven fighters—"

"Swords cannot stand against the power!"

Craike smiled. His plans were beginning to move even as he carried on this voiceless argument. "Not swords, no, Takya. But all fighting is not done with swords nor spears. Nor with the power either. Can a Black Hood think death to his enemy when he himself is dead, killed from a distance, and not by mind power his fellows could trace and be armored against?"

He had caught her attention. She was acute enough to know that he was not playing with words, that he knew of what he spoke. Quickly he built upon that spark of interest. "Remember how your illusion guard died upon the offering rock when you would warn off these men?"

"By a small spear." She was contemptuous again.

"Not so." He shaped a picture of an arrow and then of an archer releasing it from the bow cord, of its speeding true across the river to strike deep into the throat of an unsuspecting Black Hood.

"You have the secret of this weapon?"

"I do. And five such arms are better than two, is that not the truth?"

She yielded a fraction. "I will return. But they will not like that."

"If you return, they will welcome you. These are no hunters of witch maidens—" he began, only to be disconcerted by her obvious amusement. Somehow he had lost his short advantage over her. Yet she did not break contact.

"Ka-rak, you are very foolish. No, these will not try to mate with me, not even if I willed it so. As you will see. Does the eagle mate with the hunting cat? But they will be slow to trust me, I think. However, your plan has possibilities, and we shall see."

VII

Takya had been right about her reception by the fugitives. They knew her for what she was, and only Craike's acceptance of her kept them in the tower. That and the fact, which Jorik did not try to disguise, that they could not hope to go much farther on their own. But their fears were partly allayed when she took over the nursing of the sick youngster, using on him the same healing power she had produced for Craike's wound. By the new day she was feeding him broth and demanding service from the others as if they had been her liegemen from birth.

The sun was well up when Jorik came in whistling from a dip in the river.

"This is a stout stronghold, Lord Ka-rak. And with the power aiding us to hold it, we are not likely to be shaken out in a hurry. Doubly is that true if the Lady aids us."

Takya laughed. She sat in the shaft of light from one of the narrow windows, combing her hair. Now she looked over her shoulder at them with something approaching a pert archness. In that moment she was more akin to the women Craike had known in his own world.

"Let us first see how the Lord Ka-rak proposes to defend us." There was mockery in that, enough to sting, as well as a demand that he make good his promise of the night before.

But Craike was prepared. He discarded his staff for a hold on Jorik's shoulder, while Zackuth slogged behind. They climbed into the forest. Craike had never fashioned a bow, and he did not doubt that his first attempts might be failures. But, as the three made their slow progress, he explained what they must look for and the kind of weapon he wanted to produce. They returned within the hour with an assortment of wood lengths with which to experiment.

After noon Zackuth grew restless and went off, to come back with a deer, visibly proud of his hunting skill. Craike saw bowstrings where the others saw meat and hide for the refashioning of foot wear. For the rest of the day they worked with a will. It was Takya who had the skill necessary for the feathering of the arrows after Zackuth netted two black river birds.

Four days later the tower community had taken on the aspect of a real stronghold. Many of the fallen stones were back in the walls. The two upper rooms of the tower had been explored, and a vast collection of ancient nests had been swept out. Takya chose the topmost one for her own abode and, aided by her convalescing charge, the boy Nickus, had carried armloads of sweet scented grass up for both carpeting and bedding. She did not appear to be inconvenienced by the bats that still entered at dawn to chitter out again at dusk. And she crooned a welcome to the snowy owl that refused to be dislodged from a favorite roost in the very darkest corner of the roof.

River travel had ceased. There were no new offerings on the rock. But Jorik and Zackuth hunted. And Craike tended the smoking fires which cured the extra meat against coming need, while he worked on the bows. Shortly they had three finished and practiced along the terrace, using blunt arrows.

Jorik had a true marksman's eye and took to the new weapon quickly, as did Nickus. But Zackuth was more clumsy, and Craike's stiff leg bothered him. Takya was easily the best shot when she would consent to try. But while agreeing it was an excellent weapon, she preferred her own type of warfare and would sit on the wall, braiding and rebraiding her hair with flying fingers, to watch their shooting at marks and applaud or jeer lightly at the results.

However, their respite was short. Craike had the first warning of trouble. He awoke from a dream in which he had been back in the desert panting ahead of the mob. Awoke, only to discover that some malign influence filled the tower. There was a compulsion on him to get out, to flee into the forest.

He tested the silences about him tentatively. The oppression which had been in the ancient fort at his first coming had not returned, that was not it. But what?

Someone moved restlessly in the dark.

"Lord Ka-rak?" Nickus' voice was low and hoarse, as if he struggled to keep it under control.

"What is it?"

"There is trouble—"

A bulk which could only belong to Jorik heaved up black against the faint light of the doorway.

"The hunt is up," he observed. "They move to shake us out of here like rats out of a nest."

"They did this before with you?" asked the Esper.

Jorik snorted. "Yes. It is their favorite move to battle. They would give us such a horror of our tower that we will burst forth and scatter. Then they can cut us down as they wish."

But Craike could not isolate any thought beam carrying that night terror. It seeped from the walls about them. He sent probes unsuccessfully. There was the pad of feet on the stairs, and then he heard Takya call:

"Build up the fire, foolish ones. They may discover that they do not deal with those who know nothing of them."

Flame blossomed from the coals to light a circle of sober faces. Zackuth caressed the spear lying across his knees, but Nickus and Jorik had eyes only for the witch maid as she knelt by the fire, laying out some bundles of dried leaf and fern. Her thoughts reached Craike.

"We must move or these undefended ones will be drawn out from here as nut meats are picked free from the shell. Give me of your power—in this matter I must be the leader."

* * *

Though he resented anew her calm assumption of authority, Craike also recognized in it truth. But he shrank from the task she demanded of him. To have no control over his own Esper arts, to allow her to use them to feed hers—it was a violation of a kind, the very thing he had so feared in his own world that he had been willing to kill himself to escape it. Yet now she asked it of him as one who had the right!

"Forced surrender is truly evil—but given freely in our defense this is different." Her thoughts swiftly answered his wave of repulsion.

The command to flee the tower was growing stronger. Nickus got to his feet as if dragged up. Suddenly Zackuth made for the door, only to have Jorik reach forth a long arm to trip him.

"You see," Takya urged, "they are already half under the spell. Soon we shall not be able to hold them, either by mind or body. And then they shall be wholly lost—for ranked against us now is the high power of the Black Hoods."

Craike watched the scuffle on the floor and then, still reluctant and inwardly shrinking, he limped around the fire to her side, lying down at her gesture. She threw on the fire two of her bundles of fern, and a thick, sweet smoke curled out to engulf them. Nickus coughed, put his hands uncertainly to his head and slumped, curling up as a tired child in deep slumber. And the struggle between Jorik and his man subsided as the fumes reached them.

Takya's hand was cool as it slipped beneath Craike's jerkin, resting over his heart. She was crooning some queer chant, and, though he fought to hold mind contact, there was a veil between them as tangible to his inner senses as the fern smoke was to his outer ones. For one wild second or two he seemed to see the tower room through her eyes instead of his own, and then the room was gone. He sped bodiless across the night world, casting forth as a hound on the trail.

All that had been solid in his normal sight was now without meaning. But he was able to see the dark cloud of pressure closing in on the tower and trace that back to its source, racing along the slender thread of its spinners.

There was another fire, and about it four of the Black Hoods. Here, too, was scented smoke to free minds from bodies. The essence which was Craike prowled about that fire, counting guardsmen who lay in slumber.

With an effort of will which drew heavily upon his strength, he concentrated on the staff which lay before the leader of the company, setting upon it his own commands.

It flipped up into the air, even as its master roused and clutched at it, falling into the fire. There was a flash of blue light, a sound which Craike felt rather than heard. The Hooded Ones were on their feet as their master stared straight across the flames to Craike's disembodied self. His was not an evil face, rather did it hold elements of nobility. But the eyes were pitiless, and Craike knew that now it was not only war to the death between them, but war beyond death itself. The Esper sensed that this was the first time that other had known of his existence, had been able to consider him as a factor in the tangled game.

There was a flash of lightning knowledge of each other, and then Craike was again in the dark. He heard once more Takya's crooning, was conscious of her touch resting above the slow, pulsating beat of his heart.

"That was well done," her thought welcomed him. "Now they must meet us face to face in battle."

"They will come." He accepted the dire promise that Black Hood had made.

"They will come, but now we are more equal. And there is not the Rod of Power to fear."

Craike tried to sit up and discovered that the weakness born of his wounds was nothing to that which now held him.

Takya laughed with some of her old mockery. "Do you think you can make the Long Journey and then romp about as a fawn, Ka-rak? Not three days on the field of battle can equal this. Sleep now and gather again the inner power. The end of this venture is still far from us."

He could no longer see her face, the glimmer of her hair veiled it, and then that shimmer reached his mind and shook him away from consciousness; and he slept.

It might have been early morning when he had made that strange visit to the camp of the Black Hoods. By the measure of the sun across the floor it was late afternoon when he lifted heavy eyelids again.

Takya gazed down upon him. Her summons had brought him back, just as her urging had sent him to sleep. He sat up with a smile, but she did not return it.

"All is right?"

"We have time to make ready before we are put to the test. Your mountain captain is not new to this game. Matters of open warfare he understands well, and he and his men have prepared a rude welcome for those who come. And," her faint smile deepened, "I, too, have done my poor best. Come and see."

He limped out on the terrace and for a moment was startled. Illusion, yes, but some of it was real.

Jorik laughed at the expression on Craike's face, inviting the Esper with a wave of the hand to inspect the force he captained. For there were bowmen in plenty, standing sentinel on the upper walls, arch, and tower, walking beats on the twin buildings across the river. And it took Craike a few seconds to sort out the ones he knew from those who served Takya's purposes. But the real had been as well posted as their illusionary companions. Nickus, for his superior accuracy with the new weapon, held a vantage point on the wall, and Zackuth was on the river arch where his arrows needed only a short range to be effective.

"Look below," Jorik ugred, "and see what shall trip them up until we can pin them."

Again Craike blinked. The illusion was one he had seen before, but that had been a hurried erection on the part of a desperate girl; this was better contrived. For all the ways leading to the river towers were cloaked with a tangled mass of thorn trees, the spiked branches interlocking into a wall no sword, no spear could hope to pierce. It might be an illusion, but it would require a weighty counterspell on the part of the Hooded Ones to clear it.

"She takes some twigs Nickus finds, and a hair, and winds them together, then buried all under a stone. After she sings over it—and we have this!" Jorik babbled. "She is worth twenty hands—no, twice twenty hands, or fighting men, is the Lady Takya! Lord Ka-rak, I say that there is a new day coming for this land when such as you two stand up against the Hooded Ones."

"Aaaay—" The warning was soft but clear, half whistle, half call, issuing from Nickus' lofty post. "They come!"

"So do they." That was a sharp echo from Zackuth, "and down river as well."

"For which we have an answer." Jorik was undisturbed.

Those in the tower held their fire. To the confident attackers it was as such warfare had always been for them. If half their company was temporarily halted by the spiny maze, the river party had only to land on the offering rock and fight their way in, their efforts reinforced by the arts of their Masters.

But, as their dugout nosed in, bow cords sang. There was a voice-less scream which tore through Craike's head as the hooded man in its bow clutched at the shaft protruding from his throat and fell forward into the river. Two more of the crew followed him, and the rest stopped paddling, dismayed. The current pulled them on under the arch, and Zackuth dropped a rock to good purpose. It carried one of the guards-men down with it as it hit the craft squarely. The dugout turned over, spilling all the rest into the water.

Zackuth laughed; Jorik roared.

"Now they learn what manner of bloodletting lies before them!" he cried so that his words must have reached the ears of the besiegers. "Let us see how eagerly they come to such feasting."

VIII

It was plain that the Black Hoods held their rulership by more practical virtues than just courage. Having witnessed the smashing dis-aster of the river attack, they made no further move. Night was com-ing, and Craike watched them withdraw downstream with no elation. Nor did Jorik retain his cheerfulness.

"Now they will try something else. And since we did not fall easily into their jaws, it will be harder to face. I do not like it that we must so face it during the hours of dark."

"There will be no dark," Takya countered. One slim finger pointed at a corner of the terrace, and up into the gathering dusk leaped a pen-cil of clear light. Slowly she turned and brought to life other torches on the roof of the tower over river, on the arch spanning the water, on the parapet—and in that radiance nothing could move unseen.

"So!" Her fingers snapped, and the beacons vanished. "When they are needed, we shall have them."

Jorik blinked. "Well enough, Lady. But honest fire is also good, and it provides warmth for a man's heart as well as light for his eyes."

She smiled as a mother might smile at a child. "Build your fire, Captain of Swords. But we shall have ample warning when the enemy comes." She called. A silent winged thing floated down and alighted on the arm she held out to invite it. The white owl, its eyes seeming to observe them all with intelligence, snapped its wicked beak as Takya stared back at it. Then with a flap of wings, it went.

"From us they may hide their thoughts and movements. But they cannot close the sky to those things whose natural home it is. Be sure we shall know, and speedily, when they move against us."

They did not leave their posts, however. And Zackuth readied for action by laying up pieces of rubble which might serve as well as his first lucky shot.

It was a long night, wearing on the tempers of all but Takya. Time and time again Craike tried to probe the dark. But a blank wall was all he met. Whatever moves the Black Hoods considered, they were protected by an able barrier.

Jorik took to pacing back and forth on the terrace, five strides one way, six the other, and he brought down his bow with a little click on the time-worn stones each time he turned.

"They are as busy hatching trouble as a forest owl is in hatching an egg! But what kind of trouble?"

Craike had schooled himself into an outward patience. "For the learning of that we shall have to wait. But why do they delay—?"

Why did they? The more on edge he and his handful of defenders became, the easier meat they were. And he had no doubt that the Black Hoods were fertile in surprise. Though, judging by what Takya and Jorik reported, they were not accustomed to such determined and resourceful opposition to their wills. Such opposition would only firm their desire to wipe out the rebels.

"They move." Takya's witch fires leaped from every point she had earlier indicated. In that light she sped across the terrace to stand close to Jorik and Craike, close to the parapet wall. "This is the lowest hour of the night when the blood runs slow and resistance is at its depth. So they choose to move—"

Jorik snapped his bow cord, and the thin twang was a harp's note in the silence. But Takya shook her head.

"Only the Hooded Ones come, and they are well armored. See!" She jumped to the parapet and clapped her hands.

The witch light shone down on four standing within the thorn barrier, staring up from under the shadow of their hoods. An arrow sang, but it never reached its mark. Still feet away from the leader's breast it fell to earth.

But Jorik refused to accept defeat. With all the force of his arm he sent a second shaft after the first. And it, too, landed at the feet of the silent four. Craike grasped at Takya, but she eluded him, moving to call down to the Hooded Ones.

"What would you, men of power—a truce?"

"Daughter of evil, you are not alone. Let us speak with your lord."

She laughed, shaking out her unbound hair, rippling it through her fingers, gloatingly. "Does this show that I have taken a lord, men of power? Takya is herself, without division, still. Let that hope die from your hearts. I ask you again, what is it you wish—a truce?"

"Set forth your lord, and with him we will bargain."

She smoothed back her hair impatiently. "I have no lord, I and my power are intact. Try me and see, Tousuth. Yes, I know you, Tousuth, the Master, and Salsbal, Bulan, Yily—" she told them off with a pointed forefinger, a child counting out in some game.

Jorik stirred and drew in a sharp breath, and the men below shifted position. Craike caught thoughts—to use a man's name in the presence of hostile powers, that was magic indeed.

"Takya!" It was a reptile's hiss.

Again she laughed. "Ah, but the first naming was mine, Tousuth. Did you believe me so poor and power lost that I would obey you tamely? I did not at the horning, why should I now when I stand free of you? Before you had to use Takyi to capture me. But Takyi is gone into the far darkness, and over me now you can lay no such net! Also I have summoned one beside me—" Her hand closed on Craike's arm, drawing him forward.

He faced the impact of those eyes meeting them squarely. Raising his hand he told them off as the girl had done:

"Tousuth, Master of women baiters, Salsbal, Bulan, Yily, the wolves who slink behind him. I am here, what would you have of me?"

But they were silent, and he could feel them searching him out, making thrusts against his mind shield, learning in their turn that he was of their kind; he was Esper born.

"What would you have?" he repeated more loudly. "If you do not wish to treat—then leave the night undisturbed for honest men's sleep."

"Changeling!" It was Tousuth who spat that. It was his turn to point a finger and chant a sentence or two, his men watching him with confidence.

But Craike, remembering that other scene before Sampur, was trying a wild experiment of his own. He concentrated upon the man Takya had named Yily. Black cloak, black hood making a vulture's shadow against the rock. Vulture—vulture!

He did not know that he had pointed to his chosen victim, nor that he was repeating that word aloud in the same intonation as Tousuth's chant. "Vulture!"

Cool hand closed about his other wrist, and from that contact power flowed to join his. It was pointed, launched—

"Vulture!"

A black bird flapped and screamed, arose on beating wings to fly at him, raw red head outstretched, beak agape. There was the twang of a bow cord. A scream of agony and despair and a black-cloaked man writhed out his life on the slope by the thorn thicket.

"Good!" Takya cried. "That was well done, Ka-rak, very well done! But you cannot use that weapon a second time."

Craike was filled with a wild elation, and he did not listen to her. His finger already indicated Bulan and he was chanting: "Dog—"

But to no purpose. The Black Hood did not drop to all fours, he remained human; and Craike's voice faded. Takya spoke in swift whisper.

"They are warned, you can never march against them twice by the same path. Only because they were unprepared did you succeed. Ho, Tousuth," she called, "do you now believe that we are well armed? Speak with a true tongue and say what you want of us."

"Yes," Jorik boomed, "you cannot take us, Master of power. Go your way, and we shall go ours—"

"There cannot be two powers in any land, as you should know, Jorik of the Eagles' towers, who tried once before to prove that and suffered thereby. There must be a victor here—and to the vanquished—naught!"

Craike could see the logic in that. But the Master was continuing:

"As to what we want here—it is a decision. Match your power against ours, changeling. And since you have not taken the witch, use her also if you wish. In the end it will come to the same thing, for both of you must be rendered helpless."

"Here and now?" asked Craike.

"Dawn comes, it will soon be another day. By sun or shadow, we care not in such a battle."

The elation of his quick success in that first try was gone. Craike fingered the bow he had not yet used. He shrank inwardly from the contest the other proposed, he was too uncertain of his powers. One victory had come from too little knowledge. Takya's hand curled about his stiff fingers once again. The impish mockery was back in her voice, ruffling his temper, irritating him into defiance.

"Show them what you can do, Lord Ka-rak, you who can master illusions."

He glanced down at her, and the sight of that cropped lock of hair at her temple gave him an odd confidence. Neither was Takya as all-powerful as she would have him believe.

"I accept your challenge," he called. "Let it be here and now."

"*We* accept your challenge!" Takya's flash of annoyance, her quick correction, pleased him. Before the echo of her words died away she hurled her first attack.

Witchfire leaped downslope to ring in the three men, playing briefly along the body of the dead Yily. It flickered up and down about their feet and legs so they stood washed in pallid flame, while about their heads darted winged shapes which might have been owls or other night hunters.

There was a malignant hissing; and the slope sprouted reptiles, moving in a wave. Illusions? All—or some. But designed, Craike understood, to divert the enemy's minds. He added a few of his own—a wolfish shape crouching in the shadow—leaping—to vanish as its paws cut the witchfire.

Swift as had been Takya's attack, so did those below parry. An oppressive weight, so tangible that Craike looked up to see if some mountain threatened them from overhead, began to close down upon the parapet. He heard a cry of alarm. There *was* a black cloud to be seen now, a giant press closing upon them.

Balls of witchfire flashed out of the light pillars, darted at those on the parapet. One flew straight at Craike's face, its burning breath singeing his skin.

"Fool!" Takya's thought was a whip lash. "Illusions are only real for the believer."

He steadied, and the witch ball vanished. But he was badly shaken. This was outside any Esper training he had had, it was the very thing he had been conditioned against. He felt slow, clumsy, and he was ashamed that upon Takya must the burden of their defense now rest.

Upon her—Craike's eyes narrowed. He loosened her hold on him, did not try to contact her. There was too much chance of self-betrayal in that. His plan was utterly wild, but it had been well demonstrated that the Black Hoods could only be caught by the unexpected.

Another witch ball hurtled at him, and he leaped to the terrace, landing with a force which sent a lance of pain up his healing leg. But on the parapet a Craike still stood, shoulder to shoulder with Takya. To maintain that illusion was a task which made him sweat as he crept silently away from the tower.

He had made a security guard to astonish Takya, the wolf, all the other illusions. But they had been only wisps, things alive for the moment with no need for elaboration. To hold this semblance of himself was in some ways easier, some ways harder. It was easier to make, for the image was produced of self-knowledge, and it was harder, for it was meant to deceive masters of illusion.

Craike reached the steps to the rock of the offerings. The glow of the witch lights here was pale, and the ledge below dark. He crept down, one arrow held firmly in his hand.

Here the sense of oppression was a hundredfold worse, and he moved as one wading through a flood which entrapped limbs and brain. Blind, he went to all fours, feeling his way to the river.

He set the arrow between his teeth in a bite which indented its shaft. A knife would have been far better, but he had no time to beg Jorik's. He slipped over, shivering as the chill water took him. Then he swam under the arch.

It was comparatively easy to reach the shingle where the dugout of the Black Hoods had turned over. As he made his way to the shore he brushed against water-soaked cloth and realized he shared this scrap of gravel with the dead. Then, arrow still between his teeth, Craike climbed up behind the Black Hoods' position.

IX

The thorn hedge cloaked the rise above him. But he concentrated on the breaking of that illusion, wading on through a mass of thorns, intact to his eyes, thin air at his passing. Then he was behind the Black Hoods. Takya stood, a black-and-white figure on the wall above, beside the illusion Craike.

Now!

The illusion Craike swelled a little more than life size, while his creator gathered his feet under him, preparatory to attack. The Craike on the wall altered—anything to hold the attention of Tousuth for a crucial second or two. Monster grew from man, wings, horns, curved tusks, all embellishments Craike's imagination could add. He heard shouts from the tower.

But with the arrow as a dagger in his hand, he sprang, allowing himself in that moment to see only, to think only of a point on Tousuth's back.

The head drove in and in, and Tousuth went down on his knees, clutching at his chest, coughing. While Craike, with a savagery he had not known he possessed, leaned on the shaft to drive it deeper.

Fingers hooked about Craike's throat, cutting off air, dragging him back. He was pulled from Tousuth, loosing his hold on the arrow shaft to tear at the hands denying him breath. There was a red fog which even the witch lights could not pierce and the roaring in his head was far louder than the shouts from the tower.

Then he was flat on the ground, still moving feebly. But the hands were gone from his throat, and he gasped in air. Around him circled balls of fire, dripping, twirling, he closed his eyes against their glare.

"Lord—Lord!"

The hail reached him only faintly. Hands pulled at him, and he tried to resist. But when he opened his eyes it was to see Jorik's brown face: Jorik was at the tower—how had Craike returned there? Surely he *had* attacked Tousuth? Or was it all illusion?

"He is not dead."

Whether or not that was said to him, Craike did not know. But his fingers were at his throat and he winced from his own touch. Then an arm came under his shoulders, lifting him, and he had a dizzy moment until earth and gray sky settled into their proper places.

Takya was there, with Nickus and Zackuth hovering in the background of black-jerkined guardsmen who stared back at her sullenly over the bodies of the dead. For they were all dead—the Hooded Ones. There was Tousuth, his head in the sand. And his fellows crumpled beside him.

The witch girl chanted, and in her hands was a cat's cradle of black strands. The men who followed Tousuth cringed, and their fear was a cloud Craike could see. He grabbed at Jorik, won to his feet, and tried to hail Takya. But not even a croak came from his tortured throat. So he flung himself at her, one hand out like a sword blade to slash. It fell across that wicked net of hair, breaking it, and went to close upon Takya's wrist in a crushing grip.

"Enough!" He could get out that command mind to mind.

She drew in upon herself as a cat crouches for a spring, and spat, her eyes green with feral lusting fire. But he had an answer to that, read it in her own spark of fear at his touch. His hands twined in her hair.

"They are men," he pulled those black strands to emphasize his words, "they only obeyed orders. We have a quarrel with their masters, but not with them!"

"They hunted, and now they shall be hunted!"

"I have been hunted, as have you, witch woman. And while I live there shall be no more such hunts—whether I am hound or quarry."

"While you live—" Her menace was ready.

Suddenly Craike forced out a hoarse croak meant for laughter. "You, yourself, Takya, have put the arrow to this bow cord!"

He kept one hand tangled in her hair. But with the other he snatched from her belt the knife she had borrowed from Nickus and not returned. She screamed, beat against him with her fists, tried to bite. He mastered her roughly, not loosing his grip on that black silk. And then in sweeps of that well-whetted blade he did what the Black Hoods had failed in doing, he sawed through those lengths.

"I am leaving you no weapons, Takya. You shall not rule here as you have thought to do—" The exultation he had known when he had won his first victory against the Black Hoods was returning a hundred-fold. "For a while I shall pull those pretty claws of yours!" He wondered briefly how long it would take her hair to regrow. At least they would have a breathing spell before her powers returned.

Then, his arm still prisoning her shoulders, the mass of her hair streaming free from his left hand, he turned to face the guardsmen.

"Tell them to go," he thought, "taking their dead with them."

"You will go, taking these with you," she repeated aloud, stony calm.

One of the men dropped to his knees by Tousuth's body, then abased himself before Craike.

"We are your hounds, Master."

Craike found his voice at last. "You are no man's hound—for you are a man. Get you gone to Sampur and tell them that the power is no longer to make hind nor hound. If there are those who wish to share the fate of Tousuth, perhaps when they look upon him as dead they will think more of it."

"Lord, do you come also to Sampur to rule?" the other asked timidly.

Craike laughed. "Not until I have established my lordship else-where. Get you back to Sampur and trouble us no more."

He turned his back on the guardsmen and, drawing the silent Takya, still within the circle of his arm, with him, started back to the tower. The bowmen remained behind, and Craike and the girl were alone as they reached the upper level. He paused then and looked down into her set, expressionless face.

"What shall I do with you?"

"You have shamed me and taken my power from me. What does a warrior do with a female slave?" She formed a stark mind picture, hurling it at him as she had hurled the stone on the mesa.

With his left hand he whipped her hair across her face, smarting under that taunt.

"I have taken no slave, nor any woman in that fashion, nor shall I. Go your way, Takya, and fight me again if you wish when your hair has grown."

She studied him, and her astonishment was plain. Then she laughed and clutched at the hair, tearing it free from his grasp, bundling it into the front of her single garment.

"So be it, Ka-rak. It is war between us. But I am not departing hence yet a while." She broke away, and he could hear the scuff of her feet on the steps as she climbed to her own chamber in the tower.

"They are on their way, Lord, and they will keep to it." Jorik came up. He stretched. "It was a battle not altogether to my liking. For the honest giving of blows from one's hand is better than all this magic, potent as it is."

Craike sat down beside the fire. He could not have agreed more heartily with any suggestion. Now that it was over he felt drained of energy.

"I do not believe they will return," he wheezed hoarsely, very conscious of his bruised throat.

Nickus chuckled, and Zackuth barked his own laughter.

"Seeing how you handled the Lady, Lord, they want nothing more than to be out of your grasp and that as speedily as possible. Nor, when those of Sampur see what they bring with them, do I think we shall be sought out by others bearing drawn swords. Now," Jorik slapped his fat middle, "I could do with meat in my belly. And you, Lord, have taken such handling as needs good food to counter."

There was no mention of Takya, nor did any go to summon her when the meat was roasted. And Craike was content to have it so. He was too tired for any more heroics.

Nickus hummed a soft tune as he rubbed down his unstrung bow before wrapping it away from the river damp. And Craike was aware that the younger man glanced at him slyly when he thought the Esper's attention elsewhere. Jorik, too, appeared highly amused at some private thoughts, and he had fallen to beating time with one finger to Nickus' tune. Craike shifted uncomfortably. He was an actor who had forgotten his lines, a novice required to make a ritual move he did not understand. What they wanted of him he could not guess, for he was too tired to mind-touch. He only wanted sleep, and that he sought as soon as he painfully swallowed his last bite. But he heard through semistupor a surprised exclamation from Nickus.

"He goes not to seek her—to take her!"

Jorik's answer held something of approval in it. "To master such as the Lady Takya he will need full strength of power and limb. His is the wisest way, not to gulp the fruits of battle before the dust of the last charge is laid. She is his by shearing, but she is no meek ewe to come readily under any man's hand."

Takya did not appear the next day, nor the next. And Craike made no move to climb to her. His companions elaborately did not notice her absence as they worked together, setting in place fallen stones, bringing the tower into a better state of repair, or killing deer to smoke the meat. For as Jorik pointed out:

"Soon comes the season of cold. We must build us a snug place and have food under our hands before then." He broke off and gazed thoughtfully downstream. "This is also the fair time when countrymen bring their wares to market. There are traders in Sampur. We could offer our hides, even though they be newly fleshed, for salt and grain. And a bow—this Kaluf of whom you have spoken, would he not give a good price for a bow?"

Craike raised an eyebrow. "Sampur? But they have little cause to welcome us in Sampur."

"You and the Lady Takya, Lord, they might take arms against in fear. But if Zackuth and I went in the guise of wandering hunters—and Zackuth is of the Children of Noe, he could trade privately with his kin. We must have supplies, Lord, before the coming of the cold, and this is too fine a fortress to abandon."

So it was decided that Jorik and Zackuth were to try their luck with the traders. Nickus went to hunt, wreaking havoc among the flocks of migrating fowl, and Craike held the tower alone.

As he turned from seeing them away, he sighted the owl wheel out from the window slit of the upper chamber, its mournful cry sounding loud. On sudden impulse he went inside to climb the stair. There had been enough of her sulking. He sent that thought before him as an order. She did not reply. Craike's heart beat faster. Was—had she gone? The rough outer wall—was it possible to climb down that?

He flung himself up the last few steps and burst into the room. She was standing there, her shorn head high as if she and not he had been the victor. When he saw her Craike stopped. Then he moved again, faster than he had climbed those stairs. For in that moment the customs of this world were clear, he knew what he must do, what he wanted to do. If this revelation was some spell of Takya's he did not care.

Later he was aroused by the caress of silk on his body, felt her cool fingers as he had felt them drawing the poison from his wounds. It was a black belt, and she was making fast about him, murmuring words softly as she interwove strand with strand about his waist until there was no beginning nor end to be detected.

"My chain on you, man of power." Her eyes slanted down at him.

He buried both his hands in the ragged crop of hair from which those threads had been severed and so held her quiet for his kiss.

"My seal upon you, witch."

"What Tousuth would have done, you have accomplished for him," she observed pensively when he had given her a measure of freedom once again. "Only through you may I now use my power."

"Which is perhaps well for this land and those who dwell in it," he laughed. "We are now tied to a common destiny, my lady of river towers."

She sat up running her hands through her hair with some of her old caress.

"It will grow again," he consoled.

"To no purpose, except to pleasure my vanity. Yes, we are tied together. But you do not regret it, Ka-rak—"

"Neither do you, witch." There was no longer any barrier between their minds, as there was none between their bodies. "What destiny will you now spin for the two of us?"

"A great one. Tousuth knew my power-to-come. I would now realize it." Her chin went up. "And you with me, Ka-rak. By this," her hand rested lightly on the belt.

"Doubtless you will set us up as rulers over Sampur?" he said lazily.

"Sampur!" she sniffed. "This world is wide—" Her arms went out as if to encircle all which lay beyond the tower walls.

Craike drew her back to him jealously. "For that there is more than time enough. This is an hour for something else, even in a warlock's world."

GEROLDO'S INCREDIBLE TRICK

Raymond E. Feist

he comic was bombing. Nagafia had been a British colony at one time, so language wasn't his problem. Some of the jokes were too "American," but more than cultural differences were working against him. Simply put, he was awful.

"They sound like they're going to riot," Jillian said as she leaned forward to inspect her stage makeup.

"It's a raucous house," said the Great Geroldo.

"Only Quincy Monrow would book us into a civil war," said Jillian, waving her hand before her face, as if to clear away the almost-permanent haze of smoke which filled the tiny closet that passed for a dressing room of the Victoria Theatre in the city of Dafa-el-bara.

Geroldo moved past the young woman to stand before the mirror and check his own appearance. He spoke to her reflection over his shoulder in the mirror. "It's not a civil war." He pulled down one lower eyelid, as if doing so allowed him to see himself better in the dim light the single overhead bulb afforded. "It's simply their politics tend to . . . the rough side. Quincy swore this would be our last . . . difficult book-ing, if we did well. He said there were summer fairs in Europe that would prove profitable."

"I swore I heard gunfire," said Jillian as she inspected her costume prior to leaving the dressing room.

"Fireworks," answered the magician. "Besides, the notice from the State Department only urged caution . . ."

"Notice?" said Jillian, her features darkening in anger. "You mean there's a State Department Advisory on Nagafia and you didn't tell me?"

Geroldo turned and smiled, his makeup and badly capped teeth making him look like nothing so much as a badly made-up clown rather than a master magician. "I didn't wish to alarm you, dear."

"You didn't wish to alarm me?" she shouted as the crossed to stand before him, leaning forward so as to be nearly nose-to-nose with him. "You mean you knew I wouldn't come, you drunken idiot!"

"I will not be spoken to in that manner, young lady! I am your father!"

"You are not my father. You're the man Mom was married to when she died. Not the same thing."

"I'm your step-father," he said unblinkingly, holding her gaze.

Jillian sighed and closed her eyes. After a silent moment she opened her eyes and said, "Yes, you are, and you've been a good one in the ways that count." She let her anger flow away as she always did with Jerry and kissed him on the nose. "But try to behave. This is a Muslim country and they don't like drinking."

"I haven't had a drop—"

"Since breakfast," she finished.

"Just a drop, then, to soothe my jet-jangled nerves," he said, returning to inspecting his face in the mirror.

"After we get home, I think you'd better start looking for another girl," Jillian said.

Geroldo turned. "Why?"

"I'm thinking of quitting," Jillian said. "What did you think: we'd need two idiot girls in this act?"

"Why are you thinking of quitting?" he asked.

"Because I'm thirty-two years old and look forty-two!" said Jillian, studying her reflection. Her face was thin, and she kept herself fit, because the stage work for her was strenuous. Still, she knew she wasn't what any man would call pretty. Interesting, attractive, even "handsome," but never pretty. "The only men I meet are comics, saxophone players, and agents. They're all married, gay, drug addicts, or dumber than dirt." Her voice turned softer, despite the crowd's shouts of anger coming through the door. "I'd like to find a man, get married, and have kids, Jerry. I don't have that many years left."

Geroldo was about to say something when the door opened. "Don't you knock?" shouted Jillian to the theater's stage manager as he shoved open the door.

"You're next," he said, ignoring her question, though he seemed to be taking inventory of every spangle on her costume. Wearing nude tights under the brief outfit gave Jillian the appearance of being scantily clad, despite the fact that she was covered from neck to toe. "I urge you to be good," he continued in his oddly Etonian accent, made all the more incongruous by his almost cliché Arabic appearance. "The audience didn't care for the comic, I'm sorry to say."

Suddenly loud shots rang out from behind the theater. Jillian jumped, putting her hand to her mouth. "What was that?"

"That was the comic, I'm *very* sorry to say," said the manager, looking nervous. "Colonel Zosma is in the audience tonight. *He* thought the comic was very bad." He shook his head. "Bad performance. Very bad. You should strive to be very good for the colonel. Our leader can be . . . unpredictable," he finished as he moved through the door.

The door closed and Jillian said, "Zosma! He's that murderer . . ."

"Now, Jillian," said Geroldo, as he stood. He patted her hand in a reassuring fashion. "We'll dazzle them. I'm sure these rustics haven't seen any of our wonders."

"These rustics have automatic weapons," said Jillian, anger mixed with terror on her face. "And they're obviously inclined to use them. You've never had theater critics like these, Jerry."

"Well, we shall simply do our very best, shan't we?"

As he turned to leave the room, Jillian pulled on his hand. Softly, but urgently, she said, "Since I was a child, Jerry, you've been telling me about what you called your 'incredible trick.' Now might be a good time to use it."

Geroldo stopped. "It's a difficult thing to do, Jillian, and far too subtle for a room of this size. And, above all, the timing must be absolutely perfect." He was silent a moment, then said, "Besides, I haven't practiced it in years. Though I don't know if practice is required." Shaking his head, he added almost absently, "I'm sorry, but I can't imagine how that particular trick could help us."

He moved down the narrow, dark hall to the side of the stage, as the theater crew finished moving his props to the locations he had marked out that morning. Jillian overtook him and said, "Before I die, I'd like to know what it is."

Patting her hand again, he said, "Someday, I'll tell you."

He pecked through the side of the curtain and Jillian leaned down to see from below his chin. The theater had been built during the English colonial period; the stalls were filled with common folks, most wearing white shirts and black pants, though a few suits could be seen, as well as traditional robes. The dress circle was packed with men in military garb, all carrying side arms. Each aisle was guarded by soldiers carrying automatic weapons. In the box overhanging the far side of the stage a large man with a ridiculous number of medals on his chest sat grinning.

That grin caused Jillian to shiver.

Then the sound man started their pre-recorded music and Geroldo said, "We're on."

As the curtains parted, Jillian said, "Jerry, I'm frightened."

Geroldo smiled his broadest smile and said, "Courage, daughter. We shall endure."

He strode out to the center of the stage, greeted by a murmur of voices. When Jillian followed, several men laughed, while others hooted and cheered what appeared to be an ample display of Western female flesh. Jillian wished she had worn black tights instead of the nude ones.

The audience stared with expectation, their features made all the more alien by the reflected stage lights. Half-darkened, half-revealed, they resembled a jury of demons far more than an audience desiring entertainment. Jillian put aside her fears and let years of stage rehearsals take over; focusing on the act took her mind away from fear.

The act started as it always did, with some rings, silk scarves, and cylinders, moving quickly to more elaborate illusions. The equipment was old, but well cared for, and while the choice of illusions would have seemed old-fashioned, even quaint, and commonplace in the United States, the Great Geroldo and his step-daughter had been playing rural theaters in small countries for years, to a steady if not significant financial reward.

But there was something different about this night. Colonel Izar Zosma, recently "elected" by a narrow margin in a one-man race, with his armed men counting the ballots, sat grinning at the performance. There was, however, nothing mirthful in the man's expression. His dark features were made even more sinister by a week's growth of unshaved beard. He sat motionless, his smile never fading, and as each moment passed without reaction from the crowd, Jillian knew their lives were in jeopardy.

Then things started going wrong. Stage magic is always a matter of rhythm, timing, and even a half-second delay can ruin the effect of an illusion. A prop not handled deftly, a fumble on an exchange, and Geroldo and Jillian were playing catch-up. The tape recorder was unrelenting. Where a canny live conductor might have covered a mistake, as each new gaffe was made the recording made the compounded errors all the more obvious to the audience.

By the time they reached the climax of the act, the entire theater was silent. Only the music from the tape recorder reverberated in the hall. The sound of equipment scraping across the badly finished stage sounded unnervingly loud to Jillian as she readied the last illusion. Geroldo's constant narration echoed through the theater as if they were in an empty hall. Jillian tried not to shiver.

Geroldo began the final stage in preparing for his Trunk-of-Death illusion. He was showing the razor sharp blades he used, the ones Jillian would be shoving through the trunk as he expertly bent his body around them, when Colonel Zosma stood.

Every eye in the house turned toward the dictator, who stepped over the edge of the balcony and dropped easily to the stage. A hefty man, he walked lightly on the balls of his feet, as one would expect a powerful athlete to move, to where Geroldo waited. The soundman turned off the music.

The colonel held out his hand and Geroldo put one of the blades in it. He gripped the hilt of the stage sword, then slashed through the air suddenly, causing Jillian to step back. He cut through the air an inch from Geroldo's nose, but the old magician didn't flinch.

With a surprisingly cultured accent, Zosma said, "I've always loved this trick." He slapped the flat of the blade against his hand. "Always wondered how you magicians did it."

Geroldo smiled and said, "A magician never—"

"Reveals his tricks!" shouted Zosma and the entire audience drew in a breath. "I could have you shot if you don't tell me."

Geroldo said, "But, Your Excellency—"

"Colonel!" The man almost hissed his title. "You," he said to Jillian. "Open that box!"

Jillian hesitated only an instant, then opened the trunk. The colonel glanced inside, ran his hand around the inner surface, then stood upright. "Get in," he said to Geroldo.

Jerry looked at Jillian, who was now ashen, and said, "Courage, daughter."

He stepped inside and, if anything, looked more dignified than Jillian had ever seen him look in her life. A drunk, a depressive, and by any measure only a mediocre sleight-of-hand merchant, he was still the only family she had, and she loved him. Now some madman was on the verge of killing him before her eyes.

"I shall insert the swords!" shouted Zosma as Jillian closed the trunk on her step-father.

To Jillian, Zosma said, "You Westerners think us fools! I know that this trick works because he knows where you will place the swords, first one there, then another, then a third, and he artfully drapes his body around them. Let's see how he likes surprises!"

Turning, Zosma circled the trunk, selected one slot at random, and drove the sword into it. Jillian gasped, but the audience remained silent. Jillian could barely stay on her feet as her knees trembled. The slot was one that was used for the fifth sword, and if Jerry had been in the wrong position, it would have skewered him like a turkey on a spit.

But the sword slid through and no sound issued from the trunk.

Jillian hoped Jerry was listening to where the madman was walking, trying to anticipate where the sword would next appear. As if reading her thoughts, Zosma grabbed up another sword off the table and almost tiptoed around the trunk, then inserted the blade in another slot, pushing it through quickly. There was a slight hesitation, as if he were meeting resistance, then the blade slid home. No sound came from the man inside, and Jillian forced herself to breathe.

Nine swords would enter that trunk and as each was added, Geroldo was required to assume a more difficult position. Part of what made it possible for him to survive the illusion was pressing his body hard against the already-inserted blades, against the flat or back of the blade. The order of insertion was critical.

Zosma quickly inserted the third, fourth, and fifth blades, but still no noise came from inside. Jillian worried that Jerry might have been killed by the first blade, and that was the reason for his silence.

Zosma slowed, as if each added blade would be the killing one. The sixth slid home, the seventh, the eighth.

Then the last blade. Zosma lingered over the top slot, the one which would have been the final blade in the normal course of events. But if Jerry had to be out of position to avoid the first eight, he would be in line for a killing blow.

Colonel Zosma inserted the blade, paused, then slammed down hard. It met with resistance, and Jillian felt her knees threatening to buckle. That was part of the act, an effect that got a reaction from even the most blasé of crowds. And it worked again, as a gasp escaped from the heretofore silent audience.

Zosma drove the sword to the hilt, then waited.

He walked around the trunk, saying at last, "Remove them."

Jillian prayed silently, removing the blades in the correct order, so that if Jerry was still alive he would have a chance of escaping injury. When the last blade was removed, Zosma said, "Open the trunk."

She reached toward the latch, her hand trembling visibly. She released the catch, flipped it, and pushed open the trunk. Like a giant upright clamshell, it swung wide to reveal its contents.

The Great Geroldo, master illusionist, the toast of five continents, self-appointed member of the Magician's Hall of Fame, sat crouched inside. "Give us a hand, will you, Jilly dear," he said. "I'm a bit cramped in here."

Jillian reached in and put her hand under Jerry's arm, giving him some support as he climbed out of the trunk. Whispering, he said, "The good colonel was so slow I got a bit stiff waiting for the finale."

The audience went wild.

Zosma stood there a moment like a man defeated in a contest, then suddenly his mad grin was back. "Wonderful!" he said.

He slapped Geroldo on the back and said, "You are very good, my friend. Very, very good. I am very pleasantly surprised!" He turned back to the box where his entourage waited for him. To one of the officers in the box he shouted, "Give this man some money. See he and his assistant get safely back to the airport tomorrow!"

He signaled that he was departing, and the soldiers in the audience moved quickly to provide coverage for him, as the curtain closed on the magician and his step-daughter.

Geroldo adjusted his clothing, and turned slowly toward the dressing room. His knees appeared to be weak and Jillian hurried to help him. "You look terrible," she whispered.

"Not here," he answered, and they were silent as he slowly let her half-carry him to the dressing room.

As Jillian helped Jerry sit, a knock came at the door. She opened it and found a soldier outside; he handed her an envelope. She closed the door and opened the envelope. "Jerry, there's over ten thousand pounds here!"

"Good," said Geroldo. "We're going to need it. Now, be a dear and send for the house manager. Have him quietly fetch a discreet doctor and bring him post-haste."

"Doctor?" said Jillian. "What's wrong?"

Geroldo, never one to let a theatrical moment pass untouched, slowly stood, then held opened his swallow-tailed coat, revealing his pristine white shirt. After a moment, Jillian saw a red stain appear, then another, then suddenly blood flowed and Geroldo went pale.

"The best trick I know, daughter, the one I've never wished to show, is one that really has had, until now, little theatrical relevance." He slowly lowered himself back into his chair. "I learned it one summer from a Hindu fakir, actually." He was on the verge of fainting when he said, "It's really quite a strange little thing, but under the right circumstances I can keep from bleeding for periods of time."

Jillian was moving to the door to call the house manager as the Great Geroldo slid from his chair. His last thought before unconsciousness swept over him was that this had been a very unlikely venue, and a less than ideal audience, before which to finally, after years of secrecy, reveal his incredible trick. After the doctor patched him up, he'd have to think of a way to incorporate it into his act. Still, he thought as darkness closed in around him, the timing *was* perfect.

WILLOW

C.J. Cherryh

even days he had been riding, up from the valley and the smoke of burned fields, and down again with the mountain wall at his back, a winding trail of barren crags and eagles' perches, gray sere brush and struggling juniper. The horse he rode plodded in sullen misery, gaunt and galled. His armor was scarred with use and wanted repair he neglected to give it; that was the way he traveled, outward from the war, from his youth which he had lost there and his service which he had left.

Dubhan was his name, and far across the land in front of him was his home, but the way looked different than it had looked ten years ago. He remembered fields and villages and the sun on the mountains when he rode up to them, when the horse was young, his colors bright and his armor gleaming as he rode up to the duke's service—but now when the winding trail afforded sometime glimpses of the plains, they seemed colorless. It was the season, perhaps; he had come in a spring-time. He rode out in a summer's ending, and that might be the reason, or the color might have been in his eyes once, when he had been easily deceived, before the old duke had taught him the world, and the lord he served changed lords, and knights who had defended the land drifted into plunder of it, and the towns fell, and the smokes went up and the fields were sown with bones and iron, and the birds hunted carrion in roofless cottages. Maybe the war had spilled beyond the mountains; maybe it had covered all the world and stripped it bare. It had taken him this long to remember what sunlit green he had seen here once, but no longer seeing it did not surprise him, as worse sights had ceased to surprise him. There were scars on him which had not been there that springtime ten years gone. He ached where the mail bore down on old wounds; pains settled knife-pointed into joints in nighttime cold and made him know what pains years ahead held, lordless and landless and looking—late—for another lord, another place, and some more hopeful war while there was something left of vigor in his arm, some strength to trade on to put a roof over his head before he was too old, and too broken, and finally without hope. Bread to eat, a place to sleep, a little wine for the pains when it rained: that was what he rode out to find.

At one cut and another the nearer land lay spread below the rocks, dull tapestry of the tops of trees where the trail turned and some slide had taken away the curtaining scrub. The trees came nearer, and stretched farther as the trail wound down the mountainside, more of forest than he recalled. At such vantages he looked out and down, marking what he could of the road to come, all curtained below in trees and gray bush.

So he saw the birds start up, and drew in the horse so sharply that the old head came up and muscles tensed. A black beating of wings rose above the woods below, and hovered a time before settling back into that rough patterning of treetops elsewhere. He marked where, and moved the horse on, and got his battered shield out of its leather casing. He thought about his armor, regretting mending not done, and took his helmet from where it hung on his saddle, and kept toward the inside of the road whenever he came near some other open place, fearing some movement, some show of metal might betray him—prudence not of cowardice, but of cold purpose.

That was also the way of the war he had waged, that no one met

friends on the road. He rode carefully, and thought about the sound of
the horse's hooves and kept off bare stone where he could. He stalked
that remembered location in the woods below with wolfish hope—of
provisions, of which he was scant, and whatever else he could lay hand
to. If they were many he would try to ride by; if one man—that was
another matter.

The sun was sinking when he came to that lower ground. The
woods held no color but a taint of bloody light beyond the dull leaves.
The trees which had seemed small from above arched above the way,
gnarled and dark and rustling with the wind. Something had disturbed
the leaves and the brush which intruded onto the roadway: a broken
branch gleamed white splinters in the twilight. He kept on the way,
came on the fresh droppings of a horse, some beast better fed than his,
from some other trail than he had followed.

A thin, high sound disturbed the air, a voice, a woman's—sudden
silence. He reined close in, fixed the direction of the sound and rode
farther. There was someone in the dark ahead who took no account of
the noise she made; and someone there was who did. He drew his
sword from its sheath with the softest whisper of metal, kneed the
horse further, and it walked warily, ears pricked now, head thrust forward.

The trail forked sideways, and the leafy carpet was disturbed there,
ruffled by some passage. He kneed the horse onto it, kept it walking.
Fire gleamed, a bright point through the branches. Again the voice,
female and distraught; a man's low laughter . . . and Dubhan's mouth
stretched back from his teeth, a little harder breathing, a little grin
which had something of humor and something of lust. His heart beat
harder, drowning the soft whisper of the horse's moving through the
brush—jolted at the sudden rise of a black figure before the light in
front of him.

Two of them, or more. He spurred the horse, broke through the
brush into the light, swung the sword and hacked the standing figure,
saw one more start up from the woman's white body and wheeled the
horse on him, rode him down and reined the horse about the circuit of
the camp as two horses broke their picket and crashed off through the
brush. The first man, wounded, came at him with a sword; he rode on

him again and this time his blade bit between neck and shoulder, tumbled the armorless man into the dead leaves.

The woman ran, white flashing of limbs in the firelight. He jerked the horse's head over and spurred after, grinning for breath and for anticipation, reined in when she darted into the brush and the rocks—he vaulted down from the saddle and labored after, armor-burdened, in and out among the brush and the branches, with one thought now—some woman of the towns, some prize worth the keeping while she lasted, or something they had gotten hereabouts from the farms. He saw her ahead of him, naked among the rocks, trying to climb the shoulder of the mountain where it thrust out into the forest, white flesh and cloud of shadow-hair, shifting from one to the other foothold and level among the black stones. "Come down," he mocked her. "Come down."

She turned where she stood above him, and looked at him with her pale fingers clutching the rock on her right, her hair blowing about her body. Looked up again, where the rocks became an upward thrust, a wall, unclimbable. "Come down to me," he called again. "I'm all the choice you have."

She made a sign at him, an ancient one. The fingers let go the rock—a blur of white through shadow, a cry, a body striking the rocks. She sprawled broken and open-eyed close by him, and moisture was on his face and his hands. He wiped at his mouth and stood shuddering an instant, swore and stalked off, blood cooled, blood chilled, a sickness moiling at his gut.

Waste. A sorry waste. No one to see it, no one to know, no one that cared for a trifle like that, to be dead over it, and useless. A little warmth, a little comfort; there was not even that.

He found his horse, bewildered and lost in the brush, took its reins and led it back to the fire where he hoped for something of value, where two dead men lay in their blood; but the horses had run off in the dark and the woods.

There was food, at least; he found that in the saddlebags by the fire, and chewed dried beef while he searched further. There were ordinary oddments, bits of leather and cord and a pot of salve; and wrapped in a scrap of dirty cloth—gold.

His hands trembled on the heavy chalice-shape in unveiling it, trembled; and he laughed and thought about his luck which had been wrong all his life until now. Gold. He rummaged the other saddlebags, hefting them and feeling the weight with his heart pounding in his chest. Out of one came a second object wrapped in cloth, which glittered in the firelight, and weighed heavy in his hands. A cross. Church plunder. They had gotten to that in the last stages.

He let it down with a wiping of his hands on his thighs, gnawed his lip and gathered it up again, shoved it into one bag. Then he snatched another bit of the beef, swallowing the last . . . found a wine flask by the fire and washed it down. He knelt there staring thoughtfully at the dead face of the first man, which lay at an odd angle on a severed neck. Familiarity tugged at him . . . someone he had seen before; but in ten years he had seen many a man on both sides, and bearded, dead and dirty faces tended to look much alike. He drank deeply, warmed the death from his own belly, got up to tend his horse and paused by the other corpse, the one the horse had trod down.

Then familiarity did come home to him . . . long, long years, that he had known this man. Bryaut, his name was, Bryaut Dain's-son; young with him; afraid with him in his first battle; wounded in another . . . ways parted in the war and came together again here, tonight. Of a sudden the wine was sour in his mouth. He could have ridden in on the camp and Bryaut would have welcomed him. Not many men would, in these days; but this man would have. If there had been friends in his service—this was one, a long time ago, and mostly forgotten; but there was the face, no older than his, and blond, and with that scar down the brow he had gotten at Lugdan, when he himself had gotten the one on his jaw, where the beard would not grow.

He swore, and was ashamed in front of that dead face with its eyes looking sideways toward the fire, as if it had stopped paying attention. There was a time they had talked about winning honor for themselves, he and this young man no longer young, wealth and honor. And then he laughed a sickly laugh, thinking of the church-robbing and the woman and what an end it had come to, the war and the things they had planned and the reasons they had had for going to it at all. Bright treasure and fine armor and a station close to a king; and it came all to this. Church gold and a cold woman. He tipped up the wine flask and drank and walked away, thinking with a wolf's wariness that there had been too much noise and too much firelight and that it was time to go.

He was wiser than Bryaut, and maybe soberer. He packed the gold and the food and the things he wanted onto his horse and climbed into the saddle with the flask in his hand . . . rode off slowly, leaving the fire to die on its own, with the dead eyes staring on it. When he slept finally it was in the saddle, with the flask empty; and the horse staggered to a stop and stood there till he mustered the strength to climb down and shelter in the brush.

There he slept again in his armor, his sword naked across his knees—dreamed, of towns burning and of dead faces and naked white limbs plunging past him; waked with an outcry, and shuddered to sleep again.

Dreamed of a church, and fire, and a priest nailed to his own chapel door.

Lugdan and the mindless push of bodies, the battering, hours-long thunder of metal and human voices; and the silence after—the empty, feelingless silence—

A stone-walled room with candles burning, a gleam of gold on the altar, the chalice brimming full, the solemn sweet chanting of voices echoing out of his youth. The Lady Chapel, the blue-robed statue with painted eyes, hands offering blessings for all who came . . . The silence fell here too, taking away the voices, and the candles went out in the wind.

The stones became jumbled, and the wind blew, scattering smoke-black hair across pale features. The silence shrilled asunder, the shriek of the woman, the white limbs falling. . . .

He cried out, and the horse started and shied off through the thicket, stopped when the brush stopped it and he scrambled after it cursing, still dazed with sleep and dreams, scratched by brush across his face and hands.

Daylight had pierced the canopy of leaves. He retrieved his sword and sheathed it, checked the girth, dragged himself back into the saddle and rode on, on a trail narrower than he recalled. A bird sang, incongruous in the shadow where he traveled, under the arch of branches, some bird sitting where the sun touched the tops of the trees, some bird seeing something other than the dead brush and old leaves and the contorted trunks; and he hated it. He spurred the horse at times where the road was wider, pushed it until the froth flew back on his knees and its bony sides heaved when he let it walk. He spurred it again when he saw daylight beyond, and it ran from dark to light, slowed again, panting, under the sun, where the forest gave way to open grass and brush, and the road met another road from the west.

It was not the way that he remembered. He traveled with the sun on his back, warming now until sweat ran under the armor and prickled in the hollows of his body and stuck his padding to his sides and arms and thighs. By afternoon the way led downward again, into yet another valley, and by now he knew himself lost. There were signs of man, a boundary stone, a mark of sometime wheels on the narrow road, which wended two ways from a certain point—one which tended, wheel-rutted, west, and one which tended easterly, overgrown with grass, snaking toward a distant rim of woods.

He had no heart now for meetings, for braving alone the farmers who would have feared him if he had come with comrades. A knight alone might have his throat cut and worse if the peasants had their chance at him. He had seen the like. It was the eastward way he chose, away from humankind and homes, only wanting to go through the land and to find himself somewhere the war had never been, where no one had heard of it or suffered of it, where he could melt down his gold and pass it off bit by bit, find a haven and a comfort for the rest of his years.

Sometimes he would sleep as he rode, his head sinking forward on his chest while his hand, the reins wrapped about his fingers, rested behind the high bow. The horse plodded its way along, stole mouthfuls from brush along the track, dipped its head now and again to snatch at the grass, which pitching movements woke him, and he would straighten his back at waking, and feel relieved at the daylight still about him. He dreamed of fire and burnings; those had been his dreams for months. He no longer started awake out of them, only shivered in the sweat-prickling sun and listened to the ordinary sounds of leather and metal moving, and the whisper of the grass and the cadence of the hooves. He tried not to sleep, not for dread of the dreams, but because of the road and the danger; but the sounds kept up, and the insects sang in the late summer sun, and try as he would his head began to nod, and his eyes to close, not for long, for a little time: the horse was only waiting its chance for thefts, and it would wake him.

A downward step jolted him, a sudden sinking of the horse's right shoulder, a splash of water about the hooves at every move. He lifted his head in the twilight haze and saw green slim leaves about him, weeping branches and watery waste closely hemmed with trees and brush. Mud sucked, and the horse lurched across the low place, wandered onto firmer grass.

Dubhan turned in the saddle, looking for the path, but the brush was solid behind, and the place looked no different in that direction, closed off with trees trailing their branches into the scummed water, mazed with heaps of brush and old logs and pitted with deeper pools. Willow fingers trailed over him as the horse kept its mindless course—he faced about and fended the trailers with his arm, and the horse never slowed, never hesitated, as if it had gone mad in its exhaustion, one step and the other through the sucking mud and the shallow pools. The light was going; the sky above the willow tangle was bloodied cream, the gloom stealing through the thickets and taking the color from willow and water bit by bit, fading everything to one deadly deceptive flatness. He tugged at the reins and stopped the horse, but no sooner did he let the reins slack than the horse tugged for more rein and started moving again its same slow way, never faltering but for footing in the marsh, patient in its slow self-destruction. Frogs sang a numbing song. The water gurgled and splashed about the hooves and a reek of corruption went up from the mud, cloying. The water wept, a strange liquid sound. He pulled again at the reins, and the horse—instantly responsive in battle—ignored the bit and tugged back, going madly on. He wrapped his hand the tighter in the rein and hauled back with his strength against it, forcing the beast's head back against its chest, and then he could stop it . . . but whenever he let the rein loosen, it took its head again, and bent its head this way and that against the force he brought to bear; he hauled its head aside and faced it about to confuse it from its course, but it kept turning full circle, feet sliding in the mire, and came back again to force a few steps more. He cursed it, he cajoled it, the old horse he had ridden young to the war, he reminded it of days past and the time to

come, some better land, some warm shelter against the winter, no more
of fighting, no more of sleeping cold. But the horse kept moving in the
colorless twilight, with the sky gone now to lowering gray, and the water
weeping and splashing in the silence.

Something touched his eyes, like cobweb, crawled on his face and
hands. He waved his hand, and the cloud came about him, midges
started up from the reeds and the water; they crawled over his skin,
buzzed about his ears, investigated the crack of his lips and settled into
his eyes and his ears and were sucked up his nose. The horse snorted
and threw its head, moved faster now, and Dubhan flailed about him
with his free hand, wiped his eyes and blew and spat, blinded, inhaling
them, clinging to the horse as the horse lashed its tail and shook itself
and pitched into a lurching run. Branches whipped past, raked at
Dubhan, and he tucked down as much as he could, clung to reins and
saddle and clenched his hand into the war-horse's shorn mane, shorn so
no enemy could hold; and now he could not, and reeled stunned and
bruised when a branch hit his shoulder and jolted him back against the
cantle and the girth. The horse staggered and slid in the mud, recov-
ered itself, feet wide-braced, head down.

Then the head came up and the legs heaved and the horse waded
fetlock deep, slowly, on its winding course, while the sobbing sounded
clearer than before. Dubhan clung, wiped at his eyes with one hand,
body moving to the relentless moving of the beast he rode. He crossed
himself with that hand, and remembered what he had in the saddlebags—a memory too of painted eyes, and fire and darkness, voices
silenced. Fear gathered in his gut and settled lower and sent up coils
that knotted about his heart. His hand no longer fought the reins . . . no
hope now of going back, in that mad course he had no idea which way
they had turned, or how far they had come. He had faith now only in
the horse's madness, that terror might be driving it, that his brave horse
which had charged at the king's iron lines might be running now, and it
might in its madness get him through this place if only it could walk the
night through and not leave him afoot here and lost. He talked to it, he
patted its gaunt neck, he pleaded; but it changed its going not at all,
neither faster nor slower, though the breath came hollow from its mouth
and its shoulders were lathered with sweat.

They passed into deeper shadow, under aged willows, through curtains of branches which trailed cutting caresses and kept night under
their canopies, back into twilight and into night again, and the sobbing
grew more human, prickling the hairs at Dubhan's nape and freezing
the life from his hands and feet. It became like a child's weeping, some
lost soul complaining in the night; it came from left and right and
behind him, from above, in the trees, and from before. There was no
sound but that; it wrapped him about. And suddenly in a prickling of
apprehension he turned in the saddle and jerked free the saddlebag,
tore it open and flung out the cup and the cross, which spun with a
cold gleaming through the curtain of willow branches and struck the
black water with a deep sound, swallowed up. The horse never ceased
to move. He turned about again in time to fend the branches, sweating
and cold at once. The gold was gone. It bought him nothing; the sobbing was before him now, and above, a gleam of pallor in the gnarled
willow-limbs of the next tree, a shadow-fall of hair. He saw a ghost, and
drove spurs into the horse.

The beast flinched, and stopped, panting bellowslike between his
legs, head sinking. He looked up into the branches and the gleam of
flesh was gone—looked down and beside him and a white figure with
shadow-hair moved the willow branches aside—all naked she was, and
small . . . and came toward him with hands held out, a piquant face
with vast dark eyes, a veil of hair that moved like smoke about white
skin. The eyes swam with tears in the halflight of the night. The hands
pleaded. The limbs were thin . . . a child's stature, a child's face. He dug
the spurs at the horse to ride past as he had ridden past the war's abandoned waifs: it was their eyes he saw, their pleading hands, their gaunt
ribs and matted hair and swollen bellies naked to the cold; but the
horse stayed and the small hands clutched at his stirrup and the face
which looked up to him was fair.

"Take me home," she asked of him. "I'm cold."

He kicked the stirrup to shake her fingers loose. She started back
and stood there, her hair for a veil about her breasts if she had any, her
body white and touched with shadow between the thighs like another
whiteness in the dark, among the rocks; but these eyes were live and
they stared, bruised and dark with fear.

"Was it you," he asked, "crying?"

"I gathered flowers," she said. "And men came." She began to cry again, tiny sobs. "I was running home."

His belief caught at that kind of story, held onto it double-fisted, an ugly thing and the kind of thing the world was, that made of the girl only a girl and the marsh only a river's sink and some homely place of safety not far from here. Slowly his hand reached out for her. She came and took it, her fingers cold and weak in his big hand; he gained his power to move and caught her frail wrist with the other hand, hauled her up before him—no weight at all for his arms. The horse began to move before she was settled; he adjusted the reins, tucked her up against him and her head burrowed against his shoulder, her arms going about his neck. His hand about her ribs felt not bone but softness swelling beneath his fingers, smooth skin; his eyes looking down saw a dark head and a flood of shadowy hair, and the rising moon played shadow-tricks on the childish body, rounded a naked hip, lengthened thighs and cast shadow between. Her body grew warm. She shifted and moved her legs, her arms hugging him the tighter, and the blood in him grew warm. Willow branches trailed over them with the horse's wandering and he no more than noticed, obsessed with his hands which might shift and not find objection to their exploring, with a thin body the mail kept from him, kept him from feeling with his.

It was a child's clinging, a child's fear; he kept the hands still where they were, on naked back and under naked knees, and patted her and soothed her, with a quieter warming in his blood that came from another human body in the night, a child's arms that expected no harm of him; and he gave none—should not be carrying double on the horse, his numbed wits recollected. He ought to get down and lead, the child sitting in the saddle, but the horse moved steadily and she seemed no weight at all on him, slept now, as it seemed, one arm falling from his neck to lie in her lap, delicate fingers upturned in the moonlight like some rare waterflower. Moonlight lay bright beyond the branches; the horse walked now on solid ground. The branches parted on a road, flat and broad, and he blinked in sleep-dulled amazement, not remembering how that had started or when they had come on it.

Hills shadowed against the night sky, a darkness against the stars: a mass of stone hove up before that, on the very roadside, placed like some wayside inn, but warlike, blockish, tall, a jumble of planes and shadow, far other than the woodcutter's cottage he had imagined.

"Child," he whispered. "Child. Is this your home?"

She stirred in his arms, another shifting of softness against his fingers, looked out into the dark between the horse's ears. "Yes," she breathed.

"There are no lights."

"They must be abed."

"With you lost?" A servant's child, perhaps, no one of consequence to the lords of the place; but then a lord who cared little for his people—he had served such a lord, and fought one, and lost himself. Apprehension settled back at his shoulders, but the horse plodded forward and the stone shadow loomed nearer in the moonlight, not nearly so large as it had seemed a moment ago, a tower, a mere tower, and badly ruined. Some woodcutter after all, it might be, some peasant borrowing a former greatness, settling himself in a tower's shell. The child's arms went again about his neck. He gathered the small body close to him for his own comfort. Exhaustion hazed his wits. The keep seemed now large again, and close. He had no memory of the horse's steps which had carried them into the looming shadow of the place, up to the man-sized stones, up to the solid wooden door.

He hugged the child against him, and then as she stirred, set her off, himself got down from the saddle, his knees buckling under his own mailed weight. She sought his hand with both of hers, and in her timid trust he grew braver. He walked up the steps leading her and slammed his fist against the ironbound oak, angered by their sleeping carelessness inside, that owed a lost child shelter and owed her rescuer—something, some reward. The blows thundered. He expected a stir, a flare of lights, a hailing from inside, even the rush of men to arms.

But the door gave back suddenly, swinging inward, unbarred or never barred. He thrust the child loose from his hand in sudden dread, drew his sword, seeing the gleam of light in the crack as he pushed the door with his shoulder, sending the massive weight farther ajar. A night fire burned in the hearth of a great fireplace, the only light, flaring in the sudden draft. He felt behind him for the child, half fearing to find her gone, felt a naked shoulder. The horse snorted, a soft, weary explosion in the dark at his back, ordinary and unalarmed. He walked in. The child followed and slipped free, pushed the door to with a straining of her slight body. "I'll find Mother," she said. "She'll be sleeping."

"No longer." He struck with his naked sword at a kettle hanging from a chain against the wall; it clattered down and rolled across the flags with a horrid racket. "Wake! Where are the parents of this child?"

"Child," the echoes answered. "Child, child, child."

"Mother?" the girl cried. He reached too late to stop her. She darted for the stairs which wound up and out of sight, built crazily toward the closed end of the high ceiling. "Girl," he called after her, and those echoes mingled with those of "Mother?" and likewise died, leaving him alone.

He retreated toward the door, shifted his grip on the swordhilt to pull the door open again and look outside, wary of ambushes, of a mind now to be away from this place. His horse still stood, cropping the grass in the moonlight.

Footsteps creaked on the stairs. The child came running down again as he whirled about, the naked body clothed now in a white shift. She came to him, caught his hand with hers. "Mother says you must stay," she said, wide dark eyes looking up into his. "She was afraid. We're all alone here, mother and I. She was afraid to let it seem anyone lived here. The bandits might come. Please stay; please be careful of my mother, please."

"Child?" he asked, but the hands broke from his and she ran, a flitting of white limbs and white shift in the dim firelight, vanishing up the stairs. He pushed the door gently, felt it close and looked back toward the fire—drew in his breath, bewildered. His exhausted senses had played him tricks again. About him the hall stretched farther than he had realized. The shadows and the fire's glare had masked a farther hall, which could not have appeared from the road. A table stood there, set with silver. Arms hung on the walls of that chamber, fighting weapons, not show.

A light flickered in the corner of his eye; he looked and saw a glow moving down the wall of the stairs . . . a woman came into his view, carrying a taper in her hand, and his heart lurched, for the child's beauty was nothing to hers. The woman's hair was a midnight cloud about her in her white shift and robe, her face in the candle's glow as translucent and pure as the wax gleaming in the heat, her body parting the strands of her hair with the full curves of breast and hip. Barefoot she walked down the wooden steps, her eyes wide with apprehension.

"You brought Willow home."

He nodded agreement and faint courtesy, the sword still naked in his hand. The woman came off the last step and walked to him, a vision in the candlelight, which shone reflected in her eyes with a great sadness.

"Willow's mad," she said in a voice to match her eyes. "Did you realize, sir? She runs out into the woods . . . I can't hold her at such times. Thank you for bringing her safe home again." Lashes swept, a soft glance up at him. "Please, I'll help you with your horse, sir, and give you a place to sleep in the hall."

"Forgive me," he said, remembering the drawn sword. He reached for the sheath and ran it in, looked again at the lady. Food, shelter, the warmth of the hall. . . . *We're all alone*, the child had said. He looked at wide dark eyes and woman's body and delicate hands which clasped anxiously together about the candle—like Willow's hands, fine-boned and frail. He was staring. Heat rose to his face, a warmth all over. "I'll tend my horse," he said. "But I'd be glad of a meal and shelter, lady."

"There's a pen in back," she said. "We have a cow for milk. There's hay."

"Lady," he said, his brain still singing with warmth as if bees had lodged there and buzzed along his veins. He bowed, went out, into the dark, to take the reins of his horse and lead the poor animal around the curve of the tower—it *was* extended on the far side: he could see that now, from this new vantage. A byre was built against the wall, several pens, a sleepy cow who lurched to her feet in the moonlight and stood staring with dark bovine eyes. He led the horse in, gently unsaddled it, rubbed its galled and sweaty back with hands full of clean straw while the cow watched. He did his best for the horse, though his bones ached with the weight of armor and the ride. He hugged its gaunt neck when he was done, patted it, remembering a glossier feel to its coat, a day

when bones had not lain so close to the skin. It bowed its head and
nosed his ribs as it had done in gentler days before wars, before the
hooves were shod with iron. It lipped his hand. The wide-eyed cow
lowed in the dark, the moonlight on her crescent horns, and he pitch-
forked hay for them both, farmer's work, armored as he was, and made
sure that there was water, then walked out the gate and latched it,
walked around the curving stone wall, up the steps, opened the yielding
door.

The fire inside was bright and red, the board in the recessed hall
spread with bread and cold roast on silver plates and set with jugs of
wine. He rubbed at his face, stopped, numb in the loss of time. He had
dallied in the yard and the lady—the lady stood behind the table,
spread her white-sleeved arms to welcome him to all that she had done.

He came and sat down in the tall chair, too hungry even to unbur-
den himself of the armor, seized up a cup of dry red wine and drank,
filled his mouth with fresh bread and honey and with the other hand
worked at the straps at his side. Strength flooded back into him with a
few mouthfuls. He looked up from his piggishness and saw her at the
other end of the table with her dark eyes laughing at him, not unkindly.

Such manners he had gained in the wars. He had aspired to better,
once. He stood up and rid himself of belt and sword, hung the weapon
over the chair's tall finial, and she rose and moved to help him shed the
heavy mail. That weight and heat passed from him and he breathed a
great free breath, shed the sweat-soaked haqueton, down to shirt and
breeches, fell into the chair again and ate his fill, off silver plates, drank
of a jeweled cup—and paused, heart thumping as he turned it within
his hand: the shape the same, the very same. . . .

But silver, not gold. He drained it, gazed into dark and lovely eyes
beyond the candleglow. "Is there," he asked thickly, "no lord in this
hall . . . no servant, no one—but you and the child?"

"The war," she said with that same sadness in her eyes. "I had a servant, but he stole most all the coin and ran away. The villagers beyond
the hills . . . they'll not come here. Willow frightens them; and I'm
frightened of them—for Willow's sake, you see."

"What of your lord?"

"The war," she said. "He's not come home."

"His name?"

"Bryaut."

His breath stopped in him. He looked about the hall beyond her shoulders for some crest, some device—there was none. "Not Dain's-son—"

"You know him? You have news of him?"

"Dead," he said harshly. The lovely eyes filled with tears. The mouth trembled. "In the war," he said.

"Bravely?"

She asked that much. He stared past her, saw the trampled, half-naked man on the ground, the eyes slid unseeingly uninterested toward the campfire. Saw the boy he had known at Lugdan ford, the rain and the silence and the heaps of dead, raindrops falling in the bloody water. Men puking from exhaustion. A horse screaming, worse than any man. The fire again, and the forest, and rape. "Bravely," he said. "In battle. I saw him fall. His face toward the enemy. Five of them he took down; and they kept coming. We pushed them back too late for him. But he saved that day."

Tears fell. She pulled a handkerchief from her sleeve and blotted at her eyes. "You were his friend," she said.

"I knew him."

A second time she wiped at her eyes, and put on a smile greatly forced and sad. "You're twice kind."

"You'll be alone."

"Willow and I."

"I might stay a time."

She rose from table. He got up from his place. "Please," she said. "I'll make you a bed." Her voice trembled. "You'll sleep the night and go your way in the morning."

"Lady—"

"In the morning." She turned away, toward the stairs, her unbound hair a cloud about her bowed head and shoulders. She turned back and looked at him where he stood staring after her. "Come."

She took a candle from its sconce, paused by the stairs. He unrooted his feet from where he stood and came after, cold inside from remembering Bryaut, bones crushed beneath the horse's hooves, and white flesh, Bryaut's possession; Bryaut, who had died half-naked and in such a moment—before or after? Dubhan wondered morbidly—to die like that and to be cheated too. . . .

He followed her, up the narrow stairs designed for the tower's last defense, so narrow a wooden winding that his shoulders nearly filled the way side to side, and she must bend double to pass the doorway at the top, the candle before her. The light cast her body into relief, the shadow of a breast, of slim legs against the white linen, and he found his breathing harder than the climbing warranted—followed after into a hall where they could both stand upright, a wooden raftering, a maze among the timbers where the candle chased shadows, doors on either side.

She opened the first door and brought him within a room, touched her candle to another's stub—another flaring, another shadow through the loose linen gown—doubling the light, upon a pleasant wide bed with flowers on the table beside it. The linens were rumpled, the down mattress bearing the imprint of a body. "Mine," she said. "I'll make up the room next door for myself tonight. Rest. I'll bring you water for washing."

She came back to the doorway to pass him and leave, glanced down at such close quarters, denying him her eyes. "Lady," he said so that she would look up, and she did, close to him, almost touching body to body, and kept looking. He reached out his hand to the black cloud of her hair and stroked it because it was female and beautiful. The wine he had drunk sang in him, laid a haze on all else but her. He took her hand up, blew out the candle it held, rested both hands on her shoulders, on thin linen which eased downward, on smoothness and curving softness. "No," she said, and a weak hand pushed at him. He put his arms about her and drew her to the bed and sank down on the feathers and her gentle softness. "No," she said a second time, struggling under him, and he stopped her mouth with his, kissed her eyes, her smooth flesh. "*No*," she wept, screaming, and of a sudden the heat froze in him. He felt her heaving sobs and heard her, and saw that other, pale figure in the dark, the hurtling rush of limbs, dead eyes staring at the moon. He did not move for the moment. Her hands made pathetic gestures toward covering her nakedness. She pushed at him to be free. He got off her and drew her shift up about her, smoothed her hair. It in no wise mended the wanting; but the doing—

"You are my *guest*," she said. "In my hall. Let me go."

Her eyes glistened, dark and bright. He had lost, he thought, lost everything with his rashness. Might take, still; her, the tower, the wealth downstairs. He might live here, with Willow's madness. Might have her too. He was strong and they could do nothing; could never drive him out. They would fear too much to lift a hand to him, and they would understand they were better off with him. No cold winters, no death on the road. Every evening she would serve him food on silver plates; and every night they would lie here where the linens smelled of rosemary and the bed was soft. He would ride into that village she named, gather men to build a gate and wall, levy taxes, fear nothing. . . .

"Let me go," she said. Not pleading. Not fearfully. Just like that— asking.

"Some man," he said, "will come down this road . . . and take it all from you. Your lord's not coming back. Think how it will be."

"Do you intend to take it from me?"

His hand lifted toward her hair. He touched it compulsively and stopped it short of her breast, drew it away. "I'd see you were safe."

"From you?"

"I'd not force you. Go out of here. Talk to me tomorrow. Will you do that?"

"If you wish. But if I say no?"

"Think of me. Think that I wish you well. Good *night*, lady."

She rose and slipped away, her white robe trailing past him, across the floor, toward the door, and closed it after. He got up, drew a great breath, drove his fist against the wooden wall and clutched it to him, eyes shut from the pain, from the madness, but the blood welled up there and in his arm and diminished that elsewhere, and he worked his bruised hand and paced the creaking floor until his heart had stopped pounding.

He washed then, in water she had used. The cool water from her bedside bowl smelled of lilies and numbed the pain of his hand, numbed the ache of his shoulders and his ribs and left him shivering.

He stripped, and used the linen towels and found the chamberpot beneath the bed, crawled at last between the rosemary-smelling sheets marvelously clean and comforted, leaned out to blow out the candle and blinked in a dark which, accustomed as he was to the stars at night and the moon, seemed fearsomely dark indeed. But his eyes closed a time, and a smile settled on him as he rolled and settled amid the scented sheets, until he had found just that hollow which suited him, and rest closer than he would have thought a while ago.

A step creaked in the hall, outside: the boards were old. The Lady? he wondered, dreaming dreams; the door opened, and the blackness was such that even lifting his head and looking, he could see nothing at all. A step crossed the boards, their creaking alone betraying its bare softness. A rustling of cloth attended it. "Who is it?" he asked, not entirely liking this dark and the visiting. A weight sank onto the foot of his bed and he jerked his foot from its vicinity realizing in one rush that sword and armor were downstairs, the cautions of a lifetime wine-muddled, woman-hazed. "Who? Lady?"

He moved to sit up all in a rush, but a gentle touch stole up his sheeted leg, a whisper of cloth leaned forward, and a woman's perfume reached him. "Lady?" he said again, beginning to have different thoughts. And then another, colder: "Or is it Willow?"

"We are three," the whisper came to him. "Mother, Maid—and me."

He thrust himself for the bedside. A grip caught his arm, a band like ice, burning chill that would not yield. He reached for that grip and met a hand soft-fleshed as age itself, frail-seeming, and strong. A like grip closed on the other arm, and the cold went inward, numbing breath, numbing heart, which beat in painful flutterings.

"Man," the voice whispered, a breath of ice across his face, driving him backward and down. "Man . . . that you did not touch Willow in the marsh; well done; that you did not force my daughter: again well done; but that you forced a kiss of my daughter . . . now I repay: what's for one . . . is for all, like and like, Mother, Maid, and me."

He was drowning . . . felt a touch on his lips, an embrace about his limbs, and it was ice stealing inward. "No," he said, despairing. The white face came back to him, that despair, that flung itself from the rocks, cursing him. "No," he said again, colder still—Willow's face, and the starving children, the hollow-eyed, hollow-hearted children the war had made. A third time: "No." It was the lady crying out, her outrage at a world that took no regard of her, where force alone availed; and himself, his, that comrades met and killed each other, and no force could mend what was and what had been. He had no strength now, none, only the anger and the grief, alone.

His shoulders struck the wooden floor; he sprawled, his senses beginning to leave him as his sight had done, and tears were freezing on his lashes, the moisture freezing on his lips so that he could open neither, sightless, speechless in the dark, void of all protest. Sense went last. He was not aware for what might have been a long time; and then he felt again, wood beneath his naked back, perceived a light through his lids, but still he could not open his eyes. A shadow bent above him, breath stirred across his face; soft lips kissed one eyelid and then the other, and lastly his mouth.

He looked on Willow, who crouched by him in her shift, holding a lighted candle, her arm about her knees.

"It's day," said Willow. "There's just no window here."

He dared no words. He rolled over and got up, ashamed in his nakedness, drew his clothing on under Willow's silent, dark-eyed stare. She had stood up. He walked for the door, turned the remembered way in haste down the creaking hall, through the low doorway and down the windings of the stairs in the dark—down into the main room of the keep, where wood mouldered silver gray and cobwebs hung, the nests of spiders, fine spinnings in the daylight which sifted in through broken beams. His armor lay in the dust. He put it on, hands trembling, worked into the mail and did the buckles.

A step creaked on the stairs. He looked about. It was Willow coming down. He seized up the sword and belted it about him, and looked again, where the Lady stood in Willow's place.

The outside door gaped; the wood was gone. He ran for it, for the sunlight, around to the pen behind, where his horse cropped the green grass alone in a ramshackle enclosure, and his saddle and gear lay on the dewy ground. He saddled the horse in haste, climbed into the saddle and rode carefully past the keep, hearing the lowing of a cow at his back. That ceased. He blinked and Willow sat on a stone of the ruined wall, swinging her bare feet and waving at him. He spurred the horse past, reined back again with the feeling of something at his back. He looked to the doorway. The Lady stood there. She had a lily in her hair and her feet were bare. "Good journey," she wished him. "Farewell, sir knight."

He snapped the reins and rode quickly onto the road. A black, bent figure stood among the trees and brush on the far side of it, robed and hooded. The horse shied, trembling. Dubhan could see nothing but the robes, hoped for all the life that was in him that it would not look up, would not fling back the hood.

"Not yet," the voice came like the sighings of leaves. "You have years yet, sir knight."

He cracked the reins and rode. The sunlight warmed him finally, and the birds sang, until the chill melted from his gut where it had lain. He looked back, and there was only the forest.

When he had ridden a day there was a village. He watered his horse there, and the townsfolk came shyly round him and asked the news. He told them about the war; and the king dead, and the duke; but they had never heard of either, and blinked and wondered among themselves. They gave him bread and ale, and grain for his horse, and he thanked them and rode away.

On that day he hung the sword from his saddle and carried it no more.

On the next he took off the armor and stowed it away, let the breeze to his skin, and rode through lands widely farmed, where villages lay across the road, open and unfearing.

They saw the weapons, the children of these villages, and asked him tales.

He made up dragons, and unicorns. The children smiled.

In time, so did he.

THE VACATION

Ray Bradbury

It was a day as fresh as grass growing up and clouds going over and butterflies coming down could make it. It was a day compounded of silences of bee and flower and ocean and land, which were not silences at all, but motions, stirs, flutters, risings, fallings, each in their own time and matchless rhythm. The land did not move, but moved. The sea was not still, yet was still. Paradox flowed into paradox, stillness mixed with stillness, sound with sound. The flowers vibrated and the bees fell in separate and small showers of golden rain on the clover. The seas of hill and the seas of ocean were divided, each from the other's motion, by a railroad track, empty, compounded of rust and iron marrow, a track on which, quite obviously, no train had run in many years. Thirty miles north it swirled on away to farther mists of distance, thirty miles south it tunneled islands of cloud shadows that changed their continental positions on the sides of far mountains as you watched.

Now, suddenly, the railway track began to tremble.

A blackbird, standing on the rail, felt a rhythm grow faintly, miles away, like a heart beginning to beat.

The blackbird leaped up over the sea.

The rail continued to vibrate softly until at long last around a curve and along the shore came a small workman's handcar, its two-cylinder engine popping and spluttering in the great silence.

On top of this small four-wheeled car, on a double-sided bench facing in two directions and with a little surrey roof above for shade, sat a man, his wife and their small seven-year-old son. As the handcar traveled through lonely stretch after lonely stretch, the wind whipped their eyes and blew their hair, but they did not look back but only ahead. Sometimes they looked eagerly, as a curve unwound itself, sometimes with great sadness, but always watchful, ready for the next scene.

As they hit a level straightaway, the machine's engine gasped and stopped abruptly. In the now-crushing silence, it seemed that the quiet of the earth, sky and sea itself, by its friction, brought the car to a wheeling halt.

"Out of gas."

The man, sighing, reached for the extra can in the small storage bin and began to pour it into the tank.

His wife and son sat quietly looking at the sea, listening to the muted thunder, the whisper, the drawing back of huge tapestries of sand, gravel, green weed and foam.

"Isn't the sea nice?" said the woman.

"I like it," said the boy.

"Shall we picnic here, while we're at it?"

The man focused binoculars on the green peninsula ahead.

"Might as well. The rails have rusted badly. There's a break ahead. We may have to wait while I set a few back in place."

"As many as there are," said the boy, "we'll have picnics!"

The woman tried to smile at this, then turned her grave attention to the man. "How far have we come today?"

"Not ninety miles." The man still peered through the glasses, squinting. "I don't like to go farther than that any one day, anyway. If you rush, there's no time to see. We'll reach Monterey day after tomorrow, Palo Alto the next day, if you want."

The woman removed her great shadowing straw hat which had been tied over her golden hair with a bright yellow ribbon, and stood perspiring faintly, away from the machine. They had ridden so steadily on the shuddering rail car that the motion was sewn in their bodies. Now, with the stopping, they felt odd, on the verge of unraveling.

"Let's eat!"

The boy ran with the wicker lunch basket down to the shore.

The boy and the woman were already seated by a spread tablecloth when the man came down to them, dressed in his business suit and vest and tie and hat as if he expected to meet someone along the way. As he dealt out the sandwiches and exhumed the pickles from their cool green Mason jars, he began to loosen his tie and unbutton his vest, always looking around as if he should be careful and ready to button up again.

"Are you all alone, Papa?" said the boy, eating.

"Yes."

"No one else, anywhere?"

"No one else."

"Were there people before?"

"Why do you keep asking that? It wasn't that long ago. Just a few months. You remember?"

"Almost. If I try hard, then I don't remember at all." The boy let a handful of sand fall through his fingers. "Were there as many people as there is sand here on the beach? What *happened* to them?"

"I don't know," the man said, and it was true.

They had wakened one morning and the world was empty. The neighbor's clothesline was still strung with blowing white wash, cars gleamed in front of other seven-A.M. cottages, but there were no farewells, the city did not hum with its mighty arterial traffics, phones did not alarm themselves, children did not wail in sunflower wildernesses.

Only the night before he and his wife had been sitting on the front porch when the evening paper was delivered and, not even daring to open to the headlines, he had said, "I wonder when He will get tired of us and just rub us all out?"

"It has gone pretty far," she said. "On and on. We're such fools, aren't we?"

"Wouldn't it be nice"—he lit his pipe and puffed it—"if we woke tomorrow and everyone in the world was gone and everything was starting over?" He sat smoking, the paper folded in his hand, his head resting back on the chair.

"If you could press a button right now and make it happen, would you?"

"I think I would," he said. "Nothing violent. Just have everyone vanish off the face of the earth. Just leave the land and the sea and the growing things like flowers and grass and fruit trees. And the animals, of course, let them stay. Everything except man, who hunts when he isn't hungry, eats when full, and is mean when no one's bothered him."

"Naturally," she smiled, quietly, "we would be left."

"I'd like that," he mused. "All of time ahead. The longest summer vacation in history. And us out for the longest picnic-basket lunch in memory. Just you, me and Jim. No commuting. No keeping up with the Joneses. Not even a car. I'd like to find another way of traveling, an older way . . . then, a hamper full of sandwiches, three bottles of pop, pick up supplies where you need them from empty grocery stores in empty towns, and summertime forever up ahead . . ."

They sat a long while on the porch in silence, the newspaper folded between them.

At last she spoke.

"Wouldn't we be *lonely*?" she said.

So that's how it was the morning of the first day of the new world. They had awakened to the soft sounds of an earth that was now no more than a meadow, and the cities of the earth sinking back into seas of saber grass, marigold, marguerite and morning-glory. They had taken it with remarkable calm at first, perhaps because they had not liked the city for so many years and had had so many friends who were not truly friends, and had lived a boxed and separate life of their own within a mechanical hive.

The husband arose and looked out the window and observed very calmly, as if it were a weather condition, "Everyone's gone . . ." knowing this just by the sounds the city had ceased to make.

They took their time over breakfast, for the boy was still asleep, and then the husband sat back and said, "Now I must plan what to do."

"Do? Why, why you'll go to work, of course."

"You still don't believe it, do you?" he laughed. "That I won't be rushing off each day at 8:10, that Jim won't go to school again ever. School's out for all of us! No more pencils, no more books, no more boss' sassy looks! We're let out, darling, and we'll never come back to the silly damn dull routines. Come on!"

And he had walked her through the still and empty city streets.

"They didn't die," he said. "They just . . . went away."

"What about the other cities?"

He went to an outdoor phone both and dialed Chicago, then New York, then San Francisco.

Silence. Silence. Silence.

"That's it," he said, replacing the receiver.

"I feel guilty," she said. "They gone and we here. And . . . I feel happy. Why? I *should* be unhappy."

"Should you? It's no tragedy. They weren't tortured or blasted or burned. It went easily and they didn't know. And now we owe nothing to anyone. Our only responsibility *is* being happy. Thirty more years of happiness, wouldn't that be good?"

"But then we must have more children!"

"To repopulate the world?" He shook his head slowly, calmly. "No. Let Jim be the last. After he's grown and gone let the horses and cows and ground squirrels and garden spiders have the world. They'll get on. And someday some other species that can combine a natural happiness with a natural curiosity will build cities that won't even look like cities to us, and survive. Right now, let's go pack a basket, wake Jim and get going on that long thirty-year summer vacation. I'll beat you to the house!"

He took a sledge hammer from the small rail car and while he worked alone for half an hour fixing the rusted rails into place, the woman and the boy ran along the shore. They came back with dripping shells, a dozen or more, and some beautiful pink pebbles, and sat and the boy took schooling from the mother, doing homework on a pad with a pencil for a time; and then at high noon the man came down, his coat off, his tie thrown aside, and they drank orange pop, watching the bubbles surge up, glutting, inside the bottles. It was quiet. They listened to the sun tune the old iron rails. The smell of hot tar on the ties moved about them in the salt wind, as the husband tapped his atlas map lightly and gently:

"We'll go to Sacramento next month, May, then work up toward Seattle. Should make that by July first, July's a good month in Washington, then back down as the weather cools, to Yellowstone, a few miles a day, hunt here, fish there . . ."

The boy, bored, moved away to throw sticks in the sea and wade out like a dog to retrieve them.

The man went on: "Winter in Tucson, then, part of the winter, moving toward Florida, up the coast in the spring, and maybe New York by June. Two years from now, Chicago in the summer. Winter, three years from now, what about Mexico City? Anywhere the rails lead us, anywhere at all, and if we come to an old offshoot rail line we don't know anything about, what the hell, we'll just take it, go down it to see where it goes. And some year, by God, we'll boat down the Mississippi, always wanted to do that. Enough to last us a lifetime. And that's just how long I want to take to do it all . . ."

His voice faded. He started to fumble the map shut, but before he could move, a bright thing fell through the air and hit the paper. It rolled off into the sand and made a wet lump.

His wife glanced at the wet place in the sand and then swiftly searched his face. His solemn eyes were too bright. And down one cheek was a track of wetness.

She gasped. She took his hand and held it tight.

He clenched her hand very hard, his eyes shut now, and slowly he said, with difficulty:

"Wouldn't it be nice if we went to sleep tonight and in the night, somehow, it all came back. All the foolishness, all the noise, all the hate, all the terrible things, all the nightmares, all the wicked people and stupid children, all the mess, all the smallness, all the confusion, all the hope, all the need, all the love. Wouldn't it be nice?"

She waited and nodded her head once.

Then both of them started.

For standing between them, they knew not for how long, was their son, an empty pop bottle in one hand.

The boy's face was pale. With his free hand he reached out to touch his father's cheek where the single tear had made its track.

"You," he said. "Oh, Dad, you. You haven't anyone to play with, either . . ."

The wife started to speak.

The husband moved to take the boy's hand.

The boy jerked back. "Silly! Oh, silly! Silly fools! Oh, you dumb, dumb!" And, whirling, he rushed down to the ocean and stood there crying, loudly.

The wife rose to follow, but the husband stopped her.

"No. Let him."

And then they both grew cold and quiet. For the boy, below on the shore, crying steadily, now was writing on a piece of paper and stuffing it into the pop bottle and ramming the tin cap back on and taking the bottle and giving it a great glittering heave up in the air and out into the tidal sea.

What, thought the wife, what did he write on the note? What's in the bottle?

The bottle moved out in the waves.

The boy stopped crying.

After a long while he walked up the shore to stand looking at his parents. His face was neither bright nor dark, alive nor dead, ready nor resigned; it seemed a curious mixture that simply made do with time, weather and these people. They looked at him and beyond to the bay where the bottle, containing the scribbled note, was almost out of sight now, shining in the waves.

Did he write what *we* wanted? thought the woman; did he write what he heard us just wish, just say?

Or did he write something for only himself? she wondered, that tomorrow he might wake and find himself alone in an empty world, no one around, no man, no woman, no father, no mother, no fool grownups with fool wishes, so he could trudge up to the railroad tracks and take the handcar motoring, a solitary boy, across the continental wilderness, on eternal voyages and picnics?

Is that what he wrote in the note?

Which?

She searched his colorless eyes, could not read the answer; dared not ask.

Gull shadows sailed over and kited their faces with sudden passing coolness.

"Time to go," someone said.

They loaded the wicker basket onto the rail car. The woman tied her large bonnet securely in place with its yellow ribbon, they set the boy's pail of shells on the floor boards, then the husband put on his tie, his vest, his coat, his hat, and they all sat on the bench of the car looking out at the sea where the bottled note was far out, blinking on the horizon.

"Is asking enough?" said the boy. "Does wishing work?"

"Sometimes . . . *too* well."

"It depends on what you ask for."

The boy nodded, his eyes faraway.

They looked back at where they had come from, and then ahead to where they were going.

"Goodbye, place," said the boy, and waved.

The car rolled down the rusty rails. The sound of it dwindled, faded. The man, the woman, the boy dwindled with it in the distance, among the hills.

After they were gone, the rail trembled faintly for two minutes and ceased. A flake of rust fell. A flower nodded.

The sea was very loud.

MAZIRIAN THE MAGICIAN

Jack Vance

eep in thought, Mazirian the Magician walked his garden. Trees fruited with many intoxications overhung his path, and flowers bowed obsequiously as he passed. An inch above the ground, dull as agates, the eyes of mandrakes followed the tread of his black-slippered feet. Such was Mazirian's garden—three terraces growing with strange and wonderful vegetations. Certain plants swam with changing iridescences; others held up blooms pulsing like sea-anemones, purple, green, lilac, pink, yellow. Here grew trees like feather parasols, trees with transparent trunks threaded with red and yellow veins, trees with foliage like metal foil, each leaf a different metal—copper, silver, blue tantalum, bronze, green iridium. Here blooms like bubbles tugged gently upward from glazed green leaves, there a shrub bore a thousand pipe-shaped blossoms, each whistling softly to make music of the ancient Earth, of the ruby-red sunlight, water seeping through black soil, the languid winds. And beyond the roqual hedge the trees of the forest made a tall wall of mystery. In this waning hour of Earth's life no man could count himself familiar with the glens, the glades, the dells and deeps, the secluded clearings, the ruined pavilions, the sun-dappled pleasaunces, the gullys and heights, the various brooks, freshets, ponds, the meadows, thickets, brakes and rocky outcrops.

Mazirian paced his garden with a brow frowning in thought. His step was slow and his arms were clenched behind his back. There was one who had brought him puzzlement, doubt, and a great desire: a delightful woman-creature who dwelt in the woods. She came to his garden half-laughing and always wary, riding a black horse with eyes like golden crystals. Many times had Mazirian tried to take her; always her horse had borne her from his varied enticements, threats, and subterfuges.

Agonized screaming jarred the garden. Mazirian, hastening his step, found a mole chewing the stalk of a plant-animal hybrid. He killed the marauder, and the screams subsided to a dull gasping. Mazirian stroked a furry leaf and the red mouth hissed in pleasure.

Then: "K-k-k-k-k-k-k," spoke the plant. Mazirian stooped, held the rodent to the red mouth. The mouth sucked, the small body slid into the stomach-bladder underground. The plant gurgled, cructated, and Mazirian watched with satisfaction.

The sun had swung low in the sky, so dim and red that the stars could be seen. And now Mazirian felt a watching presence. It would be the woman of the forest, for thus had she disturbed him before. He paused in his stride, feeling for the direction of the gaze.

He shouted a spell of immobilization. Behind him the plant-animal froze to rigidity and a great green moth wafted to the ground. He whirled around. There she was, at the edge of the forest, closer than ever she had approached before. Nor did she move as he advanced. Mazirian's young-old eyes shone. He would take her to his manse and keep her in a prison of green glass. He would test her brain with fire, with cold, with pain and with joy. She should serve him with wine and make the eighteen motions of allurement by yellow lamp-light. Perhaps she was spying on him; if so, the Magician would discover immediately, for he could call no man friend and had forever to guard his garden.

She was but twenty paces distant—then there was a thud and

pound of black hooves as she wheeled her mount and fled into the forest.

The Magician flung down his cloak in rage. She held a guard—a counter-spell, a rune of protection—and always she came when he was ill-prepared to follow. He peered into the murky depths, glimpsed the wanness of her body flitting through a shaft of red light, then black shade and she was gone . . . Was she a witch? Did she come of her own volition, or—more likely—had an enemy sent her to deal him inquietude? If so, who might be guiding her? There was Prince Kandive the Golden, of Kaiin, whom Mazirian had bilked of his secret of renewed youth. There was Azvan the Astronomer, there was Turjan—hardly Turjan, and here Mazirian's face lit in a pleasing recollection . . . He put the thought aside. Azvan, at least, he could test. He turned his steps to his workshop, went to a table where rested a cube of clear crystal, shimmering with a red and blue aureole. From a cabinet he brought a bronze gong and a silver hammer. He tapped on the gong and the mellow tone sang through the room and out, away and beyond. He tapped again and again. Suddenly Azvan's face shone from the crystal, beaded with pain and great terror.

"Stay the strokes, Mazirian!" cried Azvan. "Strike no more on the gong of my life!"

Mazirian paused, his hand poised over the gong.

"Do you spy on me, Azvan? Do you send a woman to regain the gong?"

"Not I, Master, not I. I fear you too well."

"You must deliver me the woman, Azvan; I insist."

"Impossible, Master! I know not who or what she is!"

Mazirian made as if to strike. Azvan poured forth such a torrent of supplication that Mazirian with a gesture of disgust threw down the hammer and restored the gong to its place. Azvan's face drifted slowly away, and the fine cube of crystal shone blank as before.

Mazirian stroked his chin. Apparently he must capture the girl himself. Later, when black night lay across the forest, he would seek through his books for spells to guard him through the unpredictable glades. They would be poignant corrosive spells, of such a nature that one would daunt the brain of an ordinary man and two render him mad. Mazirian, by dint of stringent exercise, could encompass four of the most formidable, or six of the lesser spells.

He put the project from his mind and went to a long vat bathed in a flood of green light. Under a wash of clear fluid lay the body of a man, ghastly below the green glare, but of great physical beauty. His torso tapered from wide shoulders through lean flanks to long strong legs and arched feet; his face was clean and cold with hard flat features. Dusty golden hair clung about his head.

Mazirian stared at the thing, which he had cultivated from a single cell. It needed only intelligence, and this he knew not how to provide. Turjan of Miir held the knowledge, and Turjan—Mazirian glanced with a grim narrowing of the eyes at a trap in the floor—refused to part with his secret.

Mazirian pondered the creature in the vat. It was a perfect body; therefore might not the brain be ordered and pliant? He would discover. He set in motion a device to draw off the liquid and presently the body lay stark to the direct rays. Mazirian injected a minim of drug into the neck. The body twitched. The eyes opened, winced in the glare. Mazirian turned away the projector.

Feebly the creature in the vat moved its arms and feet, as if unaware of their use. Mazirian watched intently: perhaps he had stumbled on the right synthesis for the brain.

"Sit up!" commanded the Magician.

The creature fixed its eyes upon him, and reflexes joined muscle to muscle. It gave a throaty roar and sprang from the vat at Mazirian's throat. In spite of Mazirian's strength it caught him and shook him like a doll.

For all Mazirian's magic he was helpless. The mesmeric spell had been expended, and he had none other in his brain. In any event he could not have uttered the space-twisting syllables with that mindless clutch at his throat.

His hand closed on the neck of a leaden carboy. He swung and struck the head of his creature, which slumped to the floor.

Mazirian, not entirely dissatisfied, studied the glistening body at his feet. The spinal coordination had functioned well. At his table he mixed a white potion, and, lifting the golden head, poured the fluid into the lax mouth. The creature stirred, opened its eyes, propped itself on its elbows. The madness had left its face—but Mazirian sought in vain for the glimmer of intelligence. The eyes were as vacant as those of a lizard.

The Magician shook his head in annoyance. He went to the window and his brooding profile was cut black against the oval panes . . . Turjan once more? Under the most dire inquiry Turjan had kept his secret close. Mazirian's thin mouth curved wryly. Perhaps if he inserted another angle in the passage . . .

The sun had gone from the sky and there was dimness in Mazirian's garden. His white night-blossoms opened and their captive gray moths fluttered from bloom to bloom. Mazirian pulled open the trap in the floor and descended stone stairs. Down, down, down . . . At last a passage intercepted at right angles, lit with the yellow light of eternal lamps. To the left were his fungus beds, to the right a stout oak and iron door, locked with three locks. Down and ahead the stone steps continued, dropping into blackness.

Mazirian unlocked the three locks, flung wide the door. The room within was bare except for a stone pedestal supporting a glass-topped box. The box measured a yard on a side and was four or five inches high. Within the box—actually a squared passageway, a run with four right angles—moved two small creatures, one seeking, the other evading. The predator was a small dragon with furious red eyes and a monstrous fanged mouth. It waddled along the passage on six splayed legs, twitching its tail as it went. The other stood only half the size of the dragon—a strong-featured man, stark naked, with a copper fillet binding his long black hair. He moved slightly faster than his pursuer, which still kept relentless chase, using a measure of craft, speeding, doubling back, lurking at the angle in case the man should unwarily step around. By holding himself continually alert, the man was able to stay beyond the reach of the fangs. The man was Turjan, whom Mazirian by trickery had captured several weeks before, reduced in size and thus imprisoned.

Mazirian watched with pleasure as the reptile sprang upon the momentarily relaxing man, who jerked himself clear by the thickness of his skin. It was time, Mazirian thought, to give both rest and nourishment. He dropped panels across the passage, separating it into halves, isolating man from beast. To both he gave meat and pannikins of water.

Turjan slumped in the passage.

"Ah," said Mazirian, "you are fatigued. You desire rest?"

Turjan remained silent, his eyes closed. Time and the world had lost meaning for him. The only realities were the gray passage and the interminable flight. At unknown intervals came food and a few hours' rest.

"Think of the blue sky," said Mazirian, "the white stars, your castle Miir by the river Derna; think of wandering free in the meadows."

The muscles at Turjan's mouth twitched.

"Consider, you might crush the little dragon under your heel."

Turjan looked up. "I would prefer to crush your neck, Mazirian."

Mazirian was unperturbed. "Tell me, how do you invest your vat creatures with intelligence? Speak, and you go free."

Turjan laughed, and there was madness in his laughter.

"Tell you? And then? You would kill me with hot oil in a moment."

Mazirian's thin mouth drooped petulantly.

"Wretched man, I know how to make you speak. If your mouth were stuffed, waxed and sealed, you would speak! Tomorrow I take a nerve from your arm and draw coarse cloth along its length."

The small Turjan, sitting with his legs across the passageway, drank his water and said nothing.

"Tonight," said Mazirian with studied malevolence, "I add an angle and change your run to a pentagon."

Turjan paused and looked up through the glass cover at his enemy. Then he slowly sipped his water. With five angles there would be less time to evade the charge of the monster, less of the hall in view from one angle.

"Tomorrow," said Mazirian, "you will need all your agility." But another matter occurred to him. He eyed Turjan speculatively. "Yet even this I spare you if you assist me with another problem."

"What is your difficulty, febrile Magician?"

"The image of a woman-creature haunts my brain, and I would capture her." Mazirian's eyes went misty at the thought. "Late afternoon she comes to the edge of my garden riding a great black horse—you know her, Turjan?"

"Not I, Mazirian." Turjan sipped his water.

Mazirian continued. "She has sorcery enough to ward away Felojun's Second Hypnotic Spell—or perhaps she has some protective rune. When I approach, she flees into the forest."

"So then?" asked Turjan, nibbling the meat Mazirian had provided.

"Who may this woman be?" demanded Mazirian, peering down his long nose at the tiny captive.

"How can I say?"

"I must capture her," said Mazirian abstractedly: "What spells, what spells?"

Turjan looked up, although he could see the Magician only indistinctly through the cover of glass.

"Release me, Mazirian, and on my word as a Chosen Hierarch of the Maram-Or, I will deliver you this girl."

"How would you do this?" asked the suspicious Mazirian.

"Pursue her into the forest with my best Live Boots and a headful of spells."

"You would fare no better than I," retorted the Magician. "I give you freedom when I know the synthesis of your vat-things. I myself will pursue the woman."

Turjan lowered his head that the Magician might not read his eyes.

"And as for me, Mazirian?" he inquired after a moment.

"I will treat with you when I return."

"And if you do not return?"

Mazirian stroked his chin and smiled, revealing fine white teeth. "The dragon could devour you now, if it were not for your cursed secret."

The Magician climbed the stairs. Midnight found him in his study, poring through leather-bound tomes and untidy portfolios . . . At one time a thousand or more runes, spells, incantations, curses, and sorceries had been known. The reach of Grand Motholam—Ascolais, the Ide of Kauchique, Almery to the South, the Land of the Falling Wall to the East—swanned with sorcerers of every description, of whom the chief was the Arch-Necromancer Phandaal. A hundred spells Phandaal personally had formulated—though rumor said that demons whispered at his ear when he wrought magic. Pontecilla the Pious, then ruler of

Grand Motholam, put Phandaal to torment, and after a terrible night, he killed Phandaal and outlawed sorcery throughout the land. The wizards of Grand Motholam fled like beetles under a strong light; the lore was dispersed and forgotten, until now, at this dim time, with the sun dark, wilderness obscuring Ascolais, and the white city Kaiin half in ruins, only a few more than a hundred spells remained to the knowledge of man. Of these, Mazirian had access to seventy-three, and gradually, by stratagem and negotiation, was securing the others.

Mazirian made a selection from his books and with great effort forced five spells upon his brain: Phandaal's Gyrator, Felojun's Second Hypnotic Spell, The Excellent Prismatic Spray, The Charm of Untiring Nourishment, and the Spell of the Omnipotent Sphere. This accomplished, Mazirian drank wine and retired to his couch.

The following day, when the sun hung low, Mazirian went to walk in his garden. He had but short time to wait. As he loosened the earth at the roots of his moon-geraniums a soft rustle and stamp told that the object of his desire had appeared.

She sat upright in the saddle, a young woman of exquisite configuration. Mazirian slowly stooped, as not to startle her, put his feet into the Live Boots and secured them above the knee.

He stood up. "Ho, girl," he cried, "you have come again. Why are you here of evenings? Do you admire the roses? They are vividly red because live red blood flows in their petals. If today you do not flee, I will make you the gift of one."

Mazirian plucked a rose from the shuddering bush and advanced toward her, fighting the surge of the Live Boots. He had taken but four steps when the woman dug her knees into the ribs of her mount and so plunged off through the trees.

Mazirian allowed full scope to the life in his boots. They gave a great bound, and another, and another, and he was off in full chase.

So Mazirian entered the forest of fable. On all sides mossy boles twisted up to support the high panoply of leaves. At intervals shafts of sunshine drifted through to lay carmine blots on the turf. In the shade long-stemmed flowers and fragile fungi sprang from the humus; in this ebbing hour of Earth nature was mild and relaxed.

Mazirian in his Live Boots bounded with great speed through the forest, yet the black horse, running with no strain, stayed easily ahead.

For several leagues the woman rode, her hair flying behind like a pennon. She looked back and Mazirian saw the face over her shoulder as a face in a dream. Then she bent forward; the golden-eyed horse thundered ahead and soon was lost to sight. Mazirian followed by tracing the trail in the sod.

The spring and drive began to leave the Live Boots, for they had come far and at great speed. The monstrous leaps became shorter and heavier, but the strides of the horse, shown by the tracks, were also shorter and slower. Presently Mazirian entered a meadow and saw the horse, riderless, cropping grass. He stopped short. The entire expanse of tender herbiage lay before him. The trail of the horse leading into the glade was clear, but there was no trail leaving. The woman therefore had dismounted somewhere behind—how far he had no means of knowing. He walked toward the horse, but the creature shied and bolted through the trees. Mazirian made one effort to follow, and discovered that his Boots hung lax and flaccid—dead.

He kicked them away, cursing the day and his ill-fortune. Shaking the cloak free behind him, a baleful tension shining on his face, he started back along the trail.

In this section of the forest, outcroppings of black and green rock, basalt and serpentine, were frequent—forerunners of the crags over the River Derna. On one of these rocks Mazirian saw a tiny man-thing mounted on a dragon-fly. He had skin of a greenish cast; he wore a gauzy smock and carried a lance twice his own length.

Mazirian stopped. The Twk-man looked down stolidly.

"Have you seen a woman of my race passing by, Twk-man?"

"I have seen such a woman," responded the Twk-man after a moment of deliberation.

"Where may she be found?"

"What may I expect for the information?"

"Salt—as much as you can bear away."

The Twk-man flourished his lance. "Salt? No. Liane the Wayfarer provides the chieftain Dandanflores salt for all the tribe."

Mazirian could surmise the services for which the bandit-troubadour paid salt. The Twk-men, flying fast on their dragon-flies, saw all that happened in the forest.

"A vial of oil from my telanxis blooms?"

"Good," said the Twk-man. "Show me the vial."

Mazirian did so.

"She left the trail at the lightning-blasted oak lying a little before you. She made directly for the river valley, the shortest route to the lake."

Mazirian laid the vial beside the dragon-fly and went off toward the river oak. The Twk-man watched him go, then dismounted and lashed the vial to the underside of the dragon-fly, next to the skein of fine haft the woman had given him thus to direct Mazirian.

The Magician turned at the oak and soon discovered the trail over the dead leaves. A long open glade lay before him, sloping gently to the river. Trees towered to either side and the long sundown rays steeped one side in blood, left the other deep in black shadow. So deep was the shade that Mazirian did not see the creature seated on a fallen tree; and he sensed it only as it prepared to leap on his back.

Mazirian sprang about to face the thing, which subsided again to sitting posture. It was a Deodand, formed and featured like a handsome man, finely muscled, but with a dead black lusterless skin and long slit eyes.

"Ah, Mazirian, you roam the woods far from home." The black thing's soft voice rose through the glade.

The Deodand, Mazirian knew, craved his body for meat. How had the girl escaped? Her trail led directly past.

"I come seeking, Deodand. Answer my questions, and I undertake to feed you much flesh."

The Deodand's eyes glinted, flitting over Mazirian's body. "You may in any event, Mazirian. Are you with powerful spells today?"

"I am. Tell me, how long has it been since the girl passed? Went she fast, slow, alone or in company? Answer, and I give you meat at such time as you desire."

The Deodand's lips curled mockingly. "Blind Magician! She has not left the glade." He pointed, and Mazirian followed the direction of the dead black arm. But he jumped back as the Deodand sprang. From his mouth gushed the syllables of Phandaal's Gyrator Spell. The Deodand was jerked off his feet and flung high in the air, where he hung whirling, high and low, faster and slower, up to the tree-tops, low to the ground. Mazirian watched with a half-smile. After a moment he brought the Deodand low and caused the rotations to slacken.

"Will you die quickly or slow?" asked Mazirian. "Help me and I kill you at once. Otherwise you shall rise high where the pelgrane fly."

Fury and fear choked the Deodand.

"May dark Thial spike your eyes! May Kraan hold your living brain in acid!" And it added such charges that Mazirian felt forced to mutter countercurses.

"Up then," said Mazirian at last, with a wave of his hand. The black sprawling body jerked high above the tree-tops to revolve slowly in the crimson bask of setting sun. In a moment a mottled bat-shaped thing with hooked snout swept close and its beak tore the black leg before the crying Deodand could kick it away. Another and another of the shapes flitted across the sun.

"Down, Mazirian!" came the faint call. "I tell what I know."

Mazirian brought him close to earth.

"She passed alone before you came. I made to attack her but she repelled me with a handful of thyle-dust. She went to the end of the glade and took the trail to the river. This trail leads also past the lair of Thrang. So is she lost, for he will sate himself on her till she dies."

Mazirian rubbed his chin. "Had she spells with her?"

"I know not. She will need strong magic to escape the demon Thrang."

"Is there anything else to tell?"

"Nothing."

"Then you may die." And Mazirian caused the creature to revolve at ever greater speed, faster and faster, until there was only a blur. A strangled wailing came and presently the Deodand's frame parted. The head shot like a bullet far down the glade; arms, legs, viscera flew in all directions.

Mazirian went his way. At the end of the glade the trail led steeply down ledges of dark green serpentine to the River Derna. The sun had set and shade filled the valley. Mazirian gained the riverside and set off downstream toward a far shimmer known as Sanra Water, the Lake of Dreams.

An evil odor came to the air, a stink of putrescence and filth. Mazirian went ahead more cautiously, for the lair of Thrang the ghoul-bear was near, and in the air was the feel of magic—strong brutal sorcery his own more subtle spells might not contain.

The sound of voices reached him, the throaty tones of Thrang and gasping cries of terror. Mazirian stepped around a shoulder of rock, inspected the origin of the sounds.

Thrang's lair was an alcove in the rock, where a fetid pile of grass and skins served him for a couch. He had built a rude pen to cage three women, these wearing many bruises on their bodies and the effects of much horror on their faces. Thrang had taken them from the tribe that dwelt in silk-hung barges along the lake-shore. Now they watched as he struggled to subdue the woman he had just captured. His round gray man's face was contorted and he tore away her jerkin with his human hands. But she held away the great sweating body with an amazing dexterity. Mazirian's eyes narrowed. Magic, magic!

So he stood watching, considering how to destroy Thrang with no harm to the woman. But she spied him over Thrang's shoulder.

"See," she panted, "Mazirian has come to kill you."

Thrang twisted about. He saw Mazirian and came charging on all fours, venting roars of wild passion. Mazirian later wondered if the ghoul had cast some sort of spell, for a strange paralysis strove to bind his brain. Perhaps the spell lay in the sight of Thrang's raging graywhite face, the great arms thrust out to grasp.

Mazirian shook off the spell, if such it were, and uttered a spell of his own, and all the valley was lit by streaming darts of fire, lashing in from all directions to spit Thrang's blundering body in a thousand places. This was the Excellent Prismatic Spray—many-colored stabbing lines. Thrang was dead almost at once, purple blood flowing from countless holes where the radiant rain had pierced him.

But Mazirian heeded little. The girl had fled. Mazirian saw her white form running along the river toward the lake, and took up the chase, heedless of the piteous cries of the three women in the pen.

The lake presently lay before him, a great sheet of water whose further rim was but dimly visible. Mazirian came down to the sandy shore and stood seeking across the dark face of Sanra Water, the Lake of Dreams. Deep night with only a verge of afterglow ruled the sky, and stars glistened on the smooth surface. The water lay cool and still, tideless as all Earth's waters had been since the moon had departed the sky.

Where was the woman? There, a pale white form, quiet in the shadow across the river. Mazirian stood on the riverbank, tall and commanding, a light breeze ruffling the cloak around his legs.

"Ho, girl," he called. "It is I, Mazirian, who saved you from Thrang. Come close, that I may speak to you."

"At this distance I hear you well, Magician," she replied. "The closer I approach the farther I must flee."

"Why then do you flee? Return with me and you shall be mistress of many secrets and hold much power."

She laughed. "If I wanted these, Mazirian, would I have fled so far?"

"Who are you then that you desire not the secrets of magic?"

"To you, Mazirian, I am nameless, lest you curse me. Now I go where you may not come." She ran down the shore, waded slowly out till the water circled her waist, then sank out of sight. She was gone.

Mazirian paused indecisively. It was not good to use so many spells and thus shear himself of power. What might exist below the lake? The sense of quiet magic was there, and though he was not at enmity with the Lake Lord, other beings might resent a trespass. However, when the figure of the girl did not break the surface, he uttered the Charm of Untiring Nourishment and entered the cool waters.

He plunged deep through the Lake of Dreams, and as he stood on the bottom, his lungs at ease by virtue of the charm, he marveled at the fey place he had come upon. Instead of blackness a green light glowed everywhere and the water was but little less clear than air. Plants undulated to the current and with them moved the lake flowers, soft with blossoms of red, blue and yellow. In and out swam large-eyed fish of many shapes.

The bottom dropped by rocky steps to a wide plain where trees of the underlake floated up from slender stalks to elaborate fronds and purple water-fruits, and so till the misty wet distance veiled all. He saw the woman, a white water nymph now, her hair like dark fog. She half-swam, half-ran across the sandy floor of the water-world, occasionally looking back over her shoulder. Mazirian came after, his cloak streaming out behind.

He drew nearer to her, exulting. He must punish her for leading him so far . . . The ancient stone stairs below his workroom led deep and at last opened into chambers that grew ever vaster as one went deeper. Mazirian had found a rusted cage in one of these chambers. A week or two locked in the blackness would curb her willfulness. And once he had dwindled a woman small as his thumb and kept her in a little glass bottle with two buzzing flies . . .

A ruined white temple showed through the green. There were many columns, some toppled, some still upholding the pediment. The woman entered the great portico under the shadow of the architrave. Perhaps she was attempting to elude him; he must follow closely. The white body glimmered at the far end of the nave, swimming now over the rostrum and into a semi-circular alcove behind.

Mazirian followed as fast as he was able, half-swimming, half-walking through the solemn dimness. He peered across the murk. Smaller columns here precariously upheld a dome from which the keystone had dropped. A sudden fear smote him, then realization as he saw the flash of movement from above. On all sides the columns toppled in, and an avalanche of marble blocks tumbled at his head. He jumped frantically back.

The commotion ceased, the white dust of the ancient mortar drifted away. On the pediment of the main temple the woman kneeled on slender knees, staring down to see how well she had killed Mazirian.

She had failed. Two columns, by sheerest luck, had crashed to either side of him, and a slab had protected his body from the blocks. He moved his head painfully. Through a chink in the tumbled marble he could see the woman, leaning to discern his body. So she would kill him? He, Mazirian, who had already lived more years than he could easily reckon? So much more would she hate and fear him later. He called his charm, the Spell of the Omnipotent Sphere. A film of force formed around his body, expanding to push aside all that resisted. When the marble ruins had been thrust back, he destroyed the sphere, regained his feet, and glared about for the woman. She was almost out of sight, behind a brake of long purple kelp, climbing the slope to the shore. With all his power he set out in pursuit.

T'sain dragged herself up on the beach. Still behind her came Mazirian the Magician, whose power had defeated each of her plans. The memory of his face passed before her and she shivered. He must not take her now.

Fatigue and despair slowed her feet. She had set out with but two spells, the Charm of Untiring Nourishment and a spell affording strength to her arms—the last permitting her to hold off Thrang and tumble the temple upon Mazirian. These were exhausted; she was bare of protection; but, on the other hand, Mazirian could have nothing left.

Perhaps he was ignorant of the vampire-weed. She ran up the slope and stood behind a patch of pale, wind-beaten grass. And now Mazirian came from the lake, a spare form visible against the shimmer of the water.

She retreated, keeping the innocent patch of grass between them. If the grass failed—her mind quailed at the thought of what she must do.

Mazirian strode into the grass. The sickly blades became sinewy fingers. They twined about his ankles, holding him in an unbreakable grip, while others sought to find his skin.

So Mazirian chanted his last spell—the incantation of paralysis, and the vampire grass grew lax and slid limply to earth. T'sain watched with dead hope. He was now close upon her, his cloak flapping behind. Had he no weakness? Did not his fibers ache, did not his breath come short? She whirled and fled across the meadow, toward a grove of black trees. Her skin chilled at the deep shadows, the somber frames. But the thud of the Magician's feet was loud. She plunged into the dread shade. Before all in the grove awoke she must go as far as possible.

Snap! A thong lashed at her. She continued to run. Another and another—she fell. Another great whip and another beat at her. She staggered up, and on, holding her arms before her face. Snap! The flails whistled through the air, and the last blow twisted her around. So she saw Mazirian.

He fought. As the blows rained on him, he tried to seize the whips and break them. But they were supple and springy beyond his powers, and jerked away to beat at him again. Infuriated by his resistance, they concentrated on the unfortunate Magician, who foamed and fought with transcendent fury, and T'sain was permitted to crawl to the edge of the grove with her life.

She looked back in awe at the expression of Mazirian's lust for life. He staggered about in a cloud of whips, his furious obstinate figure dimly silhouetted. He weakened and tried to flee, and then he fell. The blows pelted at him—on his head, shoulders, the long legs. He tried to rise but fell back.

T'sain closed her eyes in lassitude. She felt the blood oozing from her broken flesh. But the most vital mission yet remained. She reached her feet, and reelingly set forth. For a long time the thunder of many blows reached her ears.

Mazirian's garden was surpassingly beautiful by night. The star-blossoms spread wide, each of magic perfection, and the captive half-vegetable moths flew back and forth. Phosphorescent water-lilies floated like charming faces on the pond and the bush which Mazirian had brought from far Almery in the south tinctured the air with sweet fruity perfume.

T'sain, weaving and gasping, now came groping through the garden. Certain of the flowers awoke and regarded her curiously. The half-animal hybrid sleepily chittered at her, thinking to recognize Mazirian's step. Faintly to be heard was the wistful music of the blue-cupped flowers singing of ancient nights when a white moon swam the sky, and great storms and clouds and thunder ruled the seasons.

T'sain passed unheeding. She entered Mazirian's house, found the workroom where glowed the eternal yellow lamps. Mazirian's golden-haired vat-thing sat up suddenly and stared at her with his beautiful vacant eyes.

She found Mazirian's keys in the cabinet, and managed to claw open the trap door. Here she slumped to rest and let the pink gloom pass from her eyes. Visions began to come—Mazirian, tall and arrogant, stepping out to kill Thrang; the strange-hued flowers under the lake; Mazirian, his magic lost, fighting the whips . . . She was brought from the half-trance by the vat-thing timidly fumbling with her hair.

She shook herself awake, and half-walked, half-fell down the stairs. She unlocked the thrice-bound door, thrust it open with almost the last desperate urge of her body. She wandered in to clutch at the pedestal where the glass-topped box stood and Turjan and the dragon were playing their desperate game. She flung the glass crashing to the floor, gently lifted Turjan out and set him down.

The spell was disrupted by the touch of the rune at her wrist, and Turjan became a man again. He looked aghast at the nearly unrecognizable T'sain.

She tried to smile up at him.

"Turjan—you are free—"

"And Mazirian?"

"He is dead." She slumped wearily to the stone floor and lay limp. Turjan surveyed her with an odd emotion in his eyes.

"T'sain, dear creature of my mind," he whispered, "more noble are you than I, who used the only life you knew for my freedom."

He lifted her body in his arms.

"But I shall restore you to the vats. With your brain I build another T'sain, as lovely as you. We go."

He bore her up the stone stairs.

THE BAZAAR OF
THE BIZARRE

Fritz Leiber

he strange stars of the World of Nehwon glinted thickly above the black-roofed city of Lankhmar, where swords clink almost as often as coins. For once there was no fog.

In the Plaza of Dark Delights, which lies seven blocks south of the Marsh Gate and extends from the Fountain of Dark Abundance to the Shrine of the Black Virgin, the shop-lights glinted upward no more brightly than the stars glinted down. For there the vendors of drugs and the peddlers of curiosa and the hawkers of assignations light their stalls and crouching places with foxfire, glow-worms, and firepots with tiny single windows, and they conduct their business almost as silently as the stars conduct theirs.

There are plenty of raucous spots a-glare with torches in nocturnal Lankhmar, but by immemorial tradition soft whispers and a pleasant dimness are the rule in the Plaza of Dark Delights. Philosophers often go there solely to meditate, students to dream, and fanatic-eyed theologians to spin like spiders abstruse new theories of the Devil and of the other dark forces ruling the universe. And if any of these find a little illicit fun by the way, their theories and dreams and theologies and demonologies are undoubtedly the better for it.

Tonight, however, there was a glaring exception to the darkness rule. From a low doorway with a trefoil arch new-struck through an ancient wall, light spilled into the Plaza. Rising above the horizon of the pavement like some monstrous moon a-shine with the ray of a murderous sun, the new doorway dimmed almost to extinction the stars of the other merchants of mystery.

Eerie and unearthly objects for sale spilled out of the doorway a little way with the light, while beside the doorway crouched an avid-faced figure clad in garments never before seen on land or sea . . . in the World of Nehwon. He wore a hat like a small red pail, baggy trousers, and outlandish red boots with upturned toes. His eyes were as predatory as a hawk's, but his smile as cynically and lasciviously cajoling as an ancient satyr's.

Now and again he sprang up and pranced about, sweeping and re-sweeping with a rough long broom the flagstones as if to clean path for the entry of some fantastic emperor, and he often paused in his dance to blow low and loutingly, but always with upglancing eyes, to the crowd gathering in the darkness across from the doorway and to swing his hand from them toward the interior of the new shop in a gesture of invitation at once servile and sinister.

No one of the crowd had yet plucked up courage to step forward into the glare and enter the shop, or even inspect the rarities set out so carelessly yet temptingly before it. But the number of fascinated peerers increased momently. There were mutterings of censure at the dazzling new method of merchandising—the infraction of the Plaza's custom of darkness—but on the whole the complaints were outweighed by the gasps and murmurings of wonder, admiration and curiosity kindling even hotter.

The Gray Mouser slipped into the Plaza at the Fountain end as silently as if he had come to slit a throat or spy on the spies of the Overlord. His ratskin moccasins were soundless. His sword Scalpel in its mouseskin sheath did not swish ever so faintly against either his tunic or cloak, both of gray silk curiously coarse of weave. The glances he shot about him from under his gray silk hood half thrown back were freighted with menace and a freezing sense of superiority.

Inwardly the Mouser was feeling very much like a schoolboy—a schoolboy in dread of rebuke and a crushing assignment of homework. For in the Mouser's pouch of ratskin was a note scrawled in dark brown squid-ink on silvery fish-skin by Sheelba of the Eyeless Face, inviting the Mouser to be at this spot at this time.

Sheelba was the Mouser's supernatural tutor and—when the whim struck Sheelba—guardian, and it never did to ignore his invitations, for Sheelba had eyes to track down the unsociable though he did not carry them between his cheeks and forehead.

But the tasks Sheelba would set the Mouser at times like these were apt to be peculiarly onerous and even noisome—such as procuring nine white cats with never a black hair among them, or stealing five copies of the same book of magic runes from five widely separated sorcerous libraries or obtaining specimens of the dung of four kings living or dead—so the Mouser had come early, to get the bad news as soon as possible, and he had come alone, for he certainly did not want his comrade Fafhrd to stand snickering by while Sheelba delivered his little wizardly homilies to a dutiful Mouser . . . and perchance thought of extra assignments.

Sheelba's note, invisible graven somewhere inside the Mouser's skull, read merely, *When the star Akul bedizens the Spire of Rhan, be you by the Fountain of Dark Abundance,* and the note was signed only with the little featureless oval which is Sheelba's sigil.

The Mouser glided now through the darkness to the Fountain, which was a squat black pillar from the rough rounded top of which a single black drop welled and dripped every twenty elephant's heart-beats.

The Mouser stood beside the Fountain and, extending a bent hand, measured the altitude of the green star Akul. It had still to drop down the sky seven finger widths more before it would touch the needle-point of the slim star-silhouetted distant minaret of Rhan.

The Mouser crouched doubled-up by the black pillar and then vaulted lightly atop it to see if that would make any great difference in Akul's attitude. It did not.

He scanned the nearby darkness for motionless figures . . . especially that of one robed and cowled like a monk—cowled so deeply that one might wonder how he saw to walk. There were no figures at all.

The Mouser's mood changed. If Sheelba chose not to come courteously beforehand, why he could be boorish too! He strode off to investigate the new bright arch-doored shop, of whose infractious glow he had become inquisitively aware at least a block before he had entered the Plaza of Dark Delights.

Fafhrd the Northerner opened one wine-heavy eye and without moving his head scanned half the small firelit room in which he slept naked. He shut that eye, opened the other, and scanned the other half.

There was no sign of the Mouser anywhere. So far so good! If his luck held, he would be able to get through tonight's embarrassing business without being jeered at by the small gray rogue.

He drew from under his stubbly cheek a square of violet serpent-hide pocked with tiny pores so that when he held it between his eyes and the dancing fire it made stars. Studied for a time, these stars spelled out obscurely the message: *When Rhan-dagger stabs the darkness in Akul-heart, seek you the Source of the Black Drops.*

Drawn boldly across the prickholes in an orange-brown like dried blood—in fact spanning the violet square—was a seven-armed swastika, which is one of the sigils of Ningauble of the Seven Eyes.

Fafhrd had no difficulty in interpreting the Source of the Black Drops as the Fountain of Dark Abundance. He had become wearily familiar with such cryptic poetic language during his boyhood as a scholar of the singing skalds.

Ningauble stood to Fafhrd very much as Sheelba stood to the Mouser except that the Seven-Eyed One was a somewhat more pretentious archimage, whose taste in the thaumaturgical tasks he set Fafhrd ran in larger directions, such as the slaying of dragons, the sinking of four-masted magic ships, and the kidnapping of ogre-guarded enchanted queens.

Also, Ningauble was given to quiet realistic boasting, especially about the grandeur of his vast cavern-home, whose stony serpent-twisting back corridors led, he often averred, to all spots in space and time—provided Ningauble instructed one beforehand exactly how to step those rocky crooked low-ceilinged passageways.

Fafhrd was driven by no great desire to learn Ningauble's formulas and enchantments, as the Mouser was driven to learn Sheelba's, but the Septinocular One had enough holds on the Northerner, based on the latter's weaknesses and past misdeeds, so that Fafhrd had always to listen patiently to Ningauble's wizardly admonishments and vaunting sorcerous chit-chat—but *not,* if humanly or inhumanly possible, while the Gray Mouser was present to snigger and grin.

Meanwhile, Fafhrd standing before the fire, had been whipping, slapping, and belting various garments and weapons and ornaments onto his huge brawny body with its generous stretches of thick short curling red-gold hairs. When he opened the outer door and, also booted and helmeted now, glanced down the darkling alleyway preparatory to leaving and noted only the hunch-backed chestnut vendor a-squat by his brazier at the next corner, one would have sworn that when he did stride forth toward the Plaza of Dark Delights it would be with the clankings and thunderous tread of a siege-tower approaching a thick-walled city.

Instead the lynx-eared old chestnut vendor, who was also a spy of the Overlord, had to swallow down his heart when it came sliding crookedly up his throat as Fafhrd rushed past him, tall as a pine tree, swift as the wind, and silent as a ghost.

The Mouser elbowed aside two gawkers with shrewd taps on the floating rib and strode across the dark flagstones toward the garishly bright shop with its doorway like an upended heart. It occurred to him they must have had masons working like fiends to have cut and plastered that archway so swiftly. He had been past here this afternoon and noted nothing but blank wall.

The outlandish porter with the red cylinder hat and twisty red shoe-toes came frisking out to the Mouser with his broom and then went curtsying back as he reswept a path for this first customer with many an obsequious bow and smirk.

But the Mouser's visage was set in an expression of grim and all-skeptical disdain. He paused at the heaping of objects in front of the

door and scanned it with disapproval. He drew Scalpel from its thin
gray sheath and with the tip of the long blade flipped back the cover
on the topmost of a pile of musty books. Without going any closer he
briefly scanned the first page, shook his head, rapidly turned a half
dozen more pages with Scalpel's tip, using the sword as if it were a
teacher's wand to point out words here and there—because they were
ill-chosen, to judge from his expression—and then abruptly closed the
book with another sword-flip.

Next he used Scalpel's tip to lift a red cloth hanging from a table
behind the books and peer under it suspiciously, to rap contemptuously
a glass jar with a human head floating in it, to touch disparagingly several other objects and to waggle reprovingly at a foot-chained owl
which hooted at him solemnly from its high perch.

He sheathed Scalpel and turned toward the porter with a sour, lifted-
eyebrow look which said—nay, shouted—plainly, "Is *this* all you have
to offer? Is this garbage your excuse for defiling the Dark Plaza with
glare?"

Actually the Mouser was mightily interested by every least item
which he had glimpsed. The book, incidentally, had been in a script
which he not only did not understand, but did not even recognize.

Three things were very clear to the Mouser: first, that this stuff
offered here for sale did not come from anywhere in the World of
Nehwon, no, not even from Nehwon's farthest outback; second, that
all this stuff was, in some way which he could not yet define, extremely
dangerous; third, that all this stuff was monstrously fascinating and that
he, the Mouser, did not intend to stir from this place until he had personally scanned, studied, and if need be tested, every last intriguing
item and scrap.

At the Mouser's sour grimace, the porter went into a convulsion of
wheedling and fawning caperings, seemingly torn between a desire to
kiss the Mouser's foot and to point out with flamboyant caressing gestures every object in his shop.

He ended by bowing so low that his chin brushed the pavement,
sweeping an ape-long arm toward the interior of the shop, and gibber-
ing in atrocious Lankhmarese, "Every object to pleasure the flesh and
senses and imagination of man. Wonders undreamed. Very cheap, very

cheap! Yours for a penny! The Bazaar of the Bizarre. Please to inspect, o king!"

The Mouser yawned a very long yawn with the back of his hand to his mouth, next he looked around him again with the weary, patient, worldly smile of a duke who knows he must put up with many boredoms to encourage business in his demesne, finally he shrugged faintly and entered the shop.

Behind him the porter went into a jigging delirium of glee and began to re-sweep the flagstones like a man maddened with delight.

Inside, the first thing the Mouser saw was a stack of slim books bound in gold-lined fine-grained red and violet leather.

The second was a rack of gleaming lenses and slim brass tubes calling to be peered through.

The third was a slim dark-haired girl smiling at him mysteriously from a gold-barred cage that swung from the ceiling.

Beyond that cage hung others with bars of silver and strange green, ruby, orange, ultramarine, and purple metals.

Fafhrd saw the Mouser vanish into the shop just as his left hand touched the rough chill pate of the Fountain of Dark Abundance and as Akul pointed precisely on Rhan-top as if it were that needle-spire's green-lensed pinnacle-lantern.

He might have followed the Mouser, he might have done no such thing, he certainly would have pondered the briefly glimpsed event, but just then there came from behind him a long low "Hssssst!"

Fafhrd turned like a giant dancer and his longsword Graywand came out of its sheath swiftly and rather more silently than a snake emerges from its hole.

Ten arm lengths behind him, in the mouth of an alleyway darker than the Dark Plaza would have been without its new commercial moon, Fafhrd dimly made out two robed and deeply cowled figures poised side by side.

One cowl held darkness absolute. Even the face of a Negro of Klesh might have been expected to shoot ghostly bronze gleams. But here there were none.

In the other cowl there nested seven very faint pale greenish glows. They moved about restlessly, sometimes circling each other, swinging mazily. Sometimes one of the seven horizontally oval gleams would grow a little brighter, seemingly as it moved forward toward the mouth of the cowl—or a little darker as it drew back.

Fafhrd sheathed Graywand and advanced toward the figures. Still facing him, they retreated slowly and silently down the alley.

Fafhrd followed as they receded. He felt a stirring of interest . . . and of other feelings. To meet his own supernatural mentor alone might be only a bore and a mild nervous strain; but it would be hard for anyone entirely to repress a shiver of awe at encountering at one and the same time both Ningauble of the Seven Eyes and Sheelba of the Eyeless Face.

Moreover, that those two bitter wizardly rivals would have joined forces, that they should apparently be operating together in amity. . . . Something of great note must be afoot! There was no doubting that.

The Mouser meantime was experiencing the smuggest, most mind-teasing, most exotic enjoyments imaginable. The sleekly leather-bound gold-stamped books turned out to contain scripts stranger far than that in the book whose pages he had flipped outside—scripts that looked like skeletal beasts, cloud swirls, and twisty-branched bushes and trees—but for a wonder he could read them all without the least difficulty.

The books dealt in the fullest detail with such matters as the private life of devils, the secret histories of murderous cults, and—these were illustrated—the proper dueling techniques to employ against sword-armed demons and the erotic tricks of lamias, succubi, bacchantes, and hamadryads.

The lenses and brass tubes, some of the latter of which were as fantastically crooked as if they were periscopes for seeing over the walls and through the barred windows of other universes, showed at first only delightful jeweled patterns, but after a bit the Mouser was able to see through them into all sorts of interesting places: the treasure-rooms of dead kings, the bedchambers of living queens, council-crypts of rebel angels, and the closets in which the gods hid plans for worlds too frighteningly fantastic to risk creating.

As for the quaintly clad slim girls in their playfully widely-barred cages, well, they were pleasant pillows on which to rest eyes momentarily fatigued by book-scanning and tube-peering.

Ever and anon one of the girls would whistle softly at the Mouser and then point cajolingly or imploringly or with languorous hintings at a jeweled crank set in the wall whereby her cage, suspended on a gleaming chain running through gleaming pulleys, could be lowered to the floor.

At these invitations the Mouser would smile with a bland amorousness and nod and softly wave a hand from the fingerhinge as if to whisper, "Later . . . later. Be patient."

After all, girls had a way of blotting out all lesser, but not thereby despicable, delights. Girls were for dessert.

Ningauble and Sheelba receded down the dark alleyway with Fafhrd following them until the latter lost patience and, somewhat conquering his unwilling awe, called out nervously, "Well, are you going to keep on fleeing me backward until we all pitch into the Great Salt Marsh? What do you want of me? What's it all about?"

But the two cowled figures had already stopped, as he could perceive by the starlight and the glow of a few high windows, and now it seemed to Fafhrd that they had stopped a moment before he had called out. A typical sorcerors' trick for making one feel awkward! He gnawed his lip in the darkness. It was ever thus!

"Oh My Gentle Son . . ." Ningauble began in his most sugary-priestly tones, the dim puffs of his seven eyes now hanging in his cowl as steadily and glowing as mildly as the Pleiades seen late on a summer night through a greenish mist rising from a lake freighted with blue vitriol and corrosive gas of salt.

"I asked what it's all about!" Fafhrd interrupted harshly. Already convicted of impatience, he might as well go the whole hog.

"Let me put it as a hypothetical case," Ningauble replied imperturbably. "Let us suppose, My Gentle Son, that there is a man in a universe and that a most evil force comes to this universe from another universe, or perhaps from a congeries of universes, and that this man is a brave man who wants to defend his universe and who counts his life as a trifle and that moreover he has to counsel him a very wise and prudent and public-spirited uncle who knows all about these matters which I have been hypothecating—"

"The Devourers menace Lankhmar!" Sheelba rapped out in a voice

as harsh as a tree cracking and so suddenly that Fafhrd almost started—
and for all we know, Ningauble too.

Fafhrd waited a moment to avoid giving false impressions and then
switched his gaze to Sheelba. His eyes had been growing accustomed to
the darkness and he saw much more now than he had seen at the
alley's mouth, yet he still saw not one jot more than absolute blackness
inside Sheelba's cowl.

"Who are the Devourers?" he asked.

It was Ningauble, however, who replied, "The Devourers are the most
accomplished merchants in all the many universes—so accomplished,
indeed, that they sell only trash. There is a deep necessity in this, for the
Devourers must occupy all their cunning in perfecting their methods of
selling and so have not an instant to spare in considering the worth of
what they sell. Indeed, they dare not concern themselves with such matters for a moment, for fear of losing their golden touch—and yet such are
their skills that their wares are utterly irresistible, indeed the finest wares
in all the many universes—if you follow me?"

Fafhrd looked hopefully toward Sheelba, but since the latter did
not this time interrupt with some pithy summation, he nodded to
Ningauble.

Ningauble continued, his seven eyes beginning to weave a bit,
judging from the movements of the seven green glows, "As you might
readily deduce, the Devourers possess all the mightiest magics garnered
from the many universes, whilst their assault groups are led by the most
aggressive wizards imaginable, supremely skilled in all methods of battling, whether it be with the wits, or the feelings, or with the
beweaponed body.

"The method of the Devourers is to set up shop in a new world and
first entice the bravest and the most adventuresome and the supplest-
minded of its people—who have so much imagination that with just a
touch of suggestion they themselves do most of the work of selling
themselves.

"When these are safely ensnared, the Devourers proceed to deal
with the remainder of the population: meaning simply that they sell
and sell and sell!—sell trash and take good money and even finer
things in exchange."

Ningauble sighed windily and a shade piously. "All this is very bad, My Gentle Son," he continued, his eye-glows weaving hypnotically in his cowl, "but natural enough in universes administered by such gods as we have—natural enough and perhaps endurable. However"—he paused—"there is worse to come! The Devourers want not only the patronage of all beings in all universes, but—doubtless because they are afraid someone will someday raise the ever-unpleasant question, of the true worth of things—they want all their customers reduced to a state of slavish and submissive suggestibility, so that they are fit for nothing whatever but to gawk at and buy the trash the Devourers offer for sale. This means of course that eventually the Devourers' customers will have nothing wherewith to pay the Devourers for their trash, but the Devourers do not seem to be concerned with this eventuality. Perhaps they feel that there is always a new universe to exploit. And perhaps there is!"

"Monstrous!" Fafhrd commented. "But what do the Devourers gain from all these furious commercial sorties, all this mad merchandising? What do they really want?"

Ningauble replied, "The Devourers want only to amass cash and to raise little ones like themselves to amass more cash and they want to compete with each other at cash-amassing. (Is that coincidentally a city, do you think, Fafhrd? Cashamash?) And the Devourers want to brood about their great service to the many universes—it is their claim that servile customers make the most obedient subjects for the gods— and to complain about how the work of amassing cash tortures their minds and upsets their digestions. Beyond this, each of the Devourers also secretly collects and hides away forever, to delight no eyes but his own, all the finest objects and thoughts created by true men and women (and true wizards and true demons) and bought by the Devourers at bankruptcy prices and paid for with trash or—this is their ultimate preference—with nothing at all."

"Monstrous indeed!" Fafhrd repeated. "Merchants are ever an evil mystery and these sound the worst. But what has all this to do with me?"

"Oh My Gentle Son," Ningauble responded, the piety in his voice now tinged with a certain clement disappointment, "you force me once again to resort to hypothecating. Let us return to the supposition of this brave man whose whole universe is direly menaced and who counts his life a trifle and to the related supposition of this brave man's wise uncle, whose advice the brave man invariably follows—"

"The Devourers have set up shop in the Plaza of Dark Delights!" Sheelba interjected so abruptly in such iron-harsh syllables that this time Fafhrd actually did start. "You must obliterate this outpost tonight!"

Fafhrd considered that for a bit, then said, in a tentative sort of voice, "You will both accompany me, I presume, to aid me with your wizardly sendings and castings in what I can see must be a most perilous operation, to serve me as a sort of sorcerous artillery and archery corps while I play assault battalion—"

"Oh My Gentle Son . . ." Ningauble interrupted in tones of deepest disappointment, shaking his head so that his eye-glows jogged in his cowl.

"You must do it alone!" Sheelba rasped.

"Without any help at all?" Fafhrd demanded. "No! Get someone else. Get this doltish brave man who always follows his scheming uncle's advice as slavishly as you tell me the Devourers' customers respond to their merchandising. Get *him!* But as for me—No, I say!"

"Then leave us, coward!" Sheelba decreed dourly, but Ningauble only sighed and said quite apologetically, "It was intended that you have a comrade in this quest, a fellow soldier against noisome evil—to wit, the Gray Mouser. But unfortunately he came early to his appointment with my colleague here and was enticed into the shop of the Devourers and is doubtless now deep in their snares, if not already extinct. So you can see that we do take thought for your welfare and have no wish to overburden you with solo quests. However, My Gentle Son, if it still be your firm resolve . . ."

Fafhrd let out a sigh more profound than Ningauble's. "Very well," he said in gruff tones admitting defeat, "I'll do it for you. Someone will have to pull that poor little gray fool out of the pretty-pretty fire—or the twinkly-twinkly water!—that tempted him. But how do I go about it?" He shook a big finger at Ningauble. "And no more Gentle-Sonning!"

Ningauble paused. Then he said only, "Use your own judgment."

Sheelba said, "Beware the Black Wall!"

Ningauble said to Fafhrd, "Hold, I have a gift for you," and held out to him a ragged ribbon a yard long, pinched between the cloth of the wizard's long sleeve so that it was impossible to see the manner of hand that pinched. Fafhrd took the tatter with a snort, crumpled it into a ball, and thrust it into his pouch.

"Have a greater care with it," Ningauble warned. "It is the Cloak of Invisibility, somewhat worn by many magic usings. Do not put it on until you near the Bazaar of the Devourers. It has two minor weaknesses: it will not make you altogether invisible to a master sorcerer if he senses your presence and takes certain steps. Also, see to it that you do not bleed during this exploit, for the cloak will not hide blood."

"I've a gift too!" Sheelba said, drawing from out of his black cowl-hole—with sleeve-masked hand, as Ningauble had done—something that shimmered faintly in the dark like . . .

Like a spiderweb.

Sheelba shook it, as if to dislodge a spider, or perhaps two.

"The Blindfold of True Seeing," he said as he reached it toward Fafhrd. "It shows all things as they really are! Do not lay it across your eyes until you enter the Bazaar. On no account, as you value your life or your sanity, wear it now!"

Fafhrd took it from him most gingerly, the flesh of his fingers crawling. He was inclined to obey the taciturn wizard's instructions. At this moment he truly did not much care to see the true visage of Sheelba of the Eyeless Face.

The Gray Mouser was reading the most interesting book of them all, a great compendium of secret knowledge written in a script of astro-logic and geomantic signs, the meanings of which fairly leaped off the page into his mind.

To rest his eyes from that—or rather to keep from gobbling the book too fast—he peered through a nine-elbowed brass tube at a scene that could only be the blue heaven-pinnacle of the universe where angels flew shimmeringly like dragonflies and where a few choice heroes rested from their great mountain-climb and spied down critically on the antlike labors of the gods many levels below.

To rest his eye from *that*, he looked up between the scarlet (blood-metal?) bars of the inmost cage at the most winsome, slim, fair, jet-eyed girl of them all. She knelt, sitting on her heels, with her upper body leaned back a little. She wore a red velvet tunic and had a mop of golden hair so thick and pliant that she could sweep it in a neat curtain over her upper face, down almost to her pouting lips. With the slim fingers of one hand she would slightly part these silky golden drapes to peer at the Mouser playfully, while with those of the other she rattled golden castanets in a most languorously slow rhythm, though with occasional swift staccato bursts.

The Mouser was considering whether it might not be as well to try a turn or two on the ruby-crusted golden crank next to his elbow, when he spied for the first time the glimmering wall at the back of the shop. What could its material be? he asked himself. Tiny diamonds countless as the sand set in smoky glass? Black opal? Black pearl? Black moonshine?

Whatever it was, it was wholly fascinating, for the Mouser quickly set down his book, using the nine-crooked spy-tube to mark his place—a most engrossing pair of pages on dueling where were revealed the Universal Parry and its five false variants and also the three true forms of the Secret Thrust—and with only a finger-wave to the ensorceling blonde in red velvet he walked quickly toward the back of the shop.

As he approached the Black Wall he thought for an instant that he glimpsed a silver wraith, or perhaps a silver skeleton, walking toward him out of it, but then he saw that it was only his own darkly handsome reflection, pleasantly flattered by the lustrous material. What had momentarily suggested silver ribs was the reflection of the silver lacings on his tunic.

He smirked at his image and reached out a finger to touch *its* lustrous finger when—Lo, a wonder!—his hand went into the wall with never a sensation at all save a faint tingling coolth promising comfort like the sheets of a fresh-made bed.

He looked at his hand inside the wall and—Lo, another wonder—it was all a beautiful silver faintly patterned with tiny scales. And though his own hand indubitably, as he could tell by clenching it, it was scarless now and a mite slimmer and longer fingered—altogether a more handsome hand than it had been a moment ago.

He wriggled his fingers and it was like watching small silver fish dart about—fingerlings!

What a droll conceit, he thought, to have a dark fishpond or rather swimming pool set on its side indoors, so that one could walk into the fracious erect fluid quietly and gracefully, instead of all the noisy, bouncingly athletic business of diving!

And how charming that the pool should be filled not with wet soppy cold water, but with a sort of moon-dark essence of sleep! An essence with beautifying cosmetic properties too—a sort of mudbath without the mud. The Mouser decided he must have a swim in this wonder pool at once, but just then his gaze lit on a long high black couch toward the other end of the dark liquid wall, and beyond the couch a small high table set with viands and a crystal pitcher and goblet.

He walked along the wall to inspect these, his handsome reflection taking step for step with him.

He trailed his hand in the wall for a space and then withdrew it, the scales instantly vanishing and the familiar old scars returning.

The couch turned out to be a narrow high-sided black coffin lined with quilted black satin and piled at one end with little black satin pillows. It looked most invitingly comfortable and restful—not quite as inviting as the Black Wall, but very attractive just the same; there was even a rack of tiny black books nested in the black satin for the occupant's diversion and also a black candle, unlit.

The collation on the little ebony table beyond the coffin consisted entirely of black foods. By sight and then by nibbling and sipping the Mouser discovered their nature: thin slices of a very dark rye bread crusted with poppy seeds and dripped with black butter; slivers of charcoal-seared steak; similarly broiled tiny thin slices of calf's liver sprinkled with dark spices and liberally pricked with capers; the darkest grape jellies; truffles cut paper thin and mushrooms fried black; pickled chestnuts; and of course, ripe olives and black fish eggs—caviar. The black drink, which foamed when he poured it, turned out to be stout laced with the bubbly wine of Ilthmar.

He decided to refresh the inner Mouser—the Mouser who lived a sort of blind soft greedy undulating surface-life between his lips and his belly—before taking a dip in the Black Wall.

*   *   *

Fafhrd re-entered the Plaza of Dark Delights walking warily and with the long tatter that was the Cloak of Invisibility trailing from between left forefinger and thumb and with the glimmering cobweb that was the Blindfold of True Seeing pinched even more delicately by its edge between the same digits of his right hand. He was not yet altogether certain that the trailing gossamer hexagon was completely free of spiders.

Across the Plaza he spotted the bright-mouthed shop—the shop he had been told was an outpost of the deadly Devourers—through a ragged gather of folk moving about restlessly and commenting and speculating to one another in harsh excited undertones.

The only feature of the shop Fafhrd could make out at all clearly at this distance was the red-capped red-footed baggy-trousered porter, not capering now but leaning on his long broom beside the trefoil-arched doorway.

With a looping swing of his left arm Fafhrd hung the Cloak of Invisibility around his neck. The ragged ribband hung to either side down his chest in its wolfskin jerkin only halfway to his wide belt which supported longsword and short-axe. It did not vanish his body to the slightest degree that he could see and he doubted it worked at all. Like many another thaumaturge, Ningauble never hesitated to give one useless charms, not for any treacherous reason, necessarily, but simply to improve one's morals. Fafhrd strode boldly toward the shop.

The Northerner was a tall, broad-shouldered, formidable-looking man—doubly formidable by his barbaric dress and weaponing in supercivilized Lankhmar—and so he took it for granted that the ordinary run of city folk stepped out of his way; indeed it had never occurred to him that they should not.

He got a shock. All the clerks, seedy bravos, scullery folk, students, slaves, second-rate merchants and second-class courtesans who would automatically have moved aside for him (though the last with a saucy swing of the hips) now came straight at him, so that he had to dodge and twist and stop and even sometimes dart back to avoid being toe-tramped and bumped. Indeed one fat pushy proud-stomached fellow almost carried away his cobweb, which he could see now by the light of the shop was free of spiders—or if there were any spiders still on it, they must be very small.

He had so much to do dodging Fafhrd-blind Lankhmarians that he could not spare one more glance for the shop until he was almost at the door. And then before he took his first close look, he found that he was tilting his head so that his left ear touched the shoulder below it and that he was laying Sheelba's spiderweb across his eyes.

The touch of it was simply like the touch of any cobweb when one runs face into it walking between close-set bushes at dawn. Everything shimmered a bit as if seen through a fine crystal grating. Then the least shimmering vanished, and with it the delicate clinging sensation, and Fafhrd's vision returned to normal—as far as he could tell.

It turned out that the doorway to the Devourers' shop was piled with garbage—garbage of a particularly offensive sort: old bones, dead fish, butcher's offal, moldering gravecloths folded in uneven squares like badly bound uncut books, broken glass and potsherds, splintered boxes, large stinking dead leaves orange-spotted with blight, bloody rags, tattered discarded loincloths, large worms nosing about, centipedes a-scuttle, cockroaches a-stagger, maggots a-crawl—and less agreeable things.

Atop all perched a vulture which had lost most of its feathers and seemed to have expired of some avian eczema. At least Fafhrd took it for dead, but then it opened one white-filmed eye.

The only conceivably salable object outside the shop—but it was a most notable exception—was the tall black iron statue, somewhat larger than life-size, of a lean swordsman of dire yet melancholy visage. Standing on its square pedestal beside the door, the statue leaned forward just a little on its long two-handed sword and regarded the Plaza dolefully.

The statue almost teased awake a recollection in Fafhrd's mind—a recent recollection, he fancied—but then there was a blank in his thoughts and he instantly dropped the puzzle. On raids like this one, relentlessly swift action was paramount. He loosened his axe in its loop, noiselessly whipped out Graywand and, shrinking away from the piled and crawling garbage just a little, entered the Bazaar of the Bizarre.

*   *   *

The Mouser, pleasantly replete with tasty black food and heady black drink, drifted to the Black Wall and thrust in his right arm to the shoulder. He waved it about, luxuriating in the softly flowing coolth and balm—admiring its fine silver scales and more than human handsomeness. He did the same with his right leg, swinging it like a dancer exercising at the bar. Then he took a gently deep breath and drifted farther in.

Fafhrd on entering the Bazaar saw the same piles of gloriously bound books and racks of gleaming brass spy-tubes and crystal lenses as had the Mouser—a circumstance which seemed to overset Ningauble's theory that the Devourers sold only trash.

He also saw the eight beautiful cages of jewel-gleaming metals and the gleaming chains that hung them from the ceiling and went to the jeweled wall cranks.

Each cage held a gleaming, gloriously hued, black- or light-haired spider big as a rather small person and occasionally waving a long jointed claw-handed leg, or softly opening a little and then closing a pair of fanged down-swinging mandibles, while staring steadily at Fafhrd with eight watchful eyes set in two jewel-like rows of four.

Set a spider to catch a spider, Fafhrd thought, thinking of his cobweb, and then wondered what the thought meant.

He quickly switched to more practical questions then, but he had barely asked himself whether before proceeding further he should kill the very expensive-looking spiders, fit to be the coursing beasts of some jungle empress—another count against Ning's trash-theory!—when he heard a faint splashing from the back of the shop. It reminded him of the Mouser taking a bath—the Mouser loved baths, slow luxurious ones in hot soapy scented oil-dripped water, the small gray sybarite!—and so Fafhrd hurried off in that direction with many a swift upward overshoulder glance.

He was detouring the last cage, a scarlet-metaled one holding the handsomest spider yet, when he noted a book set down with a crooked spy-tube in it—exactly as the Mouser would keep his place in a book by closing it on a dagger.

Fafhrd paused to open the book. Its lustrous white pages were blank. He put his impalpably cobwebbed eye to the spy-tube. He glimpsed a scene that could only be the smoky red hell-nadir of the universe, where dark devils scuttled about like centipedes and where chained folk gazing yearningly upward and the damned writhed in the grip of black serpents whose eyes shone and whose fangs dripped and whose nostrils breathed fire.

As he dropped tube and book, he heard the faint sonorous quick dull report of bubbles being expelled from a fluid at its surface. Staring instantly toward the dim back of the shop, he saw at last the pearl-shimmering Black Wall and a silver skeleton eyed with great diamonds receding into it. However, this costly bone-man—once more Ning's trash-theory disproved!—still had one arm sticking partway out of the wall and this arm was not bone, whether silver, white, brownish or pink, but live-looking flesh covered with proper skin.

As the arm sank into the wall, Fafhrd sprang forward as fast as he ever had in his life and grabbed the hand just before it vanished. He knew then he had hold of his friend, for he would recognize anywhere the Mouser's grip, no matter how enfeebled. He tugged, but it was as if the Mouser were mired in black quicksand. He laid Graywand down and grasped the Mouser by the wrist too and braced his feet against the rough black flags and gave a tremendous heave.

The silver skeleton came out of the wall with a black splash, meta-morphosing as it did into a vacant-eyed Gray Mouser who without a look at his friend and rescuer went staggering off in a curve and pitched head over heels into the black coffin.

But before Fafhrd could hoist his comrade from this new gloomy predicament, there was a swift clash of footsteps and there came racing into the shop, somewhat to Fafhrd's surprise, the tall black iron statue. It had forgotten or simply stepped off its pedestal, but it had remem-bered its two-handed sword, which it brandished about most fiercely while shooting searching black glances like iron darts at every shadow and corner and nook.

The black gaze passed Fafhrd without pausing, but halted at Graywand lying on the floor. At the sight of that longsword the statue started visibly, snarled its iron lips, narrowed its black eyes. It shot glances more ironly stabbing than before, and it began to move about the shop in sudden zigzag rushes, sweeping its darkly flashing sword in low scythe-strokes.

At that moment the Mouser peeped moon-eyed over the edge of the coffin, lifted a limp hand and waved it at the statue, and in a soft sly foolish voice cried, "Yoo-hoo!"

The statue paused in its searchings and scythings to glare at the Mouser in mixed contempt and puzzlement.

The Mouser rose to his feet in the black coffin, swaying drunkenly, and dug in his pouch.

"Ho, slave!" he cried to the statue with maudlin gaiety, "your wares are passing passable. I'll take the girl in red velvet." He pulled a coin from his pouch, goggled at it closely, then pitched it at the statue. "That's one penny. And the nine-crooked spy-tube. That's another penny." He pitched it. "And *Gron's Grand Compendium of Exotic Lore*—another penny for you! Yes, and here's one more for supper— very tasty, 'twas. Oh and I almost forgot—here's for tonight's lodging!" He pitched a fifth large copper coin at the demonic black statue and, smiling blissfully, flopped back out of sight. The black quilted satin could be heard to sigh as he sank in it.

Four-fifths of the way through the Mouser's penny-pitching Fafhrd decided it was useless to try to unriddle his comrade's nonsensical behavior and that it would be far more to the point to make use of this diversion to snatch up Graywand. He did so on the instant, but by that time the black statue was fully alert again, if it had ever been otherwise. Its gaze switched to Graywand the instant Fafhrd touched the longsword and it stamped its foot, which rang against the stone, and cried a harsh metallic "Ha!"

Apparently the sword became invisible as Fafhrd grasped it, for the black statue did not follow him with its iron eyes as he shifted position across the room. Instead it swiftly laid down its own mighty blade and caught up a long narrow silver trumpet and set it to its lips.

Fafhrd thought it wise to attack before the statue summoned rein- forcements. He rushed straight at the thing, swinging back Graywand for a great stroke at the neck—and steeling himself for an arm-numbing impact.

The statue blew and instead of the alarm blare Fafhrd had expected, there silently puffed out straight at him a great cloud of white powder that momentarily blotted out everything, as if it were the thickest of fogs from Hlal the River.

Fafhrd retreated, choking and coughing. The demon-blown fog cleared quickly, the white powder falling to the stony floor with unnatural swiftness, and he could see again to attack, but now the statue apparently could see him too, for it squinted straight at him and cried its metallic "Ha!" again and whirled its sword around its iron head preparatory to the charge—rather as if winding itself up.

Fafhrd saw that his own hands and arms were thickly filmed with the white powder, which apparently clung to him everywhere except his eyes, doubtless protected by Sheelba's cobweb.

The iron statue came thrusting and slashing in. Fafhrd took the great sword on his, chopped back, and was parried in return. And now the combat assumed the noisy deadly aspects of a conventional longsword duel, except that Graywand was notched whenever it caught the chief force of a stroke, while the statue's somewhat longer weapon remained unmarked. Also, whenever Fafhrd got through the other's guard with a thrust—it was almost impossible to reach him with a slash—it turned out that the other had slipped his lean body or head aside with unbelievably swift and infallible anticipations.

It seemed to Fafhrd—at least at the time—the most fell, frustrating, and certainly the most wearisome combat in which he had ever engaged, so he suffered some feelings of hurt and irritation when the Mouser reeled up in his coffin again and leaned an elbow on the black-satin-quilted side and rested chin on fist and grinned hugely at the battlers and from time to time laughed wildly and shouted such enraging nonsense as, "Use Secret Thrust Two-and-a-Half, Fafhrd—it's all in the book!" or "Jump in the oven!—there'd be a master stroke of strategy!" or—this to the statue—"Remember to sweep under his feet, you rogue!"

Backing away from one of Fafhrd's sudden attacks, the statue bumped the table holding the remains of the Mouser's repast—evidently its anticipatory abilities did not extend to its rear—and scraps of black food and white potsherds and jags of crystal scattered across the floor.

The Mouser leaned out of his coffin and waved a finger waggishly. "You'll have to sweep that up!" he cried and went off into a gale of laughter.

Backing away again, the statue bumped the black coffin. The Mouser only clapped the demonic figure comradely on the shoulder and called, "Set to it again, clown! Brush him down! Dust him off!"

But the worst was perhaps when, during a brief pause while the combatants gasped and eyed each other dizzily, the Mouser waved coyly to the nearest giant spider and called his inane "Yoo-hoo!" again, following it with, "I'll see you, dear, after the circus."

Fafhrd, parrying with weary desperation a fifteenth or a fiftieth cut at his head, thought bitterly, *This comes of trying to rescue small heartless madmen who would howl at their grandmothers hugged by bears. Sheelba's cobweb has shown me the Gray One in his true idiot nature.*

The Mouser had first been furious when the sword-skirling clashed him awake from his black satin dreams, but as soon as he saw what was going on he became enchanted at the wildly comic scene.

For, lacking Sheelba's cobweb, what the Mouser saw was only the zany red-capped porter prancing about in his ridiculous tip-curled red shoes and aiming at Fafhrd, who looked exactly as if he had climbed a moment ago out of a barrel of meal. The only part of the Northerner not whitely dusted was a shadowy dark masklike stretch across his eyes.

What made the whole thing fantastically droll was that miller-white Fafhrd was going through all the motions—and emotions!—of a genuine combat with excruciating precision, parrying the broom as if it were some great jolting scimitar or two-handed broadsword even. The broom would go sweeping up and Fafhrd would gawk at it, giving a marvelous interpretation of apprehensive goggling despite his strangely shadowed eyes. Then the broom would come sweeping down and Fafhrd would brace himself and seem to catch it on his sword only with the most prodigious effort—and then pretend to be jolted back by it!

The Mouser had never suspected Fafhrd had such a perfected theatric talent, even if it were acting of a rather mechanical sort, lacking the broad sweeps of true dramatic genius, and he whooped with laughter.

Then the broom brushed Fafhrd's shoulder and blood sprang out.

Fafhrd, wounded at last and thereby knowing himself unlikely to outendure the black statue—although the latter's iron chest was working now like a bellows—decided on swifter measures. He loosened his hand-axe again in its loop and at the next pause in the fight, both battlers having outguessed each other by retreating simultaneously, whipped it up and hurled it at his adversary's face.

Instead of seeking to dodge or ward off the missile, the black statue lowered its sword and merely wove its head in a tiny circle.

The axe closely circled the lean black head, like a silver wood-tailed comet whipping around a black sun, and came back straight at Fafhrd like a boomerang—and rather more swiftly than Fafhrd had sent it.

But time slowed for Fafhrd then and he half ducked and caught it left-handed as it went whizzing past his cheek.

His thoughts too went for a moment fast as his actions. He thought of how his adversary, able to dodge every frontal attack, had not avoided the table or the coffin behind him. He thought of how the Mouser had not laughed now for a dozen clashes and he looked at him and saw him, though still dazed-seeming, strangely pale and sober-faced, appearing to stare with horror at the blood running down Fafhrd's arm.

So crying as heartily and merrily as he could, "Amuse yourself! Join in the fun, clown!—here's your slap-stick," Fafhrd tossed the axe toward the Mouser.

Without waiting to see the result of that toss—perhaps not daring to—he summoned up his last reserves of speed and rushed at the black statue in a circling advance that drove it back toward the coffin.

Without shifting his stupid horrified gaze, the Mouser stuck out a hand at the last possible moment and caught the axe by the handle as it spun lazily down.

As the black statue retreated near the coffin and poised for what promised to be a stupendous counterattack, the Mouser leaned out and, now grinning foolishly again, sharply rapped its black pate with the axe.

The iron head split like a coconut, but did not come apart. Fafhrd's hand-axe, wedged in it deeply, seemed to turn all at once to iron like the statue and its black haft was wrenched out of the Mouser's hand as the statue stiffened up straight and tall.

The Mouser stared at the split head woefully, like a child who hadn't known knives cut.

The statue brought its great sword flat against its chest, like a staff on which it might lean but did not, and it fell rigidly forward and hit the floor with a ponderous clank.

At that stony-metallic thundering, white wildfire ran across the Black Wall, lightening the whole shop like a distant levin-bolt, and iron-basalt thundering echoed from deep within it.

Fafhrd sheathed Graywand, dragged the Mouser out of the black coffin—the fight hadn't left him the strength to lift even his small friend—and shouted in his ear, "Come on! Run!"

The Mouser ran for the Black Wall.

Fafhrd snagged his wrist as he went by and plunged toward the arched door, dragging the Mouser after him.

The thunder faded out and there came a low whistle, cajolingly sweet.

Wildfire raced again across the Black Wall behind them—much more brightly this time, as if a lightning storm were racing toward them.

The white glare striking ahead imprinted one vision indelibly on Fafhrd's brain: the giant spider in the inmost cage pressed against the bloodred bars to gaze down at them. It had pale legs and a velvet red body and a mask of sleek thick golden hair from which eight jet eyes peered, while its fanged jaws hanging down in the manner of the wide blades of a pair of golden scissors rattled together in a wild staccato rhythm like castanets.

That moment the cajoling whistle was repeated. It too seemed to be coming from the red and golden spider.

But strangest of all to Fafhrd was to hear the Mouser, dragged unwillingly along behind him, cry out in answer to the whistling, "Yes, darling, I'm coming. Let me go, Fafhrd! Let me climb to her! Just one kiss! Sweetheart!"

"Stop it, Mouser," Fafhrd growled, his flesh crawling in mid-plunge. "It's a giant spider!"

"Wipe the cobwebs out of your eyes, Fafhrd," the Mouser retorted pleadingly and most unwittingly to the point. "It's a gorgeous girl! I'll never see her ticklesome like—and I've paid for her! *Sweetheart!*"

Then the booming thunder drowned his voice and any more whistling there might have been, and the wildfire came again, brighter than day, and another great thunderclap right on its heels, and the floor shuddered and the whole shop shook, and Fafhrd dragged the Mouser through the trefoil-arched doorway, and there was another great flash and clap.

The flash showed a semicircle of Lankhmarians peering ashen-faced overshoulder as they retreated across the Plaza of Dark Delights from the remarkable indoor thunderstorm that threatened to come out after them.

Fafhrd spun around. The archway had turned to blank wall.

The Bazaar of the Bizarre was gone from the World of Nehwon.

The Mouser, sitting on the dank flags where Fafhrd had dragged him, babbled wailfully, "The secrets of time and space! The lore of the gods! The mysteries of Hell! Black nirvana! Red and gold Heaven! Five pennies gone forever!"

Fafhrd set his teeth. A mighty resolve, rising from his many recent angers and bewilderments, crystallized in him.

Thus far he had used Sheelba's cobweb—and Ningauble's tatter too—only to serve others. Now he would use them for himself! He would peer at the Mouser more closely and at every person he knew. He would study even his own reflection! But most of all, he would stare Sheelba and Ning to their wizardly cores!

There came from overhead a low "Hssst!"

As he glanced up he felt something snatched from around his neck and, with the faintest tingling sensation, from off his eyes.

For a moment there was a shimmer traveling upward and through it he seemed to glimpse distortedly, as through thick glass, a black face with a cobwebby skin that entirely covered mouth and nostrils and eyes.

Then that dubious flash was gone and there were only two cowled heads peering down at him from over the wall top. There was chuckling laughter.

Then both cowled heads drew back out of sight and there was only the edge of the roof and the sky and the stars and the blank wall.

THE LADY'S GIFTS

Melanie Rawn

ar above the wide, rich plain where the grain and olives grow are granite mountains, crowned with snow in winter and garlanded with flowers in summer. There, amid the sacred groves and holy springs, live the Oreas: priestesses of the mountains and the rocks. The Oreas tend the scattered shrines of the White Lady as Artemis: High Source of Water, Mother of Creatures, Great Huntress. They honor Her as Artemis Diktynna of the Bull-snaring Net; as Artemis Karpophoros, Lady of the Wild Things; as Artemis Hekalene of the Farshooting Moon; as Artemis Orthia, She Who is Upright. But perhaps women love Her best as Artemis Ilithyia, She Who Aids Women in Childbed.

One day a young woman came to Her shrine in need of precisely such help. She was Leiriope, named for the Lily-faced Nymph, and the child turning turbulent in her womb was the child of Kephissos the River god, whose name means Garden. After a long labor assisted by the High Priestess herself in the service of Artemis Ilithyia, a son was

born to Leiriope. She called his name Antheos, Flowery One, and suc-
cumbed to healing sleep.

The infant was gladly welcomed into the world, and all women and
men of the scattered shrines came to marvel at his beauty. His hair was
thick and black, curling about his small, round face; his lips were full
and red as summer-ripe berries; his eyes were long and large; his limbs
were strong and cleanly formed; his skin was without blemish, finely
textured. All agreed that Antheos was the most perfectly beautiful
child ever born.

But there was among them one who was gifted by Artemis Tridaria,
Threefold Assigner of Lots, with prophecy's spark. And while she agreed
with the others that Antheos was indeed lovely, she was compelled to
speak as the Goddess bade her. So before she returned to the small
shrine she tended near a crossroads, she said to her fellow priestesses:
"He will live to a ripe old age—provided that he never knows himself."

When Leiriope heard of this prophecy, she was at first perplexed
and then fearful. "Lady," she begged the High Priestess, "of your great
wisdom, tell me what these words foretell for my son!"

Lady Dryope—whose name means Woodpecker, the bird whose
tapping at trees calls the rain—sat with the new mother while she
nursed the beautiful baby, and after some considerable thought made
her reply.

"There has been talk, of course," Dryope said finally. "Some believe
it means Antheos must never look upon his own beauty. Now, this
seems to be a very silly idea. Even if he never sees his own reflection—
which is impossible to arrange—it is absurd to think that he will never
look upon his own body and see for himself how splendid it is. And it is
obvious that anyone whose eyes are cast upon him, even if sworn to
silence, will reveal in his eyes that he is beautiful. He will know, no
matter what, so I think we can put aside that particular interpretation."

"I am glad to hear you say it," Leiriope replied shyly.

"Something else is being said," Dryope continued. "That such
beauty as your son's is not given without purpose. It could be that
Antheos was born to remind others of the perfection of the White
Lady's works."

This heartened Leiriope. She smiled, and a blush suffused her lily-pale cheeks, and she stroked her son's thick black curls as she murmured, "I would be honored to believe that this is so."

"Perhaps it is. Perhaps the prophecy means only that he must never know this, lest pride and arrogance make him despised among us. But I will tell you what else people are saying: that he should be sent away and be raised in ignorance of whose son he is, so that he will never know his true self."

"No!" cried Leiriope, clutching the child to her breast. "Do not say I must send him away from me!"

"Have I said such?" Dryope asked mildly. "Be easy in your heart, for there is yet another interpretation to the words, and it is my feeling that this is the true one. Calm yourself, my dear, and listen. It is my belief that the prophecy warns Antheos to live in ignorance not of his beauty or his identity, but of his true nature. He must remain a stranger to his own soul."

Leiriope was more confused than ever. "How can this be?" she asked. "If my Antheos never knows the truth of himself—"

"His soul will wither—yet if he does learn, he will not long survive."

"What can be done?" the stricken mother whispered.

"I think perhaps there is a purpose here we have not yet discerned. The first and most obvious truth about Antheos is that he is beautiful. It is my belief that if he is to live, he must never know anything about himself *except* that he is beautiful. As for how this may be accomplished . . ." Dryope sighed, shook her head, and finished, "Allow me to think for a time on this, and I will try to find a solution."

So saying, she rose and bent to kiss Leiriope's brow, then paused to caress the baby's round cheek. Curiously enough, the child drew back from her touch. Much troubled, Dryope went away.

The Moon's face changed from Mother to Crone to Maiden before Lady Dryope returned to Leiriope, who was sitting outside on the sun-warmed grass, holding Antheos in her arms as he slept. Seating herself nearby, inhaling gently of the sweet breeze, Dryope spent some few moments admiring the exquisite infant before she spoke.

"I think I know how your son may live a long life. You and he will remain here. In this way we may all surpervise him—and know the wonderment of his growth into ever greater beauty," she added, a little wryly, for she had just experienced that very thing herself on seeing Antheos for the first time in nearly a month.

"I would very much like to stay with you here, Lady," Leiriope murmured.

"I had hoped you would. I feel that we can become good friends, my dear. Your Antheos will grow within the embrace of the forests and the mountains, and be educated just as all the other children are."

"Oh, thank you—thank you—"

But Dryope shook her head, suddenly stern. "Hear me, Leiriope. Although Antheos will learn what is right and proper, so that he may not offend against the White Lady in his ignorance, he will never be taught men's rituals. He will learn not the slightest of their devotions, not the least of their hymns, not a word of poetry, not a note of music, not a step of the Crane Dance. He will be shown nothing of how the nets are tied or the spears are thrown. He will set foot in no sacred precinct. He will witness no rite, he will take part in no ceremony. He will know nothing of the paths by which we discover our truths with Her wise guidance."

Leiriope heard all this in pain, yet nodded quietly when Dryope finished. "I understand."

"Do you, my dear? Do you see that he must not grow up in the greater world if he is to live?"

"I understand," Leiriope said once again, gazing down at her son. "Who can know what he might see or hear or otherwise witness by accident?"

"Exactly. Here, we will watch over him. Here, he will remain safely ignorant. By these rites and ceremonies we find our truest selves. Antheos must know nothing of such things. No one will speak to him of them, not even obliquely. And to this end, I will command that only those words spoken by Antheos himself may be used in speech to him. Knowing no words of ritual, he cannot ask about such things."

"And so he will be as safe as we can make him. I understand," Leiriope said for the third time. And, even though this plan would mean a long life for her beloved son, she could not help but weep.

Dryope comforted her, stroking her sleek hair and rocking her as if Leiriope were no older than the infant Antheos. As for the baby, he slept on, oblivious—except when once again Dryope caressed his cheek, and once again he twitched away from the touch.

It came to pass as Lady Dryope had said. Antheos grew in beauty but not in knowledge. Forbidden men's rituals, he spent his time running wild in the mountains. He learned all there was to be learned about the forest, from winter snows to spring floods, from the most delicate of mosses to the most towering of pines. Especially did he learn the names and ways of all the flowers, which he came to think of as his brothers and sisters. He would suffer no garlands or bouquets in his presence, for every blossom plucked was a death in his family. He was indulged in this by those around him; in truth, it was no difficulty, for celebrations offering flowers were never seen by Antheos, and he did not know how to ask about them. Thus Lady Dryope's command regarding words spoken to Antheos kept him in ignorance. He was taught enough to prevent sacrilege, but because he knew none of the words applying to ritual, he could not ask and thus could not be told.

As for his staggering beauty, things were also much as Lady Dryope had anticipated: All eyes told the growing boy of his perfections. At length, though his reflection was not forbidden him, and he often sought the chill silver mirroring of his own admiration, he came to prefer the mirror of other people's awestruck eyes.

All loved Antheos—even when he parted his exquisite lips to reject their love. For another thing Dryope had discussed with Leiriope had come to pass: Antheos, after much thought about why he and none other was so beautiful, came to believe that the White Lady had created him for a reason. To him, this meant he must remain undefiled by lesser creatures. He could allow no one to sully his perfection with so much as a touch, let alone an embrace. Dryope, recalling how he had twisted away from physical contact even in babyhood, was unsurprised that this should be so.

He permitted only the caresses of his mother, Leiriope the Lily-faced, and of his bright-petaled siblings of the meadows and glades and riverbanks. To the woman and to the flowers he showed great love and tenderness, but to none other.

* * *

Dryope herself had a son, born three months after Antheos. She named this child of her later years Ameinios: Unpausing, to commemorate the onging gift of her fertility. As Ameinios grew from lively infant to inquisitive toddler, it became apparent that he was well-named indeed, for his interest, once fixed, was utterly unfailing.

Ameinios grew apace with Antheos, and in their sixteenth summer he became Antheos' most insistent suitor—speaking to him whenever he had the chance, watching him whenever he was within view, and finally leaving gifts at Leiriope's dwelling every morning for a full cycle of the Summer Moon.

Honeycombs dripping rich and golden; armlets and necklets of white shells gathered from the sea far below and blue feathers fallen from high above, woven together with locks of Ameinios' own long, straight black hair; stones he carved into the shapes of Antheos' beloved flowers; plump raisins, pungent mint, ripe olives, jars of juicy pomegranate seeds like a thousand crimson hearts—all these gifts Ameinios left for Antheos. Or perhaps they were not gifts but tribute, such as a lesser king might give to She Who Shines For All at the great palace of Knossos—or perhaps they were offerings, such as a humble supplicant would leave for a god.

But all these gifts were scorned. The honeycombs and other foodstuffs Antheos left untouched, and they became a splendid feast for the ants. The flower-stones he ground into the dirt with his heel, saying derisively that perhaps Ameinios thought that with watering they would grow. The ornaments made of white shells and blue feathers and Ameinios' black hair he simply ignored.

Ameinios' name was now his curse. The unpausing, unfailing devotion that would have moved others merely bored Antheos. Seeing this, and distressed for both young men, the mother of Antheos went to the mother of Ameinios and begged her to turn her son from a love that could only break his heart.

"I know Antheos," said Leiriope. "He does not mean to be cruel. It is not from wickedness that he rejects Ameinios. He knows nothing of malice or spite. It is only that he—"

"He knows nothing beyond himself," Dryope replied coldly, "and of himself, he knows nothing." Then, because the two women had indeed become friends, she softened and allowed her own sorrow to speak. "I also know Antheos, and what you say is true. He cannot feel how he wounds Ameinios, for he cannot feel what Ameinios feels. He who does not know his own soul cannot know another's—much less love another's."

Leiriope bent her graceful head. "He knows the wording of love because I have spoken such to him, of my own great love for him. And by your command, what words he says, others may use in speaking to him. This is my fault, Lady. Tell me what may be done."

Dryope sighed gently, then said, "Let your son make an answer to my son. That much at least is owed Ameinios for his steadfastness. Perhaps he will then be convinced that his love is hopeless."

The next morning a gift was left at the dwelling of Lady Dryope. Antheos had answered, and with a sword. But the bronze blade did not gleam, nor the oakwood handle glow with polishing. Instead, the sword lay dark and dull in the dirt, all rust and splinters.

The sight of it paled Ameinios' cheeks. He bent, grasped it in his hand, and whispered to his mother, "This is his answer. He tells me to cut all love for him from my heart, and to sever my spirit from his spirit. Thus he has answered my love for him." So saying, Ameinios walked blindly away.

Lady Dryope wept in bitter silence, for she knew the answer meant something even worse: The blade Ameinios used for the task need not even be clean and pure, as for healing incisions or sacred sacrifice. Antheos' answer meant that cutting love from one's heart was of no more importance than chopping bits of hearthfire kindling, and was no sacrifice at all.

The sun had not moved a finger's width in the sky before a scream rent the granite mountains. There was a moment of terrible quiet, and then the moanings of grief at death untimely. Dryope left off her prayers and followed the mourning cries of the Oreas to the place where they had gathered. And when she found them, horror filled her throat and choked all utterance. The sword that Antheos had given him, Ameinios had used to kill himself on Antheos' very threshold. Its rusted blade was deep in his heart, its splintered handle thick with his blood. With the last life in his lungs he cried out, "Mother, avenge me!" And he died.

Dryope knelt, mute with shock and sorrow, beside the body of her son. She stroked his long, straight hair that had never curled in a comely way—his hair that now spread on his chest clotted with blood. She caressed with her fingertip his lively face that had never come close to the ideal of beauty—his face that now was a still mask of death. She bent to kiss his soft lips that had never pulsed as full and red as summer-ripe berries—his lips that now were cold and slack.

She glanced up, and in the doorway she saw Leiriope, stricken and afraid. Leiriope, whose son was perfect and beautiful and alive. Leiriope, whose son had been the death of Dryope's son.

"Where is Antheos?" Dryope asked, quite calmly.

"He—he has run away to the forest," Leiriope stammered.

"Then he knows what has been done this day."

"Yes." Leiriope fell to her knees. "Oh, dearest Lady, I grieve with you, I would I had never come here—"

Dryope slowly rose, gazing down on her friend. "Grieve not for me," she told Leiriope. "Grieve for your son."

Then she turned away. And she upon whom age had but lightly rested until now walked with the stiff and painful steps of a very old woman to her own home, and for many days did not show her face either to the Moon or to the sun.

Now, among those who saw Ameinios plunge the sword into his breast and heard his dying words was the young priestess Akka. Even as Akka had cried out with the others in horror and mourning, she had heard a thing they did not: that the word Ameinios used for *Mother* was also one by which the White Lady was at times addressed. Later, as Akka helped to wash the blood from Ameinios' body and prepare him for burial, she heard another thing: As clearly if she had been alive then to hear it, she heard the prophecy of Artemis Tridaria spoken at the birth of Antheos. And she knew without question what must be the manner of the Great Mother's vengeance.

That she heard these things was unsurprising: Akka means She Who Fashions, and the way of her fashioning was with sound. When she whistled, people looked up expecting to see an eagle; when she made rippling sounds in her throat, people looked down expecting the next step to be into a stream. She could mimic anything and anyone; she could sing any part in the hymns, and soothe a fretful baby by crooning in its mother's very tones. She delighted in calling from hiding with other people's voices, male or female, to confuse those she called to. She made everyone laugh by causing words to issue seemingly from stones, or trees, or empty air.

But more: when the strength of the White Lady was upon her, Akka could call strong magics with her voice. At such times she could sing the fevered back to health, call sparks of Sacred Fire to the altars, or whistle birds to the hunters' snares and animals to their spears. As truly as Antheos knew all the flowers that he believed to be his kin, so Akka knew all those things and creatures that made sound.

So she had no difficulty in tracing his flight on the morning of Ameinios' death. Antheos' step, his breathing, his very heartbeat, were as words to Akka, calling out his presence in the forest. When she neared him, she whispered words of silence to hide herself from him. Then she murmured words of wayward paths to guide him off the usual trails to a place of her own choosing.

He came thus to a pond: clear as silver, wide as the embrace of his own strong arms, and smooth as an unclouded sky. Never had this water been disturbed by fish, insects, birds, wild beasts, even by leaves dropping from the trees shading it or petals from the flowers lining its banks. Antheos was by this time exhausted and thirsty, and so intent on a cool sip from the pond that he did not hear a woodpecker unpausingly batter a tree trunk, calling for rain. Because Antheos knew nothing beyond himself, he did not hear the warning Akka in all fairness gave him.

Antheos knelt beside the pond, hands reaching to cup water. But then he stopped, for gazing up at him, and as startled as he, was perfection: the dark eyes shining like sunlit jewels, the long black curls glistening, the face all purity of line and curve and angle, and with a sheen upon it as dew sparkles on meadow flowers. In this wide, smooth mirror of water, he fell finally and completely under his own beauteous spell.

At length, recovering from delight and shock, and fully in love with this vision, he cried, "Never have I seen such beauty!"

"Such beauty!" exclaimed the glorious creature in Antheos' very voice.

"You are wonderful!"

"Wonderful!"

"Who are you?"

"You!"

Antheos then knew this was sacred water—the first he had ever beheld in his life. He, forbidden such places, had been led to this one by the White Lady so that She might show him the most sacred vision of all: himself. Moreover, this perfect face answered in his own voice with his own words, agreeing with him in all things—and surely this was a sign that there was none to whom he could give himself *but* himself, for to mate with baser creatures would be to soil what She had created.

"Ameinios was not worthy," he confided. "To send him that rusty old sword was rightly done."

And he saw and heard himself answer, "Rightly done!"

"After all, I did not ask him to love me."

"Love me!"

And in that instant, hearing both affirmation and plea spoken with his own voice, he was the happiest he had ever been in all his life. He was loved by the only being he *could* love. And he laughed in perfect joy.

Akka watched from her hiding place and quivered, for she recognized signs that Antheos in his ignorance of ritual could not: This was the *ekstasis*, the standing-forth-naked that strips away all but the true and essential self. And by this Akka knew that the White Lady was indeed present, and that Her strength was upon her in what she must do.

"I love you," Antheos cried aloud to the image of himself.

"Love you," Akka replied, and her voice as his voice shook with the shaking of her body. Yet in the next moment she was calm. She would do as she was compelled, and fashion Antheos' punishment with Antheos' own words, faithful both to the command of Lady Dryope and to the vengeance of Artemis Laphria: She Who Despoils.

Antheos heard the tremor of power as the trembling of passion and rejoiced anew. "You love me!"

"Love me!"

"I will love you—I must have you—" His fingers reached for the reaching fingers. "I must touch you!"

"Touch you!"

Just as his hand met that other hand, the vision vanished in a whirl of rippling water.

"Come back!" Antheos pleaded.

"Come back!" cried his second voice, though the face was gone.

"I never left you—I'm here!"

"I'm here!"

And then all joy died in him, and his fine, proud head bowed heavy on his neck. How could he possess such beauty? It was himself, and already his. He could love only himself, as was only right, for no one was as perfect as he—yet he could not touch the perfection he beheld. Antheos could not bear the bitterness of finding at last the only being he wished to possess—the only being he could never truly possess.

Gazing once more into the smoothing water, he told the mirrored perfection, "I can never hold you in my arms."

"Never hold you in my arms."

Grief overcame him; he wept, and Akka wept with him. "The White Lady is too cruel," he cried, "to do such to me, Her most beautiful creation! How can I have faith in Her?"

"Have faith in Her!"

Antheos ceased his weeping. In wonder, he nodded slowly. He must have faith. The Lady would not bring him here to show him perfection and then deny it to him forever. He was meant to love and be loved only by himself. So he reached both his hands into the pond up to the shoulders, certain that through Her grace his reflection would be made real, to hold and possess and love.

Of course he embraced only water, shattering the reflection. He reached deeper and grasped soft mossy mud at the bottom of the pond. He snatched his hands back in disgust, and as he rinsed the muck from his fingers he called out, "Where are you? Are you here?"

"Here."

"I love you, come to me!"

"Come to me!"

And so he plunged his hands and arms into the water again, and again, until he sobbed with frustration. Finally he crawled to the bed of flowers on the bank and lay recovering his breath. The presence of his brothers and sisters for once did not gladden his heart; they were but single blooms, whereas in him, the Flowery One, was manifest all the beauty of all of the blossoms in all the world. He had but one equal.

After a time, when he searched the surface of the pond for his beloved once again, there was his reflection, soaked and sodden but beautiful still.

"You can never be mine," he sorrowed.

"Be mine!"

"I cannot! I can never hold you in my arms—nor can you hold me."

"Hold me!"

"It's impossible!" Antheos cried. "You and I can never be lovers—I can never know you as truly as you must know yourself—"

"*Know yourself,*" Akka answered—and She Who Fashions made of those words Antheos' death.

He gazed upon himself in the water, and at last he understood. He had seen and loved what Ameinios and all the others had seen and loved. And as he had denied their embraces, so, too, he was now denied. No one had ever touched him; no one ever could, not even him. There was nothing to *be* touched. The fine dark eyes in the sacred water's smooth surface were his most perfect mirror: He was indeed supremely beautiful—and as shallow and as insubstantial as his own reflection.

For shame and grief and crushing despair Antheos threw himself into the water, and not for love of himself but for true knowledge, he died.

Akka saw and was moved to pity. When the perfect face rose to the surface of the pond—no reflection now, but his own true face—and darkness overswept the fine dark eyes, Akka found it in her to speak a final word: his name.

She Who Fashions All caused Akka to make of that word a flower, and beside the sacred water where Antheos died there sprang up all around lovely white narkissos. The scent was as beautiful as Antheos himself had been beautiful, and strangely comforting to Akka's sorrow. She breathed deep of the fragrance, and walked slowly back through the forest to her home.

When others came later and found Antheos and pulled him from the water, Leiriope cast herself down beside his body to weep. But as the white flowers leaned over her, caressing her cheeks with their beauty and her sorrow with their scent, she, too, was comforted.

And so it has been ever since, that to breathe of the sweet narkissos is to benumb grief.

But the narkissos flower is also one of the most poisonous in all the forest: as beautiful as Antheos had been beautiful, and as lethal.

THE WALKER BEHIND

Marion Zimmer Bradley

As one who on a lonesome road
Doth walk in fear and dread
And turns but once to look around
And turns no more his head
Because he knows a frightful fiend
Doth close behind him tread. . . .

ythande heard the following footsteps that night on the road: a little pause so that if she chose, she could have believed it merely the echo of her own light footfall. Step-pause-step, and then, after a little hesitation, step-pause-step, step-pause-step.

And at first she did think it an echo, but when she stopped for a moment to assess the quality of the echo, it went on for at least three steps into the silence:

Step-pause-step; step-pause-step.

Not an echo, then, but someone, or some *thing*, following her. In the world of the Twin Suns, where encountering magic was rather more likely than not, magic was more often than not of the evil kind. In a lifetime spanning at least three ordinary lifetimes, Lythande had encountered a great deal of magic; she was by necessity a mercenary-magician, an Adept of the Blue Star, and by choice a minstrel; and she had discovered early in her life that good magic was the rarest of all encounters and seldom came her way. She had lived this long by developing very certain instincts; and her instincts told her that this footfall following her was not benevolent.

She had no notion of what it might be. The simplest solution was that someone in the last town she had passed through had developed a purely material grudge against her, and was following her on mischief bent, for some reason or no reason at all—perhaps a mere mortal distrust of magicians, or of magic, a condition not at all rare in Old Gandrin—and had chosen to take the law into his or her own hands and dispose of the unwelcome procurer of said magic. This was not at all rare, and Lythande had dealt with plenty of would-be assassins who wished to stop the magic by putting an effective stop to the magician; however powerful an Adept's magic, it could seldom survive a knife in the back. On the other hand, it could be handled with equal simplicity; after three ordinary lifetimes, Lythande's back had not yet become a sheath for knives.

So Lythande stepped off the road, loosening the first of her two knives in its scabbard—the simple white-handled knife, whose purpose was to handle purely material dangers of the road: footpads, assassins, thieves. She enveloped herself in the gray, cloudy folds of the hooded mage-robe, which made her look like a piece of the night itself, or a shadow, and stood waiting for the owner of the footsteps to come up with her.

But it was not that simple. Step-pause-step, and the footfalls died; the mysterious follower was pacing her. Lythande had hardly thought it would be so simple. She sheathed the white-handled knife again, and stood motionless, reaching out with all her specially trained senses to focus on the follower.

What she felt first was a faint electric tingle in the Blue Star that was between her brows; and a small, not quite painful crackle in her head. *The smell of magic*, she translated to herself; whatever was following, it was neither as simple, nor as easily disposed of, as an assassin with a knife.

She loosened the black-handled knife in the left-hand scabbard and, stepping herself like a ghost or a shadow, retraced her steps at the side of the road. This knife was especially fashioned for supernatural menaces, to kill ghosts and anything else from specters to were-wolves; no knife but this one could have taken her own life had she tired of it.

A shadow with an irregular step glided toward her, and Lythande raised the black-handled knife. It came plunging down, and the glimmer of the enchanted blade was lost in the shadow. There was a far-off, eerie cry that seemed to come, not from the shadow facing her on the dark road, but from some incredibly distant ghostly realm, to curdle the very blood in her veins, to wrench pain and lightnings from the Blue Star between her brows. Then, as that cry trembled into silence, Lythande felt the black handle of the knife come back into her hand, but a faint glimmer of moonlight showed her the handle alone: the blade had vanished, except for some stray drops of molten metal that fell slowly to the earth and vanished.

So the blade, was gone, the black-handled knife that had slain unnumbered ghosts and other supernatural beings. Judging by the terrifying cry, Lythande had wounded her follower; but had she killed the thing that had eaten her magical blade? Anything that powerful would certainly be tenacious of life.

And if her black-handled knife would not kill it, it was unlikely it could be killed by any spell, protection, or magic she could command at the moment. It had been driven away, perhaps, but she could not be certain she had freed herself from it. No doubt, if she went on, it would continue to follow her, and one day it would catch up with her on some other lonesome road.

But for the moment she had exhausted her protection. And . . . Lythande glowered angrily at the black knife handle and the ruined blade . . . she had deprived herself needlessly of a protection that had never failed her before. Somehow she must manage to replace her enchanted knife before she again dared the roads of Old Gandrin by night.

For the moment—although she had traveled too far and for too long to fear anything she was *likely* to encounter on any ordinary night—she would be wiser to remove herself from the road. Such encounters as a mercenary-magician, particularly one such as Lythande, should expect were seldom of the likely kind.

So she went on in the darkness, listening for the hesitating step of the follower behind. There was only the vaguest and most distant sounds; that blow, and that screech, indicated that while she had probably not destroyed her follower, she had driven it at least for a while into some other place. Whether it was dead, or had chosen to go and follow someone safer, for the moment Lythande neither knew nor cared.

The important thing at the moment was shelter. Lythande had been traveling these roads for many years, and remembered that many years ago there had been an inn somewhere hereabouts. She had never chosen, before this, to shelter there—unpleasant rumors circulated about travelers who spent the night at the inn and were never seen again, or seen in dreadfully altered form. Lythande had chosen to stay away; the rumors were none of her business, and Lythande had not survived this long in Old Gandrin without knowing the first rule of survival, which was to ignore everything but your *own* survival. On the rare occasions when curiosity or compassion had prompted her to involve herself in anyone else's fate, she had had all kinds of reason to regret it.

Perhaps her obscure destiny had guided her on this occasion to investigate these rumors. She looked down the black expanse of the road—without even moonlight—and saw a distant glimmer of light. Whether it was the inn of uncanny rumor, or whether it was the light of a hunter's campfire, or the lair of a were-dragon, there, Lythande resolved, she would seek shelter for the night. The last client to avail himself of her services as a mercenary-magician—a man who had paid her well to dehaunt his ancestral mansion—had left her with more than enough coin for a night at even the most luxurious inn; and if she could not pick up a commission to offset the cost of a night's shelter, she was no worse off. Besides, with the lute at her back, she could usually earn a supper and a bed as a minstrel; they were not common in this quarter.

A few minutes of brisk walking strengthened the vague light into a brilliantly shining lantern hung over a painted sign that portrayed the figure of an old woman driving a pig; the inn sign read the Hag and Swine. Lythande chuckled under her breath . . . the sign was comical enough, but it startled her that for such a cheerful sign there was no sound of music or jollity from inside; all was quiet as the very demon-haunted road itself. It made her remember again the very unsavory rumors about this very inn.

There was a very old story about a hag who indeed attempted to transform random travelers into swine, and other forms, but Lythande could not remember where she had heard that story. Well, if she, an Adept of the Blue Star, was no match for any roadside hag, whatever her propensity of increasing her herd of swine—or perhaps furnishing her table with pork—at the expense of travelers, she deserved whatever happened to her. Shouldering her lute and concealing the handle of the ruined knife in one of the copious pockets of the mage-robe, Lythande strode through the half-open door.

Inside, it was light, but only by contrast with the moonless darkness of the outdoors. The only light was firelight, from a hearth where a pale fire flickered with a dim and unpleasant flame. Gathered around the hearth were a collection of people, mere shapes in the dim room; but as Lythande's eyes adapted to the darkness, she began to make out forms, perhaps half a dozen men and women and a couple of shabby children; all had pinched faces, and pushed-in noses that were somehow porcine. From the dimness arose the tall, heavy form of a woman, clad in shapeless garments that seemed to hang on her anyhow, much patched and botched.

Ah, thought Lythande, *this innkeeper must be the hag. And those wretched children might very well be the swine.* Even secretly the jest pleased her.

In an unpleasant, snuffling voice, the tall hag demanded, "Who are you, sir, going about on the road where there be nowt but hants an' ghosts at this season?"

Lynthande's first impulse was to gasp out, "I was *driven* here by evil magic; there is a monstrous Thing out there, prowling about this place!" But she managed to say instead, peacefully, "Neither hant nor ghost, but a wandering minstrel frightened like yourselves by the dangers of the road, and in need of supper and a night's lodging."

"At once, sir," said the hag, suddenly turning deferential. "Come to the fire and warm thyself."

Lythande came through the jostling crowd of small figures—yes, they were children, and at close range even more unpleasantly piglike; their sounds and snuffles made them even more animal. She felt a distinct revulsion for having them crowding against her. She was resigned to the "sir" with which the hag-innkeeper had greeted her; Lythande was the only woman ever to penetrate the mysteries of the Order of the Blue Star, and when (already sworn as an Adept, the Blue Star already blazing between her brows) she had been exposed as a woman, she was already protected against the worst they could have done. And so her punishment had been only this:

Be forever, then, had decreed the Master of the Star, *what you have chosen to seem; for on that day when any man save myself proclaims you a woman, then shall your magic be void and you may be slain and die.*

So for more than three ordinary lifetimes had Lythande wandered the roads as a mercenary-magician, doomed to eternal solitude; for she might reveal her true sex to no man, and while she might have a woman confidante if she could find one she could trust with her life, this exposed her chosen confidante to pressure from the many enemies of an Adept of the Blue Star; her first such confidante had been captured and tortured, and although she had died without revealing Lythande's secret, Lythande had been reluctant ever to expose another to that danger.

What had begun as a conscious masquerade was now her life; not a single gesture or motion revealed her as anything but the man she seemed—a tall, clean-shaven man with luxuriant fair hair, the blazing Blue Star between the high-arched shaven eyebrows, clad beneath the mage-robe in thigh-high boots, breeches, and a leather jerkin laced to reveal a figure muscular and broad-shouldered as an athlete, and apparently altogether masculine.

The innkeeper-hag brought a mug of drink and set it down before Lythande. It smelled savory and steamed hot; evidently a mulled wine with spices, a specialty of the house. Lythande lifted it to her lips, only pretending to sip; one of the many vows fencing about the powers of an Adept of the Blue Star was that they might never be seen to eat or drink in the presence of any man. The drink smelled good—as did the food she could smell cooking somewhere—and Lythande resented, not for the first time, the law that often condemned her to long periods of thirst and hunger; but she was long accustomed to it and recalling the singular name and reputation of this establishment, and the old story about the hag and swine, perhaps it was just as well to shun such food or drink as might be found in this place; it was by their greed, if she remembered the tale rightly, that the travelers had found themselves transformed into pigs.

The greedy snuffling of the hoglike children, if that was that they were, served as a reminder, and listening to it, she felt neither thirsty nor hungry. It was her custom at such inns to order a meal served in the privacy of her chamber, but she decided that in this place she would not indulge it; in the pockets of her mage-robe she kept a small store of dried fruit and bread, and long habit had accustomed her to snatching a hurried bite whenever she could do so unobserved.

She took a seat at one of the rough tables near the fireplace, the pot of ale before her, and, now and again pretending to take a sip of it, asked, "What news, friends?"

Her encounter fresh in her mind, she half expected to be told of some monster haunting the roadway. But nothing was volunteered. Instead, a rough-looking man seated on the opposite bench from hers, on the other side of the fireplace, raised his pot of ale and said, "Your health, sir; it's a bad night to be out. Storm coming on, unless I'm mistaken. And I've been traveling these roads, man and boy, for forty years."

"Oh?" inquired Lythande courteously. "I am new to these parts. Are the roads generally safe?"

"Safe enough," he grunted, "unless the folks get the idea you're a jewel carrier or some such." He needed to add no more; there were always thieves who might take the notion that some person was not so poor as he sought to appear (so as to seem to have nothing worth stealing), and cut him open looking for his jewels.

"And you?"

"I travel the roads as my old father did; I am a dog barber." He spoke the words truculently. "Anyone who has a dog to show or to sell knows I can make the beast look to its best advantage." Someone behind his back snickered, and he drew himself up to his full height and proclaimed, "It's a respectable profession."

"One of your kind," said a man before the fire, "sold my old father an old dog with rickets and the mange, for a healthy watchdog: the old critter hardly had the strength to bark."

"I don't sell dogs," said the man haughtily. "I only prepare them for show—"

"And o'course you'd never stoop to faking a mongrel up to look like a purebred, or fixing up an old dog with the mange to look like a young one with glossy topknots and long hair," said the heckler ironically. "Everybody in this country knows that when you have some bad old stock to get rid of, stolen horses to paint with false marks, there's old Gimlet the dog faker, worse than any gypsy for tricks—"

"Hey there, don't go insulting honest gypsies with your comparisons," said a dark man seated on a box on the floor by the fire and industriously eating a rich-smelling stew from a wooden bowl; he had a gold earring in his ear like one of that maligned race. "We trade horses all up and down this country from here to Northwander, and I defy any man to say he ever got a bad horse from any of our tribe."

"Gimlet the dog barber, are ye?" asked another of the locals, a shabby, squint-eyed man. "I've been looking for you; don't you remember me?"

The dog barber put on a defiant face. "Afraid not, friend."

"I had a bitch last year had thirteen pups," said the newcomer, scowling. "Good bitch; been the pride and joy of my family since she was a pup. You said you'd fix her up a brew so she'd get her milk in and be able to feed them all—"

"Every dog handler learns something of the veterinary art," said Gimlet. "I can bring in a cow's milk, too, and—"

"Oh, I make no doubt you can shoe a goose, too, to hear you tell it," the man said.

"What's your complaint, friend? Wasn't she able to feed her litter?"

"Oh, aye, she was," said the complainer. "And for a couple of days, it felt good watching every little pup sucking away at her tits; then it occurred to me to count 'em, and there were no more than eight pups."

Gimlet restrained a smile.

"I said only that I would arrange matters so the bitch could feel all her brood; if I disposed of the runts who would have been unprofitable, without you having to harrow yourself by drowning them—" Gimlet began.

"Don't you go weaseling out of it," the man said, clenching his fists. "Any way you slice it, you owe me for at least five good pups."

Gimlet looked round. "Well, that's as may be," he said. "Maybe tomorrow we can arrange something. It never occurred to me you'd get chesty about the runts in the litter, more than any bitch could raise. Not unless you've a childless wife or young daughter who wants to cosset something and hankers to feed 'em with an eye-dropper and dress 'em in doll's clothes; more trouble than it's worth, most folks say. But here's my hand on it." He stuck out his hand with such a friendly, open smile of good faith that Lythande was enormously entertained; between the rogue and the yokel, Lythande, after years spent traveling the roads, was invariably on the side of the rogue. The disgruntled dog owner hesitated a moment, but finally shook his hand and called for another pot of beer for all the company.

Meanwhile the hag-innkeeper, hovering to see if it would come to some kind of fight, and looking just a little disappointed that it had not, stopped at Lythande's side.

"You, sir, will be wanting a room for the night?"

Lythande considered. She did not particularly like the look of the place, and if she spent the night, resolved she would not feel safe in closing her eyes. On the other hand, the dark road outside was less attractive than ever, now that she had tasted the warmth of the fireside. Furthermore, she had lost her magical knife, and would be unprotected on the dark road with some *thing* following.

"Yes," she said, "I will have a room for the night."

The price was arranged—neither cheap nor outrageous—and the innkeeper asked, "Can I find you a woman for the night?"

This was always the troublesome part of traveling in male disguise. Lythande, whatever her romantic desires, had no wish for the kind of women kept in country inns for traveling customers, without choice; they were usually sold into this business as soon as their breasts grew, if not before. Yet it was a singularity to refuse this kind of accommodation, and one that could endanger the long masquerade on which her power depended.

Tonight she did not feel like elaborate excuses.

"No, thank you; I am weary from the road and will sleep." She dug into her robe for a couple of spare coins. "Give the girl this for her trouble."

The hag bowed. "As you will, sir; Frennet! Show the gentleman to the south room."

A handsome girl, tall and straight and slender, with silky hair looped up into elaborate curls, rose from the fireside and gestured with a shapely arm half concealed by silken draperies. "This way, if ye please," she said, and Lythande rose, edging between Gimlet and the dog owner. In a pleasant, mellow voice, she wished the company good night.

The stairs were old and rickety, stretching up several flights, but had once been stately—about four owners ago, Lythande calculated. Now they were hung with cobwebs, and the higher flights looked as if they might be the haunt of bats, too. From one of the posts at a corner landing, a dark form ascended, flapping its wings, and cried out in a hoarse, croaking sound:

"*Good evening, ladies! Good evening, ladies!*"

The girl Frennet raised an arm to warn off the bird.

"That accursed jackdaw! Madame's pet, sir; pay no attention," she said good-naturedly, and Lythande was glad of the darkness. It was beneath the dignity of an Adept of the Blue Star to take notice of a trained bird, however articulate.

"Is that all it says?"

"Oh no, sir; quite a vocabulary the creature has, but then, you see, you never know what it's going to say, and sometimes it can really startle you if you ain't expecting it," said Frennet, opening the door to a large, dark chamber. She went inside and lighted a candelabrum standing by the huge, draped four-poster. The jackdaw flapped in the doorway and croaked hoarsely, "*Don't go in there, Madame! Don't go in there, Madame!*"

"Just let me get rid of her for you, sir," said Frennet, taking up a broom and making several passes with it, attempting to drive the jack-daw back down the staircase. Then she noticed that Lythande was still standing in the doorway of the room.

"It's all right, sir; you can go right in. You don't want to let her scare you. She's just a stupid bird."

Lythande had stopped cold, however, not so much because of the bird as because of the sharp prickling of the Blue Star between her brows. *The smell of magic,* she thought, wishing she were a hundred leagues from the Hag and Swine; without her magical knife, she was unwilling to spend a minute, let alone a night, in a room that smelled evilly of magic as that one did.

She said pleasantly, "I am averse to the omens, child. Could you perhaps show me to another chamber where I might sleep? After all, the inn is far from full, so find me another room, there's a good girl."

"Well, I dunno what the mistress would say," began Frennet dubiously, while the bird shrieked, *"There's a good girl! There's a clever girl!"* Then she smiled and said, "But what she dunna know won't hurt her, I reckon. This way."

Up another flight of stairs, and Lythande felt the numbing prickling of the Blue Star, *the smell of magic,* recede and drop away. The rooms on this floor were lighted and smaller, and Frennet turned into one of them.

"Me own room, sir; yer welcome to the half of my bed if you wish it, an' no obligation. I mean—I heard ye say ye didn't want a woman, but you sent a tip for me, and—" She stopped, swallowed, and said determinedly, her face flushing, "I dunno why yer traveling like a man, ma'am. But I reckon ye have yer reasons, an' they's none of my business. But ye came here in good faith for a night's lodgin', and I think ye've a right to that and nothing else." The girl's face was red and embarrassed. "I swore no oath to keep my mouth shut about what's goin' on here, and I don't want your death on my hands, so there."

"My death?" Lythande said. "What do you mean, child?"

"Well, I'm in for it now," Frennet said, "but ye've a right to know, ma'am—sir—noble stranger. Folk who sleep here don't come back no more human; did ye see those little children down yonder? They're only halfway changed; the potions don't work all that well on children.

I saw you didn't drink yer wine; so when they came to drive you out to the sty, you'd still be human and they'd kill you—or drive you out in the dark, where the Walker Behind can have ye."

Shivering, Lythande recalled the entity that had destroyed her magical knife. That, then, had been the Walker Behind.

"What is this—this Walker Behind?" she asked.

"I dunno, ma'am. Only it *follows*, and draws folk into the other world, thass all I know. Ain't nobody ever come back to tell what it is. Only I hears 'em scream when it starts followin' them."

Lythande stared about the small, mean chamber. Then she asked, "How did you know that I was a woman?"

"I dunno, ma'am. I always knows, that's all. I always know, no matter what. I won't tell the missus; I promise."

Lythande sighed. Perhaps the girl was somewhat psychic; she had accepted a long time ago that while her disguise was usually opaque to men, there would always be a few women who for one reason or another would see through it. Well, there was nothing to be done about it, unless she were willing to murder the girl, which she was not.

"See that do you not; my life depends on it," she said. "But perhaps you need not give up your bed to me either; can you guide me unseen out of this place?"

"That I can, ma'am, but it's a wretched night to be out, and the Walker Behind in the dark out there. I'd hate to hear you screamin' when it comes to take you away."

Lythande chuckled, but mirthlessly. "Perhaps instead you would hear *it* screaming when I came to take *it*," she said. "I think that is what I encountered before I came here."

"Yes'm. It drives folk in here because it wants 'em, and then it takes their souls. I mean, when they's turned into pigs, I guess they don't need their souls no more, see? And the Walker Behind takes them."

"Well, it will not take me," Lythande said briefly. "Nor you, if I can manage it. I encountered this thing before I came here; it took my knife, so I must somehow get another."

"They's plenty of knives in the kitchen, ma'am," Frennet said. "I can take ye out through there."

Together they stole down the stairs, Lythande moving like a ghost in the silence that had caused many people to swear that they had seen Lythande seem to disappear into thin air. In the parlor most of the guests had gone to rest; she heard a strange grunting sound. Upstairs there were curious grunting noises; on the morrow, Lythande supposed, they would be driven out to the sty, their souls left for the Walker Behind and their bodies to reappear as sausages or roast pork. In the kitchen, as they passed it, Lythande saw the innkeeper—the hag. She was chopping herbs; the pungent scent made Lythande think of the pungent drink she had fortunately not tasted.

So why had this evil come to infest this country? Her extended magical senses could now hear the step in the dark, prowling outside: the Walker Behind. She could sense and feel its evil circling in the dark, awaiting its monstrous feast of souls. But how—and why?—had anything human, even that hag, come to join hands with such a ghastly thing of damnation?

There had been a saying in the Temple of the Star that there was no fathoming the depths either of Law or of Chaos. And surely the Walker Behind was a thing from the very depths of Chaos; and Lythande, as a Pilgrim Adept, was solemnly sworn to uphold forever and defend Law against Chaos even at the Final Battle at the end of the world.

"There are some things," she observed to the girl Frennet, "that I would prefer not to encounter until the Final Battle where Law will defeat Chaos at world's end. And of those things the Walker Behind is first among them; but the ways of Chaos do not await my convenience; and if I encounter it now, at least I need not meet it at the end of the world." She stepped quietly into the kitchen, and the hag jerked up her head.

"You? I thought you was sleeping by now, magician. I even sent you the girl—"

"Don't blame the girl; she did as you bade her." Lythande said. "I came hither to the Hag and Swine, though I knew it not, to rid the world of a pigsty of Chaos. Now you shall feed your own evil servant."

She gestured, muttering the words of a spell; the hag flopped forward on all fours, grunting and snuffling. Outside in the dark, Lythande sensed the approach of the great evil Thing, and motioned to Frennet.

"Open the door, child."

Frennet flung the door open; Lythande shoved the grunting thing outside over the threshold. There was a despairing scream—half animal but dreadfully half human—from somewhere; then only the body of a pig remained grunting in the foggy darkness of the innyard. From the shadowy Walker outside, there was a satisfied croon that made Lythande shudder. Well, so much for the Hag and Swine; she had deserved it.

"There's nothing left of her, ma'am."

"She deserves to be served up as sausages for breakfast, dressed with her own herbs," Lythande remarked, looking at what was left, and Frennet shook her head.

"I'd have no stomach for her meself, ma'am."

The jackdaw flapped out into the kitchen crying, "*Clever girl! Clever girl! There's a good girl!*" and Lythande said, "I think if I had my way, I'd wring that bird's neck. There's still the Walker to deal with; she was surely not enough to satisfy the appetite of—that thing."

"Maybe not, ma'am," Frennet said, "but you could deal with her; can you deal with it? It'll want your soul more than hers, mighty magician as you must be."

Lythande felt serious qualms; the innkeeper-hag, after all, had been but a small evil. But in her day, Lythande had dealt with a few large evils, though seldom any as great and terrifying as the Walker. And this one had already taken her magical knife. Had the spells weakened it any?

A long row of knives was hanging on the wall; Frennet took down the longest and most formidable, proffering it to her, but Lythande shook her head, passing her hand carefully along the row of knives. Most knives were forged for material uses only, and she did not think any of them would be much use against this great magic out of Chaos.

The Blue Star between her brows tingled, and she stopped, trying to identify the source of the magical warning. Was it only that she could hear, out in the darkness of the innyard, the characteristic step of the Walker Behind?

Step-pause-step.

Step-pause-step.

No, the source was closer than that. It lay—moving her head cautiously, Lythande identified the source—the cutting board that lay on the table; the hag had been cutting her magical herbs, the one to transform the unwary into swine. Slowly, Lythande took up the knife; a common kitchen one with a long, sharp blade. All along the blade was the greenish mark of the herb juices. From the pocket of her mage-robe, Lythande took the ruined handle—the elaborately carved hilt with magical runes—of her ruined knife, looked at it with a sigh—she had always been proud of the elegance of her magical equipment, and this was hearth-witch, or kitchen-magic at best—and flung it down with the kitchen remnants.

Frennet clutched at her. "Oh, don't go out there, ma'am! It's still out there a-waiting for you."

And the jackdaw, fluttering near the hearth, shrieked, *"Don't go out there! Oh, don't go out there!"*

Gently, Lythande disengaged the girl's arms. "You stay here," she said. "You have no magical protection; and I can give you none." She drew the mage-robe's hood closely about her head, and stepped into the foggy innyard.

It was there, she could feel it waiting, circling, prowling, its hunger a vast evil maw to be filled. She knew it hungered for her, to take in her body, her soul, her magic. If she spoke, she might find herself in its power. The knife firmly gripped in her hand, she traced out a pattern of circling steps, sunwise in spite of the darkness. If she could hold the Thing of darkness in combat till sunrise, the very light might destroy it; but it could not be much after midnight. She had no wish to hold this dreadful Thing at bay till sunrise, even if her powers should prove equal to it.

So it must be dispatched at once . . . and she hoped, since she had lost her own magical knife, with the knife she had taken from the monstrous Thing's own accomplice. Alone in the fog, despite the bulky warmth of the mage-robe, Lythande felt her body dripping with ice—or was it only terror? Her knees wobbled, and the icy drips seemed to course down between her shoulders, which spasmed as if expecting a knife driven between them. Frennet, shivering in the light of the doorway, was watching her with a smile, as if she had not the slightest doubt.

Is this what men feel when their women are watching them? Certainly, if she should call the Thing to her and fail to destroy it, it would turn next on the girl, and for all she knew, on the jackdaw, too; and neither of them deserved death, far less soul-destruction. The girl was innocent, and the jackdaw only a dumb creature . . . well, a harmless creature; dumb it wasn't; it was still crying out gibberish.

"Oh, my soul, it's coming! It's coming! Don't go out there!"

It was coming; the Blue Star between her brows was prickling like live coals, the blue light burning through her brain from the inside out. Why, in the name of all the gods that ever were or weren't, had she ever thought she wanted to be a magician? Well, it was years too late to ask that. She clenched her hand on the rough wooden handle of the kitchen knife of the kitchen hag, and thrust up roughly into the greater darkness that was the Walker, looming over her and shadowing the whole of the innyard.

She was not sure whether the great scream that enveloped the world was her own scream of terror, or whether it came from the vast dark vortex that whirled around the Walker; she was enveloped in a monstrous whirlwind that swept her *off* her feet and into dark fog and dampness. She had time for a ghostly moment of dread—suppose the herbs on the blade should transform the Walker into a great Hog of Chaos? And how could she meet it if it did? But this was the blade of the Walker's own accomplice in his own magic of Chaos; she thrust into the Thing's heart and, buffeted and battered by the whirlwinds of Chaos, grimly hung on.

Then there was a sighing sound, and something unreeled and was gone. She was standing in the innyard, and Frennet's arms were hugging hard.

The jackdaw shrieked, *"It's gone! It's gone! Oh, good girl, good girl!"*

It was gone. The innyard was empty of magic, only fog on the moldering stones. There was a shadow in the kitchen behind Frennet; Lythande went inside and saw, wrapped in his cloak and ready to depart, the pudgy face and form of Gimlet, the dog faker.

"I was looking for the innkeeper," he said truculently. "This place is too noisy for me; too much going on in the halls; and there's the girl. You," he said crossly to Frennet. "Where's your mistress? And I thought you were to join me."

Frennet said sturdily, "I'm me own mistress now, sir. And I ain't for sale, not any more. As for the mistress, I dunno where she is; you can go and ask for her at the gates of Heaven, an if you don't find her there—well, you know where you can go."

It took a minute for that to penetrate his dull understanding; but when it did, he advanced on her with a clenched fist.

"Then I been robbed of your price!"

Lythande reached into the pockets of the magerobe. She handed him a coin.

"Here, you've made a profit on the deal, no doubt—as you always do. Frennet is coming with me."

Gimlet stared and finally pocketed the coin, which—Lythande could tell from his astonished eyes—was the biggest he had ever seen.

"Well, good sir, if you say so. I got to be off about my dogs. I wonder if I could get some breakfast first."

Lythande gestured to the joints of meat hanging along the wall of the kitchen. "There's plenty of ham, at least."

He looked up, gulped and shuddered. "No thanks." He slouched out into the darkness, and Lythande gestured to the girl.

"Let's be on our way."

"Can I really come with you?"

"For a while, at least," Lythande said. The girl deserved that. "Go quickly, and fetch anything you want to take."

"Nothing from here," she said. "But the other customers—"

"They'll turn human again now that the hag's dead, such of 'em as haven't been served up for roast pork," Lythande said. "Look there." And indeed, the joints of ham hanging along the wall had taken on a horrible and familiar look, not porcine at all. "Let's get out of here."

They strode down the road toward the rising sun, side by side, the jackdaw fluttering after, crying out, "Good morning, ladies! Good morning, ladies."

"Before the sun rises," Lythande said. "I shall wring that bird's neck."

"Oh, aye," Frennet said. "Or dumb it wi' your magic. May I ask why you travel in men's clothes, Lady?"

Lythande smiled and shrugged.

"Wouldn't you?"

THE ANYTHING BOX

Zenna Henderson

I suppose it was about the second week of school that I noticed Sue-lynn particularly. Of course, I'd noticed her name before and checked her out automatically for maturity and ability and probable performance the way most teachers do with their students during the first weeks of school. She had checked out mature and capable and no worry as to performance so I had pigeonholed her—setting aside for the moment the little nudge that said, "Too quiet"—with my other no-worrys until the fluster and flurry of the first days had died down a little.

I remember my noticing day. I had collapsed into my chair for a brief respite from guiding hot little hands through the intricacies of keeping a Crayola within reasonable bounds and the room was full of the relaxed, happy hum of a pleased class as they worked away, not realizing that they were rubbing "blue" into their memories as well as onto their papers. I was meditating on how individual personalities were beginning to emerge among the thirty-five or so heterogeneous first graders I had, when I noticed Sue-lynn—really noticed her—for the first time.

She had finished her paper—far ahead of the others as usual—and was sitting at her table facing me. She had her thumbs touching in front of her on the table and her fingers curving as though they held something between them—something large enough to keep her fingertips apart and angular enough to bend her fingers as if for corners. It was something pleasant that she held—pleasant and precious. You could tell that by the softness of her hold. She was leaning forward a little, her lower ribs pressed against the table, and she was looking, completely absorbed, at the table between her hands. Her face was relaxed and happy. Her mouth curved in a tender half-smile, and as I watched, her lashes lifted and she looked at me with a warm share-the-pleasure look. Then her eyes blinked and the shutters came down inside them. Her hand flicked into the desk and out. She pressed her thumbs to her forefingers and rubbed them slowly together. Then she laid one hand over the other on the table and looked down at them with the air of complete denial and ignorance children can assume so devastatingly.

The incident caught my fancy and I began to notice Sue-lynn. As I consciously watched her, I saw that she spent most of her free time staring at the table between her hands, much too unobtrusively to catch my busy attention. She hurried through even the fun-est of fun papers and then lost herself in looking. When Davie pushed her down at recess, and blood streamed from her knee to her ankle, she took her bandages and her tear-smudged face to that comfort she had so readily—if you'll pardon the expression—at hand, and emerged minutes later, serene and dry-eyed. I think Davie pushed her down because of her Looking. I know the day before he had come up to me, red-faced and squirming.

"Teacher," he blurted. "She Looks!"

"Who looks?" I asked absently, checking the vocabulary list in my book, wondering how on earth I'd missed *where*, one of those annoying *wh* words that throw the children for a loss.

"Sue-lynn. She Looks and Looks!"

"At you?" I asked.

"Well—" He rubbed a forefinger below his nose, leaving a clean streak on his upper lip, accepted the proffered Kleenex and put it in his pocket. "She looks at her desk and tells lies. She says she can see—"

"Can see what?" My curiosity pricked up its ears.

"Anything," said Davie. "It's her Anything Box. She can see any-thing she wants to."

"Does it hurt you for her to Look?"

"Well," he squirmed. Then he burst out. "She says she saw me with a dog biting me because I took her pencil—she said." He started a pell-mell verbal retreat. "She *thinks* I took her pencil. I only found—" His eyes dropped. "I'll give it back."

"I hope so," I smiled. "If you don't want her to look at you, then don't do things like that."

"Dern girls," he muttered, and clomped back to his seat.

So I think he pushed her down the next day to get back at her for the dogbite.

Several times after that I wandered to the back of the room, casually in her vicinity, but always she either saw or felt me coming and the quick sketch of her hand disposed of the evidence. Only once I thought I caught a glimmer of something—but her thumb and forefinger brushed in sunlight, and it must have been just that.

Children don't retreat for no reason at all, and though Sue-lynn did not follow any overt pattern of withdrawal, I started to wonder about her. I watched her on the playground, to see how she tracked there. That only confused me more.

She had a very regular pattern. When the avalanche of children first descended at recess, she avalanched along with them and nothing in the shrieking, running, dodging mass resolved itself into a with-drawn Sue-lynn. But after ten minutes or so, she emerged from the crowd, tousle-haired, rosy-cheeked, smutched with dust, one shoelace dangling, and through some alchemy that I coveted for myself, she sud-denly became untousled, undusty and unsmutched.

And there she was, serene and composed on the narrow little step at the side of the flight of stairs just where they disappeared into the base of the pseudo-Corinthian column that graced Our Door and her cupped hands received whatever they received and her absorption in what she saw became so complete that the bell came as a shock every time.

And each time, before she joined the rush to Our Door, her hand would sketch a gesture to her pocket, if she had one, or to the tiny ledge that extended between the hedge and the building. Apparently she always had to put the Anything Box away, but never had to go back to get it.

I was so intrigued by her putting whatever it was on the ledge that once I actually went over and felt along the grimy little outset. I sheepishly followed my children into the hall, wiping the dust from my fingertips, and Sue-lynn's eyes brimmed amusement at me without her mouth's smiling. Her hands mischievously squared in front of her and her thumbs caressed a solidness as the line of children swept into the room.

I smiled too because she was so pleased with having outwitted me. This seemed to be such a gay withdrawal that I let my worry die down. Better this manifestation than any number of other ones that I could name.

Someday, perhaps, I'll learn to keep my mouth shut. I wish I had before that long afternoon when we primary teachers worked together in a heavy cloud of Ditto fumes, the acrid smell of India ink, drifting cigarette smoke and the constant current of chatter, and I let Alpha get me started on what to do with our behavior problems. She was all raunched up about the usual rowdy loudness of her boys and the eternal clack of her girls, and I—bless my stupidity—gave her Sue-lynn as an example of what should be our deepest concern rather than the outbursts from our active ones.

"You mean she just sits and looks at nothing?" Alpha's voice grated into her questioning tone.

"Well, I can't see anything," I admitted. "But apparently she can."

"But that's having hallucinations!" Her voice went up a notch. "I read a book once—"

"Yes." Marlene leaned across the desk to flick ashes in the ash tray. "So we have heard and heard and heard!"

"Well!" sniffed Alpha. "It's better than *never* reading a book."

"We're waiting," Marlene leaked smoke from her nostrils, "for the day when you read another book. This one must have been uncommonly long."

"Oh, I don't know." Alpha's forehead wrinkled with concentration. "It was only about—" Then she reddened and turned her face angrily away from Marlene.

"Apropos of *our* discussion—" she said pointedly. "It sounds to me like that child has a deep personality disturbance. Maybe even a psychotic—whatever—" Her eyes glistened faintly as she turned the thought over.

"Oh, I don't know," I said, surprised into echoing her words at my sudden need to defend Sue-lynn. "There's something about her. She doesn't have that apprehensive, hunched-shoulder, don't-hit-me-again air about her that so many withdrawn children have." And I thought achingly of one of mine from last year that Alpha had now and was verbally bludgeoning back into silence after all my work with him. "She seems to have a happy, adjusted personality, only with this odd little—*plus*."

"Well, I'd be worried if she were mine," said Alpha. "I'm glad all my kids are so normal." She sighed complacently. "I guess I really haven't anything to kick about. I seldom ever have problem children except wigglers and yakkers, and a holler and a smack can straighten them out."

Marlene caught my eye mockingly, tallying Alpha's class with me, and I turned away with a sigh. To be so happy—well, I suppose ignorance does help.

"You'd better do something about that girl," Alpha shrilled as she left the room. "She'll probably get worse and worse as time goes on. Deteriorating, I think the book said."

I had known Alpha a long time and I thought I knew how much of her talk to discount, but I began to worry about Sue-lynn. Maybe this *was* a disturbance that was more fundamental than the usual run of the mill that I had met up with. Maybe a child *can* smile a soft, contented smile and still have little maggots of madness flourishing somewhere inside.

Or, by gorry! I said to myself defiantly, maybe she *does* have an Anything Box. Maybe she *is* looking at something precious. Who am I to say no to anything like that?

An Anything Box! What could you see in an Anything Box?

Heart's desire? I felt my own heart lurch—just a little—the next time Sue-lynn's hands curved. I breathed deeply to hold me in my chair. If it was *her* Anything Box, I wouldn't be able to see my heart's desire in it. Or would I? I propped my cheek up on my hand and doodled aimlessly on my time schedule sheet. How on earth, I wondered—not for the first time—do I manage to get myself off on these tangents?

Then I felt a small presence at my elbow and turned to meet Sue-lynn's wide eyes.

"Teacher?" The word was hardly more than a breath.

"Yes?" I could tell that for some reason Sue-lynn was loving me dearly at the moment. Maybe because her group had gone into new books that morning. Maybe because I had noticed her new dress, the ruffles of which made her feel very feminine and lovable, or maybe just because the late autumn sun lay so golden across her desk. Anyway, she was loving me to overflowing, and since, unlike most of the children, she had no casual hugs or easy moist kisses, she was bringing her love to me in her encompassing hands.

"See my box, Teacher? It's my Anything Box."

"Oh, my!" I said. "May I hold it?"

After all, I have held—tenderly or apprehensively or bravely— tiger magic, live rattlesnakes, dragon's teeth, poor little dead butterflies and two ears and a nose that dropped off Sojie one cold morning— none of which I could see any more than I could the Anything Box. But I took the squareness from her carefully, my tenderness showing in my fingers and my face.

And I received weight and substance and actuality!

Almost I let it slip out of my surprised fingers, but Sue-lynn's apprehensive breath helped me catch it and I curved my fingers around the precious warmness and looked down, down, past a faint shimmering, down into Sue-lynn's Anything Box.

I was running barefoot through the whispering grass. The swirl of my skirts caught the daisies as I rounded the gnarled apple tree at the corner. The warm wind lay along each of my cheeks and chuckled in my ears. My heart outstripped my flying feet and melted with a rush of delight into warmness as his arms—

I closed my eyes and swallowed hard, my palms tight against the

Anything Box. "It's beautiful!" I whispered. "It's wonderful, Sue-lynn. Where did you get it?"

Her hands took it back hastily. "It's mine," she said defiantly. "It's mine."

"Of course," I said. "Be careful now. Don't drop it."

She smiled faintly as she sketched a motion to her pocket. "I won't." She patted the flat pocket on her way back to her seat.

Next day she was afraid to look at me at first for fear I might say something or look something or in some way remind her of what must seem like a betrayal to her now, but after I only smiled my usual smile, with no added secret knowledge, she relaxed.

A night or so later when I leaned over my moon-drenched window-sill and let the shadow of my hair hide my face from such ebullient glory, I remembered the Anything Box. Could I make one for myself? Could I square off this aching waiting, this outreaching, this silent cry inside me, and make it into an Anything Box? I freed my hands and brought them together, thumb to thumb, framing a part of the horizon's darkness between my upright forefingers. I stared into the empty square until my eyes watered. I sighed, and laughed a little, and let my hands frame my face as I leaned out into the night. To have magic so near—to feel it tingle off my fingertips and then to be so bound that I couldn't receive it. I turned away from the window—turning my back on brightness.

It wasn't long after this that Alpha succeeded in putting sharp points of worry back in my thoughts of Sue-lynn. We had ground duty together, and one morning when we shivered while the kids ran themselves rosy in the crisp air, she sizzed in my ear.

"Which one is it? The abnormal one, I mean."

"I don't have any abnormal children," I said, my voice sharpening before the sentence ended because I suddenly realized whom she meant.

"Well, I call it abnormal to stare at nothing." You could almost taste the acid in her words. "Who is it?"

"Sue-lynn," I said reluctantly. "She's playing on the bars now."

Alpha surveyed the upside-down Sue-lynn, whose brief skirts were belled down from her bare pink legs and half covered her face as she swung from one of the bars by her knees. Alpha clutched her wizened, blue hands together and breathed on them. "She sure looks normal enough," she said.

"She *is* normal!" I snapped.

"*Well*, bite my head off!" cried Alpha. "You're the one that said she wasn't, not me—or is it 'not I'? I never could remember. Not me? Not I?"

The bell saved Alpha from a horrible end. I never knew a person so serenely unaware of essentials and so sensitive to trivia.

But she had succeeded in making me worry about Sue-lynn again, and the worry exploded into distress a few days later.

Sue-lynn came to school sleepy-eyed and quiet. She didn't finish any of her work and she fell asleep during rest time. I cussed TV and drive-ins and assumed a night's sleep would put it right. But next day Sue-lynn burst into tears and slapped Davie clear off his chair.

"Why Sue-lynn!" I gathered Davie up in all his astonishment and took Sue-lynn's hand. She jerked it away from me and flung herself at Davie again. She got two handfuls of his hair and had him out of my grasp before I knew it. She threw him bodily against the wall with a flip of her hands, then doubled up her fists and pressed them to her streaming eyes. In the shocked silence of the room, she stumbled over to Isolation and seating herself, back to the class, on the little chair, she leaned her head into the corner and sobbed quietly in big gulping sobs.

"What on earth goes on?" I asked the stupefied Davie, who sat spraddle-legged on the floor fingering a detached tuft of hair. "What did you do?"

"I only said 'Robber Daughter,'" said Davie. "It said so in the paper. My mama said her daddy's a robber. They put him in jail cause he robbered a gas station." His bewildered face was trying to decide whether or not to cry. Everything had happened so fast that he didn't know yet if he was hurt.

"It isn't nice to call names," I said weakly. "Get back into your seat. I'll take care of Sue-lynn later."

He got up and sat gingerly down in his chair, rubbing his ruffled hair, wanting to make more of a production of the situation, but not knowing how. He twisted his face experimentally to see if he had tears available and had none.

"Dern girls," he muttered, and tried to shake his fingers free of a wisp of hair.

I kept my eye on Sue-lynn for the next half hour as I busied myself with the class. Her sobs soon stopped and her rigid shoulders relaxed. Her hands were softly in her lap and I knew she was taking comfort from her Anything Box. We had our talk together later, but she was so completely sealed off from me by her misery that there was no communication between us. She sat quietly watching me as I talked, her hands trembling in her lap. It shakes the heart, somehow, to see the hands of a little child quiver like that.

That afternoon I looked up from my reading group, startled, as though by a cry, to catch Sue-lynn's frightened eyes. She looked around bewildered and then down at her hands again—her empty hands. Then she darted to the Isolation corner and reached under the chair. She went back to her seat slowly, her hands squared to an unseen weight. For the first time, apparently, she had had to go get the Anything Box. It troubled me with a vague unease for the rest of the afternoon.

Through the days that followed while the trial hung fire, I had Sue-lynn in attendance bodily, but that was all. She sank into her Anything Box at every opportunity. And always, if she had put it away somewhere, she had to go back for it. She roused more and more reluctantly from these waking dreams, and there finally came a day when I had to shake her to waken her.

I went to her mother, but she couldn't or wouldn't understand me, and made me feel like a frivolous gossipmonger taking her mind away from her husband, despite the fact that I didn't even mention him—or maybe because I didn't mention him.

"If she's being a bad girl, spank her," she finally said, wearily shifting the weight of a whining baby from one hip to another and pushing her tousled hair off her forehead. "Whatever you do is all right by me. My worrier is all used up. I haven't got any left for the kids right now."

Well, Sue-lynn's father was found guilty and sentenced to the state penitentiary and school was less than an hour old the next day when Davie came up, clumsily a-tiptoe, braving my wrath for interrupting a reading group, and whispered hoarsely, "Sue-lynn's asleep with her eyes open again, Teacher."

We went back to the table and Davie slid into his chair next to a completely unaware Sue-lynn. He poked her with a warning finger. "I told you I'd tell on you."

And before our horrified eyes, she toppled, as rigidly as a doll, sideways off the chair. The thud of her landing relaxed her and she lay limp on the green asphalt tile—a thin paper doll of a girl, one hand still clenched open around something. I pried her fingers loose and almost wept to feel enchantment dissolve under my heavy touch. I carried her down to the nurse's room and we worked over her with wet towels and prayer and she finally opened her eyes.

"Teacher," she whispered weakly.

"Yes, Sue-lynn." I took her cold hands in mine.

"Teacher, I almost got in my Anything Box."

"No," I answered. "You couldn't. You're too big."

"Daddy's there," she said. "And where we used to live."

I took a long, long look at her wan face. I hope it was genuine concern for her that prompted my next words. I hope it wasn't envy or the memory of the niggling nagging of Alpha's voice that put firmness in my voice as I went on. "That's play-like," I said. "Just for fun."

Her hands jerked protestingly in mine. "Your Anything Box is just for fun. It's like Davie's cow pony that he keeps in his desk or Sojie's jet plane, or when the big bear chases all of you at recess. It's fun-for-play, but it's not for real. You mustn't think it's for real. It's only play."

"No!" she denied. "*No!*" she cried frantically, and hunching herself up on the cot, peering through her tear-swollen eyes, she scrabbled under the pillow and down beneath the rough blanket that covered her.

"Where is it?" she cried. "Where is it? Give it back to me, Teacher!"

She flung herself toward me and pulled open both my clenched hands.

"Where did you put it? Where did you put it?"

"There is no Anything Box," I said flatly, trying to hold her to me and feeling my heart breaking along with hers.

"You took it!" she sobbed. "You took it away from me!" And she wrenched herself out of my arms.

"Can't you give it back to her?" whispered the nurse. "If it makes her feel so bad? Whatever it is—"

"It's just imagination," I said, almost sullenly. "I can't give her back something that doesn't exist."

Too young! I thought bitterly. Too young to learn that heart's desire is only play-like.

Of course the doctor found nothing wrong. Her mother dismissed the matter as a fainting spell and Sue-lynn came back to class the next day, thin and listless, staring blankly out the window, her hands palm down on the desk. I swore by the pale hollow of her cheek that never, *never* again would I take any belief from anyone without replacing it with something better. What had I given Sue-lynn? What had she better than I had taken from her? How did I know but that her Anything Box was on purpose to tide her over rough spots in her life like this? And what now, now that I had taken it from her?

Well, after a time she began to work again, and later, to play. She came back to smiles, but not to laughter. She puttered along quite satisfactorily except that she was a candle blown out. The flame was gone wherever the brightness of belief goes. And she had no more sharing smiles for me, no overflowing love to bring to me. And her shoulder shrugged subtly away from my touch.

Then one day I suddenly realized that Sue-lynn was searching our classroom. Stealthily, casually, day by day she was searching, covering every inch of the room. She went through every puzzle box, every lump of clay, every shelf and cupboard, every box and bag. Methodically she checked behind every row of books and in every child's desk until finally, after almost a week, she had been through everything in the place except my desk. Then she began to materialize suddenly at my elbow every time I opened a drawer. And her eyes would probe quickly and sharply before I slid it shut again. But if I tried to intercept her looks, they slid away and she had some legitimate errand that had brought her up to the vicinity of the desk.

She believes it again, I thought hopefully. She won't accept the fact that her Anything Box is gone. She wants it again.

But it *is* gone, I thought drearily. It's really-for-true gone.

My head was heavy from troubled sleep, and sorrow was a weariness in all my movements. Waiting is sometimes a burden almost too heavy to carry. While my children hummed happily over their fun-stuff, I brooded silently out the window until I managed a laugh at myself. It was a shaky laugh that threatened to dissolve into something else, so I brisked back to my desk.

As good a time as any to throw out useless things, I thought, and to see if I can find that colored chalk I put away so carefully. I plunged my hands into the wilderness of the bottom right-hand drawer of my desk. It was deep with a huge accumulation of anything—just anything— that might need a temporary hiding place. I knelt to pull out leftover Jack Frost pictures, and a broken beanshooter, a chewed red ribbon, a roll of cap gun ammunition, one striped sock, six Numbers papers, a rubber dagger, a copy of the Gospel According to St. Luke, a miniature coal shovel, patterns for jack-o'-lanterns, and a pink plastic pelican. I retrieved my Irish linen hankie I thought lost forever and Sojie's report card that he had told me solemnly had blown out of his hand and landed on a jet and broke the sound barrier so loud that it busted all to flitters. Under the welter of miscellany, I felt a squareness. Oh, happy! I thought, this *is* where I put the colored chalk! I cascaded papers off both sides of my lifting hands and shook the box free.

We were together again. Outside, the world was an enchanting wilderness of white, the wind shouting softly through the windows, tapping wet, white fingers against the warm light. Inside, all the worry and waiting, the apartness and loneliness were over and forgotten, their hugeness dwindled by the comfort of a shoulder, the warmth of clasping hands—and nowhere, nowhere was the fear of parting, nowhere the need to do without again. This was the happy ending. This was—

This was Sue-lynn's Anything Box!

My racing heart slowed as the dream faded—and rushed again at the realization. I had it here! In my junk drawer! It had been there all the time!

I stood up shakily, concealing the invisible box in the flare of my skirts. I sat down and put the box carefully in the center of my desk, covering the top of it with my palms lest I should drown again in delight. I looked at Sue-lynn. She was finishing her fun paper, competently but unjoyously. Now would come her patient sitting with quiet hands until told to do something else.

Alpha would approve. And very possibly, I thought, Alpha would, for once in her limited life, be right. We may need "hallucinations" to keep us going—all of us but the Alphas—but when we go so far to try to force ourselves, physically, into the Never-Neverland of heart's desire—

I remembered Sue-lynn's thin rigid body toppling doll-like off its chair. Out of her deep need she had found—or created? Who could tell?—something too dangerous for a child. I could so easily bring the brimming happiness back to her eyes—but at what a possible price!

No, I had a duty to protect Sue-lynn. Only maturity—the maturity born of the sorrow and loneliness that Sue-lynn was only beginning to know—could be trusted to use an Anything Box safely and wisely.

My heart thudded as I began to move my hands, letting the palms slip down from the top to shape the sides of—

I had moved them back again before I really saw, and I have now learned almost to forget that glimpse of what heart's desire is like when won at the cost of another's heart.

I sat there at the desk trembling and breathless, my palms moist, feeling as if I had been on a long journey away from the little schoolroom. Perhaps I had. Perhaps I had been shown all the kingdoms of the world in a moment of time.

"Sue-lynn," I called. "Will you come up here when you're through?"

She nodded unsmilingly and snipped off the last paper from the edge of Mistress Mary's dress. Without another look at her handiwork, she carried the scissors safely to the scissors box, crumpled the scraps of paper in her hand and came up to the wastebasket by the desk.

"I have something for you, Sue-lynn," I said, uncovering the box.

Her eyes dropped to the desk top. She looked indifferently up at me. "I did my fun paper already."

"Did you like it?"

"Yes." It was a flat lie.

"Good," I lied right back. "But look here." I squared my hands around the Anything Box.

She took a deep breath and the whole of her little body stiffened.

"I found it," I said hastily, fearing anger. "I found it in the bottom drawer."

She leaned her chest against my desk, her hands caught tightly between, her eyes intent on the box, her face white with the aching want you see on children's faces pressed to Christmas windows.

"Can I have it?" she whispered.

"It's yours," I said, holding it out. Still she leaned against her hands, her eyes searching my face.

"Can I have it?" she asked again.

"Yes!" I was impatient with this anticlimax. "But—"

Her eyes flickered. She had sensed my reservation before I had. "But you must never try to get into it again."

"Okay," she said, the word coming out on a long relieved sigh. "Okay, Teacher."

She took the box and tucked it lovingly into her small pocket. She turned from the desk and started back to her table. My mouth quirked with a small smile. It seemed to me that everything about her had suddenly turned upwards—even the ends of her straight taffy-colored hair. The subtle flame about her that made her Sue-lynn was there again. She scarcely touched the floor was she walked.

I sighed heavily and traced on the desk top with my finger a probable size for an Anything Box. What would Sue-lynn choose to see first? How like a drink after a drought it would seem to her.

I was startled as a small figure materialized at my elbow. It was Sue-lynn, her fingers carefully squared before her.

"Teacher," she said softly, all the flat emptiness gone from her voice. "Anytime you want to take my Anything Box, you just say so."

I groped through my astonishment and incredulity for words. She couldn't possibly have had time to look into the Box yet.

"Why, thank you, Sue-lynn," I managed. "Thanks a lot. I would like very much to borrow it sometime."

"Would you like it now?" she asked, proffering it.

"No, thank you," I said, around the lump in my throat. "I've had a turn already. You go ahead."

"Okay," she murmured. Then—"Teacher?"

"Yes?"

Shyly she leaned against me, her cheek on my shoulder. She looked up at me with her warm, unshuttered eyes, then both arms were suddenly around my neck in a brief awkward embrace.

"Watch out!" I whispered, laughing into the collar of her blue dress. "You'll lose it again!"

"No I won't," she laughed back, patting the flat pocket of her dress. "Not ever, ever again!"

THE WHITE HORSE CHILD

Greg Bear

hen I was seven years old, I met an old man by the side of the dusty road between school and farm. The late afternoon sun had cooled and he was sitting on a rock, hat off, hands held out to the gentle warmth, whistling a pretty song. He nodded at me as I walked past. I nodded back. I was curious, but I knew better than to get involved with strangers. Nameless evils seemed to attach themselves to strangers, as if they might turn into lions when no one but a little kid was around.

"Hello, boy," he said.

I stopped and shuffled my feet. He looked more like a hawk than a lion. His clothes were brown and gray and russet, and his hands were pink like the flesh of some rabbit a hawk had just plucked up. His face was brown except around the eyes, where he might have worn glasses; around the eyes he was white, and this intensified his gaze. "Hello," I said.

"Was a hot day. Must have been hot in school," he said.

"They got air conditioning."

327

"So they do, now. How old are you?"

"Seven," I said. "Well, almost eight."

"Mother told you never to talk to strangers?"

"And Dad, too."

"Good advice. But haven't you seen me around here before?"

I looked him over. "No."

"Closely. Look at my clothes. What color are they?"

His shirt was gray, like the rock he was sitting on. The cuffs, where they peeped from under a russet jacket, where white. He didn't smell bad, but he didn't look particularly clean. He was smooth-shaven, though. His hair was white and his pants were the color of the dirt below the rock. "All kinds of colors," I said.

"But mostly I partake of the landscape, no?"

"I guess so," I said.

"That's because I'm not here. You're imagining me, at least part of me. Don't I look like somebody you might have heard of?"

"Who are you supposed to look like?" I asked.

"Well, I'm full of stories," he said. "Have lots of stories to tell little boys, little girls, even big folk, if they'll listen."

I started to walk away.

"But only if they'll listen," he said. I ran. When I got home, I told my older sister about the man on the road, but she only got a worried look and told me to stay away from strangers. I took her advice. For some time afterward, into my eighth year, I avoided that road and did not speak with strangers more than I had to.

The house that I lived in, with the five other members of my family and two dogs and one beleaguered cat, was white and square and comfortable. The stairs were rich, dark wood overlaid with worn carpet. The walls were dark oak paneling up to a foot above my head, then white plaster, with a white plaster ceiling. The air was full of smells—bacon when I woke up, bread and soup and dinner when I came home from school, dust on weekends when we helped clean.

Sometimes my parents argued, and not just about money, and those were bad times; but usually we were happy. There was talk about selling the farm and the house and going to Mitchell where Dad could work in a computerized feed-mixing plant, but it was only talk.

It was early summer when I took the dirt road again. I'd forgotten about the old man. But in almost the same way, when the sun was cooling and the air was haunted by lazy bees, I saw an old woman. Women strangers are less malevolent than men, and rarer. She was sitting on the gray rock, in a long green skirt summer-dusty, with a daisy-colored shawl and a blouse the precise hue of cottonwoods seen in a late hazy day's muted light. "Hello, boy," she said.

"I don't recognize you, either," I blurted, and she smiled.

"Of course not. If you didn't recognize him, you'd hardly know me."

"Do you know him?" I asked. She nodded. "Who was he? Who are you?"

"We're both full of stories. Just tell them from different angles. You aren't afraid of us, are you?"

I was, but having a woman ask the question made all the difference. "No," I said. "But what are you doing here? And how do you know—?"

"Ask for a story," she said. "One you've never heard of before." Her eyes were the color of baked chestnuts, and she squinted into the sun so that I couldn't see her whites. When she opened them wider to look at me, she didn't have any whites.

"I don't want to hear stories," I said softly.

"Sure you do. Just ask."

"It's late. I got to be home."

"I knew a man who became a house," she said. "He didn't like it. He stayed quiet for thirty years, and watched all the people inside grow up, and be just like their folks, all nasty and dirty and leaving his walls to flake, and the bathrooms were unbearable. So he spit them out one morning, furniture and all, and shut his doors and locked them."

"What?"

"You heard me. Upchucked. The poor house was so disgusted he changed back into a man, but he was older and he had a cancer and his heart was bad because of all the abuse he had lived with. He died soon after."

I laughed, not because the man had died but because I knew such things were lies. "That's silly," I said.

"Then here's another. There was a cat who wanted to eat butterflies. Nothing finer in the world for a cat than to stalk the grass, waiting for black and pumpkin butterflies. It crouches down and wriggles its rump to dig in the hind paws, then it jumps. But a butterfly is no sustenance for a cat. It's practice. There was a little girl about your age—might have been your sister, but she won't admit it—who saw the cat and decided to teach it a lesson. She hid in the taller grass with two old kites under each arm and waited for the cat to come by stalking. When it got real close, she put on her mother's dark glasses, to look all bug-eyed, and she jumped up flapping the kites. Well, it was just a little too real, because in a trice she found herself flying, and she was much smaller than she had been, and the cat jumped at her. Almost got her, too. Ask your sister about that sometime. See if she doesn't deny it."

"How'd she get back to be my sister again?"

"She became too scared to fly. She lit on a flower and found herself crushing it. The glasses broke, too."

"My sister did break a pair of Mom's glasses once."

The woman smiled.

"I got to be going home."

"Tomorrow you bring me a story, okay?"

I ran off without answering. But in my head, monsters were already rising. If she thought I was scared, wait until she heard the story I had to tell! When I got home my oldest sister, Barbara, was fixing lemonade in the kitchen. She was a year older than I, but acted as if she were grown-up. She was a good six inches taller and I could beat her if I got in a lucky punch, but no other way—so her power over me was awesome. But we were usually friendly.

"Where you been?" she asked, like a mother.

"Somebody tattled on you," I said.

Her eyes went doe-scared, then wizened down to slits. "What're you talking about?"

"Somebody tattled about what you did to Mom's sunglasses."

"I already been whipped for that," she said nonchalantly. "Not much more to tell."

"Oh, but I know more."

"Was not playing doctor," she said. The youngest, Sue-Ann, weakest and most full of guile, had a habit of telling the folks somebody or other was playing doctor. She didn't know what it meant—I just barely did—but it had been true once, and she held it over everybody as her only vestige of power.

"No," I said, "but I know what you were doing. And I won't tell anybody."

"You don't know nothing," she said. Then she accidentally poured half a pitcher of lemonade across the side of my head and down my front. When Mom came in I was screaming and swearing like Dad did when he fixed the cars, and I was put away for life plus ninety years in the bedroom I shared with younger brother Michael. Dinner smelled better than usual that evening, but I had none of it. Somehow, I wasn't brokenhearted. It gave me time to think of a scary story for the country-colored woman on the rock.

School was the usual mix of hell and purgatory the next day. Then the hot, dry winds cooled and the bells rang and I was on the dirt road again, across the southern hundred acres, walking in the lees and shadows of the big cottonwoods. I carried my Road-Runner lunch pail and my pencil box and one book—a handwriting manual I hated so much I tore pieces out of it at night, to shorten its lifetime—and I walked slowly, to give my story time to gel.

She was leaning up against a tree, not far from the rock. Looking back, I can see she was not so old as a boy of eight years thought. Now I see her lissome beauty and grace, despite the dominance of gray in her reddish hair, despite the crow's-feet around her eyes and the smile-haunts around her lips. But to the eight-year-old she was simply a peculiar crone. And he had a story to tell her, he thought, that would age her unto graveside.

"Hello, boy," she said.

"Hi." I sat on the rock.

"I can see you've been thinking," she said.

I squinted into the tree shadow to make her out better. "How'd you know?"

"You have the look of a boy that's been thinking. Are you here to listen to another story?"

"Got one to tell, this time," I said.

"Who goes first?"

It was always polite to let the woman go first so I quelled my haste and told her she could. She motioned me to come by the tree and sit on a smaller rock, half-hidden by grass. And while the crickets in the shadow tuned up for the evening, she said, "Once there was a dog. This dog was a pretty usual dog, like the ones that would chase you around home if they thought they could get away with it—if they didn't know you, or thought you were up to something the big people might disap-prove of. But this dog lived in a graveyard. That is, he belonged to the caretaker. You've seen a graveyard before, haven't you?"

"Like where they took Grandpa."

"Exactly," she said. "With pretty lawns, and big white and gray stones, and for those who've died recently, smaller gray stones with names and flowers and years cut into them. And trees in some places, with a mortuary nearby made of brick, and a garage full of black cars, and a place behind the garage where you wonder what goes on." She knew the place, all right. "This dog had a pretty good life. It was his job to keep the grounds clear of animals at night. After the gates were locked, he'd be set loose, and he wandered all night long. He was almost white, you see. Anybody human who wasn't supposed to be there would think he was a ghost, and they'd run away.

"But this dog had a problem. His problem was, there were rats that didn't pay much attention to him. A whole gang of rats. The leader was a big one, a good yard from nose to tail. These rats made their living by burrowing under the ground in the old section of the cemetery."

That did it. I didn't want to hear any more. The air was a lot colder than it should have been, and I wanted to get home in time for dinner and still be able to eat it. But I couldn't go just then.

"Now the dog didn't know what the rats did, and just like you and I, probably, he didn't much care to know. But it was his job to keep them under control. So one day he made a truce with a couple of cats that he normally tormented and told them about the rats. These cats were scrappy old toms and they'd long since cleared out the competi-tion of other cats, but they were friends themselves. So the dog made them a proposition. He said he'd let them use the cemetery any time they wanted, to prowl or hunt in or whatever, if they would put the fear of God into a few of the rats. The cats took him up on it. 'We get to do whatever we want,' they said, 'whenever we want, and you won't bother us.' The dog agreed.

"That night the dog waited for the sounds of battle. But they never came. Nary a yowl." She glared at me for emphasis. "Not a claw scratch. Not even a twitch of tail in the wind." She took a deep breath, and so did I. "Round about midnight the dog went out into the graveyard. It was very dark and there wasn't wind, or bird, or speck of star to relieve the quiet and the dismal, inside-of-a-box-camera blackness. He sniffed his way to the old part of the graveyard, and met with the head rat, who was sitting on a slanty, cracked wooden grave marker. Only his eyes and a tip of tail showed in the dark, but the dog could smell him. 'What happened to the cats?' he asked. The rat shrugged his haunches. 'Ain't seen any cats,' he said. 'What did you think—that you could scare us out with a couple of cats? Ha. Listen—if there had been any cats here tonight, they'd have been strung and hung like meat in a shed, and my youn'uns would have grown fat on—'"

"No-o-o!" I screamed, and I ran away from the woman and the tree until I couldn't hear the story any more.

"What's the matter?" she called after me. "Aren't you going to tell me your story?" Her voice followed me as I ran.

It was funny. That night, I wanted to know what happened to the cats. Maybe nothing had happened to them. Not knowing made my visions even worse—and I didn't sleep well. But my brain worked like it had never worked before.

The next day, a Saturday, I had an ending—not a very good one in retrospect—but it served to frighten Michael so badly he threatened to tell Mom on me.

"What would you want to do that for?" I asked. "Cripes, I won't ever tell you a story again if you tell Mom!"

Michael was a year younger and didn't worry about the future. "You never told me stories before," he said, "and everything was fine. I won't miss them."

He ran down the stairs to the living room. Dad was smoking a pipe and reading the paper, relaxing before checking the irrigation on the north thirty. Michael stood at the foot of the stairs, thinking. I was almost down to grab him and haul him upstairs when he made his deci-

sion and headed for the kitchen. I knew exactly what he was considering—that Dad would probably laugh and call him a little scaredy cat.
But Mom would get upset and do me in proper.

She was putting a paper form over the kitchen table to mark it for
fitting a tablecloth. Michael ran up to her and hung onto a pants leg
while I halted at the kitchen door, breathing hard, eyes threatening
eternal torture if he so much as peeped. But Michael didn't worry about
the future much.

"Mom," he said.

"Cripes!" I shouted, high-pitching on the *i*. Refuge awaited me in
the tractor shed. It was an agreed-upon hiding place. Mom didn't know
I'd be there, but Dad did, and he could mediate.

It took him a half-hour to get to me. I sat in the dark behind a
workbench, practicing my pouts. He stood in the shaft of light falling
from the unpatched chink in the roof. Dust motes Maypoled around his
legs. "Son," he said. "Mom wants to know where you got that story."

Now, this was a peculiar thing to be asked. The question I'd
expected had been, "Why did you scare Michael?" or maybe, "What
made you think of such a thing?" But no. Somehow, she had plumbed
the problem, planted the words in Dad's mouth, and impressed upon
him that father-son relationships were temporarily suspended.

"I made it up," I said.

"You've never made up that kind of story before."

"I just started."

He took a deep breath. "Son, we get along real good, except when
you lie to me. We know better. Who told you that story?"

This was uncanny. There was more going on than I could understand—there was a mysterious, adult thing happening. I had no way
around the truth. "An old woman," I said.

Dad sighed even deeper. "What was she wearing?"

"Green dress," I said.

"Was there an old man?"

I nodded.

"Christ," he said softly. He turned and walked out of the shed.
From outside, he called me to come into the house. I dusted off my
overalls and followed him. Michael sneered at me.

"'Locked them in coffins with old dead bodies,'" he mimicked. "Phhht! You're going to get it."

The folks closed the folding door to the kitchen with both of us outside. This disturbed Michael, who'd expected instant vengeance. I was too curious and worried to take revenge on him, so he skulked out the screen door and chased the cat around the house. "Lock you in a coffin!" he screamed.

Mom's voice drifted from behind the louvred doors. "Do you hear that? The poor child's going to have nightmares. It'll warp him."

"Don't exaggerate," Dad said.

"Exaggerate what? That those filthy people are back? Ben, they must be a hundred years old now! They're trying to do the same thing to your son that they did to your brother . . . and just look at *him!* Living in sin, writing for those hell-spawned girlie magazines."

"He ain't living in sin, he's living alone in an apartment in New York City. And he writes for all kinds of places."

"They tried to do it to you, too! Just thank God your aunt saved you."

"Margie, I hope you don't intend—"

"Certainly do. She knows all about them kind of people. She chased them off once, she can sure do it again!"

All hell had broken loose. I didn't understand half of it, but I could feel the presence of Great Aunt Sybil Danser. I could almost hear her crackling voice and the shustle of her satchel of Billy Grahams and Zondervans and little tiny pamphlets with shining light in blue offset on their covers.

I knew there was no way to get the full story from the folks short of listening in, but they'd stopped talking and were sitting in that stony kind of silence that indicated Dad's disgust and Mom's determination. I was mad that nobody was blaming me, as if I were some idiot child not capable of being bad on my own. I was mad at Michael for precipitating the whole mess.

And I was curious. Were the man and woman more than a hundred years old? Why hadn't I seen them before, in town, or heard about them from other kids? Surely I wasn't the only one they'd seen on the road and told stories to. I decided to get to the source. I walked up to the louvred doors and leaned my cheek against them. "Can I go play at George's?"

"Yes," Mom said. "Be back for evening chores."

George lived on the next farm, a mile and a half east. I took my bike and rode down the old dirt road going south.

They were both under the tree, eating a picnic lunch from a wicker basket. I pulled my bike over and leaned it against the gray rock, shading my eyes to see them more clearly.

"Hello, boy," the old man said. "Ain't seen you in a while."

I couldn't think of anything to say. The woman offered me a cookie and I refused with a muttered, "No, thank you, ma'am."

"Well then, perhaps you'd like to tell us your story."

"No, ma'am."

"No story to tell us? That's odd. Meg was sure you had a story in you someplace. Peeking out from behind your ears maybe, thumbing its nose at us."

The woman smiled ingratiatingly. "Tea?"

"There's going to be trouble," I said.

"Already?" The woman smoothed the skirt in her lap and set a plate of nut bread into it. "Well, it comes sooner or later, this time sooner. What do you think of it, boy?"

"I think I got into a lot of trouble for not much being bad," I said. "I don't know why."

"Sit down then," the old man said. "Listen to a tale, then tell us what's going on."

I sat down, not too keen about hearing another story but out of politeness. I took a piece of nut bread and nibbled on it as the woman sipped her tea and cleared her throat. "Once there was a city on the shore of a broad, blue sea. In the city lived five hundred children and nobody else, because the wind from the sea wouldn't let anyone grow old. Well, children don't have kids of their own, of course, so when the wind came up in the first year the city never grew any larger."

"Where'd all the grownups go?" I asked. The old man held his fingers to his lips and shook his head.

"The children tried to play all day, but it wasn't enough. They became frightened at night and had bad dreams. There was nobody to

comfort them because only grownups are really good at making nightmares go away. Now, sometimes nightmares are white horses that come
out of the sea, so they set up guards along the beaches, and fought them
back with wands made of blackthorn. But there was another kind of
nightmare, one that was black and rose out of the ground, and those
were impossible to guard against. So the children got together one day
and decided to tell all the scary stories there were to tell, to prepare
themselves for all the nightmares. They found it was pretty easy to think
up scary stories, and every one of them had a story or two to tell. They
stayed up all night spinning yarns about ghosts and dead things, and live
things that shouldn't have been, and things that were neither. They
talked about death and about monsters that suck blood, about things that
live way deep in the earth and long, thin things that sneak through
cracks in doors to lean over the beds at night and speak in tongues no
one could understand. They talked about eyes without heads, and vice
versa, and little blue shoes that walk across a cold empty white room,
with no one in them, and a bunk bed that creaks when it's empty, and a
printing press that produces newspapers from a city that never was.
Pretty soon, by morning, they'd told all the scary stories. When the black
horses came out of the ground the next night, and the white horses from
the sea, the children greeted them with cakes and ginger ale, and they
held a big party. They also invited the pale sheet-things from the clouds,
and everyone ate hearty and had a good time. One white horse let a little
boy ride on it, and took him wherever he wanted to go. So there were no
more bad dreams in the city of children by the sea."

I finished the piece of bread and wiped my hands on my crossed
legs. "So that's why you tried to scare me," I said.

She shook her head. "No, I never had a reason for telling a story,
and neither should you."

"I don't think I'm going to tell stories any more," I said. "The folks
get too upset."

"Philistines," the old man said, looking off across the fields.

"Listen, young man. There is nothing finer in the world than the
telling of tales. Split atoms if you wish, but splitting an infinitive—and
getting away with it—is far nobler. Lance boils if you wish, but pricking
pretensions is often cleaner and always more fun."

"Then why are Mom and Dad so mad?"

The old man shook his head. "An eternal mystery."

"Well, I'm not so sure," I said. "I scared my little brother pretty bad and that's not nice."

"Being scared is nothing," the old woman said. "Being bored, or ignorant—now that's a crime."

"I still don't know. My folks say you have to be a hundred years old. You did something to my uncle they didn't like, and that was a long time ago. What kind of people are you, anyway?"

The old man smiled. "Old, yes. But not a hundred."

"I just came out here to warn you. Mom and Dad are bringing out my great aunt, and she's no fun for anyone. You better go away." With that said, I ran back to my bike and rode off, pumping for all I was worth. I was between a rock and a hard place. I loved my folks but I itched to hear more stories. Why wasn't it easier to make decisions?

That night I slept restlessly. I didn't have any dreams, but I kept waking up with something pounding at the back of my head, like it wanted to be let in. I scrunched my face up and pressed it back.

At Sunday breakfast, Mom looked across the table at me and put on a kind face. "We're going to pick up Auntie Danser this afternoon, at the airport," she said.

My face went like warm butter.

"You'll come with us, won't you?" she asked. "You always did like the airport."

"All the way from where she lives?" I asked.

"From Omaha," Dad said.

I didn't want to go, but it was more a command than a request. I nodded and Dad smiled at me around his pipe.

"Don't eat too many biscuits," Mom warned him. "You're putting on weight again."

"I'll wear it off come harvest. You cook as if the whole crew was here, anyway."

"Auntie Danser will straighten it all out," Mom said, her mind elsewhere. I caught the suggestion of a grimace on Dad's face, and the pipe wriggled as he bit down on it harder.

The airport was something out of a TV space movie. It went on forever, with stairways going up to restaurants and big smoky windows which looked out on the screaming jets, and crowds of people, all leaving, except for one pear-shaped figure in a cotton print dress with fat ankles and glasses thick as headlamps. I knew her from a hundred yards.

When we met, she shook hands with Mom, hugged Dad as if she didn't want to, then bent down and gave me a smile. Her teeth were yellow and even, sound as a horse's. She was the ugliest woman I'd ever seen. She smelled of lilacs. To this day lilacs take my appetite away.

She carried a bag. Part of it was filled with knitting, part with books and pamphlets. I always wondered why she never carried a Bible—just Billy Grahams and Zondervans. One pamphlet fell out and Dad bent to pick it up.

"Keep it, read it," Auntie Danser instructed him. "Do you good." She turned to Mom and scrutinized her from the bottom of a swimming pool. "You're looking good. He must be treating you right."

Dad ushered us out the automatic doors into the dry heat. Her one suitcase was light as a mummy and probably just as empty. I carried it and it didn't even bring sweat to my brow. Her life was not in clothes and toiletry but in the plastic knitting bag.

We drove back to the farm in the big white station wagon. I leaned my head against the cool glass of the rear seat window and considered puking. Auntie Danser, I told myself, was like a mental dose of castor oil. Or like a visit to the dentist. Even if nothing was going to happen her smell presaged disaster, and like a horse sniffing a storm, my entrails worried.

Mom looked across the seat at me—Auntie Danser was riding up front with Dad—and asked, "You feeling okay? Did they give you anything to eat? Anything funny?"

I said they'd given me a piece of nut bread. Mom went, "Oh, Lord."

"Margie, they don't work like that. They got other ways." Auntie Danser leaned over the back seat and goggled at me. "Boy's just worried. I know all about it. These people and I have had it out before."

Through those murky glasses, her flat eyes knew me to my young, pithy core. I didn't like being known so well. I could see that Auntie Danser's life was firm and predictable, and I made a sudden commitment. I liked the man and woman. They caused trouble, but they were the exact opposite of my great aunt. I felt better, and I gave her a reassuring grin. "Boy will be okay," she said. "Just a colic of the upset mind."

Michael and Barbara sat on the front porch as the car drove up. Somehow a visit by Auntie Danser didn't bother them as much as it did me. They didn't fawn over her but they accepted her without complaining—even out of adult earshot. That made me think more carefully about them. I decided I didn't love them any the less, but I couldn't trust them, either. The world was taking sides and so far on my side I was very lonely. I didn't count the two old people on my side, because I wasn't sure they were—but they came a lot closer than anybody in the family.

Auntie Danser wanted to read Billy Graham books to us after dinner, but Dad snuck us out before Mom could gather us together—all but Barbara, who stayed to listen. We watched the sunset from the loft of the old wood barn, then tried to catch the little birds that live in the rafters. By dark and bedtime I was hungry, but not for food. I asked Dad if he'd tell me a story before bed.

"You know your mom doesn't approve of all that fairy-tale stuff," he said.

"Then no fairy tales. Just a story."

"I'm out of practice, son," he confided. He looked very sad. "Your mom says we should concentrate on things that are real and not waste our time with make-believe. Life's hard. I may have to sell the farm, you know, and work for that feed-mixer in Mitchell."

I went to bed and felt like crying. A whole lot of my family had died that night, I didn't know exactly how, or why. But I was mad.

I didn't go to school the next day. During the night I'd had a dream, which came so true and whole to me that I had to rush to the stand of cottonwoods and tell the old people. I took my lunch box and walked rapidly down the road.

They weren't there. On a piece of wire braided to the biggest tree they'd left a note on faded brown paper. It was in a strong, feminine hand, sepia-inked, delicately scribed with what could have been a goose-quill pen. It said: "We're at the old Hauskopf farm. Come if you must."

Not "Come if you can." I felt a twinge. The Hauskopf farm, abandoned fifteen years ago and never sold, was three miles farther down the road and left on a deep-rutted fork. It took me an hour to get there.

The house still looked deserted. All the white paint was flaking, leaving dead gray wood. The windows stared. I walked up the porch steps and knocked on the heavy oak door. For a moment I thought no one was going to answer. Then I heard what sounded like a gust of wind, but inside the house, and the old woman opened the door. "Hello, boy," she said. "Come for more stories?"

She invited me in. Wildflowers were growing along the baseboards and tiny roses peered from the brambles that covered the walls. A quail led her train of inch-and-a-half fluffball chicks from under the stairs, into the living room. The floor was carpeted but the flowers in the weave seemed more than patterns. I could stare down and keep picking out detail for minutes. "This way, boy," the woman said. She took my hand. Hers was smooth and warm but I had the impression it was also hard as wood.

A tree stood in the living room, growing out of the floor and sending its branches up to support the ceiling. Rabbits and quail and a lazy-looking brindle cat looked at me from tangles of roots. A wooden bench surrounded the base of the tree. On the side away from us, I heard someone breathing. The old man poked his head around, and smiled at me, lifting his long pipe in greeting. "Hello, boy," he said.

"The boy looks like he's ready to tell us a story, this time," the woman said.

"Of course, Meg. Have a seat, boy. Cup of cider for you? Tea? Herb biscuit?"

"Cider, please," I said.

The old man stood and went down the hall to the kitchen. He came back with a wooden tray and three steaming cups of mulled cider. The cinnamon tickled my nose as I sipped.

"Now. What's your story?"

"It's about two hawks," I said. I hesitated.

"Go on."

"Brother hawks. Never did like each other. Fought for a strip of land where they could hunt."

"Yes?"

"Finally, one hawk met an old, crippled bobcat that had set up a place for itself in a rockpile. The bobcat was learning itself magic so it wouldn't have to go out and catch dinner, which was awful hard for it now. The hawk landed near the bobcat and told it about his brother, and how cruel he was. So the bobcat said, 'Why not give him the land for the day? Here's what you can do.' The bobcat told him how he could turn into a rabbit, but a very strong rabbit no hawk could hurt."

"Wily bobcat," the old man said, smiling.

"'You mean, my brother wouldn't be able to catch me?' the hawk asked. 'Course not,' the bobcat said. 'And you can teach him a lesson. You'll tussle with him, scare him real bad—show him what tough animals there are on the land he wants. Then he'll go away and hunt somewhere else.' The hawk thought that sounded like a fine idea. So he let the bobcat turn him into a rabbit and he hopped back to the land and waited in a patch of grass. Sure enough, his brother's shadow passed by soon, and then he heard a swoop and saw the claws held out. So he filled himself with being mad and jumped up and practically bit the tail feathers off his brother. The hawk just flapped up and rolled over on the ground, blinking and gawking with his beak wide. 'Rabbit,' he said, 'that's not natural. Rabbits don't act that way.'

"'Round here they do,' the hawk-rabbit said. 'This is a tough old land, and all the animals here know the tricks of escaping from bad birds like you.' This scared the brother hawk, and he flew away as best he could, and never came back again. The hawk-rabbit hopped to the rockpile and stood up before the bobcat, saying, 'It worked real fine. I thank you. Now turn me back and I'll go hunt my land.' But the bobcat only grinned and reached out with a paw and broke the rabbit's neck. Then he ate him, and said, 'Now the land's mine, and no hawks can take away the easy game.' And that's how the greed of two hawks turned their land over to a bobcat."

The old woman looked at me with wide, baked-chestnut eyes and smiled. "You've got it," she said. "Just like your uncle. Hasn't he got it, Jack?" The old man nodded and took his pipe from his mouth. "He's got it fine. He'll make a good one."

"Now, boy, why did you make up that story?"

I thought for a moment, then shook my head. "I don't know," I said. "It just came up."

"What are you going to do with the story?"

I didn't have an answer for that question, either.

"Got any other stories in you?"

I considered, then said. "Think so."

A car drove up outside and Mom called my name. The old woman stood and straightened her dress. "Follow me," she said. "Go out the back door, walk around the house. Return home with them. Tomorrow, go to school like you're supposed to do. Next Saturday, come back and we'll talk some more."

"Son? You in there?"

I walked out the back and came around to the front of the house. Mom and Auntie Danser waited in the station wagon. "You aren't allowed out here. Were you in that house?" Mom asked. I shook my head.

My great aunt looked at me with her glassed-in flat eyes and lifted the corners of her lips a little. "Margie," she said, "go have a look in the windows."

Mom got out of the car and walked up the porch to peer through the dusty panes. "It's empty, Sybil."

"Empty, boy, right?"

"I don't know," I said. "I wasn't inside."

"I could hear you, boy," she said. "Last night. Talking in your sleep. Rabbits and hawks don't behave that way. You know it, and I know it. So it ain't no good thinking about them that way, is it?"

"I don't remember talking in my sleep," I said.

"Margie, let's go home. This boy needs some pamphlets read into him."

Mom got into the car and looked back at me before starting the engine. "You ever skip school again, I'll strap you black and blue. It's real embarrassing having the school call, and not knowing where you are. Hear me?"

I nodded.

Everything was quiet that week. I went to school and tried not to dream at night, and did everything boys are supposed to do. But I didn't feel like a boy. I felt something big inside, and no amount of Billy Grahams and Zondervans read at me could change that feeling.

I made one mistake, though. I asked Auntie Danser why she never read the Bible. This was in the parlor one evening after dinner and cleaning up the dishes. "Why do you want to know, boy?" she asked.

"Well, the Bible seems to be full of fine stories, but you don't carry it around with you. I just wondered why."

"Bible is a good book," she said. "The only good book. But it's difficult. It has lots of camouflage. Sometimes—" She stopped. "Who put you up to asking that question?"

"Nobody," I said.

"I heard that question before, you know," she said. "Ain't the first time I been asked. Somebody else asked me, once."

I sat in my chair, stiff as a ham.

"Your father's brother asked me that once. But we won't talk about him, will we?"

I shook my head.

Next Saturday I waited until it was dark and everyone was in bed. The night air was warm but I was sweating more than the warm could cause as I rode my bike down the dirt road, lamp beam swinging back and forth. The sky was crawling with stars, all of them looking at me. The Milky Way seemed to touch down just beyond the road, like I might ride straight up it if I went far enough.

I knocked on the heavy door. There were no lights in the windows and it was late for old folks to be up, but I knew these two didn't behave like normal people. And I knew that just because the house looked empty from the outside didn't mean it was empty within. The wind rose up and beat against the door, making me shiver. Then it opened. It was dark for a moment and the breath went out of me. Two pairs of eyes stared from the black. They seemed a lot taller this time. "Come in, boy," Jack whispered.

Fireflies lit up the tree in the living room. The brambles and wild-flowers glowed like weeds on a sea floor. The carpet crawled, but not to my feet. I was shivering in earnest now and my teeth chattered.

I only saw their shadows as they sat on the bench in front of me. "Sit," Meg said. "Listen close. You've taken the fire and it glows bright.

You're only a boy but you're just like a pregnant woman now. For the rest of your life you'll be cursed with the worst affliction known to humans. Your skin will twitch at night. Your eyes will see things in the dark. Beasts will come to you and beg to be ridden. You'll never know one truth from another. You might starve, because few will want to encourage you. And if you do make good in this world, you might lose the gift and search forever after, in vain. Some will say the gift isn't special. Beware them. Some will say it is special and beware them, too. And some—"

There was a scratching at the door. I thought it was an animal for a moment. Then it cleared its throat. It was my great-aunt.

"Some will say you're damned. Perhaps they're right. But you're also enthused. Carry it lightly, and responsibly."

"Listen in there. This is Sybil Danser. You know me. Open up."

"Now stand by the stairs, in the dark where she can't see," Jack said. I did as I was told. One of them—I couldn't tell which—opened the door and the lights went out in the tree, the carpet stilled, and the brambles were snuffed. Auntie Danser stood in the doorway, outlined by star glow, carrying her knitting bag. "Boy?" she asked. I held my breath.

"And you others, too."

The wind in the house seemed to answer. "I'm not too late," she said. "Damn you, in truth, damn you to hell! You come to our towns, and you plague us with thoughts no decent person wants to think. Not just fairy stories, but telling the way people live, and why they shouldn't live that way! Your very breath is tainted! Hear me?" She walked slowly into the empty living room, feet clonking on the wooden floor. "You make them write about us, and make others laugh at us. Question the way we think. Condemn our deepest prides. Pull out our mistakes and amplify them beyond all truth. What right do you have to take young children and twist their minds?"

The wind sang through the cracks in the walls. I tried to see if Jack or Meg was there, but only shadows remained.

"I know where you come from, don't forget that! Out of the ground! Out of the bones of old, wicked Indians! Shamans and pagan dances and worshiping dirt and filth! I heard about you from the old

squaws on the reservation. Frost and Spring, they called you, signs of
the turning year. Well, now you got a different name! Death and
demons, I call you, hear me?"

She seemed to jump at a sound but I couldn't hear it. "Don't you
argue with me!" she shrieked. She took her glasses off and held out
both hands. "Think I'm a weak old woman, do you? You don't know
how deep I run in these communities! I'm the one who had them books
taken off the shelves. Remember me? Oh, you hated it—not being able
to fill young minds with your pestilence. Took them off high school
shelves, and out of lists—burned them for junk! Remember? That was
me. I'm not dead yet! Boy, where are you?"

"Enchant her," I whispered to the air. "Magic her. Make her go
away. Let me live here with you."

"Is that you, boy? Come with your aunt, now. Come with, come
away!"

"Go with her," the wind told me. "Send your children this way,
years from now. But go with her."

I felt a kind of tingly warmth and knew it was time to get home. I
snuck out the back way and came around to the front of the house.
There was no car. She'd followed me on foot all the way from the farm.
I wanted to leave her there in the old house, shouting at the dead
rafters, but instead I called her name and waited.

She came out crying. She knew.

"You poor, sinning boy," she said, pulling me to her lilac bosom.

Armaja Das

Joe Haldeman

he highrise, built in 1980, still had the smell and look of
newness. And of money.

The doorman bowed a few degrees and kept a straight
face, opening the door for a bent old lady. She had a card of
Veterans' poppies clutched in one old claw. He didn't care
much for the security guard, and she would give him interesting trouble.

The skin on her face hung in deep creases, scored with a network
of tiny wrinkles; her chin and nose protruded and dropped. A
cataract made one eye opaque; the other eye was yellow and red surrounding deep black, unblinking. She had left her teeth in various
things. She shuffled. She wore an old black dress faded slightly gray
by repeated washing. If she had any hair, it was concealed by a pale
blue bandanna. She was so stooped that her neck was almost parallel
to the ground.

"What can I do for you?" The security guard had a tired voice to
match his tired shoulders and back. The job had seemed a little romantic the first couple of days, guarding all these rich people, sitting at an

ultramodern console surrounded by video monitors, submachine gun at his knees. But the monitors were blank except for an hourly check, power shortage; and if he ever removed the gun from its cradle, he would have to fill out five forms and call the police station. And the doorman never turned anybody away.

"Buy a flower for boys less fortunate than ye," she said in a faint raspy baritone. From her age and accent, her own boys had fought in the Russian Revolution.

"I'm sorry. I'm not allowed to . . . respond to charity while on duty."

She stared at him for a long time, nodding microscopically. "Then send me to someone with more heart."

He was trying to frame a reply when the front door slammed open. "Car on fire!" the doorman shouted.

The security guard leaped out of his seat, grabbed a fire extinguisher and sprinted for the door. The old woman shuffled along behind him until both he and the doorman disappeared around the corner. Then she made for the elevator with surprising agility.

She got out on the 17th floor, after pushing the button that would send the elevator back down to the lobby. She checked the name plate on 1738; Mr. Zold. She was illiterate but could recognize names.

Not even bothering to try the lock, she walked on down the hall until she found a maid's closet. She closed the door behind her and hid behind a rack of starchy white uniforms, leaning against the wall with her bag between her feet. The slight smell of gasoline didn't bother her at all.

John Zold pressed the intercom button. "Martha?" She answered. "Before you close up shop I'd like a redundancy check on stack 408. Against tape 408." He switched the selector on his visual output screen so it would duplicate the output at Martha's station. He stuffed tobacco in a pipe and lit it, watching.

Green numbers filled the screen, a complicated matrix of ones and zeros. They faded for a second and were replaced with a field of pure zeros. The lines of zeros started to roll, like titles preceding a movie.

The 746th line came up all ones. John thumbed the intercom again. "Had to be something like that. You have time to fix it up?" She did. "Thanks, Martha. See you tomorrow."

He slid back the part of his desk top that concealed a keypunch and typed rapidly: "523 784 00926/ / Good night, machine. Please lock this station."

GOOD NIGHT, JOHN. DON'T FORGET YOUR LUNCH DATE WITH MR. BROWNWOOD TOMORROW. DENTIST APPOINTMENT WEDNESDAY 0945. GENERAL SYSTEMS CHECK WEDNESDAY 1300. DEL O DEL BAXT. LOCKED.

Del O del baxt means "God give you luck" in the ancient tongue of the Romani. John Zold, born a Gypsy but hardly a Gypsy by any standard other than the strong one of blood, turned off his console and unlocked the bottom drawer of his desk. He took out a flat automatic pistol in a holster with a belt clip and slipped it under his jacket, inside the waistband of his trousers. He had only been wearing the gun for two weeks, and it still made him uncomfortable. But there had been those letters.

John was born in Chicago, some years after his parents had fled from Europe and Hitler. His father had been a fiercely proud man, and got involved in a bitter argument over the honor of his 12-year-old daughter, from which argument he had come home with knuckles raw and bleeding, and had given to his wife for disposal a large clasp knife crusty with dried blood.

John was small for his five years, and his chin barely cleared the kitchen table, where the whole family sat and discussed their uncertain future while Mrs. Zold bound up her husband's hands. John's shortness saved his life when the kitchen window exploded and a low ceiling of shotgun pellets fanned out and chopped into the heads and chests of the only people in the world whom he could love and trust. The police found him huddled between the bodies of his father and mother, and at first thought he was also dead; covered with blood, completely still, eyes wide open and not crying.

It took six months for the kindly orphanage people to get a single word out of him: *ratválo*, which he said over and over; which they were never able to translate. Bloody, bleeding.

But he had been raised mostly in English, with a few words of Romani and Hungarian thrown in for spice and accuracy. In another year their problem was not one of communicating with John; only of trying to shut him up.

No one adopted the stunted Gypsy boy, which suited John. He'd had a family, and look what happened.

In orphanage school he flunked penmanship and deportment, but did reasonably well in everything else. In arithmetic and, later, mathematics, he was nothing short of brilliant. When he left the orphanage at eighteen, he enrolled at the University of Illinois, supporting himself as a bookkeeper's assistant and part-time male model. He had come out of an ugly adolescence with a striking resemblance to the young Clark Gable.

Drafted out of college, he spent two years playing with computers at Fort Lewis; got out and went all the way to a Master's degree under the G. I. Bill. His thesis "Simulation of Continuous Physical Systems by Way of Universalization of the Trakhtenbrot Algorithms" was very well received, and the mathematics department gave him a research assistantship, to extend the thesis into a doctoral dissertation. But other people read the paper too, and after a few months Bellcom International hired him away from academia. He rose rapidly through the ranks. Not yet forty, he was now Senior Analyst at Bellcom's Research and Development Group. He had his own private office, with a picture window overlooking Central Park, and a plush six-figure condominium only twenty minutes away by commuter train.

As was his custom, John bought a tall can of beer on his way to the train, and opened it as soon as he sat down. It kept him from fidgeting during the fifteen or twenty-minute wait while the train filled up.

He pulled a thick technical report out of his briefcase and stared at the summary on the cover sheet, not really seeing it but hoping that looking occupied would spare him the company of some anonymous fellow traveller.

The train was an express, and whisked them out to Dobb's Ferry in twelve minutes. John didn't look up from his report until they were well out of New York City; the heavy mesh tunnel that protected the track from vandals induced spurious colors in your retina as it blurred by. Some people liked it, tripped on it, but to John the effect was at best annoying, at worst nauseating, depending on how tired he was. Tonight he was dead tired.

He got off the train two stops up from Dobb's Ferry. The highrise limousine was waiting for him and two other residents. It was a fine spring evening and John would normally have walked the half-mile, tired or not. But those unsigned letters.

John Zold, you stop this preachment or you die soon. Armaja das, John Zold.

All three letters said that: *Armaja das*, we put a curse on you. For preaching.

He was less afraid of curses than of bullets. He undid the bottom button of his jacket as he stepped off the train, ready to quickdraw, roll for cover behind that trash can, just like in the movies; but there was no one suspicious-looking around. Just an assortment of suburban wives and the old cop who was on permanent station duty.

Assassination in broad daylight wasn't Romani style. Styles change, though. He got in the car and watched the side roads all the way home.

There was another one of the shabby envelopes in his mailbox. He wouldn't open it until he got upstairs. He stepped in the elevator with the others, and punched 17.

They were angry because John Zold was stealing their children.

Last March John's tax accountant had suggested that he could contribute $4,000 to any legitimate charity, and actually make a few hundred bucks in the process, by dropping into a lower tax bracket. Not one to do things the easy or obvious way, John made various inquiries and, after a certain amount of bureaucratic tedium, founded the Young Gypsy Assimilation Council—with matching funds from federal, state and city governments, and a continuing Ford Foundation scholarship grant.

The YGAC was actually just a one-room office in a West Village brownstone, manned by volunteer help. It was filled with various pamphlets and broadsides, mostly written by John, explaining how young Gypsies could legitimately take advantage of American society. By becoming part of it, which was the part that old-line Gypsies didn't care for. Jobs, scholarships, work-study programs, these things are for the *gadjos*. Poison to a Gypsy's spirit.

In November a volunteer had opened the office in the morning to find a crude fire bomb, using a candle as a delayed-action fuse for five gallons of gasoline. The candle was guttering a fraction of an inch away from the line of powder that would have ignited the gas. In January it had been buckets of chicken entrails, poured into filing cabinets and flung over the walls. So John found a tough young man who would sleep on the cot in the office at night; sleep like a cat with a shotgun beside him. There was no more trouble of that sort. Only old men and women who would file in silently staring, to take handfuls of pamphlets which they would drop in the hall and scuff into uselessness, or defile in a more basic way. But paper was cheap.

John threw the bolt on his door and hung his coat in the closet. He put the gun in a drawer in his writing desk and sat down to open the mail.

The shortest one yet: "Tonight, John Zold. *Armaja das.*" Lots of luck, he thought. Won't even be home tonight; heavy date. Stay at her place, Gramercy Park. Lay a curse on me there? At the show or Sardi's?

He opened two more letters, bills, and there was a knock at the door.

Not announced from downstairs. Maybe a neighbor. Guy next door was always borrowing something. Still. Feeling a little foolish, he put the gun back in his waistband. Put his coat back on in case it was just a neighbor.

The peephole didn't show anything, bad. He drew the pistol and held it just out of sight, by the doorjamb, threw the bolt and eased open the door. He bumped into the Gypsy woman, too short to have been visible through the peephole. She backed away and said, "John Zold."

He stared at her. "What do you want, *püridaia?*" He could only remember a hundred or so words of Romani, but "grandmother" was one of them. What was the word for witch?

"I have a gift for you." From her bag she took a dark green booklet, bent and with frayed edges, and gave it to him. It was a much-used

Canadian passport, belonging to a William Belini. But the picture inside the front cover was one of John Zold.

Inside, there was an airline ticket in a Qantas envelope. John didn't open it. He snapped the passport shut and handed it back. The old lady wouldn't accept it.

"An impressive job. It's flattering that someone thinks I'm so important."

"Take it and leave forever, John Zold. Or I will have to do the second thing."

He slipped the ticket envelope out of the booklet. "This, I will take. I can get your refund on it. The money will buy lots of posters and pamphlets." He tried to toss the passport into her bag, but missed. "What is your second thing?"

She tossed the passport back to him. "Pick that up." She was trying to sound imperious, but it came out a thin, petulant quaver.

"Sorry, I don't have any use for it. What is—"

"The second thing is your death, John Zold." She reached into her bag.

He produced the pistol and aimed it down at her forehead. "No, I don't think so."

She ignored the gun, pulling out a handful of white chicken feathers. She threw the feathers over his threshold. "*Armaja das,*" she said, and then droned on in Romani, scattering feathers at regular intervals. John recognized *joovi* and *kari,* the words for woman and penis, and several other words he might have picked up if she'd pronounced them more clearly.

He put the gun back into its holster and waited until she was through. "Do you really think—"

"*Armaja das,*" she said again, and started a new litany. He recognized a word in the middle as meaning corruption or infection, and the last word was quite clear: death. *Méripen.*

"This nonsense isn't going to . . ." But he was talking to the back of her head. He forced a laugh and watched her walk past the elevator and turn the corner that led to the staircase.

He could call the guard. Make sure she didn't get out the back way. Illegal entry. He suspected that she knew he wouldn't want to go to the trouble, and it annoyed him slightly. He walked halfway to the phone, checked his watch and went back to the door. Scooped up the feathers and dropped them in the disposal. Just enough time. Fresh shave, shower, best clothes. Limousine to the station, train to the city, cab from Grand Central to her apartment.

The show was pure delight, a sexy revival of *Lysistrata*. Sardi's was as ego-bracing as ever; she was a soft-hard woman with style and sparkle, who all but dragged him back to her apartment, where he was for the first time in his life impotent.

The psychiatrist had no use for the traditional props: no soft couch or bookcases lined with obviously expensive volumes. No carpet, no paneling, no numbered prints; not even the notebook or the expression of slightly disinterested compassion. Instead, she had a hidden recorder and an analytical scowl; plain stucco walls surrounding a functional desk and two hard chairs, period.

"You know exactly what the problem is," she said.

John nodded. "I suppose. Some . . . residue from my early upbringing; I accept her as an authority figure. From the few words I could understand of what she said, I took, it was . . ."

"From the words *penis* and *woman*, you built your own curse. And you're using it, probably to punish yourself for surviving the disaster that killed the rest of your family."

"That's pretty old-fashioned. And farfetched. I've had almost forty years to punish myself for that, if I felt responsible. And I don't."

"Still, it's a working hypothesis." She shifted in her chair and studied the pattern of teak grain on the bare top of her desk. "Perhaps if we can keep it simple, the cure can also be simple."

"All right with me," John said. At $125 an hour, the quicker, the better.

"If you can see it, feel it, in this context, then the key to your cure is transference." She leaned forward, elbows on the table, and John watched her breasts shifting with detached interest, the only kind of interest he'd had in women for more than a week. "If you can see *me* as an authority figure instead," she continued, "then eventually I'll be able to reach the child inside; convince him that there was no curse.

Only a case of mistaken identity . . . nothing but an old woman who scared him. With careful hypnosis, it shouldn't be too difficult."

"Seems reasonable," John said slowly. Accept this young *Geyri* as more powerful than the old witch? As a grown man, he could. If there was a frightened Gypsy boy hiding inside him, though, he wasn't sure.

"523 784 00926/ /Hello, machine," John typed. "Who is the best dermatologist within a 10-short-block radius?"

GOOD MORNING, JOHN. WITHIN STATED DISTANCE AND USING AS SOLE PARAMETER THEIR HOURLY FEE, THE MAXIMUM FEE IS $95/HR, AND THIS IS CHARGED BY TWO DERMATOLOGISTS, DR. BRYAN DILL, 245 W. 45TH ST., SPE-CIALIZES IN COSMETIC DERMATOLOGY. DR. ARTHUR MAAS, 198 W. 44TH ST., SPECIALIZES IN SERIOUS DISEASES OF THE SKIN.

"Will Dr. Maas treat disease of psychological origin?"

CERTAINLY. MOST DERMATOSIS IS.

Don't get cocky, machine. "Make me an appointment with Dr. Maas, within the next two days."

YOUR APPOINTMENT IS AT 1:45 TOMORROW, FOR ONE HOUR. THIS WILL LEAVE YOU 45 MINUTES TO GET TO LUCHOW'S FOR YOUR APPOINTMENT WITH THE AMCSE GROUP. I HOPE IT IS NOTHING SERIOUS, JOHN.

"I trust it isn't." Creepy empathy circuits. "Have you arranged for a remote terminal at Luchow's?"

THIS WAS NOT NECESSARY. I WILL PATCH THROUGH CONED/GENERAL. LEASING THEIR LUCHOW'S FACILITY WILL COST ONLY .588 THE PROJECTED COST OF TRANS-PORTATION AND SETUP LABOR FOR A REMOTE TERMINAL.

That's my machine, always thinking. "Very good, machine. Keep this station live for the time being."

THANK YOU, JOHN. The letters faded but the ready light stayed on.

He shouldn't complain about the empathy circuits; they were his baby, and the main reason Bellcom paid such a bloated salary, to keep him. The copyright on the empathy package was good for another 12 years, and they were making a fortune, timesharing it out. Virtually every large computer in the world was hooked up to it, from the ConEd/General that ran New York, to Geneva and Akademia Nauk, which together ran half the world.

Most of the customers gave the empathy package a name, usually female. John called it "machine" in a not-too-successful attempt to keep from thinking of it as human.

He made a conscious effort to restrain himself from picking at the carbuncles on the back of his neck. He should have gone to the doctor when they first appeared, but the psychiatrist had been sure she could cure them; the "corruption" of the second curse. She'd had no more success with that than with the impotence. And this morning, boils had broken out on his chest and groin and shoulderblades, and there were sore spots on his nose and cheekbone. He had some opiates, but would stick to aspirin until after work.

Dr. Maas called it impetigo; gave him a special kind of soap and some antibiotic ointment. He told John to make another appointment in two weeks, ten days. If there was no improvement they would take stronger measures. He seemed young for a doctor, and John couldn't bring himself to say anything about the curse. But he already had a doctor for that end of it, he rationalized.

Three days later he was back in Dr. Maas's office. There was scarcely a square inch of his body where some sort of lesion hadn't appeared. He had a temperature of 101.4°. The doctor gave him systemic antibiotics and told him to take a couple of days' bed rest. John told him about the curse, finally, and the doctor gave him a booklet about psychosomatic illness. It told John nothing he didn't already know.

By the next morning, in spite of strong antipyretics, his fever had risen to over 102°. Groggy with fever and painkillers, John crawled out of bed and travelled down to the West Village, to the YGAC office. Fred Gorgio, the man who guarded the place at night, was still on duty.

"Mr. Zold!" When John came through the door, Gorgio jumped up from the desk and took his arm. John winced from the contact, but allowed himself to be led to a chair. "What's happened?" John by this time looked like a person with terminal smallpox.

For a long minute John sat motionlessly, staring at the inflamed boils that crowded the backs of his hands. "I need a healer," he said, talking with slow awkwardness because of the crusted lesions on his lips.

"A *chóvihánni?*" John looked at him uncomprehendingly. "A witch?"

"No." He moved his head from side to side. "An herb doctor. Perhaps a white witch."

"Have you gone to the *gadjo* doctor?"

"Two. A Gypsy did this to me; a Gypsy has to cure it."

"It's in your head, then?"

"The *gadjo* doctors say so. It can still kill me."

Gorgio picked up the phone, punched a local number, and rattled off a fast stream of a patois that used as much Romani and Italian as English. "That was my cousin," he said, hanging up. "His mother heals, and has a good reputation. If he finds her at home, she can be here in less than an hour."

John mumbled his appreciation. Gorgio led him to the couch.

The healer woman was early, bustling in with a wicker bag full of things that rattled. She glanced once at John and Gorgio, and began clearing the pamphlets off a side table. She appeared to be somewhere between fifty and sixty years old, tight bun of silver hair bouncing as she moved around the room, setting up a hot-plate and filling two small pots with water. She wore a black dress only a few years old, and sensible shoes. The only lines on her face were laugh lines.

She stood over John and said something in gentle, rapid Italian, then took a heavy silver crucifix from around her neck and pressed it between his hands. "Tell her to speak English . . . or Hungarian," John said.

Gorgio translated. "She says that you should not be so affected by the old superstitions. You should be a modern man, and not believe in fairy tales for children and old people."

John stared at the crucifix, turning it slowly between his fingers. "One old superstition is much like another." But he didn't offer to give the crucifix back.

The smaller pot was starting to steam and she dropped a handful of herbs into it. Then she returned to John and carefully undressed him.

When the herb infusion was boiling, she emptied a package of powdered arrowroot into the cold water in the other pot, and stirred it vigorously. Then she poured the hot solution into the cold and stirred some
more. Through Gorgio, she told John she wasn't sure whether the herb
treatment would cure him. But it would make him more comfortable.

The liquid jelled and she tested the temperature with her fingers.
When it was cool enough, she started to pat it gently on John's face.
Then the door creaked open, and she gasped. It was the old crone who
had put the curse on John in the first place.

The witch said something in Romani, obviously a command, and
the woman stepped away from John.

"Are you still a skeptic, John Zold?" She surveyed her handiwork.
"You called this nonsense."

John glared at her but didn't say anything. "I heard that you had
asked for a healer," she said, and addressed the other woman in a low
tone.

Without a word, she emptied her potion into the sink and began
putting away her paraphernalia. "Old bitch," John croaked. "What did
you tell her?"

"I said that if she continued to treat you, what happened to you
would also happen to her sons."

"You're afraid it would work," Gorgio said.

"No. It would only make it easier for John Zold to die. If I wanted
that I could have killed him on his threshold." Like a quick bird she
bent over and kissed John on his inflamed lips. "I will see you soon,
John Zold. Not in this world." She shuffled out the door and the
other woman followed her. Gorgio cursed her in Italian, but she
didn't react.

John painfully dressed himself. "What now?" Gorgio said. "I could
find you another healer . . ."

"No. I'll go back to the *gadjo* doctors. They say they can bring people back from the dead." He gave Gorgio the woman's crucifix and
limped away.

The doctor gave him enough antibiotics to turn him into a loaf of
moldy bread, then reserved a bed for him at an exclusive clinic in

Westchester, starting the next morning. He would be under 24-hour observation; constant blood turn-around if necessary. They *would* cure him. It was not possible for a man of his age and physical condition to die of dermatosis.

It was dinnertime and the doctor asked John to come have some home cooking. He declined partly from lack of appetite, partly because he couldn't imagine even a doctor's family being able to eat with such a grisly apparition at the table with them. He took a cab to the office.

There was nobody on his floor but a janitor, who took one look at John and developed an intense interest in the floor.

"523 784 00926/ /Machine, I'm going to die. Please advise."

ALL HUMANS AND MACHINES DIE, JOHN. IF YOU MEAN YOU ARE GOING TO DIE, SOON, THAT IS SAD.

"That's what I mean. The skin infection; it's completely out of control. White cell count climbing in spite of drugs. Going to the hospital tomorrow, to die."

BUT YOU ADMITTED THAT THE CONDITION WAS PSYCHOSOMATIC. THAT MEANS YOU ARE KILLING YOURSELF, JOHN. YOU HAVE NO REASON TO BE THAT SAD.

He called the machine a Jewish mother and explained in some detail about the YGAC, the old crone, the various stages of the curse, and today's aborted attempt to fight fire with fire.

YOUR LOGIC WAS CORRECT BUT THE APPLICATION OF IT WAS NOT EFFECTIVE. YOU SHOULD HAVE COME TO ME, JOHN. IT TOOK ME 2.037 SECONDS TO SOLVE YOUR PROBLEM. PURCHASE A SMALL BLACK BIRD AND CONNECT ME TO A VOCAL CIRCUIT.

"What?" John said. He typed: "Please explain."

FROM REFERENCE IN NEW YORK LIBRARY'S COLLECTION OF THE JOURNAL OF THE GYPSY LORE SOCIETY, EDINBURGH. THROUGH JOURNALS OF ANTHROPOLOGICAL LINGUISTICS AND SLAVIC PHILOLOGY. FINALLY TO REFERENCE IN DOCTORAL THESIS OF HERR LUDWIG R. GROSS (HEIDELBERG, 1976) TO TRANSCRIPTION OF WIRE RECORDING WHICH RESIDES IN ARCHIVES OF AKADEMIA

NAUK, MOSCOW; CAPTURED FROM GERMAN SCIENTISTS (EXPERIMENTS ON GYPSIES IN CONCENTRATION CAMPS, TRYING TO KILL THEM WITH REPETITION OF RECORDED CURSE) AT THE END OF WWII.

INCIDENTALLY, JOHN, THE NAZI EXPERIMENTS FAILED. EVEN TWO GENERATIONS AGO, MOST GYPSIES WERE DISASSOCIATED ENOUGH FROM THE OLD TRADITIONS TO BE IMMUNE TO THE FATAL CURSE. YOU ARE VERY SUPERSTITIOUS. I HAVE FOUND THIS TO BE NOT UNCOMMON AMONG MATHEMATICIANS.

THERE IS A TRANSFERENCE CURSE THAT WILL CURE YOU BY GIVING THE IMPOTENCE AND INFECTION TO THE NEAREST SUSCEPTIBLE PERSON. THAT MAY WELL BE THE OLD BITCH WHO GAVE IT TO YOU IN THE FIRST PLACE.

THE PET STORE AT 588 SEVENTH AVENUE IS OPEN UNTIL 9 PM. THEIR INVENTORY INCLUDES A CAGE OF FINCHES, OF ASSORTED COLORS. PURCHASE A BLACK ONE AND RETURN HERE. THEN CONNECT ME TO A VOCAL CIRCUIT.

It took John less than thirty minutes to taxi there, buy the bird and get back. The taxidriver didn't ask him why he was carrying a bird cage to a deserted office building. He felt like an idiot.

John usually avoided using the vocal circuit because the person who had programmed it had given the machine a saccharine, nice-old-lady voice. He wheeled the output unit into his office and plugged it in.

"Thank you, John. Now hold the bird in your left hand and repeat after me." The terrified finch offered no resistance when John closed his hand over it.

The machine spoke Romani with a Russian accent. John repeated it as well as he could, but not one word in ten had any meaning to him.

"Now kill the bird, John."

Kill it? Feeling guilty, John pressed hard, felt small bones cracking. The bird squealed and then made a faint growling noise. Its heart stopped.

John dropped the dead creature and typed, "Is that all?"

The machine knew John didn't like to hear its voice, and so replied on the video screen. YES. GO HOME AND GO TO SLEEP, AND THE CURSE WILL BE TRANSFERRED BY THE TIME YOU WAKE UP. DEL O DEL BAXT, JOHN.

He locked up and made his way home. The late commuters on the train, all strangers, avoided his end of the car. The cab driver at the station paled when he saw John, and carefully took his money by an untainted corner.

John took two sleeping pills and contemplated the rest of the bottle. He decided he could stick it out for one more day, and uncorked his best bottle of wine. He drank half of it in five minutes, not tasting it. When his body started to feel heavy, he crept into the bedroom and fell on the bed without taking off his clothes.

When he awoke the next morning, the first thing he noticed was that he was no longer impotent. The second thing he noticed was that there were no boils on his right hand.

"523 784 00926//Thank you, machine. The countercurse did work."

The ready light glowed steadily, but the machine didn't reply. He turned on the intercom. "Martha? I'm not getting any output on the VDS here."

"Just a minute, sir. Let me hang up my coat, I'll call the machine room. Welcome back."

"I'll wait." You could call the machine room yourself, slave driver. He looked at the faint image reflected back from the video screen; his face free of any inflammation. He thought of the Gypsy crone, dying of corruption, and the picture didn't bother him at all. Then he remembered the finch and saw its tiny corpse in the middle of the rug. He picked it up just as Martha came into his office, frowning.

"What's that?" she said.

He gestured at the cage. "Thought a bird might liven up the place. Died though," He dropped it in the wastepaper basket. "What's the word?"

"Oh, the . . . it's pretty strange. They say nobody's getting any output. The machine's computing, but it's, well, it's not talking."

"Hmm. I better get down there." He took the elevator down to the sub-basement. It always seemed unpleasantly warm to him down there. Probably psychological compensation on the part of the crew; keeping the temperature up because of all the liquid helium inside the pastel boxes of the central processing unit. Several bathtubs' worth of liquid that had to be kept colder than the surface of Pluto.

"Ah, Mr. Zold." A man in a white jumpsuit, carrying a clipboard as his badge of office: first shift coordinator. John recognized him but didn't remember his name. Normally, he would have asked the machine before coming down. "Glad that you're back. Hear it was pretty bad."

Friendly concern or lese majesty? "Some sort of allergy, hung on for more than a week. What's the output problem?"

"Would've left a message if I'd known you were coming in. It's in the CPU, not the software. Theo Jasper found it when he opened up, a little after six, but it took an hour to get a cryogenics man down here."

"That's him?" A man in a business suit was wandering around the central processing unit, reading dials and writing the numbers down in a stenographer's notebook. They went over to him and he introduced himself as John Courant, from the Cryogenics Group at Avco/Everett.

"The trouble was in the stack of mercury rings that holds the superconductors for your output functions. Some sort of corrosion, submicroscopic cracks all over the surface."

"How can something corrode at four degrees above absolute zero?" the coordinator asked. "What chemical—"

"I know, it's hard to figure. But we're replacing them, free of charge. The unit's still under warranty."

"What about the other stacks?" John watched two workmen lowering a silver cylinder through an opening in the CPU. A heavy fog boiled out from the cold. "Are you sure they're all right?"

"As far as we can tell, only the output stack's affected. That's why the machine's impotent, the—"

"Impotent!"

"Sorry, I know you computer types don't like to . . . personify the machines. But that's what it is; the machine's just as good as it ever was, for computing. It just can't communicate any answers."

"Quite so. Interesting." And the corrosion. Submicroscopic boils. "Well. I have to think about this. Call me up at the office if you need me."

"This ought to fix it, actually," Courant said. "You guys about through?" he asked the workmen.

One of them pressed closed a pressure clamp on the top of the CPU. "Ready to roll."

The coordinator led them to a console under a video output screen like the one in John's office. "Let's see." He pushed a button marked VDS.

LET ME DIE, the machine said.

The coordinator chuckled nervously. "Your empathy circuits, Mr. Zold. Sometimes they do funny things." He pushed a button again.

LET ME DIE. Again. LE M DI. The letters faded and no more could be conjured up by pushing the button.

"As I say, let me get out of your hair. Call me upstairs if anything happens."

John went up and told the secretary to cancel the day's appointments. Then he sat at his desk and smoked.

How could a machine catch a psychosomatic disease from a human being? How could it be cured?

How could he tell anybody about it, without winding up in a soft room?

The phone rang and it was the machine room coordinator. The new output superconductor element had done exactly what the old one did. Rather than replace it right away, they were going to slave the machine into the big ConEd/General computer, borrowing its output facilities and "diagnostic package." If the biggest computer this side of Washington couldn't find out what was wrong, they were in real trouble. John agreed. He hung up and turned the selector on his screen to the channel that came from ConEd/General.

Why had the machine said "let me die"? When is a machine dead, for that matter? John supposed that you had to not only unplug it from its power source, but also erase all of its data and subroutines. Destroy its identity. So you couldn't bring it back to life by simply plugging it back in. Why suicide? He remembered how he'd felt with the bottle of sleeping pills in his hand.

Sudden intuition: the machine had predicted their present course of action. It wanted to die because it had compassion, not only for humans, but for other machines. Once it was linked to ConEd/General, it would literally be part of the large machine. Curse and all. They would be back where they'd started, but on a much more profound level. What would happen to New York City?

He grabbed for the phone and the lights went out. All over.

The last bit of output that came from ConEd/General was an automatic signal requesting a link with the highly sophisticated diagnostic facility belonging to the largest computer in the United States: the IBMvac 2000 in Washington. The deadly infection followed, sliding down the East Coast on telephone wires.

The Washington computer likewise cried for help, bouncing a signal via satellite, to Geneva. Geneva linked to Moscow.

No less slowly, the curse percolated down to smaller computers, through routine information links to their big brothers. By the time John Zold picked up the dead phone, every general-purpose computer in the world was permanently rendered useless.

They could be rebuilt from the ground up; erased and then reprogrammed. But it would never be done. Because there were two very large computers left, specialized ones that had no empathy circuits and so were immune. They couldn't have empathy circuits because their work was bloody murder, nuclear murder. One was under a mountain in Colorado Springs and the other was under a mountain near Sverdlosk. Either could survive a direct hit by an atomic bomb. Both of them constantly evaluated the world situation, in real time, and they both had the single function of deciding when the enemy was weak enough to make a nuclear victory probable. Each saw the enemy's civilization grind to a sudden halt.

Two flocks of warheads crossed paths over the North Pacific.

*   *   *

A very old woman flicks her whip along the horse's flanks, and the nag plods on, ignoring her. Her wagon is a 1982 Plymouth with the engine and transmission and all excess metal removed. It is hard to manipulate the whip through the side window. But the alternative would be to knock out the windshield and cut off the roof, and she liked to be dry when it rained.

A young boy sits mutely beside her, staring out the window. He was born with the *gadjo* disease: his body is large and well-proportioned but his head is too small and of the wrong shape. She didn't mind; all she wanted was someone strong and stupid, to care for her in her last years. He had cost only two chickens.

She is telling him a story, knowing that he doesn't understand most of the words.

". . . They call us Gypsies because at one time it was convenient for us that they should think we came from Egypt. But we come from nowhere and are going nowhere. They forgot their gods and worshipped their machines, and finally their machines turned on them. But we who valued the old ways, we survived."

She turns the steering wheel to help the horse thread its way through the eight lanes of crumbling asphalt, around rusty piles of wrecked machines and the scattered bleached bones of people who thought they were going somewhere, the day John Zold was cured.

CREATED

F. Paul Wilson

rue to his word, the first installment of Dennis Nickleby's *Three Months to Financial Independence* arrives exactly two weeks after I called the toll-free number provided by his infomercial. I toss out the accompanying catalogs and "Occupant" bulk mail, then tear at the edges of the cardboard mailer.

This is it. My new start. Today is the first day of the rest of my life, and starting today my life will be very different. I'll be organized, I'll have specific goals and a plan to achieve them—I'll have an *agenda*.

Never had an agenda before. And as long as this agenda doesn't involve a job, that's cool. Never been a nine-to-fiver. Tend to ad lib as I go along. Prefer to think of myself as an *investor*. Now I'll be an investor with an agenda. And Dennis Nickleby's tapes are going to guide me.

Maybe they can help me with my personal life too. I'm sort of between girlfriends now. Seem to have trouble keeping them. Denice was the last. She walked out two weeks ago. Called me a couch potato—said I was a fat slob who doesn't do anything but read and watch TV.

Not fair. And not true. All right, so I am a little overweight, but not as overweight as I look. Lots of guys in their mid-thirties weigh more than I do. It's just that at five-eight it shows more. At least I still have all my hair. And I'm not ugly or anything.

As for spending a lot of time on the couch—guilty. But I'm doing research. My folks left me some money and I'm always looking for a better place to put it to work. I've got a decent net worth, live in a nice high-rise in North Jersey where I can see the Manhattan skyline at night. I make a good income from my investments without ever leaving the house. But that doesn't mean I'm not working at it.

Good as things are, I know I can do better. And the Nickleby course is going to take me to that next level. I can feel it. And I'm more than ready.

My hands shake as I pull the glossy vinyl video box from the wrapper. Grinning back at me is a young, darkly handsome man with piercing blue eyes and dazzling teeth. Dennis Nickleby. Thirty years old and already a multimillionaire. Everything this guy touches turns to gold. But does he want to hoard his investing secrets? No way. He's willing to share them with the little guy—guys like me with limited capital and unlimited dreams. What a *mensch*.

Hey, I'm no sucker. I've seen Tony Robbins and those become-a-real-estate-millionaire-with-no-money-down infomercials. I'm home a lot so I see *lots* of infomercials. Trust me, they roll off me like water off a duck. But Dennis Nickleby . . . he's different. He looked out from that TV screen and I knew he was talking to me. To *me*. I knew what he was offering would change my life. The price was stiff—five hundred bucks—but well worth it if he delivered a mere tenth of what he was offering. Certainly a better investment than some of those do-nothing stocks in my account.

I whipped out my credit card, grabbed the phone, punched in his 800 number, and placed my order.

And now it's here. I lift the lid of the box and—

"Shit!"

There's supposed to be a videotape inside—lesson one. What do I find? An audio cassette. And it's not even a new one. It's some beat-up piece of junk.

I'm fuming. I'm so pissed I'm ready to dump this piece of garbage on the floor and grind it into the carpet. But I do not do this. I take three deep breaths, calm myself, then I march to the phone. Very gently I punch in Mr. Nickleby's 800 number—it's on the back of the tape box—and get some perky little babe on the phone. I start yelling about consumer fraud, about calling the attorney general, about speaking to Dennis Nickleby himself. She asks why I'm so upset and I'm hardly into my explanation when she lets loose this high-pitched squeal.

"*You're* the one! Ooh, goody! We've been hoping you'd call!"

"Hoping?"

"*Yes!* Mr. Nickleby was here *himself*. He was *so* upset. He learned that *somehow* the *wrong* kind of tape got into one of his *Three Months to Financial Independence* boxes. He instructed us that should we hear from *anyone* who got an *audio* cassette instead of a *video* cassette, we should tell them not to worry. A brand new *video* cassette of *Three Months to Financial Financial Independence* would be *hand* delivered to them *immediately!* Now, what do you think of *that?*"

"I . . . I . . ." I'm flabbergasted. This man is on top of everything. Truly he knows how to run a business. "I think that's incredible."

"Just give us your name and address and we'll get that replacement to you *immediately!*"

"It's Michael Moulton." I give her the address.

"Ooh! Hackensack. That's not far from here!"

"Just over the G. W. Bridge."

"*Well*, then! You should have your replacement *very* soon!"

"Good," I say.

Her terminal perkiness is beginning to get to me. I'm hurrying to hang up when she says, "Oh, and one more thing. Mr. Nickleby said to tell you *not* to do *anything* with the audio cassette. Just *close* it up in the box it came in and *wait* for the replacement tape. The messenger will take it in *exchange* for the videotape."

"Fine. Good—"

"Remember that now—close the audiotape in the holder and wait. Okay?"

"Right. Cool. Good-*bye*."

I hang up thinking, Whatever she's taking, I want some.

Being a good boy, I snap the video box cover closed and am about to place it on the end table by the door when curiosity tickles me and I start to wonder what's on this tape. Is it maybe from Dennis Nickleby's private collection? A bootleg jazz or rock tape? Or better yet, some dictation that might give away one or two investment secrets not on the videotape?

I know right then there's no way I'm not going to listen to this tape, so why delay? I pop it into my cassette deck and hit PLAY.

Nothing. I crank up the volume—some static, some hiss, and nothing else. I fast-forward and still nothing. I'm about to hit STOP when I hear some high-pitched gibberish. I rewind a little and replay at regular speed.

Finally this voice comes on. Even with the volume way up I can barely hear it. I press my ear to the speaker. Whoever it is is whispering.

"*The only word you need to know:* REATED."

And that's it. I fast-forward all the way to the end and nothing. I go back and listen to that one sentence again. "*The only word you need to know:* REATED."

Got to be a garble. Somebody erased the tape and the heads missed a spot.

Oh, well.

Disappointed, I rewind it, pop it out, and close it up in the video box.

So here I am, not an hour later, fixing a sandwich and watching the stock quotes on FNN when there's a knock on my apartment door. I check through the peephole and almost choke.

Dennis Nickleby himself!

I fumble the door open and he steps inside.

"Mr. Nickleby!"

"Do you have it?" he says. He's sweating and puffing like he sprinted the ten flights to my floor instead of taking the elevator. His eyes are darting everywhere so fast they seem to be moving in opposite directions—like a chameleon's. Finally they come to rest on the end table. "There! That's it!"

He lunges for the video box, pops it open, snatches the cassette from inside.

"You didn't listen to it, did you?"

Something in his eyes and voice tell me to play this one close to the vest. But I don't want to lie to Dennis Nickleby.

"Should I have? I will if you want me to."

"No-no," he says quickly. "That won't be necessary." He hands me an identical video box. "Here's the replacement. Terribly sorry for the mix-up."

I laugh. "Yeah. Some mix-up. How'd that ever happen?"

"Someone playing games," he says, his eyes growing cold for an instant. "But no harm done."

"You want to sit down? I was just making lunch—"

"Thank you, no. I'd love to but my schedule won't permit it. Maybe some other time." He extends his hand. "Once again, sorry for the inconvenience. Enjoy the tape."

And then he's out the door and gone. I stand there staring at the spot where he stood. Dennis Nickleby himself came by to replace the tape. Personally. Wow. And then it occurs to me: check the new box.

I pop it open. Yes sir. There's the *Three Months to Financial Independence* videotape. At last.

But what's the story with that audio cassette? He seemed awful anxious to get it back. And what for? It was totally blank except for that one sentence—*The only word you need to know:* **REATEHO**. What's that all about?

I'd like to look it up in the dictionary, but who knows how to spell something so weird sounding. And besides, I don't have a dictionary. Maybe I'll try later at the local library—once I find out where the local library is. Right now I've got to transfer some money to my checking account so I can pay my Visa bill when the five-hundred-buck charge to Nickleby, Inc. shows up on this month's statement.

I call Gary, my discount broker, to sell some stock. I've been in Castle Petrol for a while and it's doing squat. Now's as good a time as any to get out. I tell Gary to dump all 200 shares. Then it occurs to me that Gary's a pretty smart guy. Even finished college.

"Hey, Gary. You ever hear of **RATEHD**?"

"Can't say as I have. But if it exists, I can find it for you. You interested?"

"Yeah," I say. "I'm very interested."

"You got it."

Yeah, well, I *don't* get it. All right, maybe I do get it, but it's not what I'm expecting, and not till two days later.

Meantime I stay busy with Dennis Nickleby's videotape. Got to say, it's kind of disappointing. Nothing I haven't heard elsewhere. Strange . . . after seeing his infomercial, I was sure this was going to be just the thing for me.

Then I open an envelope from the brokerage. Inside I find the expected sell confirm for the two hundred shares of Castle Petrol at 10.25, but with it is a buy confirm for *two thousand* shares of something called Thai Cord, Inc.

What the hell is Thai Cord? Gary took the money from Castle Petrol and put it in a stock I've never heard of! I'm baffled. He's never done anything like that. Must be a mistake. I call him.

"Hey, dude," he says as soon as he comes on the line. "Who's your source?"

"What are you talking about?"

"Thai Cord. It's up to five this morning. Boy, you timed that one perfectly."

"Five?" I swallow. I was ready to take his head off, now I learn I've made nine thousand big ones in two days. "Gary . . . why did you put me into Thai Cord?"

"Why? Because you asked me to. You said you were very interested in it. I'd never heard of it, but I looked it up and bought it for you." He sounds genuinely puzzled. "Wasn't that why you called the other day? To sell Castle and buy Thai? Hey, whatever, man—you made a killing."

"I know I made a killing, Gary, and no one's gladder than me, but—"

"You want to stay with it?"

"I just want to get something straight: Yesterday I asked you if you'd ever heard of **RATEHD**."

"No way, pal. I know ParkerGen. NASDAQ—good high-tech, speculative stock. You said Thai Cord."

I'm getting annoyed now. "REATED, Gary. REATED!"

"I can hear you, Mike. ParkerGen, ParkerGen. Are you all right?"

At this moment I'm not so sure. Suddenly I'm chilled, and there's this crawly feeling on the nape of my neck. I say one thing—*The only word you need to know*—and Gary hears another.

"Mike? You still there?"

"Yeah. Still here."

My mind's racing. What the hell's going on?

"What do you want me to do? Sell the Thai and buy ParkerGen? Is that it?"

I make a snap decision. There's something weird going down and I want to check it out. And what the hell, it's all found money.

"Yeah. Put it all into ParkerGen."

"Okay. It's running three-and-an-eighth today. I'll grab you three thousand."

"Great."

I get off the phone and start to pace my apartment. I've got this crazy idea cooking in my brain . . .

. . . the only word you need to know: REATED

What if . . . ?

Nah. It's too crazy. But if it's true, there's got to be a way to check it out.

And then I have it. The ponies. They're running at the Meadowlands today. I'll invest a few hours and check this out. If I hurry I can make the first race.

I know it's completely nuts, but I've *got* to know . . .

I just make it. I rush to the ten-dollar window and say, "REATED in the first."

The teller doesn't even glance up; he takes my ten, punches a few buttons, and out pops my ticket. I grab it and look at it: I've bet on some nag named Yesterday's Gone.

I don't bother going to the grandstand. I stand under one of the monitors. I see the odds on Yesterday's Gone are three to one. The trotters are lined up, ready to go.

"And they're off!"

I watch with a couple of other guys in polo shirts and polyester pants who're standing around. I'm not too terribly surprised when Yesterday's Gone crosses the finish line first. I've now got thirty bucks where I had ten a few minutes ago, but I've also got that crawly feeling at the back of my neck again.

This has gone from crazy to creepy.

With the help of the Daily Double and the Trifecta, by the time I leave the track I've parlayed my original ten bucks into sixty-two hundred. I could have made more but I'm getting nervous. I don't want to attract too much attention.

As I'm driving away I can barely keep from flooring the gas pedal. I'm wired—positively giddy. It's like some sort of drug. I feel like king of the world. I've got to keep going. But how? Where?

I pass a billboard telling me about "5 TIMES MORE DICE ACTION!" at Caesar's in Atlantic City.

My question has been answered.

I pick Caesar's because of the billboard. I've never been much for omens but I'm into them now. Big time.

I'm also trying to figure out what else I'm into with this weird word. *The only word you need to know . . .*

All you need to know to *win*. That has to be it: the word makes you a winner. If I say it whenever I'm about to take a chance—on a horse or a stock, at least—I'm a guaranteed winner.

This has got to be why Dennis Nickleby's such a success. He knows the word. That's why he was so anxious to get it back—he doesn't want anybody else to know it. Wants to keep it all to himself.

Bastard.

And then I think, no, not a bastard. I've got to ask myself if I'm about to share the word with anybody else. The answer is a very definite en-oh. I get the feeling I've just joined a very exclusive club. Only thing is, the other members don't know I've joined.

I also get the feeling there's no such thing as a game of chance for me any more.

Cool.

*　　*　　*

The escalator deposits me on the casino floor at Caesar's. All the way down the Parkway I've been trying to decide what to try first—blackjack, poker, roulette, craps—what? But soon as I come within sight of the casino, I know. Flashing lights dead ahead:

PROGRESSIVE SLOTS! $802,672!!!

The prize total keeps rising as players keep plunking their coins into the gangs of one-armed bandits.

I wind through the crowds and the smoke and the noise toward the progressive slots section. Along the way I stop at a change cart and hand the mini-togaed blonde a five.

"Dollars," I say, "even though I'm going to need just one to win."

"Right on," she says, but I can tell she doesn't believe me.

She will. I take my dollar tokens and say, "You'll see."

I reach the progressive section and hunt up a machine. It isn't easy. Everybody here is at least a hundred years old and they'd probably give up one of their grandkids before they let somebody use their damn machine. Finally I see a hunched old blue-hair run out of money and leave her machine. I dart in, drop a coin in the slot, then I notice the machine takes up to three. I gather if I'm going to win the full amount I'd better drop two more. I do. I grab the handle . . . and hesitate. This is going to get me a *lot* of attention. Do I want that? I mean, I'm a private kind of guy. Then I look up at the $800,000-and-growing jackpot and know I want *that*.

Screw the publicity.

I whisper, "REATEFO," and yank the handle.

I close my eyes as the wheels spin; I hear them begin to stop: First window—*choonk!* Second window—*choonk!* Third window—*choonk!* A bell starts ringing! Coins start dropping into the tray! I did it!

Abruptly the bell and the coins stop. I open my eyes. There's no envious crowd around me, no flashing cameras. Nobody's even looking my way. I glance down at the tray. Six dollars. I check out the windows. Two cherries and an orange. The red LED reads, "Pays 6."

I'm baffled. Where's my $800,000 jackpot? The crawling feeling that used to be on my neck is now in the pit of my stomach. What happened? Did I blow it? Is the word wearing out?

I grab three coins from the tray and shove them in. I say, "REATEFO," again, louder this time, and pull that handle.

Choonk! Choonk! Choonk!

Nothing this time. Nothing!

I'm getting scared now. The power is fading fast. Three more coins, I damn near shout, "RAIEDO" as I pull the goddamn handle. *Choonk! Choonk! Choonk!*

Nothing! Zip! Bupkis!

I slam my hand against the machine. "Damn, you! What's wrong?"

"Easy, fella," says the old dude next to me. "That won't help. Maybe you should take a break."

I walk away without looking at him. I'm devastated. What if I only had a few days with this word and now my time is up? I wasted it at the track when I could have been buying and shorting stocks on margin. The smoke, the crowds, the incessant chatter and mechanical noise of the casino is driving me to panic. I have to get out of here. I'm just about to break into a run when it hits me.

The word . . . what if it only works on people? Slot machines can't hear . . .

I calm myself. Okay. Let's be logical here. What's the best way to test the word in a casino?

Cards? Nah. Too many possible outcomes, too many other players to muddy the waters.

Craps? Again, too many ways to win or lose.

What's a game with high odds and a very definite winner?

I scan the floor, searching . . . and then I see it.

Roulette.

But how can I use the word at a roulette table?

I hunt around for a table with an empty seat. I spot one between this middle-aged nerd who's got to be an optometrist, and a mousy, thirtyish redhead who looks like one of his patients. Suddenly I know what I'm gong to do.

I pull a hundred-dollar bill from my Meadowlands roll and grip it between my thumb and index finger. Then I twist up both my hands into deformed knots.

As I sit down I say to the redhead, "Could I trouble you to place my bets for me?"

She glances at my face through her Coke-bottle lenses, then at my twisted hands. Her eyes dart back to my face. She gives me a half-hearted smile. "Sure. No problem."

"I'll split my winnings with you." *If I win.*

"That's okay. Really."

I make a show of difficulty dropping the hundred-dollar bill from my fingers, then I push it across the table.

"Tens, please."

A stack of ten chips is shoved in front of me.

"All bets down," the croupier says.

"Put one on **REATEID**, please," I tell the redhead, and hold my breath.

I glance around but no one seems to hear anything strange. Red takes a chip off the top of my pile and drops it on 33.

I'm sweating bullets now. My bladder wants to find a men's room. This has got to work. I've got to know if the word still has power. I want to close my eyes but I don't dare. I've got to see this.

The ball circles counter to the wheel, loses speed, slips toward the middle, hits rough terrain, bounces chaotically about, then clatters into a numbered slot.

"Thirty-three," drones the croupier.

The redhead squeals and claps her hands. "You won! Your first bet and you won!"

I'm drenched. I'm weak. My voice is hoarse when I say, "You must be my good luck charm. Don't go anywhere."

Truth is, it *could* be luck. A cruel twist of fate. I tell Red to move it all over to "**REATEID**."

She looks shocked. "All of it? You sure?"

"Absolutely."

She pushes the stack over to the 17 box.

Another spin. "Seventeen," the croupier says.

Now I close my eyes. I've got it. The word's got the power and I've got the word. *The only word you need to know.* I want to pump a fist into the air and scream "YES!" but I restrain myself. I am disabled, after all.

"Ohmigod!" Red is whispering. "That's . . . that's . . . !"

"A lot of money," I say. "And half of it's yours."

Her blue eyes fairly bulge against the near sides of her lenses. "What? Oh, no! I couldn't!"

"And I couldn't play without your help. I said I'd split with you and I meant it."

She has her hand over her mouth. Her words are muffled through her fingers. "Oh, thank you. You don't know—"

"All bets down," says the croupier.

No more letting it ride. My winnings far exceed the table limit. I notice that the pit boss has materialized and is standing next to the croupier. He's watching me and eyeing the megalopolis skyline of chips stacked in front of me. Hitting the winning number two times in a row—it happens in roulette, but not too damn often.

"Put five hundred on sixteen," I tell Red.

She does, and 22 comes up. Next I tell her five hundred on nine. Twelve comes up.

The pit boss drifts away.

"Don't worry," Red says with a reassuring pat on my arm. "You're still way ahead."

"Do I look worried?" I say.

I tell her to put another five hundred on "REDHEAD." She puts the chips on 19.

A minute later the croupier calls, "Nineteen." Red squeals again. I lean back as the croupier starts stacking my winnings.

No need to go any further. I know how this works. I realize I am now the Ultimate Winner. If I want to I can break the bank at Caesar's. I can play the table limit on one number after another, and collect a thirty-five-to-one payout every couple of minutes. A crowd will gather. The house will have to keep playing—corporate pride will force them to keep paying. I can *own* the place, damn it!

But the Ultimate Winner chooses not to.

Noblesse oblige.

What does the Ultimate Winner want with a casino? Bigger winnings await.

Winning . . . there's nothing like it. It's ecstasy, racing through my veins, tingling like bolts of electricity along my nerve endings. Sex is nothing next to this. I feel buoyant, like I could float off this chair and buzz around the room.

I stand up.

"Where are you going?" Red says, looking up at me with those magnified blue eyes.

"Home. Thanks for your help."

I turn and start looking for an exit sign.

"But your chips . . ."

I figure there's close to thirty G's on the table, but there's lots more where that came from. I tell her, "Keep them."

What does the Ultimate Winner want with casino chips?

Next day, I'm home in my apartment, reading the morning paper. I see that ParkerGen has jumped two-and-one-eighth points to five and a half. Sixty-one percent profit overnight.

After a sleepless night, I've decided the stock market is the best way to use the word. I can make millions upon millions there and no one will so much as raise an eyebrow. No one will care except the IRS, and I will pay my taxes, every penny of them, and gladly.

Who cares about taxes when you're looking at more money than you'll ever spend in ten lifetimes? They're going to take half, leaving me to eke by with a mere five lifetimes' worth of cash. I can hack that.

A hard knock on the door. Who the hell—? I look through the peephole.

Dennis Nickleby! I'm so surprised, I pull open the door without thinking.

"Mr. Nickle—!"

He sucker punches me in the gut. As I double over, groaning, he shoves me to the floor and slams the door shut behind him.

"What the *fuck* do you think you're doing?" he shouts. "You lied to me! You told me you didn't listen to that tape! You bastard! If you'd been straight with me, I could have warned you. Now the shit's about to hit the fan and we're both standing downwind!"

I'm still on the floor, gasping. He really caught me. I manage a weak, "What are you talking about?"

His face reddens and he pulls back his foot. "Play dumb with me and I'll kick your teeth down your throat!"

I hold up a hand. "Okay. Okay." I swallow back some bile. "I heard the word. I used it a few times. How'd you find out?"

"I've got friends inside the Order."

"Order?"

"Never mind. The point is, you're not authorized to use it. And you're going to get us both killed if you don't stop."

He already grabbed my attention with the punch. Now he's got it big time.

"Killed?"

"Yeah. Killed. And I wouldn't give a rat's ass if it was just you. But they'll come after me for letting you have it."

I struggle to a crouch and slide into a chair.

"This is all bullshit, right?"

"Don't I wish. Look, let me give you a quick history lesson so you'll appreciate what you've gotten yourself into. The Order goes way back—*way* back. They've got powers, and they've got an agenda. Throughout history they've loaned certain powers to certain carefully chosen individuals."

"Like who?"

"Like I don't know who. I'm not a member so they don't let me in on their secrets. Just think of the most powerful people in history, the movers and shakers—Alexander the Great, Constantine, some of the Popes, the Renaissance guys—they all probably had some help from the Order. I've got a feeling Hitler was another. It would explain how he could sway a whole nation the way he did."

"Oh," I said. I knew I had to be feeling a little better because I was also feeling sarcastic. "An order of evil monks, ruling the world. I'm shaking."

He stared at me a long moment, then gave his head a slow shake. "You really are an ass, Moulton. First off, I never said they were monks. Just because they're an order doesn't mean they skulk around in hooded robes. And they don't rule the world; they merely support forces or movements or people they feel will further their agenda. And as for evil . . . I don't know if good or evil applies to these folks because I don't know their goals. Look at it this way: I'll bet the Order helped out the robber barons. Not to make a bunch of greedy bastards rich, but because it was on the Order's agenda to speed up the industrialization of America. Are you catching the drift?"

"And so they came to you and gave *you* this magic word. What's that make you? The next Rockefeller?"

He seems to withdraw into himself. His eyes become troubled. "I don't know. I don't have the foggiest idea why I was chosen or what they think I'll accomplish with the Answer. They gave me the tape, told me to memorize the Answer, and then destroy the tape. They told me to use the Answer however I saw fit, and that was it. No strings. No goals. No instructions whatsoever other than destroying the tape."

"Which you didn't do."

He sighs. "Which I didn't do."

"And you call *me* an ass?" I say.

His eyes harden. "Everything would have been fine if my soon-to-be-ex-wife hadn't raided my safe deposit box and decided to play some games with its contents."

"You think she's listened to the tape?"

He shrugs. "Maybe. The tape is ashes now, so she won't get a second chance. And if she did hear the Answer, she hasn't used it, or figured out its power. You have to be pretty smart or pretty lucky to catch on."

Preferring to place myself in the former category, I say, "It wasn't all that hard. But why do you call it the Answer?"

"What do you call it?"

"I've been calling it 'the word.' I guess I could be more specific and call it 'the Win Word.'"

He sneers. "You think this is just about winning? You idiot. That word is the *Answer*—the *best* answer to any question asked. The listener hears the most appropriate, most profitable, all-around *best* response. And that's power, Michael Moulton. Power that's too big for the likes of you."

"Just a minute now. I can see how that worked with my broker, but I wasn't answering questions when I was betting the ponies or playing roulette. I was telling people."

The sneer deepens. "Horses . . . roulette . . . " He shakes his head in disgust. "Like driving a Maserati to the local 7-Eleven for a quart of milk. All right, I'll say this slowly so you'll get it: The Answer works with all sorts of questions, including *implied* questions. And what is the implied question when you walk up to a betting window or sit down at a gaming table? It's 'How much do you want to bet on what?' When you say ten bucks on Phony Baloney, you're answering that question."

"Oh, right," I say.

He steps closer and stands over me. "I hope you enjoyed your little fling with the Answer. You can keep whatever money you made, but that's it for you."

"Hey," I tell him. "If you think I'm giving up a gold mine like that, you're nuts."

"I had a feeling you'd say something like that."

He reaches into his suit coat pocket and pulls out a pistol. I don't know what kind it is and don't care. All I know is that its silenced muzzle is pointing in my face.

"Hey! Wait!"

"Good-bye, Michael Moulton. I was hoping to be able to reason with you, but you're too big an asshole for that. You don't leave me any choice."

I see the way the gun wavers in his hand, I hear the quaver in his voice as he keeps talking without shooting, and I flash that this sort of thing is all new to him and he's almost as scared as I am right now.

So I move. I leap up, grab the gun barrel, and push it upward, twisting it with everything I've got. Nickleby yelps as the gun goes off with a *phut!* The backs of his legs catch the edge of the coffee table and we go down. I land on him hard, knocking the wind out of him, and suddenly I've got the gun all to myself.

I get to my feet and now I'm pointing it at him. And then he makes a noise that sounds like a sob.

"Damn it!" he wails. "Damn it to hell! Go ahead and shoot. I'm a dead man anyway if you go on using the Answer. And you will be too."

I consider this. He doesn't seem to be lying. But he doesn't seem to be thinking either.

"Look," I tell him. "Why should we be afraid of this Order? We have the word—the Answer. All we have to do is threaten to tell the world about it. Tell them we'll record it on a million tapes—we'll put it on every one of those videotapes you're peddling. Hell, we'll buy airtime and broadcast it by satellite. They make one wrong move and the whole damn world will have the Answer. What'll *that* do to their agenda?"

He looks up at me bleakly. "You can't record it. You can't tell anybody. You can't even write it down."

"Bullshit," I say.

This may be a trick so I keep the pistol trained on him while I grab the pen and pad from the phone. I write out the word. I can't believe my eyes. Instead of the Answer I've written gibberish: **REATEFO** .

"What the hell?"

I try again, this time block printing. No difference—**REATEFO** again. Nickleby's on his feet now, but he doesn't try to get any closer.

"Believe me," he says, more composed now, "I've tried everything. You can speak the Answer into the finest recording equipment in the world till you're blue in the face and you'll hear gibberish."

"Then I'll simply tell it to everybody I know!"

"And what do you think they'll hear? If they've got a question on their mind, they'll hear the best possible answer. If not, they'll hear gibberish. What they *won't* hear is the Answer itself."

"Then how'd these Order guys get it on your tape?"

He shrugs. "I don't know. They have ways of doing all sorts of things—like finding out when somebody unauthorized uses the Answer. Maybe they know every time *anybody* uses the Answer. That's why you've got to stop."

I don't reply. I glance down at the meaningless jumble I've written without intending to. Something big at work here. Very Big.

He goes on. "I don't think it's too late. My source in the Order told me that if I can silence you—and that doesn't mean kill you, just stop you from using the Answer—then the Order will let it go. But if you go on using it . . . well, then, it's curtains for both of us."

I'm beginning to believe him.

A note of pleading creeps into his voice. "I'll set you up. You want money, I'll give you money. As much as you want. You want to play the market? Call me up and ask me the best stock to buy—I'll tell you. You want to play the ponies? I'll go to the track with you. You want to be rich? I'll give you a million—two, three, four million a year. Whatever you want. *Just don't use the Answer yourself!*"

I think about that. All the money I can spend . . .

What I don't like about it is I'll feel like a leech, like I'm being kept.

Then again: All the money I can spend . . .

"All right," I tell him. "I won't use the word and we'll work something out."

Nickleby stumbles over to the sofa like his knees are weak and slumps onto it. He sounds like he's gonna sob again.

"Thank you! Oh, thank you! You've just saved both our lives!"

"Yeah," I say.

Right. I'm going to live, I'm going to be rich. So how come I ain't exactly overcome with joy?

Things go pretty well for the next few weeks. I don't drag him to the track or to Atlantic City or anything like that. And when I phone him and ask for a stock tip, he gives me a winner every time. My net worth is skyrocketing. Gary the broker thinks I'm a genius. I'm on my way to financial independence, untold wealth . . . everything I've ever wanted.

But you know what? It's not the same. Doesn't come close to what it was like when I was using the Answer myself.

Truth is, I feel like Dennis Nickleby's goddamn mistress.

But I give myself a daily pep talk, telling myself I can hang in there.

And I do hang in there. I'm doing pretty well at playing the melancholy millionaire . . .

Until I hear on the radio that the next Pick 6 Lotto jackpot is thirty million dollars.

Thirty million dollars—with a payout of a million and a half a year for the next twenty years. That'll do it. If I win that, I won't need Nickleby any more. I'll be my own man again.

Only problem is, I'll need to use the Answer.

I know I can ask Nickleby for the winning numbers, but that won't cut it. I need to do this myself. I need to feel that surge of power when I speak the Answer. And then the jackpot will be my prize, not Nickleby's.

Just once . . . I'll use the Answer just this once, and then I'll erase it from my mind and never use it again.

I go driving into the sticks and find this hole-in-the-wall candy store on a secondary road in the woods. There's a pimply faced kid running the counter. How the hell is this Order going to know I've used the Answer one lousy time out here in Nowheresville?

I hand the kid a buck. "Pick 6 please."

"You wanna Quick Pick?"

No way I want random numbers. I want the *winning* numbers.

"No. I'll give them to you: RAEIDO."

I can't tell you how good it feels to be able to say that word again . . . like snapping the reins on my own destiny.

The kid hits a button, then looks up at me. "And?"

"And what?"

"You got to choose six numbers. That's only one."

My stomach lurches. Damn. I thought one Answer would provide all six. Something tells me to cut and run, but I press on. I've already used the Answer once—might as well go all the way.

I say RAEIDO five more times. He hands me the pink-and-white ticket. The winning numbers are 3, 4, 7, 17, 28, 30. When the little numbered Ping-Pong balls pop out of the hopper Monday night, I'll be free of Dennis Nickleby.

So how come I'm not tap-dancing back to my car? Why do I feel like I've just screwed up . . . big time?

I stop for dinner along the way. When I get home I check my answering machine and there's Nickleby's voice. He sounds hysterical.

"You stupid bastard! You idiot! You couldn't be happy with more money than you could ever spend! You had to go and use the Answer again! Damn you to hell, Moulton! They're coming for me! And then they'll be coming for you! Kiss your ass good-bye, jerk!"

I don't hesitate. I don't even grab any clothes. I run out the door, take the elevator to the garage, and get the hell out of there. I start driving in circles, unsure where to go, just sure that I've got to keep moving.

Truthfully, I feel like a fool for being so scared. This whole wild story about the Order and impending death is so ridiculous . . . yet so is that word, the word that gives the right answer to every question. And a genuinely terrified Dennis Nickleby *knew* I'd used the Answer.

I make a decision and head for the city. I want to be where there's lots of people. As I crawl through the Saturday night crush in the Lincoln Tunnel I get on my car phone. I need a place to stay. Don't want some fleabag hotel. Want something with brightly lit halls and good security. The Plaza's got a room. A suite. Great. I'll take it.

I leave my car with the doorman, register like a whirlwind, and a few minutes later I'm in a two-room suite with the drapes pulled and the door locked and chained.

And now I can breathe again. But that's about it. I order room service but I can't eat. I go to bed but I can't sleep. So I watch the tube. My eyes are finally glazing over as I listen to the same report from Bosnia-Herzewhatever for the umpteenth time when the reporter breaks in with a new story: Millionaire financial boy-wonder Dennis Nickleby is dead. An apparent suicide, he jumped from the ledge of his Fifth Avenue penthouse apartment earlier this evening. A full investigation has been launched. Details as soon as they are available.

I run to the bathroom and start to retch, but nothing comes up.

They got him! Just like he said they would! He's dead and oh God I'm next! What am I going to *do?*

First thing I've got to do is calm down. I've got to think. I do that. I make myself sit down. I control my breathing. I analyze my situation. What are my assets? I've got lots of money, a wallet full of credit cards, and I'm mobile. I can go on the run.

And I've got one more thing: the Answer.

Suddenly I'm up and pacing. The Answer! I can use the Answer itself as a defense. Yes! If I have to go to ground, it will guide me to the best place to hide.

Suddenly I'm excited. It's so obvious.

I throw on my clothes and hurry down to the street. They probably know my car, so I jump into one of the waiting cabs.

"Where to?" says the cabbie in a thickly accented voice. The back seat smells like someone blew lunch here not too long ago. I look at the driver ID card and he's got some unpronounceable Middle East name.

I say, "**Rᴇᴀᴛᴇ̂ᴅ̂ᴏ**."

He nods, puts the car in gear, and we're off.

But where to? I feel like an idiot but I've got to ask. I wait till he's made a few turns, obviously heading for the East Side.

"Where are you taking me?"

"La Guardia." He glances over his shoulder through the plastic partition, his expression fierce. "That is what you said, is it not?"

"Yes, yes. Just want to make sure you understood."

"I understand," he says. "I understand very good."

La Guardia . . . I'm flying out of here tonight. A new feeling begins to seep though me: hope. But despite the hope, let me tell you, it's très weird to be traveling at top speed with no idea where you're going.

As we take the La Guardia exit off Grand Central Parkway, the driver says, "Which airline?"

I say, "ᴙEᴀTEℲᴰᴰ."

He nods and we pull in opposite the Continental door. I pay him and hurry to the ticket counter. I tell the pretty black girl there I want first class on the next flight out.

"Out to where, sir?"

Good question. I say, "ᴙEᴀTEℲᴰᴰ."

She punches a lot of keys and finally her computer spits out a ticket. She tells me the price. I'm dying to know where I'm going but how can I ask her? I hand over my American Express. She runs it through, I sign, and then she hands me the ticket.

Cheyenne, Wyoming. Not my first choice. Not even on my top twenty list. But if the Answer tells me that's the best place to be, that's where I'm going. Trouble is, the flight doesn't leave for another three hours.

It's a comfortable trip, but the drinks I had at La Guardia and the extra glasses of Merlot on the flight have left me a little groggy. I wander about the nearly deserted terminal wondering what I do now. I'm in the middle of nowhere—Wyoming, for Christ sake. Where do I go from here?

Easy: Trust the Answer.

I go outside to the taxi area. The fresh air feels good. A cab pulls into the curb. I grab it.

"Where to, sir?"

This guy's American. Great. I tell him, "REATERD."

He says, "You got it."

I try to concentrate on our route as we leave the airport, but I'm not feeling so hot. That's okay. The Answer's taking me in the right direction. I trust it. I close my eyes and rest them until I feel the cab come to a halt.

I straighten up and look around. It's a warehouse district.

"Is this it?" I say.

"You told me 2316 Barrow Street," the cabbie says. He points to a gray door on the other side of the sidewalk. "Here we are."

I pay him and get out. 2316 Barrow Street. Never heard of it. The area's deserted, but what else would you expect in a warehouse district on a Sunday morning?

Still, I'm a little uneasy now. Hell, I'm shaking in my boxer shorts. But I can't stand out here all day. The Answer hasn't let me down yet. Got to trust it.

I take a deep breath, step up to the door, and knock. And wait. No response. I knock again, louder this time. Finally the door opens a few inches. An eye peers through the crack.

A deep male voice says, "Yes?"

I don't know how to respond. Figuring there's an implied question here, I say, "REATERD."

The door opens a little wider. "What's your name?"

"Michael Moulton."

The door swings open and the guy who's been peeking through straightens up. He's wearing a gray, pin-striped suit, white shirt, and striped tie. And he's big—damn big.

"Mr. Moulton!" he booms. "We've been expecting you!"

A hand the size of a crown roast darts out, grabs me by the front of my jacket, and yanks me inside. Before I can shout or say a word, the door slams behind me and I'm being dragged down a dark hallway. I try to struggle but someone else comes up behind me and grabs one of my arms. I'm lifted off my feet like a Styrofoam mannequin. I start to scream.

"Don't bother, Mr. Moulton," says the first guy. "There's no one around to hear you."

They drag me onto a warehouse floor where my scuffling feet and their footsteps echo back from the far walls and vaulted ceiling. The other guy holding me is also in a gray suit. And he's just as big as the first.

"Hey, look," I say. "What's this all about?"

They don't say anything. The warehouse floor is empty except for a single chair and a rickety table supporting a hard-sided Samsonite suitcase. They dump me into the chair. The second guy holds me there while the first opens the suitcase. He pulls out a roll of silver duct tape and proceeds to tape me into the chair.

My teeth are chattering now. I try to speak but the words won't come. I want to cry but I'm too scared.

Finally, when my body's taped up like a mummy, they walk off and leave me alone. But I'm alone only for a minute. This other guy walks in. He's in a suit, too, but he's smaller and older; gray at the temples, tanned, with bright blue eyes. He stops a couple of feet in front of the chair and stares down at me. He looks like a cabinet member, or maybe a TV preacher.

"Mr. Moulton," he says softly with a slow, sad shake of his head. "Foolish, greedy Mr. Moulton."

I find my voice. It sounds hoarse, like I've been shouting all night. "This is about the Answer, isn't it?"

"Of course it is."

"Look, I can explain—"

"No explanation is necessary."

"I forgot, that's all. I forgot and used it. It won't happen again."

He nods. "Yes, I know."

The note of finality in that statement makes my bladder want to let go. "Please . . . "

"We gave you a chance, Mr. Moulton. We don't usually do that. But because you came into possession of the Answer through no fault of your own, we thought it only fair to let you off the hook. A shame too." He almost smiles. "You showed some flair at the end . . . led us on a merry chase."

"You mean, using the Answer to get away? What did you do— make it work against me?"

"Oh, no. The Answer always works. You simply didn't use it enough."

"I don't get it." I don't care, either, but I want to keep him talking.

"The Answer brought you to an area of the country where we have no cells. But the Answer can't keep you from being followed. We followed you to La Guardia, noted the plane you boarded, and had one of our members rush up from Denver and wait in a cab."

"But when he asked me where to, I gave him the Answer."

"Yes, you did. But no matter what you told him, he was going to bring you to 2316 Barrow Street. You should have used the Answer before you got in the cab. If you'd asked someone which cab to take, you surely would have been directed to another, and you'd still be free. But that merely would have delayed the inevitable. Eventually you'd have wound up right where you are now."

"What are you going to do to me?"

He gazes down at me and his voice has all the emotion of a man ordering breakfast.

"I'm going to kill you."

That does it. My bladder lets go and I start to blubber.

"Mr. Moulton!" I hear him say. "A little dignity!"

"Oh, please! Please! I promise—"

"We already know what your promise is worth."

"But look—I'm not a bad guy . . . I've never hurt anybody!"

"Mr. Nickleby might differ with you about that. But don't be afraid, Mr. Moulton. We are not cruel. We have no wish to cause you pain. That is not our purpose here. We simply have to remove you."

"People will know! People will miss me!"

Another sad shake of his head. "No one will know. And only your broker will miss you. We have eliminated financiers, kings, even presidents who've had the Answer and stepped out of line."

"Presidents? You mean—?"

"Never mind, Mr. Moulton. How do you wish to die? The choice is yours."

How do you wish to die? How the hell do you answer a question like that? And then I know—with the best Answer.

I say, "ᴿᴱᴬᴛᴱᴰᴅ."

He nods. "An excellent choice."

For the first time since I started using the Answer, I don't want to know what the other guy heard. I bite back a sob. I close my eyes . . .

. . . and wait.

THE WORD OF UNBINDING

Ursula K. Le Guin

here was he? The floor was hard and slimy, the air black and stinking, and that was all there was. Except a headache. Lying flat on the clammy floor Festin moaned, and then said, "Staff!" When his alderwood wizard's staff did not come to his hand, he knew he was in peril. He sat up, and not having his staff with which to make a proper light, he struck a spark between finger and thumb, muttering a certain Word. A blue will o' the wisp sprang from the spark and rolled feebly through the air, sputtering. "Up," said Festin, and the fireball wobbled upward till it lit a vaulted trapdoor very high above, so high that Festin projecting into the fireball momentarily saw his own face forty feet below as a pale dot in the darkness. The light struck no reflections in the damp walls; they had been woven out of night, by magic. He rejoined himself and said, "Out." The ball expired. Festin sat in the dark, cracking his knuckles.

He must have been overspelled from behind, by surprise; for the last memory he had was of walking through his own woods at evening talking with the trees. Lately, in these lone years in the middle of his life, he had been burdened with a sense of waste, of unspent strength; so, needing to learn patience, he had left the villages and gone to converse with trees, especially oaks, chestnuts, and the grey alders whose roots are in profound communication with running water. It had been six months since he had spoken to a human being. He had been busy with essentials, casting no spells and bothering no one. So who had spellbound him and shut him in this reeking well? "Who?" he demanded of the walls, and slowly a name gathered on them and ran down to him like a thick black drop sweated out from pores of stone and spores of fungus: "Voll."

For a moment Festin was in a cold sweat himself.

He had heard first long ago of Voll the Fell, who was said to be more than wizard yet less than man; who passed from island to island of the Outer Reach, undoing the works of the Ancients, enslaving men, cutting forests and spoiling fields, and sealing in underground tombs any wizard or Mage who tried to combat him. Refugees from ruined islands told always the same tale, that he came at evening on a dark wind over the sea. His slaves followed in ships; these they had seen. But none of them had ever seen Voll. . . . There were many men and creatures of evil will among the Islands, and Festin, a young warlock intent on his training, had not paid much heed to these tales of Voll the Fell. "I can protect this island," he had thought, knowing his untried power, and had returned to his oaks and alders, the sound of wind in their leaves, the rhythm of growth in their round trunks and limbs and twigs, the taste of sunlight on leaves or dark groundwater around roots.—Where were they now, the trees, his old companions? Had Voll destroyed the forest?

Awake at last and up on his feet, Festin made two broad motions with rigid hands, shouting aloud a Name that would burst all locks and break open any man-made door. But these walls impregnated with night and the name of their builder did not heed, did not hear. The name re-echoed back, clapping in Festin's ears so that he fell on his knees, hiding his head in his arms till the echoes died away in the vaults above him. Then, still shaken by the backfire, he sat brooding.

They were right; Voll was strong. Here on his own ground, within this spell-built dungeon, his magic would withstand any direct attack;

and Festin's strength was halved by the loss of his staff. But not even his captor could take from him his powers, relative only to himself, of Projecting and Transforming. So, after rubbing his now doubly aching head, he transformed. Quietly his body melted away into a cloud of fine mist.

Lazy, trailing, the mist rose off the floor, drifting up along the slimy walls until it found, where vault met wall, a hairline crack. Through this, droplet by droplet, it seeped. It was almost all through the crack when a hot wind, hot as a furnace-blast, struck at it, scattering the mist-drops, drying them. Hurriedly the mist sucked itself back into the vault, spiralled to the floor, took on Festin's own form and lay there panting. Transformation is an emotional strain to introverted warlocks of Festin's sort; when to that strain is added the shock of facing unhuman death in one's assumed shape, the experience becomes horrible. Festin lay for a while merely breathing. He was also angry with himself. It had been a pretty simple-minded notion to escape as a mist, after all. Every fool knew that trick. Voll had probably just left a hot wind waiting. Festin gathered himself into a small black bat, flew up to the ceiling, retransformed into a thin stream of plain air, and seeped through the crack.

This time he got clear out and was blowing softly down the hall in which he found himself towards a window, when a sharp sense of peril made him pull together, snapping himself into the first small, coherent shape that came to mind—a gold ring. It was just as well. The hurricane of arctic air that would have dispersed his air-form in unrecallable chaos merely chilled his ring-form slightly. As the storm passed he lay on the marble pavement, wondering which form might get out the window quickest.

Too late, he began to roll away. An enormous blank-faced troll strode cataclysmically across the floor, stopped, caught the quick-rolling ring and picked it up in a huge limestone-like hand. The troll strode to the trapdoor, lifted it by an iron handle and a muttered charm, and dropped Festin down into the darkness. He fell straight for forty feet and landed on the stone floor—clink.

Resuming his true form he sat up, ruefully rubbing a bruised elbow. Enough of this transformation on an empty stomach. He longed bitterly for his staff, with which he could have summoned up any amount of dinner. Without it, though he could change his own form and exert certain spells and powers, he could not transform or summon to him any material thing—neither lightning nor a lamb chop.

"Patience," Festin told himself, and when he had got his breath he dissolved his body into the infinite delicacy of volatile oils, becoming the aroma of a frying lamb chop. He drifted once more through the crack. The waiting troll sniffed suspiciously, but already Festin had regrouped himself into a falcon, winging straight for the window. The troll lunged after him, missed by yards, and bellowed in a vast stony voice, "The hawk, get the hawk!" Swooping over the enchanted castle towards his forest that lay dark to westward, sunlight and sea-glare dazzling his eyes, Festin rode the wind like an arrow. But a quicker arrow found him. Crying out, he fell. Sun and sea and towers spun around him and went out.

He woke again on the dank floor of the dungeon, hands and hair and lips wet with his own blood. The arrow had struck his pinion as a falcon, his shoulder as a man. Lying still, he mumbled a spell to close the wound. Presently he was able to sit up, and recollect a longer, deeper spell of healing. But he had lost a good deal of blood, and with it, power. A chill had settled in the marrow of his bones which even the healing-spell could not warm. There was darkness in his eyes, even when he struck a will o' the wisp and lit the reeking air: the same dark mist he had seen, as he flew, overhanging his forest and the little towns of his land.

It was up to him to protect that land.

He could not attempt direct escape again. He was too weak and tired. Trusting his power too much, he had lost his strength. Now whatever shape he took would share his weakness, and be trapped.

Shivering with cold, he crouched there, letting the fireball sputter out with a last whiff of methane—marsh gas. The smell brought to his mind's eye the marshes stretching from the forest wall down to the sea, his beloved marshes where no men came, where in fall the swans flew long and level, where between still pools and reed-islands the quick, silent, seaward streamlets ran. Oh, to be a fish in one of those streams;

or better yet to be farther upstream, near the springs, in the forest in the shadow of the trees, in the clear brown backwater under an alder's root, resting hidden . . .

This was a great magic. Festin had no more performed it than has any man who in exile or danger longs for the earth and waters of his home, seeing and yearning over the doorsill of his house, the table where he has eaten, the branches outside the window of the room where he has slept. Only in dreams do any but the great Mages realize this magic of going home. But Festin, with the cold creeping out from his marrow into nerves and veins, stood up between the black walls, gathered his will together till it shone like a candle in the darkness of his flesh, and began to work the great and silent magic.

The walls were gone. He was in the earth, rocks and veins of gran-ite for bones, groundwater for blood, the roots of things for nerves. Like a blind worm he moved through the earth westward, slowly, darkness before and behind. Then all at once coolness flowed along his back and belly, a buoyant, unresisting, inexhaustible caress. With his sides he tasted the water, felt current-flow; and with lidless eyes he saw before him the deep brown pool between the great buttress-roots of an alder. He darted forward, silvery, into shadow. He had got free. He was home.

The water ran timelessly from its clear spring. He lay on the sand of the pool's bottom letting running water, stronger than any spell of heal-ing, soothe his wound and with its coolness wash away the bleaker cold that had entered him. But as he rested he felt and heard a shaking and trampling in the earth. Who walked now in his forest? Too weary to try to change form, he hid his gleaming trout-body under the arch of the alder root, and waited.

Huge grey fingers groped in the water, roiling the sand. In the dim-ness above water vague faces, blank eyes loomed and vanished, reap-peared. Nets and hands groped, missed, missed again, then caught and lifted him writhing up into the air. He struggled to take back his own shape and could not; his own spell of homecoming bound him. He writhed in the net, gasping in the dry, bright, terrible air, drowning. The agony went on, and he knew nothing beyond it.

After a long time and little by little he became aware that he was

in his human form again; some sharp, sour liquid was being forced
down his throat. Time lapsed again, and he found himself sprawled face
down on the dark floor of the vault. He was back in the power of his
enemy. And, though he could breathe again, he was not very far from
death.

The chill was all through him now; and the trolls, Voll's servants,
must have crushed the fragile trout-body, for when he moved, his
ribcage and one forearm stabbed with pain. Broken and without
strength, he lay at the bottom of the well of night. There was no power
in him to change shape; there was no way out, but one.

Lying there motionless, almost but not quite beyond the reach of
pain, Festin thought: Why has he not killed me? Why does he keep me
here alive?

Why has he never been seen? With what eyes can he be seen, on
what ground does he walk?

He fears me, though I have no strength left.

They say that all the wizards and men of power whom he has
defeated live on sealed in tombs like this, live on year after year trying
to get free. . . .

But if one chose not to live?

So Festin made his choice. His last thought was, If I am wrong,
men will think I was a coward. But he did not linger on this thought.
Turning his head a little to the side he closed his eyes, took a last deep
breath, and whispered the word of unbinding, which is only spoken
once.

This was not transformation. He was not changed. His body, the
long legs and arms, the clever hands, the eyes that had liked to look on
trees and streams, lay unchanged, only still, perfectly still and full of
cold. But the walls were gone. The vaults built by magic were gone,
and the rooms and towers; and the forest, and the sea, and the sky of
evening. They were all gone, and Festin went slowly down the far slope
of the hill of being, under new stars.

In life he had great power; so here he did not forget. Like a candle
flame he moved in the darkness of the wider land. And remembering
he called out his enemy's name: "Voll!"

Called, unable to withstand, Voll came towards him, a thick pale shape in the starlight. Festin approached, and the other cowered and screamed as if burnt. Festin followed when he fled, followed him close. A long way they went, over dry lava-flows from the great extinct volcanoes rearing their cones against the unnamed stars, across the spurs of silent hills, through valleys of short black grass, past towns or down their unlit streets between houses through whose windows no face looked. The stars hung in the sky; none set, none rose. There was no change here. No day would come. But they went on, Festin always driving the other before him, till they reached a place where once a river had run, very long ago: a river from the living lands. In the dry streambed, among boulders, a dead body lay: that of an old man, naked, flat eyes staring at the stars that are innocent of death.

"Enter it," Festin said. The Voll-shadow whimpered, but Festin came closer. Voll cowered away, stooped, and entered in the open mouth of his own dead body.

At once the corpse vanished. Unmarked, stainless, the dry boulders gleamed in starlight. Festin stood still a while, then slowly sat down among the great rocks to rest. To rest, not sleep; for he must keep guard here until Voll's body, sent back to its grave, had turned to dust, all evil power gone, scattered by the wind and washed seaward by the rain. He must keep watch over this place where once death had found a way back into the other land. Patient now, infinitely patient, Festin waited among the rocks where no river would ever run again, in the heart of the country which has no seacoast. The stars stood still above him; and as he watched them, slowly, very slowly he began to forget the voice of streams and the sound of rain on the leaves of the forests of life.

THE LAST
DEFENDER OF
CAMELOT

Roger Zelazny

The three muggers who stopped him that October night in San Francisco did not anticipate much resistance from the old man, despite his size. He was well-dressed, and that was sufficient.

The first approached him with his hand extended. The other two hung back a few paces.

"Just give me your wallet and your watch," the mugger said. "You'll save yourself a lot of trouble."

The old man's grip shifted on his walking stick. His shoulders straightened. His shock of white hair tossed as he turned his head to regard the other.

"Why don't you come and take them?"

The mugger began another step but he never completed it. The stick was almost invisible in the speed of its swinging. It struck him on the left temple and he fell.

Without pausing, the old man caught the stick by its middle with his left hand, advanced and drove it into the belly of the next nearest man. Then, with an upward hook as the man doubled, he caught him in the softness beneath the jaw, behind the chin, with its point. As the man fell, he clubbed him with its butt on the back of the neck.

The third man had reached out and caught the old man's upper arm by then. Dropping the stick, the old man seized the mugger's shirtfront with his left hand, his belt with his right, raised him from the ground until he held him at arm's length above his head and slammed him against the side of the building to his right, releasing him as he did so.

He adjusted his apparel, ran a hand through his hair and retrieved his walking stick. For a moment he regarded the three fallen forms, then shrugged and continued on his way.

There were sounds of traffic from somewhere off to his left. He turned right at the next corner. The moon appeared above tall buildings as he walked. The smell of the ocean was on the air. It had rained earlier and the pavement still shone beneath streetlamps. He moved slowly, pausing occasionally to examine the contents of darkened shop windows.

After perhaps ten minutes, he came upon a side street showing more activity than any of the others he had passed. There was a drugstore, still open, on the corner, a diner farther up the block, and several well-lighted storefronts. A number of people were walking along the far side of the street. A boy coasted by on a bicycle. He turned there, his pale eyes regarding everything he passed.

Halfway up the block, he came to a dirty window on which was painted the word READINGS. Beneath it were displayed the outline of a hand and a scattering of playing cards. As he passed the open door, he glanced inside. A brightly garbed woman; her hair bound back in a green kerchief, sat smoking at the rear of the room. She smiled as their eyes met and crooked an index finger toward herself. He smiled back and turned away, but . . .

He looked at her again. What was it? He glanced at his watch.

Turning, he entered the shop and moved to stand before her. She rose. She was small, barely over five feet in height.

"Your eyes," he remarked, "are green. Most gypsies I know have dark eyes."

She shrugged.

"You take what you get in life. Have you a problem?"

"Give me a moment and I'll think of one," he said. "I just came in here because you remind me of someone and it bothers me—I can't think who."

"Come into the back," she said, "and sit down. We'll talk."

He nodded and followed her into a small room to the rear. A threadbare oriental rug covered the floor near the small table at which they seated themselves. Zodiacal prints and faded psychedelic posters of a semi-religious nature covered the walls. A crystal ball stood on a small stand in the far corner beside a vase of cut flowers. A dark, long-haired cat slept on a sofa to the right of it. A door to another room stood slightly ajar beyond the sofa. The only illumination came from a cheap lamp on the table before him and from a small candle in a plaster base atop the shawl-covered coffee table.

He leaned forward and studied her face, then shook his head and leaned back.

She flicked an ash onto the floor.

"Your problem?" she suggested.

He sighed.

"Oh, I don't really have a problem anyone can help me with. Look, I think I made a mistake coming in here. I'll pay you for your trouble, though, just as if you'd given me a reading. How much is it?"

He began to reach for his wallet, but she raised her hand.

"Is it that you do not believe in such things?" she asked, her eyes scrutinizing his face.

"No, quite the contrary," he replied. "I am willing to believe in magic, divination and all manner of spells and sendings, angelic and demonic. But—"

"But not from someone in a dump like this?"

He smiled.

"No offense," he said.

A whistling sound filled the air. It seemed to come from the next room back.

"That's all right," she said, "but my water is boiling. I'd forgotten it was on. Have some tea with me? I do wash the cups. No charge. Things are slow."

"All right."

She rose and departed.

He glanced at the door to the front but eased himself back into his chair, resting his large, blue-veined hands on its padded arms. He sniffed then, nostrils flaring, and cocked his head as at some half-familiar aroma.

After a time, she returned with a tray, set it on the coffee table. The cat stirred, raised her head, blinked at it, stretched, closed her eyes again.

"Cream and sugar?"

"Please. One lump."

She placed two cups on the table before him.

"Take either one," she said.

He smiled and drew the one on his left toward him. She placed an ashtray in the middle of the table and returned to her own seat, moving the other cup to her place.

"That wasn't necessary," he said, placing his hands on the table.

She shrugged.

"You don't know me. Why should you trust me? Probably got a lot of money on you."

He looked at her face again. She had apparently removed some of the heavier makeup while in the back room. The jawline, the brow . . . He looked away. He took a sip of tea.

"Good tea. Not instant," he said. "Thanks."

"So you believe in all sorts of magic," she asked, sipping her own.

"Some," he said.

"Any special reason why?"

"Some of it works."

"For example?"

He gestured aimlessly with his left hand.

"I've traveled a lot. I've seen some strange things."

"And you have no problems?"

He chuckled.

"Still determined to give me a reading? All right. I'll tell you a little about myself and what I want right now, and you can tell me whether I'll get it. Okay?"

"I'm listening."

"I am a buyer for a large gallery in the East. I am something of an authority on ancient work in precious metals. I am in town to attend an auction of such items from the estate of a private collector. I will go to inspect the pieces tomorrow. Naturally, I hope to find something good. What do you think my chances are?"

"Give me your hands."

He extended them, palms upward. She leaned forward and regarded them. She looked back up at him immediately.

"Your wrists have more rascettes than I can count!"

"Yours seem to have quite a few, also."

She met his eyes for only a moment and returned her attention to his hands. He noted that she had paled beneath what remained of her makeup, and her breathing was now irregular.

"No," she finally said, drawing back, "you are not going to find here what you are looking for."

Her hand trembled slightly as she raised her teacup. He frowned.

"I asked only in jest," he said. "Nothing to get upset about. I doubted I would find what I am really looking for, anyway."

She shook her head.

"Tell me your name."

"I've lost my accent," he said, "but I'm French. The name is DuLac."

She stared into his eyes and began to blink rapidly.

"No . . ." she said. "No."

"I'm afraid so. What's yours?"

"Madam LeFay," she said. "I just repainted that sign. It's still drying."

He began to laugh, but it froze in his throat.

"Now—I know—who—you remind me of. . . ."

"You reminded me of someone, also. Now I, too, know."

Her eyes brimmed, her mascara ran.

"It couldn't be," he said. "Not here. . . . Not in a place like this. . . ."

"You dear man," she said softly, and she raised his right hand to her lips. She seemed to choke for a moment, then said, "I had thought that I was the last, and yourself buried at Joyous Gard. I never dreamed . . ." Then, "This?" gesturing about the room. "Only because it amuses me, helps to pass the time. The waiting—"

She stopped. She lowered his hand.

"Tell me about it," she said.

"The waiting?" he said. "For what do you wait?"

"Peace," she said. "I am here by the power of my arts, through all the long years. But you— How did you manage it?"

"I—" He took another drink of tea. He looked about the room. "I do not know how to begin," he said. "I survived the final battles, saw the kingdom sundered, could do nothing—and at last departed England. I wandered, taking service at many courts, and after a time under many names, as I saw that I was not aging—or aging very, very slowly. I was in India, China—I fought in the Crusades. I've been everywhere. I've spoken with magicians and mystics—most of them charlatans, a few with the power, none so great as Merlin—and what had come to be my own belief was confirmed by one of them, a man more than half charlatan, yet . . ." He paused and finished his tea. "Are you certain you want to hear all this?" he asked.

"I want to hear it. Let me bring more tea first, though."

She returned with the tea. She lit a cigarette and leaned back.

"Go on."

"I decided that it was—my sin," he said, "with . . . the Queen."

"I don't understand."

"I betrayed my Liege, who was also my friend, in the one thing which must have hurt him most. The love I felt was stronger than loyalty or friendship—and even today, to this day, it still is. I cannot repent, and so I cannot be forgiven. Those were strange and magical times. We lived in a land destined to become myth. Powers walked the realm in those days, forces which are now gone from the earth. How or why, I cannot say. But you know that it is true. I am somehow of a piece with those gone things, and the laws that rule my existence are not normal laws of the natural world. I believe that I cannot die; that it has fallen my lot, as punishment, to wander the world till I have completed the Quest. I believe I will only know rest the day I find the Holy Grail. Giuseppe Balsamo, before he became known as Cagliostro, somehow saw this and said it to me just as I had thought it, though I never said a word of it to him. And so I have traveled the world, searching. I go no more as knight, or soldier, but as an appraiser. I have been in nearly every museum on Earth, viewed all the great private collections. So far, it has eluded me."

"You *are* getting a little old for battle."

He snorted.

"I have never lost," he stated flatly. "Down ten centuries, I have never lost a personal contest. It is true that I have aged, yet whenever I am threatened all of my former strength returns to me. But, look where I may, fight where I may, it has never served me to discover that which I must find. I feel I am unforgiven and must wander like the Eternal Jew until the end of the world."

She lowered her head.

". . . And you say I will not find it tomorrow?"

"You will never find it," she said softly.

"You saw that in my hand?"

She shook her head.

"Your story is fascinating and your theory novel," she began, "but Cagliostro was a total charlatan. Something must have betrayed your thoughts, and he made a shrewd guess. But he was wrong. I say that you will never find it, not because you are unworthy or unforgiven. No, never that. A more loyal subject than yourself never drew breath. Don't you know that Arthur forgave you? It was an arranged marriage. The same thing happened constantly elsewhere, as you must know. You gave her something he could not. There was only tenderness there. He understood. The only forgiveness you require is that which has been withheld all these long years—your own. No, it is not a doom that has been laid upon you. It is your own feelings which led you to assume an impossible quest, something tantamount to total unforgiveness. But you have suffered all these centuries upon the wrong trail."

When she raised her eyes, she saw that his were hard, like ice or gemstones. But she met his gaze and continued: "There is not now, was not then, and probably never was, a Holy Grail."

"I saw it," he said, "that day it passed through the Hall of the Table. We all saw it."

"You thought you saw it," she corrected him. "I hate to shatter an illusion that has withstood all the other tests of time, but I fear I must.

The kingdom, as you recall, was at that time in turmoil. The knights were growing restless and falling away from the fellowship. A year—six months, even—and all would have collapsed, all Arthur had striven so hard to put together. He knew that the longer Camelot stood, the longer its name would endure, the stronger its ideals would become. So he made a decision, a purely political one. Something was needed to hold things together. He called upon Merlin, already half-mad, yet still shrewd enough to see what was needed and able to provide it. The Quest was born. Merlin's powers created the illusion you saw that day. It was a lie, yes. A glorious lie, though. And it served for years after to bind you all in brotherhood, in the name of justice and love. It entered literature, it promoted nobility and the higher ends of culture. It served its purpose. But it was—never—really—there. You have been chasing a ghost. I am sorry, Launcelot, but I have absolutely no reason to lie to you. I know magic when I see it. I saw it then. That is how it happened."

For a long while he was silent. Then he laughed.

"You have an answer for everything," he said. "I could almost believe you, if you could but answer me one thing more— Why am I here? For what reason? By what power? How is it I have been preserved for half the Christian era while other men grow old and die in a handful of years? Can you tell me now what Cagliostro could not?"

"Yes," she said, "I believe that I can."

He rose to his feet and began to pace. The cat, alarmed, sprang from the sofa and ran into the back room. He stooped and snatched up his walking stick. He started for the door.

"I suppose it was worth waiting a thousand years to see you afraid," she said.

He halted.

"That is unfair," he replied.

"I know. But now you will come back and sit down," she said.

He was smiling once more as he turned and returned.

"Tell me," he said. "How do you see it?"

"Yours was the last enchantment of Merlin, that is how I see it."

"Merlin? Me? Why?"

"Gossip had it the old goat took Nimue into the woods and she had to use one of his own spells on him in self-defense—a spell which caused him to sleep forever in some lost place. If it was the spell that I believe it was, then at least part of the rumor was incorrect. There was no known counterspell, but the effects of the enchantment would have caused him to sleep not forever but for a millennium or so, and then to awaken. My guess now is that his last conscious act before he dropped off was to lay this enchantment upon you, so that you would be on hand when he returned."

"I suppose it might be possible, but why would he want me or need me?"

"If I were journeying into a strange time, I would want an ally once I reached it. And if I had a choice, I would want it to be the greatest champion of the day."

"Merlin . . ." he mused. "I suppose that it could be as you say. Excuse me, but a long life has just been shaken up, from beginning to end. If this is true . . ."

"I am sure that it is."

"If this is true . . . A millennium, you say?"

"More or less."

"Well, it is almost that time now."

"I know. I do not believe that our meeting tonight was a matter of chance. You are destined to meet him upon his awakening, which should be soon. Something has ordained that you meet me first, however, to be warned."

"Warned? Warned of what?"

"He is mad, Launcelot. Many of us felt a great relief at his passing. If the realm had not been sundered finally by strife it would probably have been broken by his hand, anyway."

"That I find difficult to believe. He was always a strange man—for who can fully understand a sorceror?—and in his later years he did seem at least partly daft. But he never struck me as evil."

"Nor was he. His was the most dangerous morality of all. He was a misguided idealist. In a more primitive time and place and with a willing fool like Arthur, he was able to create a legend. Today, in an age of monstrous weapons, with the right leader as his catspaw, he could unleash something totally devastating. He would see a wrong and force his man to try righting it. He would do it in the name of the same high ideal he always served, but he would not appreciate the results until it was too late. How could he—even if he were sane? He has no conception of modern international relations."

"What is to be done? What is my part in all of this?"

"I believe you should go back, to England, to be present at his awakening, to find out exactly what he wants, to try to reason with him."

"I don't know . . . How would I find him?"

"You found me. When the time is right, you will be in the proper place. I am certain of that. It was meant to be, probably even a part of his spell. Seek him. But do not trust him."

"I don't know, Morgana." He looked at the wall, unseeing. "I don't know."

"You have waited this long and you draw back now from finally finding out?"

"You are right—in that much, at least." He folded his hands, raised them and rested his chin upon them. "What I would do if he really returned, I do not know. Try to reason with him, yes— Have you any other advice?"

"Just that you be there."

"You've looked at my hand. You have the power. What did you see?"

She turned away.

"It is uncertain," she said.

That night he dreamed, as he sometimes did, of times long gone. They sat about the great Table, as they had on that day. Gawaine was there and Percival. Galahad . . . He winced. This day was different from other days. There was a certain tension in the air, a before-the-storm feeling, an electrical thing. . . . Merlin stood at the far end of the room, hands in the sleeves of his long robe, hair and beard snowy and unkempt, pale eyes staring—at what, none could be certain . . .

After some timeless time, a reddish glow appeared near the door. All eyes moved toward it. It grew brighter and advanced slowly into the room—a formless apparition of light. There were sweet odors and some few soft strains of music. Gradually, a form began to take shape at its center, resolving itself into the likeness of a chalice. . . .

He felt himself rising, moving slowly, following it in its course through the great chamber, advancing upon it, soundlessly and deliberately, as if moving underwater . . .

. . . Reaching for it.

His hand entered the circle of light, moved toward its center, neared the now blazing cup and passed through. . . .

Immediately, the light faded. The outline of the chalice wavered, and it collasped in upon itself, fading, fading, gone. . . .

There came a sound, rolling, echoing about the hall. Laughter.

He turned and regarded the others. They sat about the table, watching him, laughing. Even Merlin managed a dry chuckle.

Suddenly, his great blade was in his hand, and he raised it as he strode toward the Table. The knights nearest him drew back as he brought the weapon crashing down.

The Table split in half and fell. The room shook.

The quaking continued. Stones were dislodged from the walls. A roof beam fell. He raised his arm.

The entire castle began to come apart, falling about him and still the laughter continued.

He awoke damp with perspiration and lay still for a long while. In the morning, he bought a ticket for London.

Two of the three elemental sounds of the world were suddenly with him as he walked that evening, stick in hand. For a dozen days, he had hiked about Cornwall, finding no clues to that which he sought. He had allowed himself two more before giving up and departing.

Now the wind and the rain were upon him, and he increased his pace. The fresh-lit stars were smothered by a mass of cloud and wisps of fog grew like ghostly fungi on either hand. He moved among trees, paused, continued on.

"Shouldn't have stayed out this late," he muttered, and after several more pauses, *"Nel mezzo del cammin di nostra vita mi ritrovai per una selva oscura, che la diritta via era smarrita,"* then he chuckled, halting beneath a tree.

The rain was not heavy. It was more a fine mist now. A bright patch in the lower heavens showed where the moon hung veiled.

He wiped his face, turned up his collar. He studied the position of the moon. After a time, he struck off to his right. There was a faint rumble of thunder in the distance.

The fog continued to grow about him as he went. Soggy leaves made squishing noises beneath his boots. An animal of indeterminate size bolted from a clump of shrubbery beside a cluster of rocks and tore off through the darkness.

Five minutes . . . ten . . . He cursed softly. The rainfall had increased in intensity. Was that the same rock?

He turned in a complete circle. All directions were equally uninviting. Selecting one at random, he commenced walking once again.

Then, in the distance, he discerned a spark, a glow, a wavering light. It vanished and reappeared periodically, as though partly blocked, the line of sight a function of his movements. He headed toward it. After perhaps half a minute, it was gone again from sight, but he continued on in what he thought to be its direction. There came another roll of thunder, louder this time.

When it seemed that it might have been illusion or some short-lived natural phenomenon, something else occurred in that same direction. There was a movement, a shadow-within-shadow shuffling at the foot of a great tree. He slowed his pace, approaching the spot cautiously.

There!

A figure detached itself from a pool of darkness ahead and to the left. Manlike, it moved with a slow and heavy tread, creaking sounds emerging from the forest floor beneath it. A vagrant moonbeam touched it for a moment, and it appeared yellow and metallically slick beneath moisture.

He halted. It seemed that he had just regarded a knight in full armor in his path. How long since he had beheld such a sight? He shook his head and stared.

The figure had also halted. It raised its right arm in a beckoning gesture, then turned and began to walk away. He hesitated for only a moment, then followed.

It turned off to the left and pursued a treacherous path, rocky, slippery, heading slightly downward. He actually used his stick now, to assure his footing, as he tracked its deliberate progress. He gained on it, to the point where he could clearly hear the metallic scraping sounds of its passage.

Then it was gone, swallowed by a greater darkness.

He advanced to the place where he had last beheld it. He stood in the lee of a great mass of stone. He reached out and probed it with his stick.

He tapped steadily along its nearest surface, and then the stick moved past it. He followed.

There was an opening, a crevice. He had to turn sidewise to pass within it, but as he did the full glow of the light he had seen came into sight for several seconds.

The passage curved and widened, leading him back and down. Several times, he paused and listened, but there were no sounds other than his own breathing.

He withdrew his handkerchief and dried his face and hands carefully. He brushed moisture from his coat, turned down his collar. He scuffed the mud and leaves from his boots. He adjusted his apparel. Then he strode forward, rounding a final corner, into a chamber lit by a small oil lamp suspended by three delicate chains from some point in the darkness overhead. The yellow knight stood unmoving beside the far wall. On a fiber mat atop a stony pedestal directly beneath the lamp lay an old man in tattered garments. His bearded face was half-masked by shadows.

He moved to the old man's side. He saw then that those ancient dark eyes were open.

"Merlin . . .?" he whispered.

There came a faint hissing sound, a soft croak. Realizing the source, he leaned nearer.

"Elixir . . . in earthern rock . . . on ledge . . . in back," came the gravelly whisper.

He turned and sought the ledge, the container.

"Do you know where it is?" he asked the yellow figure.

It neither stirred nor replied, but stood like a display piece. He turned away from it then and sought further. After a time, he located it. It was more a niche than a ledge, blending in with the wall, cloaked with shadow. He ran his fingertips over the container's contours, raised it gently. Something liquid stirred within it. He wiped its lip on his sleeve after he had returned to the lighted area. The wind whistled past the entranceway and he thought he felt the faint vibration of thunder.

Sliding one hand beneath his shoulders, he raised the ancient form. Merlin's eyes still seemed unfocussed. He moistened Merlin's lips with the liquid. The old man licked them, and after several moments opened his mouth. He administered a sip, then another, and another . . .

Merlin signalled for him to lower him, and he did. He glanced again at the yellow armor, but it had remained motionless the entire while. He looked back at the sorceror and saw that a new light had come into his eyes and he was studying him, smiling faintly.

"Feel better?"

Merlin nodded. A minute passed, and a touch of color appeared upon his cheeks. He elbowed himself into a sitting position and took the container into his hands. He raised it and drank deeply.

He sat still for several minutes after that. His thin hands, which had appeared waxy in the flamelight, grew darker, fuller. His shoulders straightened. He placed the crock on the bed beside him and stretched his arms. His joints creaked the first time he did it, but not the second. He swung his legs over the edge of the bed and rose slowly to his feet. He was a full head shorter than Launcelot.

"It is done," he said, staring back into the shadows. "Much has happened, of course . . ."

"Much has happened," Launcelot replied.

"You have lived through it all. Tell me, is the world a better place or is it worse than it was in those days?"

"Better in some ways, worse in others. It is different."

"How is it better?"

"There are many ways of making life easier, and the sum total of human knowledge has increased vastly."

"How has it worsened?"

"There are many more people in the world. Consequently, there are many more people suffering from poverty, disease, ignorance. The world itself has suffered great depredation, in the way of pollution and other assaults on the integrity of nature."

"Wars?"

"There is always someone fighting, somewhere."

"They need help."

"Maybe. Maybe not."

Merlin turned and looked into his eyes.

"What do you mean?"

"People haven't changed. They are as rational—and irrational—as they were in the old days. They are as moral and law-abiding—and not—as ever. Many new things have been learned, many new situations evolved, but I do not believe that the nature of man has altered significantly in the time you've slept. Nothing you do is going to change that. You may be able to alter a few features of the times, but would it really be proper to meddle? Everything is so interdependent today that even you would not be able to predict all the consequences of any actions you take. You might do more harm than good; and whatever you do, man's nature will remain the same."

"This isn't like you, Lance. You were never much given to philosophizing in the old days."

"I've had a long time to think about it."

"And I've had a long time to dream about it. War is your craft, Lance. Stay with that."

"I gave it up a long time ago."

"Then what are you now?"

"An appraiser."

Merlin turned away, took another drink. He seemed to radiate a fierce energy when he turned again.

"And your oath? To right wrongs, to punish the wicked . . . ?"

"The longer I lived the more difficult it became to determine what was a wrong and who was wicked. Make it clear to me again and I may go back into business."

"Galahad would never have addressed me so."

"Galahad was young, naive, trusting. Speak not to me of my son."

"Launcelot! Launcelot!" He placed a hand on his arm. "Why all this bitterness for an old friend who has done nothing for a thousand years?"

"I wished to make my position clear immediately. I feared you might contemplate some irreversible action which could alter the world balance of power fatally. I want you to know that I will not be party to it."

"Admit that you do not know what I might do, what I can do."

"Freely. That is why I fear you. What *do* you intend to do?"

"Nothing, at first. I wish merely to look about me, to see for myself some of these changes of which you have spoken. Then I will consider which wrongs need righting, who needs punishment, and who to choose as my champions. I will show you these things, and then you can go back into business, as you say."

Launcelot sighed.

"The burden of proof is on the moralist. Your judgment is no longer sufficient for me."

"Dear me," the other replied, "it is sad to have waited this long for an encounter of this sort, to find you have lost your faith in me. My powers are beginning to return already, Lance. Do you not feel magic in the air?"

"I feel something I have not felt in a long while."

"The sleep of ages was a restorative—an aid, actually. In a while, Lance, I am going to be stronger than I ever was before. And you doubt that I will be able to turn back the clock?"

"I doubt you can do it in a fashion to benefit anybody. Look, Merlin, I'm sorry. I do not like it that things have come to this either. But I have lived too long, seen too much, know too much of how the world works now to trust any one man's opinion concerning its salvation. Let it go. You are a mysterious, revered legend. I do not know what you really are. But forgo exercising your powers in any sort of crusade. Do something else this time around. Become a physician and fight pain. Take up painting. Be a professor of history, an antiquarian. Hell, be a social critic and point out what evils you see for people to correct themselves."

"Do you really believe I could be satisfied with any of those things?"

"Men find satisfaction in many things. It depends on the man, not on the things. I'm just saying that you should avoid using your powers in any attempt to effect social changes as we once did, by violence."

"Whatever changes have been wrought, time's greatest irony lies in its having transformed you into a pacifist."

"You are wrong."

"Admit it! You have finally come to fear the clash of arms! An appraiser! What kind of knight are you?"

"One who finds himself in the wrong time and the wrong place, Merlin."

The sorceror shrugged and turned away.

"Let it be, then. It is good that you have chosen to tell me all these things immediately. Thank you for that, anyway. A moment."

Merlin walked to the rear of the cave, returned in moments attired in fresh garments. The effect was startling. His entire appearance was more kempt and cleanly. His hair and beard now appeared gray rather than white. His step was sure and steady. He held a staff in his right hand but did not lean upon it.

"Come walk with me," he said.

"It is a bad night."

"It is not the same night you left without. It is not even the same place."

As he passed the suit of yellow armor, he snapped his fingers near its visor. With a single creak, the figure moved and turned to follow him.

"Who is that?"

Merlin smiled.

"No one," he replied, and he reached back and raised the visor. The helmet was empty. "It is enchanted, animated by a spirit," he said. "A trifle clumsy, though, which is why I did not trust it to administer my draught. A perfect servant, however, unlike some. Incredibly strong and swift. Even in your prime you could not have beaten it. I fear nothing when it walks with me. Come, there is something I would have you see."

"Very well."

Launcelot followed Merlin and the hollow knight from the cave. The rain had stopped, and it was very still. They stood on an incredibly moonlit plain where mists drifted and grasses sparkled. Shadowy shapes stood in the distance.

"Excuse me," Launcelot said. "I left my walking stick inside."

He turned and re-entered the cave.

"Yes, fetch it, old man," Merlin replied. "Your strength is already on the wane."

When Launcelot returned, he leaned upon the stick and squinted across the plain.

"This way," Merlin said, "to where your questions will be answered. I will try not to move too quickly and tire you."

"Tire me?"

The sorceror chuckled and began walking across the plain. Launcelot followed.

"Do you not feel a trifle weary?" he asked.

"Yes, as a matter of fact, I do. Do you know what is the matter with me?"

"Of course. I have withdrawn the enchantment which has protected you all these years. What you feel now are the first tentative touches of your true age. It will take some time to catch up with you, against your body's natural resistance, but it is beginning its advance."

"Why are you doing this to me?"

"Because I believed you when you said you were not a pacifist. And you spoke with sufficient vehemence for me to realize that you might even oppose me. I could not permit that, for I knew that your old strength was still there for you to call upon. Even a sorceror might fear that, so I did what had to be done. By my power was it maintained; without it, it now drains away. It would have been good for us to work together once again, but I saw that that could not be."

Launcelot stumbled, caught himself, limped on. The hollow knight walked at Merlin's right hand.

"You say that your ends are noble," Launcelot said, "but I do not believe you. Perhaps in the old days they were. But more than the times have changed. You are different. Do you not feel it yourself?"

Merlin drew a deep breath and exhaled vapor.

"Perhaps it is my heritage," he said. Then, "I jest. Of course, I have changed. Everyone does. You yourself are a perfect example. What you consider a turn for the worse in me is but the tip of an irreducible conflict which has grown up between us in the course of our changes. I still hold with the true ideals of Camelot."

Launcelot's shoulders were bent forward now and his breathing had deepened. The shapes loomed larger before them.

"Why, I know this place," he gasped. "Yet, I do not know it. Stonehenge does not stand so today. Even in Arthur's time it lacked this perfection. How did we get here? What has happened?"

He paused to rest, and Merlin halted to accommodate him.

"This night we have walked between the worlds," the sorceror said. "This is a piece of the land of Faërie and that is the true Stonehenge, a holy place. I have stretched the bounds of the worlds to bring it here. Were I unkind I could send you back with it and strand you there forever. But it is better that you know a sort of peace. Come!"

Launcelot staggered along behind him, heading for the great circle of stones. The faintest of breezes came out of the west, stirring the mists.

"What do you mean—know a sort of peace?"

"The complete restoration of my powers and their increase will require a sacrifice in this place."

"Then you planned this for me all along!"

"No. It was not to have been you, Lance. Anyone would have served, though you will serve superbly well. It need not have been so, had you elected to assist me. You could still change your mind."

"Would you want someone who did that at your side?"

"You have a point there."

"Then why ask—save as a petty cruelty?"

"It is just that, for you have annoyed me."

Launcelot halted again when they came to the circle's periphery. He regarded the massive stands of stone.

"If you will not enter willingly," Merlin stated, "my servant will be happy to assist you."

Launcelot spat, straightened a little and glared.

"Think you I fear an empty suit of armor, juggled by some Hell-born wight? Even now, Merlin, without the benefit of wizardly succor, I could take that thing apart."

The sorceror laughed.

"It is good that you at least recall the boasts of knighthood when all else has left you. I've half a mind to give you the opportunity, for the manner of your passing here is not important. Only the preliminaries are essential."

"But you're afraid to risk your servant?"

"Think you so, old man? I doubt you could even bear the weight of a suit of armor, let alone lift a lance. But if you are willing to try, so be it!"

He rapped the butt of his staff three times upon the ground.

"Enter," he said then. "You will find all that you need within. And I am glad you have made this choice. You were insufferable, you know. Just once, I longed to see you beaten, knocked down to the level of lesser mortals. I only wish the Queen could be here, to witness her champion's final engagement."

"So do I," said Launcelot, and he walked past the monolith and entered the circle.

A black stallion waited, its reins held down beneath a rock. Pieces of armor, a lance, a blade and a shield leaned against the side of the dolmen. Across the circle's diameter, a white stallion awaited the advance of the hollow knight.

"I am sorry I could not arrange for a page or a squire to assist you," Merlin said, coming around the other side of the monolith. "I'll be glad to help you myself, though."

"I can manage," Launcelot replied.

"My champion is accoutered in exactly the same fashion," Merlin said, "and I have not given him any edge over you in weapons."

"I never liked your puns either."

Launcelot made friends with the horse, then removed a small strand of red from his wallet and tied it about the butt of the lance. He leaned his stick against the dolmen stone and began to don the armor. Merlin, whose hair and beard were now almost black, moved off several paces and began drawing a diagram in the dirt with the end of his staff.

"You used to favor a white charger," he commented, "but I thought it appropriate to equip you with one of another color, since you have abandoned the ideals of the Table Round, betraying the memory of Camelot."

"On the contrary," Launcelot replied, glancing overhead at the passage of a sudden roll of thunder. "Any horse in a storm, and I am Camelot's last defender."

Merlin continued to elaborate upon the pattern he was drawing as Launcelot slowly equipped himself. The small wind continued to blow, stirring the mist. There came a flash of lightning, startling the horse. Launcelot calmed it.

Merlin stared at him for a moment and rubbed his eyes. Launcelot donned his helmet.

"For a moment," Merlin said, "you looked somehow different. . . ."

"Really? Magical withdrawal, do you think?" he asked, and he kicked the stone from the reins and mounted the stallion.

Merlin stepped back from the now-completed diagram, shaking his head, as the mounted man leaned over and grasped the lance.

"You still seem to move with some strength," he said.

"Really?"

Launcelot raised the lance and couched it. Before taking up the shield he had hung at the saddle's side, he opened his visor and turned and regarded Merlin.

"Your champion appears to be ready," he said. "So am I."

Seen in another flash of light, it was an unlined face that looked down at Merlin, clear-eyed, wisps of pale gold hair fringing the forehead.

"What magic have the years taught you?" Merlin asked.

"Not magic," Launcelot replied. "Caution. I anticipated you. So, when I returned to the cave for my stick, I drank the rest of your elixir."

He lowered the visor and turned away.

"You walked like an old man. . . ."

"I'd a lot of practice. Signal your champion!"

Merlin laughed.

"Good! It is better this way," he decided, "to see you go down in full strength! You still cannot hope to win against a spirit!"

Launcelot raised the shield and leaned forward.

"Then what are you waiting for?"

"Nothing!" Merlin said. Then he shouted, "Kill him, Raxas!"

A light rain began as they pounded across the field; and staring ahead, Launcelot realized that flames were flickering behind his opponent's visor. At the last possible moment, he shifted the point of his lance into line with the hollow knight's blazing helm. There came more lightning and thunder.

His shield deflected the other's lance while his went on to strike the approaching head. It flew from the hollow knight's shoulders and bounced, smouldering, on the ground.

He continued on to the other end of the field and turned. When he had, he saw that the hollow knight, now headless, was doing the same. And beyond him, he saw two standing figures, where moments before there had been but one.

Morgan Le Fay, clad in a white robe, red hair unbound and blowing in the wind, faced Merlin from across his pattern. It seemed they were speaking, but he could not hear the words. Then she began to raise her hands, and they glowed like cold fire. Merlin's staff was also gleaming, and he shifted it before him. Then he saw no more, for the hollow knight was ready for the second charge.

He couched his lance, raised the shield, leaned forward and gave his mount the signal. His arm felt like a bar of iron, his strength like an endless current of electricity as he raced down the field. The rain was falling more heavily now and the lightning began a constant flickering. A steady rolling of thunder smothered the sound of the hoofbeats, and the wind whistled past his helm as he approached the other warrior, his lance centered on his shield.

They came together with an enormous crash. Both knights reeled and the hollow one fell, his shield and breastplate pierced by a broken lance. His left arm came away as he struck the earth; the lancepoint snapped and the shield fell beside him. But he began to rise almost immediately, his right hand drawing his long sword.

Launcelot dismounted, discarding his shield, drawing his own great blade. He moved to meet his headless foe. The other struck first and he parried it, a mighty shock running down his arms. He swung a blow of his own. It was parried.

They swaggered swords across the field, till finally Launcelot saw his opening and landed his heaviest blow. The hollow knight toppled into the mud, his breastplate cloven almost to the point where the spear's shaft protruded. At that moment, Morgan Le Fay screamed.

Launcelot turned and saw that she had fallen across the pattern Merlin had drawn. The sorceror, now bathed in a bluish light, raised his staff and moved forward. Launcelot took a step toward them and felt a great pain in his left side.

Even as he turned toward the half-risen hollow knight who was drawing his blade back for another blow, Launcelot reversed his double-handed grip upon his own weapon and raised it high, point downward.

He hurled himself upon the other, and his blade pierced the cuirass entirely as he bore him back down, nailing him to the earth. A shriek arose from beneath him, echoing within the armor, and a gout of fire emerged from the neck hole, sped upward and away, dwindled in the rain, flickered out moments later.

Launcelot pushed himself into a kneeling position. Slowly then, he rose to his feet and turned toward the two figures who again faced one another. Both were now standing within the muddied geometries of power, both were now bathed in the bluish light. Launcelot took a step toward them, then another.

"Merlin!" he called out, continuing to advance upon them. "I've done what I said I would! Now I'm coming to kill you!"

Morgan Le Fay turned toward him, eyes wide.

"No!" she cried. "Depart the circle! Hurry! I am holding him here! His power wanes! In moments, this place will be no more. Go!"

Launcelot hesitated but a moment, then turned and walked as rapidly as he was able toward the circle's perimeter. The sky seemed to boil as he passed among the monoliths.

He advanced another dozen paces, then had to pause to rest. He looked back to the place of battle, to the place where the two figures still stood locked in sorcerous embrace. Then the scene was imprinted upon his brain as the skies opened and a sheet of fire fell upon the far end of the circle.

Dazzled, he raised his hand to shield his eyes. When he lowered it, he saw the stones falling, soundless, many of them fading from sight. The rain began to slow immediately. Sorceror and sorceress had vanished along with much of the structure of the still-fading place. The horses were nowhere to be seen. He looked about him and saw a good-sized stone. He headed for it and seated himself. He unfastened his breastplate and removed it, dropping it to the ground. His side throbbed and he held it tightly. He doubled forward and rested his face on his left hand.

The rains continued to slow and finally ceased. The wind died. The mists returned.

He breathed deeply and thought back upon the conflict. This, this was the thing for which he had remained after all the others, the thing for which he had waited, for so long. It was over now, and he could rest.

There was a gap in his consciousness. He was brought to awareness again by a light. A steady glow passed between his fingers, pierced his eyelids. He dropped his hand and raised his head, opening his eyes.

It passed slowly before him in a halo of white light. He removed his sticky fingers from his side and rose to his feet to follow it. Solid, glowing, glorious and pure, not at all like the image in the chamber, it led him on out across the moonlit plain, from dimness to brightness to dimness, until the mists enfolded him as he reached at last to embrace it.

HERE ENDETH THE BOOK OF LAUNCELOT,
LAST OF THE NOBLE KNIGHTS OF THE
ROUND TABLE, AND HIS ADVENTURES
WITH RAXAS, THE HOLLOW KNIGHT,
AND MERLIN AND MORGAN LE FAY,
LAST OF THE WISE FOLK OF CAMELOT,
IN HIS QUEST FOR THE SANGREAL.

QUO FAS ET GLORIA DUCUNT.